"Up-and-coming mastermind of forensic auditing mystery-crime author Gary L. Kreigh incorporates corrupt Hoosier history with elusive characters and a complex plot in his fourth Callan Morrow mystery. Kreigh's approach to storytelling draws readers from the get-go. As with any good mystery, Silence the Past opens with a scene that quickly turns sinister. Little by little, characters mixed with misperception enter the narrative since the cast swiftly mirrors red herrings.

Volunteering his expertise, native Indianian Callan Morrow keeps his investigation lowkey while attempting to identify clues, and clues tend to get muddied up fast. Kreigh begins twisting his storyline by highlighting his flawed cast, including Callan, his principal character. Callan may be excellent in his line of work; however, he shares a common struggle with the remaining cast - dealing with the past, but as the title suggests, there are deeper issues. It is a trick and a half for both Callan and readers to figure out the true culprits behind the chaos that unfolds. Nonetheless, Kreigh smartly employs relatable themes of forgiveness and facing one's fears amid alternating character scenes and page-turning, cliffhanging chapter endings.

For mystery-crime lovers looking for their next best read, turn to Gary Kreigh's *Silence the Past* ."

—Pacific Book Review

Silence the Past

A Callan Morrow Mystery

Gary L. Kreigh

AIA PUBLISHING

Chapter One

William Davisly pulled back the sheers of an upstairs window and looked out across his shaded lawn. Despite the trees, he could see where his driveway met the road in front of his house. He looked at his watch. The men with the box truck he'd ordered were now fifteen minutes late. He breathed deeply and exhaled as he closed the curtains, nervous about the bureau downstairs, which he desperately wanted out of the middle of his foyer.

The bureau was a handsome piece—a late eighteenth- or early nineteenth-century George III mahogany chest. Its four graduated drawers with blind-fret carving dominated the front, and it stood on similarly carved bracket feet. The slanted front cover opened to cubbyholes and cupboards that concealed a drawer large enough to store important personal documents. He'd managed to negotiate a good price, one below its appraised value, because the previous owner had to sell it quickly to pay a debt, or so he was told.

His wife, Camille, had questioned whether that was a good enough reason to buy the bureau. She reminded him that they already had an ample number of such antique bureaus and armoires in their home. Where was he planning to put it? And, no, she told him, the bronze-patinated German candlesticks depicting armored and helmeted knights that he set on its surface did nothing to enhance its appeal. It had to go.

That was fine with him. He wasn't going to keep it anyway. William only bought it because he had to. In fact, he wanted it out of his house, sent back to Cottage Gallery where it came from, as soon as possible.

William paced in a circle as if the tedium of his anxious steps would hasten the arrival of the truck. He walked into the hallway and focused on a small wooden tobacco stand. He opened its lone drawer. The envelope he'd stuffed into the drawer to keep hidden from Camille was still there. It was the same envelope he'd pulled from the bureau's concealed compartment when he'd brought it home from Cottage Gallery. He opened the envelope carefully, scanned the note, and shook his head in disbelief.

How did they know this?

The information within the note was comprehensive and complete, yet it was so long ago. He wondered who would take such care to document so thoroughly each minute detail of a past he longed to forget.

William read the note again. Something peculiar about the wording suddenly caught his eye. As he deciphered the clues hidden between the lines, the blood drained from his face. Perhaps the person who wrote the note knew more of the facts than he gave them credit for. They were intimate facts, facts from someone powerful who meant business if he didn't comply with the note's demands.

Nausea consumed him.

He thought carefully, rubbing the palms of his hands over his shaved chin. There was a solution. It wasn't a simple solution, but it could be done quickly and absolutely.

William hurried to a nightstand in the bedroom on his wife's side of the bed and reached inside its top drawer. The snub-nosed Colt .38 was still where he'd placed it for Camille's protection when he was out of town on business. They'd never needed it until now.

The unmistakable sound of a large truck rumbled up the winding drive to the house. He sped down the stairs and bolted to the bureau, lifting the slanted lid in frantic search of the cubbyhole where he'd placed a tightly sealed envelope to be opened when the bureau reached its destination. He heard two doors of the truck open and shut and footsteps approaching. He'd barely found the envelope and emptied it of its cash when the doorbell rang. Quickly, he stuffed the bills into an inside suit pocket, and on the surface of the envelope, he scribbled the first words that came to his mind: *Go to hell. You'll get nothing from me.*

The doorbell rang again as he placed the empty envelope back into the compartment and closed the lid. He answered the door with an indignant grunt, wiping sweat from across his forehead.

Two men garbed similarly in dull gray jumpsuits stood before him.

"North Crow's Nest," the older, larger man said to the disheveled William. "I didn't know Crow's Nest was big enough to have a north side."

William ignored the frivolous comment about the suburb of Indianapolis where he lived. The less said about the exclusive neighborhood, the better.

That didn't stop the man, who favored talk over work. He rambled incessantly about getting lost on the wooded lane that wound through the neighborhood's rolling hills and posh estates.

"The bureau is in here," William said impatiently.

The young Latino man who accompanied the driver followed William into the house. He appeared tired of the older man's prolific rambling and eager to put his muscles to work.

"Anyway, that's why we were late, sir. Sorry about that." The large man stared at the bureau as if he'd never seen such an ornate piece of furniture in his life.

"Do you mind giving your partner a hand?" William asked the man. "I'd like to get it out of here. It must go back as is—intact."

Ignoring the large man who talked too much, William handed the Latino two Grants as an incentive to follow his instructions. "You'll see that it happens?"

The young man nodded.

"I'll see that it gets there, too, sir, safe and sound," the large man bellowed. "You can count on us."

"Don't get lost. I don't want you weaving in and out of the neighborhood."

The driver laughed. "Oh, no, sir, no, sir. I know how to get out of here now. Next time, I'll—"

"There won't be a next time." William stood by the door to assist the movers out of the house, then added, "Remember, I need the bureau to arrive at Cottage Gallery just as it is—intact and unscathed." He shut the door firmly upon the movers' heels.

~

"Well, if he wasn't the oddest screwball I ever did meet," the large man said as they climbed into the cab. "Makes ya wonder how people like that ever get to be so high and mighty." He scanned the delivery instructions before starting the engine. "Oh, darn. Just a sec, kid. I forgot to have him sign the pickup slip. What'd he call it? A bureau? Well, he ain't gonna be too happy to see me again, and I can't say I'm lookin' forward to hearing him hiss at me like a cornered 'possum. Geez. Be right back."

The young man pulled his ball cap over his eyes and rested his head against the back of the seat while the driver made his way to the front door. The large man paused as he reached for the doorbell, second-guessing whether he'd brought the proper form with him. He wasn't sure, but it didn't matter. A signature anywhere on the paper was all he needed to be rid of the indignant customer.

He didn't get his stubby finger to the doorbell before a deafening pop came from within the house. Loud and distinctive, he recognized the sound immediately. He jumped and turned toward his partner in the truck.

His partner had heard it, too, catching his hat in his hand as it vaulted off his head. He poked his head through the passenger side of the truck.

The men's eyes met in wild confusion and horror.

Without hesitation, the man in the truck pulled his cell phone out of his pants pocket and called the police.

Chapter Two

Kate O'Neal disliked afternoons. She sat at her desk and stared blankly out of her office window toward the blazing sun. She turned away to finish the rest of the lukewarm sugar-free cola at the bottom of her glass. A glance at her watch made her sigh. To make it look as if she'd accomplished something, she shuffled papers to clear a space on the desk.

She rubbed the shiny surface with her hand. Oh, how she loved her desk, a stately fluted frieze-centered table with swag carving and a faux marbled breakfront top. Most Hoosiers hardly considered it to be a desk, but it suited her. Simple, rich, and exquisitely unique; that's what she wanted. More importantly, it afforded no clutter. She placed her unfinished work in an armoire set to one side of the room against a wall, a perfect place for clutter to hide—an illusion, of course, but it made her feel better.

Kate needed to feel better. Her brain swam with confusion over the recent events at Cottage Gallery. She didn't know what to do or what was expected of her.

Footsteps approached her office. She looked toward

the doorway.

Gabe Kimmerman peeked in, brushing strands of dark brown hair from his eyes and presenting a halfhearted smile. "You okay?"

She nodded and tried to return the smile.

He used his thumb to gesture toward the outdoors. "Going to grab a sandwich. I've closed the showroom, but I'll be back to straighten up for tomorrow. Want anything?"

Kate glanced at her watch again. "No, I don't have time. I have a board meeting for Open Arms in about fifteen minutes. You won't be long, will you?"

He reassured her he wouldn't and turned to leave, but she called him back.

She drew a breath but hesitated.

He looked at her intently as if trying to determine what was on her mind. "If it's about the bureau," he said.

"It is," she replied, "but I don't know what to ask. There wasn't anything . . . unusual . . . about it, was there?"

"No, ma'am, not that I noticed."

"And Mr. Davisly?"

"Business as usual. He came in, seeming to know what he wanted."

Kate frowned, puzzled. "You mean, he came into the gallery, knowing he wanted a bureau?"

"No, I mean that he wanted that *particular* bureau on consignment in the showroom."

She gasped.

"Is there a problem?"

"There shouldn't be," she said, looking away, "but there'll be questions, I'm sure."

Gabe started to say something but appeared to have second thoughts.

Kate prompted him to say it anyway.

"You're right," he said. "There shouldn't be questions, but we should take better care about what goes on between Cottage Gallery and . . ."

"Between the gallery and what?"

"Open Arms."

"I don't see what you mean. I own the gallery, Gabe. I can do with it what I want."

"But not with Open Arms. You're the executive director of Open Arms. It has charity status. Transactions between the two have to be operated separately to avoid the appearance of a conflict of interest."

"We do operate them separately. There are no conflicts of interest."

"Yes, ma'am," he said tactfully, "but we could do a better job. We should make sure we do it . . . more transparently."

Kate scrutinized him momentarily before asking, "Don't you believe we do?"

"We try our best. I'm just saying that if you're worried about questions—"

"I'm not."

"But if you were, that's where questions could center."

She frowned. "You better get your sandwich," she said, turning her attention to her empty glass. "Don't be long."

Gabe left quietly.

Kate stood and walked to the window to look at the side yard. The sun shone in her eyes, making it hard to see the many people walking on the trail toward Broad Ripple, an eclectic village of shops and eateries on Indianapolis's north side, along the Indiana Central Canal.

Gabe's short but candid comments had upset her. She'd worked hard at Cottage Gallery to build a reputation throughout the Midwest as a dealer of fine antiques. She was so renowned that potential consignees (who Kate called proprietors) waited patiently on a list to display and sell their furniture and accessories. She chose only high-quality antiques from proprietors who could speak knowledgeably about their client base and the antiques they sold.

But now, she felt as though her hard work and reputation was slipping away . . . all because William Davisly had brought back the bureau he'd purchased.

She returned to her desk and rubbed her hand over its smooth surface once again. Touching it comforted her. It was hers, solid and tangible. She could claim it as hers. Even the outdated streamline phone, with its long, unwieldy cord hanging over the edge, comforted her. Permanent, attached, and grounded. Kate needed that this afternoon.

She couldn't claim William Davisly's misfortune, and she didn't want to do so. After all, what happened to William may not have been related to her or Cottage Gallery. *Of course not*, she thought. It made no sense.

Still, Kate felt shallow for trying to dismiss a connection so easily. She'd worked hard not to be superficial, and her apparent success at that endeavor was the reason she'd volunteered to be the executive director of Open Arms—a retail thrift store with not-for-profit tax status managed by a board of directors including prominent Indianapolis businessmen and women. Open Arms accepted items of all kinds, including clothing. They repaired what they could and sold the items to donate the proceeds to charitable causes, mostly toward the reconciliation of homeless youths with their families, or to agencies that could provide young adults with the resources to become self-sufficient.

Open Arms took work to make it function efficiently and effectively. Sometimes it took more work than Kate thought the venture was worth. She wondered if she'd made the right choice, getting involved with an organization in which she really didn't have an interest. She wondered if potential customers saw through her facade, appearing to be benevolent and charitable when, in reality, she just wanted to make more money at Cottage Gallery. She hoped she didn't appear as shallow as she felt.

Kate was in no mood for the Open Arms board of directors meeting that was to begin in just a few minutes. Perhaps the other directors were as devastated as she was about William's death. She hoped there would be solace in their company and a reason not to blame the afternoon for her tired spirit.

Kate sighed, rose from her seat with briefcase in hand, and walked down the hall to the room where the board's meetings were held. The room was designed for professional and community meetings, although not for more than twelve or so people comfortably. A cherry bookcase had been custom built along the wall opposite the window. Cherry wainscoting covered the remaining walls. A whiteboard hung prominently at the far end, behind a rectangular conference table surrounded by leather executive chairs.

She was surprised to see Alex Aubert and Marilyn Wells-Brewer sitting quietly at the table. She hadn't heard them enter through the gallery's showroom, although she prided herself in greeting all patrons who entered her business.

"Gabe let us in," Marilyn said in a tone that indicated she was pleased her presence was a surprise. "He was going out as we were coming in, and I'm very glad he was there." She didn't elaborate and didn't bother lifting her head to acknowledge Kate. Instead, she pecked something on her cell phone. "That obnoxious little bell you keep over the door clangs far too loudly, my dear. It was a relief not to have to listen to it."

Kate stood at the head of the table and glowered at Marilyn

before turning to smile at Alex, who'd risen courteously from his seat upon her entrance and offered a solemn greeting. She took a seat on the same side of the table as Marilyn, next to where Beth Kimmerman, the board chair, would sit when she arrived to start the meeting.

Roger Montrose, a prominent real estate investor and philanthropist from Carmel, rushed into the room and stood behind a vacant chair next to Alex without saying a word or looking at anyone around the table. Marilyn lifted her eyes and watched him remove his suit coat. He wiped perspiration from his balding head, seated himself, and removed from his briefcase the binder of reports and spreadsheets Kate had couriered to his office earlier in the day. He scanned the materials as if he were reading them for the first time.

Kate glanced around the table. Marilyn continued to preoccupy herself with her texting, Roger with his reading. Her eyes met young Alex Aubert's by accident, and he shifted them uncomfortably to some bottles of water that had been left on the table from a previous meeting.

"May I?" he asked, reaching for one of the bottles.

"Of course," Kate responded. "They're probably warm, though. Shall I get you a cold one? It's one of those days." She looked toward the window. The oppressive May sun was magnified through the glass. "Rather warm, isn't it? It had to have been miserable on the track during practice this afternoon for the race drivers, don't you think?"

"Oh, that's right. The 500-Mile Race is in a couple of weeks." Alex seemed grateful for some small talk to break the silence. "Wonderful time of year, the Indianapolis 500. A whole month of festivities. Did you run in the mini marathon this year, Roger?"

Upon hearing his name, Mr. Montrose lifted his gray head.

He looked gaunt and pale from a weary day, and it appeared to Kate as if he wondered if he'd heard his name being called. He responded with a confused grunt of impertinence.

"You usually run the mini marathon each year as part of the 500, don't you?" Alex repeated.

"Yes, why do you ask? Did something happen at the marathon I was unaware of?"

"No, not that I know of. I was just inquiring, is all."

"Oh, yes, yes, well, I'm sorry, Alex, forgive me. Yes, I ran. I didn't do as well as in past years. I thought I'd trained just as hard, but I simply didn't have it in me this year. I'm not getting any younger. That's what I told my wife, anyway. Too much has been going on." Roger Montrose returned to his board material but politely asked, "Were you there? Do you run, by any chance?"

Alex shook his head in such a way as to assure his colleague that he had no interest in running. "Only after a three-year-old, I'm afraid."

Kate smiled. She liked the young Alex Aubert. His boyish looks were in sharp contrast to the profound business success he'd experienced in the development and sales of healthcare software that he and a Wabash College colleague had incubated from his garage.

"I shouldn't have run either," Roger said. "Too much has been going on."

"With your projects, you mean?" Alex asked.

Roger shot him a bewildered glance. "What? How do you know about them?" Alex opened his mouth to answer, but Roger lifted his hand. "Ah, yes, I remember now. Your father. I quite forgot. He's the center of all that goes on in this town."

"I do a fair amount of networking myself, Roger," Alex replied, holding his own. "I happen to know Chase VanderPelt too. He's who you're in partnership with, isn't he?"

Roger's left eye twitched. "Why? What has he been saying?" He wiped more perspiration from his brow.

The question appeared to take Alex off guard.

"He has a son, doesn't he?" Kate blurted out of thin air to mask the void. "Mr. VanderPelt, that is. Brian's his name."

The room stilled. Footsteps plodded toward them from the hall.

Patricia Reinholdt entered, sucking in wafts of air as she dumped a large satchel onto an empty chair between Kate and Marilyn. She brushed her hair back from her face and took a moment to ease her heart rate.

"Are you okay?" Kate asked.

"Yes, quite," Patricia reassured her. "Just out of shape, I'm ashamed to say. I haven't shed the pounds I promised to lose for summer; yet here it is May already, and I'm still out of shape, out of energy, out of breath, and out of time. Memorial Day is fast approaching. Summer is almost here."

"No wonder you're out of breath, Patty. That's quite a haul you brought in," Alex commented jovially.

Patricia continued to situate herself and ignored the comment.

"I don't suppose you've found it necessary to hoard all your things in those bags—given the recent robberies," Marilyn said.

"Robberies?" young Alex asked with alarm.

Marilyn stopped her texting and looked up. "Yes. Surely, you've heard. Robberies. Petty break-ins in search of jewels."

"That's not so petty. No, I hadn't heard. Here in Broad Ripple?"

"Oh, no, dear, not in Broad Ripple. There's no money like that in Broad Ripple. No, further north into the Crow's Nests, Williams Creek, and Meridian Hills. Places like that." She laughed condescendingly. "Oh, no, Alex, not in Broad Ripple. Don't be silly."

"I don't think it's silly at all," Patricia responded, setting her satchel on the floor. "There are very nice homes in Broad Ripple."

"I wonder what they're after," Alex said.

"Jewels, like I said," Marilyn said. "From what I've heard, thieves disconnected the alarms and surveillance cameras, entered the homes when they were unoccupied, and took valuable collections such as jewelry and silver."

Alex frowned. "Silver? That's hardly a take nowadays with its deflating value. Are you sure?"

Marilyn didn't have a chance to answer. Financier Andrew Gammon burst into the room. Tall and stately, he perused the members around the table and asked, "Am I late? I hope I wasn't keeping everyone."

"No," Kate answered. "Beth hasn't arrived yet. You're fine, Andrew." She glanced at her watch. "I haven't heard from Beth, by the way. She's usually early. I wonder if I should call her to see how long she'll be."

Patricia stopped fanning long enough to reflect. "I think I saw her crossing the bridge over the canal at Guilford. She should be here shortly, unless she turned down Sugar Bob to go to Open Arms."

"Why would she go to the store? She knows we have our board meetings here at the gallery."

"I don't know." Patricia shrugged, then resumed her fanning. "I'm just relating what I saw."

"Do you think that's what she did—go to Open Arms?"

"I wonder," Patricia said. "I tried to catch up to her after she crossed the bridge. I thought we could walk to the gallery together, but I lost sight of her. I assumed she turned left onto Sugar Bob to go to the store to see her daughter. Lauren is working there now, isn't she?"

"Not until after school is out," Kate said. "Finals at Vermillion College aren't until the end of the week or the first of next. I don't know anymore. Anyway, she'll be working part-time during the summer once she gets home. We can use the help. I'm expecting a busy summer in the village."

Andrew tapped his fingers on the table and shot glimpses at those sitting around him. "Other than Beth, we're all here, I see," he stated.

The directors hushed. Kate's mouth gaped but emitted no words. Marilyn stopped texting and set her phone quietly on the table. Patricia stopped fanning. Roger looked up from the material he was reading. Alex sipped his water.

Kate didn't believe Andrew was prone to blushing, but she detected a tinge of redness on his neck as he realized his blunder.

"Oh, I'm sorry," he said. "Yes, poor William, of course."

Marilyn took in a deep breath and stated what she thought was the obvious. "Well, it's not as if we can't talk about it. We're eventually going to have to discuss a suitable replacement for William at some point in time."

The hushed stillness continued until Roger countered, "Yes, that's true, but not today, not at this meeting."

"I haven't called Camille yet. Have you, Kate?" Patricia asked, fanning even harder than before. "I suppose it's a bit too soon, but I'm worried about her, the poor dear. I hope she's getting along."

"A stunning set of events, if you ask me," Marilyn added. "She's probably still trying to fathom it all."

"We all are," Kate replied. "It was all so sudden."

"What happened, exactly?" Andrew asked. "I haven't heard the official report, only rumors from acquaintances. Am I to understand Cottage Gallery was involved in some way?"

Kate sat upright in her chair. Although the financier's question was indirect and vague, she took sharp offense at the suggestion of a connection between the gallery and William

Davisly's death.

"I'm sorry. My words seem to be poorly chosen this afternoon," he said. "I didn't mean to imply anything by my comment."

"Oh, I think we understood what you meant, Andrew," Marilyn retorted, "and you aren't far from the mark, if you ask me."

"What do you mean, Marilyn?"

"Kate can confirm the details, but it appears that William ordered a truck to return a piece of furniture he purchased from the gallery only yesterday. When the truck arrived, the men placed the item in the back, and when they started to leave, they heard a lone shot coming from within his house. They called the police, and the authorities made the grisly discovery. There you go. Kate can fill in the rest of the details for you."

Kate turned slowly toward Marilyn and gave her a dirty look. "I have no details," she said emphatically. "I didn't even know he had come into the gallery to make a purchase. Beth's son, Gabe, was working the showroom yesterday. If William came into the shop and purchased a bureau, Gabe didn't tell me and probably didn't have a reason to tell me."

"Wasn't there anything at all odd about it?" Marilyn asked.

"No, it was an ordinary sale like all of the others yesterday. Furthermore, I don't know why William wished to return it after he got it home any more than any of you know the reason. All I know is that a bureau was purchased, and it was returned like any other item on any other day at the gallery."

"Except that he took his life the moment it left his home," Marilyn replied.

Kate slammed the palm of her hand onto the surface of the conference table in protest. Marilyn turned away from the executive director's scowl and picked up her phone to resume texting.

"Here, here, Marilyn," Roger chimed in. "I must agree with Kate on this one. You're jumping to conclusions and being a bit unreasonable without knowing all the facts, don't you think?"

"Was it determined to be self-inflicted?" Andrew asked before Marilyn could respond.

Alex nodded. "Yes, it's true."

"I see. That makes sense to me now. Yes, it does."

"What do you mean?"

"Well," Andrew replied, "at first, I wondered if it was a burglary gone bad like the other burglaries they've been having in the area. You've all heard about them, I'm sure. Most uncharacteristic for Crow's Nest. Although I'm not any happier about the real reason he died than I am about my probable explanation."

Marilyn snorted. "It's next to murder, if you ask me."

The room became still once again as the board members turned to look at Marilyn. She continued to look at her phone as if she'd said nothing at all.

Roger tightened his jaw and clenched a fist.

Patricia's eyes, wide with astonishment, glanced at the others around the table.

"Murder?" Roger asked. "Marilyn, don't be absurd."

Patricia nodded. "I agree. I don't know how you could say such a thing."

"Don't tell me it didn't cross your minds as well?"

Kate shook her head. "It certainly did not."

Marilyn looked at Andrew and Alex but received no indication from them that they supported her comment. "Very well," she conceded.

"I think we should change the subject," Kate said.

"Yes," Patricia said. "This conversation adds no value to our already somber mood, and it fails to acknowledge the torment

William must have suffered in the moments leading up to his decision. Nothing good can come of it."

"Very well. Conversation dropped," Marilyn said in a tone that implied she'd already conceded, and further admonishment wasn't necessary.

"No," Andrew said with authority. "Let's hear what Marilyn has to say. I want to know. William was a man close to all of us on the board. He purchased something from the gallery, returned it, and then, quite by surprise to all of us, he saw the need to take his own life. We may be able to learn something from what Marilyn has to say. I think she should continue." He turned his attention directly to Marilyn. "Tell us. You have our attention. What do you know that makes you conclude that murder took William's life?"

"Oh, I didn't say it *was* murder. Clearly, he committed suicide. No, I meant that if it was murder, I wouldn't have been surprised."

"On what grounds do you say that?" Alex asked. "I didn't know the man well, only having been on the board just a few months, but I knew of him, and his reputation in this city was highly regarded."

"You're very young, Alex."

"Your point?"

"My point is that in every city, there are closets of history that have never been cleaned out, but you're too young to know about them."

Alex threw his hands in the air. "What is she talking about? Someone, please explain to me what her parable means."

Roger Montrose glared at Marilyn who sat directly across the table from him.

Marilyn smiled when she saw his face. "You know what I'm talking about," she said. "You remember, don't you, Roger?"

"I vaguely remember something, yes, I do, but just enough to make a fool out of myself. I remember something from a long time ago, and I repeat, *a long time ago*. It was something horrific in which he was implicated. It wasn't good. I remember now, but that's all I remember."

"Murder is never good, Roger. You're thinking of the Brookside Park murders, I believe."

Andrew Gammon lifted his finger as if he, too, remembered the incident. "Brookside Park? Yes, Brookside Park, decades ago. It was an eerie execution-style murder, and it had it all, didn't it? Sex, scandal, bribes, kickbacks, stolen property, political ties, organized crime—you name it."

"But that was quite a long time ago," Patricia said.

"Yes, it was, but I remember when those young men were killed. There were so many angles to the crime that a single motive or suspect was impossible to narrow down. It's still unsolved to this day, if I'm correct, but I find it hard to believe that William had any connection to that crime. In fact, he wasn't even in Indianapolis at the time of the murders. He lived somewhere up north, I believe. Yes, up north around Lafayette or someplace like that."

"Delphi," Roger said.

"What? Was it Delphi? Yes, I believe you're right, Roger. Delphi. He only came to Indy within the past decade. Why, those murders are as old as—as old as young Alex here."

"As you said, Andrew, there were so many angles," Marilyn said in an apologetic tone. "Look, everyone, I'm terribly sorry I brought it up. Really, I am."

Kate pursed her lips and scoffed. "A little too late for sorry, Marilyn. We asked you not to go there, but you insisted, and now you're conveniently sorry. It's too late. My memory of dear William is tainted and associated with something utterly horrible."

Short, rapid steps by a woman in heels were heard suddenly from the hallway.

Alex turned to the board members and implored, "No more talk of this. Not another word."

Elizabeth Kimmerman entered the room with a light briefcase. She wiped a bead of sweat from her brow, smiled to greet the board, and offered an apology for her tardiness. She didn't make tardiness a habit, but this afternoon couldn't be helped, she said. She had business that couldn't wait, and she begged for the board's indulgence.

Kate reassured her the board understood, but Kate wouldn't have said anything different even if the board was in an uproar. Beth was her friend as well as colleague, a personable woman and practical at fiscal matters. Kate often wondered why Beth sat on the Indianapolis City Council and dabbled in the affairs of the community rather than trying her hand as Chief Executive Officer at a for-profit organization. She was a good councilwoman, Kate admitted, which was one of the reasons why heads of the political party with which she was affiliated had tapped her as their candidate for the upcoming mayoral election, but Kate didn't believe Beth had her sights set high enough. If Beth used her connections within the community to her advantage, she could land a position within an organization where she could make some *real* money—one of the reasons Kate was glad Beth was board chair and kept her close at hand as one of her friends.

Beth removed the packet of board information from her briefcase. She lifted her head periodically to acknowledge each member in attendance. Sometimes she smiled as she glanced in their direction, sometimes she let the smile wane with a confused sense of concern. The feedback she received from the faces of the members was solemn—a demeanor atypical of the group.

Kate held her breath at the board's response to Beth's engagement. She also noticed Beth eyeing the vacant chair at the end of the table. Everyone sat in their normal seats—men on one side, women on the other—everyone but William Davisly. He usually sat at the end.

Beth turned to Kate, sitting next to her on her left, and asked, "Did William say he was running late? Should we get started without him?"

Kate's eyes widened with an awareness that Beth was uninformed about his death. She stammered slightly before Alex interjected, "You must not have heard."

Beth's eyes darted about the table in bewilderment. "Heard what?" she asked sullenly. "Is something wrong?"

Chapter Three

Beth returned home immediately following the meeting at Cottage Gallery. White tea steeped in a cup as she trod into the den, where she slumped into a leather sofa. She buried her head in the palm of her hand while she rested the cup on her leg. Beth didn't know what to do with such a day. There would be more like them, she was sure. How many? And would she be able to handle them?

She'd stayed longer at the gallery than she'd anticipated, not because of the meeting's agenda but because of her conversation with Kate after the adjournment. Beth didn't know what she found more disturbing from that conversation—the details of William Davisly's death, or the conversation the board had had before her arrival. Kate told her everything about Marilyn Wells-Brewer's accusation. She'd recited the conversation as if she had a transcript of the discussion in front of her.

The meeting left Beth hopelessly sad. *Poor William*, she thought. She knew how desperate he must've felt when he made the decision to pull the trigger. She'd felt it too, in recent days.

I am the law in Indiana.

The six words sickened her. She didn't know why they came into her mind. Beth rubbed her temple with her free hand and tried to remember back to her conversation with Kate.

How unfair of Marilyn to drag William's name into a conversation in the manner she did so soon after his death. Had she no compassion for Camille? Could she not hear how damaging her words sounded to those around the table? Were the words true? Could they be true? If so, how did Marilyn of all people come to have such information?

Marilyn's accusations weren't fair, and the timing of them upset Beth greatly.

She gave Marilyn credit for one thing, however. If her intent was malice—and Beth wasn't sure that wasn't the case—Marilyn certainly knew how to work the board members to get the reaction and response she sought. Beth saw that probing characteristic in her. Yes, she believed Marilyn was a master at pushing the right buttons at the right time of those she wanted to intimidate.

The six words came to mind again.

She shook them from her head and wondered if the rumors could be true. If they were not, how sad, but if they were, and must've been to some extent for William to feel such hopelessness, what repercussions could there have been for him? The Brookside Park murders were such a long time ago. At the time of the murders, Beth was still a child at her parents' home near Kokomo and could recall nothing of the gruesome details. The little town of Russiaville where she lived wasn't isolated, but it was devoid of many outside influences that impacted larger cities. Perhaps the shelter of living in a small town exacerbated her naivety.

Beth placed her teacup on a nearby end table and picked up her cell phone. There was a way to get information to either confirm or dispel the rumors about William. She used the search engine on her phone and typed the words *Brookside Park murders*. Articles from the *Indianapolis Star* contained mostly pictures of the bungalow where the murders had occurred. People stood on the front lawn, aghast at the atrocity. She wasn't interested in sensational pictures of the scene. If gruesome photographs inside the bungalow existed, she wanted to see even less of those. What she was interested in was information on the suspects the police department identified from their investigation. Beth held her breath. She'd be devastated if William's name popped up in any of the archives she reviewed, but fortunately, his name did not appear, and she didn't recognize any other names either.

She grew weary of searching online without meaningful success and noticed that her phone's battery capacity was at 35 percent. She'd better stop while she still had juice in her phone, but the compulsion to look at one more site was overwhelming. This one contained a summary of the evidence investigators had gathered to determine a motive for the crime. The find intrigued her, not the additional facts she discovered, but the depth of evidence investigators had to sift through for plausible suspects.

Beth read that the three victims could have been killed by an array of suspects within the city and beyond. They had numerous affairs. Each of the women—and their husbands—had been investigated thoroughly. The use of stolen equipment in the men's microfilm business suggested ties to an underground market most likely from Chicago. Drunken brawls were a common activity of the three men. On more than one occasion, cronies, operating under the bar owners, searched for the men to repay damages to the inside of their establishments or, as she read later, to collect on gambling debts left behind by their indiscriminate spending on anything that ran, raced, rolled, or scored.

The men were only in their late twenties, but their brains

were fried by recreational drugs, their livers hardened by strong liquor, and their arteries clogged by excessive gluttony. They loved fast cars and spent an enormous amount of money to associate themselves with the drivers at the Indianapolis Motor Speedway. They owed mortgages, second mortgages, lines of credit, revolving credit, secured and unsecured credit, and IOUs in consequence of their business and personal spending lifestyles. More than that, they used the good nature of their friends and family to squander their savings after vowing to them that they would clean up their act.

Beth saw nothing, though, to substantiate Marilyn's claims implicating William Davisly. How sad that she would present herself as a colleague to William when he was alive, then turn against him on the day of his death.

Could it happen to me?

Beth squirmed on the sofa, debating whether Marilyn would do the same to her given the chance. A dull pang grew from deep within. She knew the answer. Yes, Marilyn Wells-Brewer would turn against her in a heartbeat.

Her stomach churned. She picked up her cup and took a small sip of tea to quell the ache. It did its trick, and so she took another sip, and yet another, but she couldn't swallow the six words that drew a lump in her throat.

Beth didn't hear two feet cross the hardwood floor toward her, but when the footsteps stopped, she felt the warmth of two strong arms wrapping gently over her shoulders to caress her. She recognized the cologne but was too tired to appreciate the man wearing it. As much as she wanted this time to be alone, she needed to know her husband was there for her, whether she wanted him there or not.

Barry ambled from behind the sofa to the easy chair that he often sat in to watch the evening news. Tonight, the news would be more disturbing than usual, and he was wise enough to leave the television off. The news and rumors of William Davisly's death disturbed him as much as they did Beth. He was the Senior Vice President of Commercial Lending at one of the major banks downtown, and he knew many of the people Davisly's life touched.

He also knew William Davisly well.

"I figured you'd be late getting home tonight," he said.

"I'm sorry I didn't call."

"Don't worry about it. I didn't expect you to. I grabbed a bite without you, though. If you're hungry, we can—"

Beth lifted her hand to stop him. "Food is that last thing on my mind. I just want tea."

A lull stretched between them.

"Do you want to get out of here for the weekend, just the two of us?" he finally asked.

She shook her head. "Lauren's coming home."

He cocked his head as if to ask her to reconsider.

"It wouldn't be right," she said. "Her coming home to an empty house after she's been gone all semester would be cruel."

He smiled and almost laughed.

"Stop it," she said playfully. "I know what you're thinking. We haven't exactly been good company lately."

"She might relish the fact that we've left town."

"I know, but I seriously doubt it, Barry. I talked with her this afternoon, before the board meeting. I think she's ready for some stability at home."

"I daresay she's not going to find an abundance of that in this house."

"She doesn't know it," Beth countered.

Barry gave his wife a look as if she was being naive. "She's not a child anymore, Beth. Give her credit for some adult perception. If she hasn't grasped it by now, Gabe will clue her in. He certainly gets it."

"He's older than she is, smart and inquisitive. I suspect he's even done some of his own research."

"On what?"

"You know very well on what, Barry."

"Your great-grandparents? How would he know?"

"Because he gets it. You said so yourself. That's why I don't think it's a good idea that he and Lauren should share that house in the Oxbow when she returns. She should be with us. Whatever happens, she should be with her parents so that we can keep an eye on her."

"There you go again with the mother smothering. Let her grow up. Besides, they'll be in Rocky Ripple, not the Oxbow."

"It doesn't matter, Barry."

"I think it does. You always get the two places confused, and you get Rocky Ripple confused with Broad Ripple on top of that. It's because you don't want to face the fact that Gabe and Lauren are adults and on their own, so you make it sound as if they live in some obscure place on the edge of the earth and should move back home."

Beth took a deep breath.

"Look, hon," Barry said, leaning forward, "I think it's good Lauren took Gabe up on his offer to move in with him during the summer. They're good kids. They'll take care of each other. It'll give us time for your campaign. You don't want Lauren smack-dab in the middle of your mayoral race. You won't be here at the house much anyway. I won't be here. She'll be alone most of the time. Let her stay with Gabe."

Beth couldn't argue his point.

I am the law in Indiana.

She twitched.

"What's the matter?" Barry asked.

Beth jerked her head his direction. "Nothing. Why?"

"You shuddered and had that look again. Far away and fearful."

"It was nothing."

Barry sighed. "Beth, it's me. I know that look."

She drew a breath. Tears welled in her eyes. "I can't shake it." Beth swallowed hard so that she could continue. "They won't go away, Barry. Thoughts of the past. The visions. Flashbacks of my imagination. They get longer and more vivid each time."

"We have a doctor. Perhaps—"

"No," she blurted. "Oh, God, Barry, no. How could you even suggest I see a psychologist at a time when I'm running for mayor?"

"It doesn't have to be a psychologist, Beth, and even so, people see such doctors all the time."

She rubbed her temples. "You're right. I'm sorry. I'll be fine. I wouldn't be so bothered right now about all of this, but Kate, well, we had a disturbing conversation this evening."

"About William?"

"Not only about William but about Open Arms."

"Beth, you shouldn't talk to Kate. She's your best friend, I know, and I realize you're comforted by talking to her, but you two have a love-hate relationship sometimes. You can't trust why she says what she says to you. What was it this time?"

"We're having trouble with inventory, it appears. It seems getting an accurate inventory of what's coming in and going out of the store is becoming more difficult without an automated inventory system. We don't have a good manual system either."

"That's imperative, Beth. Working from a manual inventory system is archaic and unnecessary, especially when Kate's system at Cottage Gallery is automated. Why isn't she doing something about it? She's the executive director."

"I don't think she wants to appear as if there's a conflict of interest."

"I didn't say Open Arms had to use *her* system. Kate simply has to use her knowledge about the system that would be best for Open Arms."

Beth curled her upper lip. "Kate is incapable of doing that. You know it's Gabe that handles all her automation at the gallery."

"Then get Gabe to help."

"We can't and don't want to at Open Arms. Gabe works for the gallery. We must be careful that we don't use him at Open Arms. We're a not-for-profit, Barry. The gallery is not. We have to be sure all transactions and interactions are separate."

"I get that, but how do you know merchandise isn't being hustled out of the door behind your backs by either customers or employees, or both?"

"You're right, we don't."

"What did the board have to say about it?"

"The board doesn't know, not entirely. Not yet. We didn't discuss it tonight. William's death took our attention away from material board matters for most of the meeting except for the financials. We talked about how much we'll miss him on the board, but Kate told me later that the board had a completely different conversation in my absence, one that wasn't very complimentary of him."

"Let me guess who mediated the unpleasant conversation."

"You don't need to guess. Chef Marilyn stirred the pot and served the stew. I'm not sure what I'm going to do with her, Barry. She has Kate terribly upset. She practically implicated the gallery as the cause for William's death."

"She's trouble, Beth."

"I know she's trouble." Beth sighed and rubbed her temple.

"Oh, please, let's not discuss it anymore."

Barry sat back in his chair, appearing to concede, but he worked his lower jaw from side to side. Beth knew he loathed Marilyn as much as she did. He also loathed her husband, Cole, even more.

"Cole Brewer is a spineless, weaseling, do-nothing shadow of a man," he said.

She requested silence again.

Barry resumed gritting his teeth.

"I had the strangest thing happen to me this afternoon," she said, filling the void. "I don't know what to make of it, really."

"Make of what, dear?"

"The strange thing that happened to me today. I got to Broad Ripple early this afternoon so that I'd have some time to spend in the village before the meeting. As I was crossing the Central Canal on Guilford, I saw Patricia Reinholdt standing on the sidewalk in front of the bistro. You remember Patty, don't you?"

"Doesn't she walk around like a bag lady or something?"

"That's beside the point. I like Patricia and all. She really is a sweet person, but she's not much of a conversationalist. Sometimes you can get free from her quite easily, and other times you can be stuck in a drawn-out discussion on topics of no importance about people you don't even know. Anyway, I didn't have time to talk to her, but I heard her call my name. I pretended I didn't hear her and continued on my way."

"I'm not sure I'm following the oddity of the story."

"I'm not finished. After the board meeting when I was talking to Kate, Kate mentioned in passing when I apologized for my delay that Patty saw me as she was standing on Guilford. She told the board she saw me cross the canal and turn down Sugar Bob."

"What's wrong with Patty standing on a sidewalk, calling

your name?"

"That's just it. She didn't just stand there. She followed me."

"Followed you?"

"Yes, she told Kate that she stood on Guilford and watched me walk down Sugar Bob, but that's not true. She actually followed me down the street. I walked about three-quarters of a block before I turned back around to see if she'd lost interest in my whereabouts, but there she was, following closely behind. She's not easy to miss on a street, Barry. You said it yourself; she's a bag lady. She carries her possessions in oversized satchels that are half her size. You couldn't miss her if you tried."

"What did you do?"

"Instead of going left on Ferguson like I wanted, I turned right. She didn't need to know my business, so I tried to confuse her. I walked a couple of blocks on Ferguson to Sixty-Fourth Street, turned left, and walked to Carrollton. I looked back again, and she was still behind me."

"That's odd, even for Patty."

"Yes, even for Patty." Beth felt like laughing but couldn't. "So I turned left again on Carrollton and headed back toward the canal greenway. One might think her behavior was funny, but I don't think it was funny at all. In fact, it was rather disturbing, so I zigzagged into a parking lot toward the American Legion. She probably thought at that point I had lost my mind. I wanted to stop and ask her what she was doing, but I'm sure she would've asked me the same thing. Strangely, though, she stopped without entering the parking lot and looked north as if she contemplated going somewhere else."

"Where did she go?"

"I don't know. There are bushes and a couple of large trees at the corner of one of the buildings. I managed to stand out of sight."

"You hid in the bushes?"

"Don't make it sound so childish. I didn't hide *in* the bushes, Barry. I just stood a little behind them. What would you have done if you had a lunatic following you around town?"

"Confront the crazy-assed—"

"Barry, please."

"I would've asked her what she was doing following me around town."

"Oh, you would not."

"Well, I sure wouldn't have been hiding behind some bushes in broad daylight. You're running for mayor, for crying out loud, Beth. You have to think of these things."

Beth set her cup of tea on an end table and shook her head. "There's just too much going on for me to think clearly anymore, Barry."

He gave her a sorrowful but supportive look. "I know. I don't blame you. I really don't. We both haven't been thinking clearly lately, but we have to focus. We must be on our guard. We can't let people like Patty Reinholdt get the best of us. We can't let . . ." Barry stopped and gritted his teeth.

Beth gave him an icy stare. "You might as well say it,and get it out into the open."

"Okay," he said, taking a deep breath. "We can't let *them* get to us either. What were you doing going down Sugar Bob in the first place?"

"I went to Open Arms."

Barry tried not to look annoyed. "Why?"

"No reason."

"I asked why."

"If you must know, I decided to take a second look at that bureau we returned. You thought it would be a nice investment. I scoffed at you at first, but later I thought you were right. I should give it a second look."

Barry frowned. "I'm never right, Beth. You know that. That's not the reason you went."

"It's the story I told them at Open Arms."

"I don't think that was a good idea."

"Why not? I think it shows I'm not afraid."

"No, it shows that the bureau we bought and returned is still on your mind, that it still bothers you."

"Nonsense. I don't believe that."

"Believe it. They'll never leave us alone if they think it bothers us."

Beth shook her head as if Barry's opinion was unfounded. In truth, however, she was afraid he was right.

"Tell me something else," Barry asked. "Why didn't you go to the gallery? The gallery is where the note told us to buy and return the bureau."

Beth shrugged and glanced away briefly. "I looked in the gallery yesterday, but I didn't see the piece they sold us. I asked Gabe about it, and he said it had been taken back to the workshop at Open Arms for repairs."

"Repairs? Is that what they call it?"

Beth shrugged again.

"You shouldn't have gone," he replied, getting up from his chair to pace the den.

"I think you're being silly."

"Who did you see? Did you talk to anyone?"

"No, just that young woman who works the counter. What's her name? Amy, that's it. Amy said Eddie had stepped out, and Chuck had gone for the day. Gone where, I don't know. There's nowhere for him to go. And Eddie stepped out to meet with Kate. I told Amy why I'd come, and I asked if I could go into the back to look for the piece, and she said I could."

"She shouldn't have let you."

"I know," Beth said. "I have no more business being in the back without an employee with me than a regular customer, but she said it would be okay, me being the board chair and all. I wish people wouldn't let me do that. It's so patronizing and wrong. Board chair or not, I didn't have any business being back there."

"But you went anyway."

Beth nodded shamefully. "Yes, I went anyway."

"And?"

"And I didn't see it."

"Not in Chuck's workshop?"

She shook her head and shook it again when Barry asked if the bureau had been prepared for transport back to Cottage Gallery. "No, Barry, I said I didn't see it."

"Perhaps it went out again," he said.

Beth bit her bottom lip. "I suppose it did."

"I wonder who it went out to?"

"I don't know," she replied. "I guess we'll have to wait for the next death to find out."

Chapter Four

Callan Morrow entered his Victorian home and set his briefcase inside the front door. He removed his suit coat and hung it on a hall tree before making his way toward the light shining from the kitchen. He'd accepted a prominent position at a small liberal arts college in west central Indiana, following a fraud case he'd solved in Chicago that drew national attention. Callan often arrived home weary, second-guessing his decision to develop a forensic accounting curriculum to interest young students in the field. Today, however, there was hope he'd made the right choice to get out of the corporate world and into academia. His students were attentive, alive, and eager. He rubbed the palms of his hands vigorously across his face, adding a blushed hue, hoping his expression now matched his mood.

His wife stood at the island in the middle of the room, dabbing at a dish of butter pecan ice cream as she watched a sitcom on a portable television. She wore dull gray sweats over a pair of fuzzy pink slippers. Her hair drooped in strings on one side of her face as the other side clung for dear life across the top of her ear. The rest was wadded into a haphazard bun on the back of her head.

She waved her spoon when Callan entered as if to ask if he wanted some of her treat.

He approached the carton that was nearby and looked in. "It's empty," he said.

"Yeah, I know, but I'd give you some from my dish."

He stepped around the island and gave her a kiss. Her offering was an act of love. Terese didn't give up ice cream easily.

"How was your class?" she asked, licking the spoon as she turned down the television sound. "Did you enlighten their minds?"

He lifted his hands toward her head as if manipulating her brain and said teasingly, "We discussed the psyche of the white-collar fraudster." He lowered his hands and added, "They were into it this evening. It was the most fun I've had since I started teaching this *Intro to Fraud* class at the college." Callan gave her another kiss on her cheek but backed away slowly.

"What's the matter?" she asked, detecting something wrong with his demeanor.

"Nothing. I was just thinking. Class went well tonight, and everyone appeared to be into my lecture and case studies, but there was this one student, I didn't know what to make of her."

"Was she not paying attention?"

"Oh, no, she was paying a great deal of attention, perhaps a little too much so. I mean, there were times the intensity in her eyes and the drawn look on her face concerned me. I couldn't tell what she was thinking."

"What was the topic again?"

"The behavior of fraudsters during an audit, and what to look for," he said. "I tried to catch her after class, but she got away too soon. It was as if she *had* to get out of the classroom because she couldn't stand it any longer."

"How odd," Terese said, setting her spoon inside her dish. "What are you going to do?"

"I don't know. I only have this class two times a week. I don't want to wait till the next one to speak with her. I may send her a quick email tomorrow and say that I'm checking up with students to see if there are any questions from tonight's lecture. Maybe that'll prompt something. In the meantime, you finish your ice cream. I'm pouring some brandy then heading upstairs to my study. I'd like to finish some genealogy work on my great-grandparents."

"Sure you wouldn't care for some ice cream? I still have some left."

Callan looked in her dish and frowned. "You've eaten all the pecans, and the ice cream has practically melted. All you've got left is a buttery swirl."

She lifted her spoon to her mouth. Some of the creamy dessert dropped off the edge and dribbled down the side of her chin. "So is that a yes or a no?"

~

Callan poured Brandy de Jerez into a snifter. The Andalusian aroma tantalized him as he walked upstairs to his study. Terese soon followed him with a cup of decaf coffee in her hand, steam rolling over the top of her fingers. He wanted to be alone to unwind after his intense classroom discussion, but he could sense Terese wanted—or needed—to be with him.

He sat at his desk and stared at vintage pictures of his great-grandparents until she joined him, then he turned his attention to his wife, taking a second look at her casual appearance. "You asked me earlier if I was okay. What about you? How are you doing?"

Terese lifted her legs onto the cushion of the chair next to his desk. "I'm fine." She took a sip from her cup, then admitted, "I'm a little bored. Brandon's at college, and Gil's involved with baseball. I hardly see anyone. Hopefully, as the semester winds down at each of your schools, I'll have all three of you back in the house soon."

"I thought we drove you crazy."

"You do, but I've since realized that your craziness keeps me moving. Without it, I do nothing. I've been almost tempted to use that gym membership I have." She wiped dust off the edge of his desk with her fingertips. "When is school out for you? Are you taking some time off?"

"I plan to, but aren't you going to work at that physician's office on the square in town?"

"They don't need my help for another month," she said disparagingly. "Not for another . . . whole . . . month."

Callan gave her an empathetic look, then turned to his photographs.

She craned her neck to see. "Who do you have there?" she asked, genuinely interested.

"Photos of some of my great-grandparents. I've done some research on them already, but I haven't included a write-up in my journal."

"I didn't know you knew who your great-grandparents were."

"I do now," Callan said. "It's almost been an obsession with me to find out about them."

"You were so young when your parents died. It's no wonder. You're bound to be curious, don't you think? Wasn't there anyone who could tell you something as you were growing up?"

"My uncle did. I remember when I was a kid he used to take me to old pioneer cemeteries. He knew where some of the family graves were. We used to take paper and charcoal and rub over the tombstones to read what was engraved. It intrigued me, but I was too young to fully appreciate what we were doing."

"I haven't seen you working on it for a while, though."

Callan nodded. "I guess family, career, household tasks, and other life diversions have a way of putting things off. Genealogy had to take a back seat."

A picture of a younger Callan with a woman a few years older than him lay off to the side. Callan glanced at the photograph then turned it facedown. "She's the other reason I stopped."

"I didn't get a good look at the picture," Terese said. "Was that you with your sister?"

Callan pushed the photo farther away.

"Why is she so against your genealogy work?"

"It's simple. She doesn't want to know if there's anything bad in our history."

"So you're also not to know, is that it?"

"Essentially. She believes if it's not researched, it won't be documented, and if it's not documented, it didn't happen."

"But what if you find out something wonderful?"

"I already have. Interesting too."

"Such as?"

"The hardships they went through. I'm not only documenting the good stuff, but I'm jotting down the hardships as well. My sister doesn't want to know of the hardships. She doesn't want to believe they even existed."

Terese resituated her legs. "That's shortsighted. When I think back to some of the hardships we've had in our own lives, they've only made us stronger."

"Tell that to my sister." Callan gathered some of the photographs in his hands. "Some difficulties do have permanent consequences. I think that's what she's trying to avoid. This great-grandfather, for instance, was killed at a railroad crossing in Preble. His horse died too. His buggy was obliterated by a freight train. As tragic as that was, the State of Indiana improved railroad crossing warnings following his death. Some long-term positive gains happened, but it took his death for that to occur."

He showed Terese another photo.

"Who's he?"

"The person my sister is ashamed of, our great-grandfather."

Terese took the photograph from Callan's hands. "Handsome man, Callan. He doesn't look evil. What does she have against him?"

"He was an inventor."

Terese's eyes widened with interest. "A successful one?"

"Very. He and his sons, including my grandfather, perfected a device for fighter planes."

"Were they in the Armed Forces?"

Callan shook his head. "He was an electrician. He invented a mechanism that enabled the accurate release of bombs."

Terese's studied the photo again.

"What's on your mind?" Callan asked.

"Well," she said reluctantly, "on one hand, I'm glad we won the war by your family's ingenuity, but on the other, it's quite a notorious invention for your family to hang their hat on."

"Exactly," Callan said. "My family was lauded for the accomplishment."

"Except by your sister."

"Not only that, but she looks at the destruction and loss of life the invention caused and considers it an embarrassment. We defeated the Nazis. She forgets that, but it doesn't matter. She's angry anyway."

Terese changed her focus to another photograph. "What about this woman? Was she noted for something good?"

Callan looked at the water-stained photo of a great-grandmother fashionably dressed in a 1920s-period ensemble, standing with other women in similar attire. "I hope so," he said.

"You hope?" Terese raised her eyebrows. "That's an odd thing to say, Callan. She was your great-grandmother. I don't see how anything bad could come from this group of women."

Callan's face turned grave. "They're not friends."

Terese frowned. "Then who were they?"

"I don't know."

She tilted her head and narrowed her eyes. "I think you do know. You're an auditor and a fraud examiner by profession. It's in your nature to find out what you don't know."

Callan tossed the photograph aside. "I said I don't know."

Terese sat back in the chair, holding her cup firmly, and studied her husband's change in demeanor. "You're not the only one who understands the psyche of people who aren't being honest."

Callan knew she was referring to him.

"Why won't you tell me? If you won't tell me, Cal, then you're speaking out of both sides of your mouth. A minute ago, you criticized your sister for her opinion on your grandfathers, but in the next, you're on board about your grandmother. Do you know what I think? I don't think your sister is at all bothered by your great-grandfather and his bombing mechanism. I think it has to do entirely with your great-grandmother—this particular great-grandmother. She doesn't want to know about her, and you don't, either."

"That's not true. That period of time was just . . . difficult to understand and comprehend, Terese."

"It was the twenties, Cal. What's so hard to understand? The twenties were full of prosperity and good times. Everyone was full of life. What are you talking about?"

"Not in Indiana. On the surface, all was grand, but that's all it was to some people." He glanced at his wife's alarmed expression.

"Can you give me a clue as to what you're talking about?" she asked.

Callan took a sip of his brandy. "I haven't sorted it all out yet, so bear with me. This is what I know: My great-grandfather worked in the coal mines in the southwestern part of the state. His job was dangerous as you can imagine. He was often injured. None of his injuries were fatal, but collectively, they contributed to his premature death."

"So do you think this photo is of your grandmother and other women whose husbands worked in the mines?"

"I'm pretty sure of it. It would make sense. As far as I could tell, they spent a lot of time together, lobbying for better conditions. The men were their livelihoods. When the City Coal Mine exploded in 1925 near Sullivan, these women formed an auxiliary to help the widows and children of the men who were killed."

Terese waited for more of the story, but none came. She grew impatient. "So far, I've heard nothing that would compel me to believe your grandmother was anyone but an honorable and civic-minded individual."

"Then you're not remembering your history very well."

"Obviously not. What am I missing?"

"I just gave you a clue," he said impatiently. "It was subtle, mind you, but I told you all was *grand*."

Callan's cell phone rang from his pants' pocket. He pulled the phone out but didn't recognize the number. He normally didn't answer numbers he didn't recognize, but the area code was from the Indianapolis area. He took a chance it was someone of importance he knew.

"Mr. Morrow?" a meek voice asked. "This is Lauren Kimmerman, from class."

Callan mouthed to Terese that the young woman who acted oddly in his class was now on the phone. Terese indicated she should leave, but Callan insisted she stay by pointing to the chair.

"Is something the matter, Lauren?" he asked. "Are you okay?"

"Oh, yes, Mr. Morrow, thank you. I'm fine, sort of, in a way."

"That wasn't very convincing."

"No, I suppose it wasn't. It's just, well, I thought it could wait, but it really can't. It's rather urgent for me. Your class this evening on the psyche of a fraudster. It got me to thinking. It hit me hard."

"Class wasn't meant to hit you. It was meant to enlighten you on the profile of white-collar predators."

"Oh, I know, Mr. Morrow, and it did all that, it really did, but when coupled with what I'm seeing back home, well, it was difficult to sit in class without feeling desperate and frightened."

"I'm sorry, Lauren. What can I do to help?"

"It's my mother, Mr. Morrow."

"Your mother? You're worried about her?"

"Yes," Lauren said emphatically, "for all the reasons you discussed in class."

"I see, but why? What's bringing this on?"

Callan could tell the young woman didn't know where to begin or how to say what she needed to say to convey the urgency of her situation.

Lauren stammered before blurting, "My mother's embezzling, Mr. Morrow. She's embezzling a great deal of money. I know she is. You have to help me."

Chapter Five

Callan arranged to meet the distraught student at an off-campus coffee shop not far from the college.

Lauren entered the shop, looking pale. Red, puffy eyes under unkempt bangs accentuated her gaunt features. The evening was warm, but she dressed as if there was a chill in the air, wearing a light cardigan sweater. Though long enough to wrap around her waist, she let it hang and tucked her hands under her arms to warm them.

Callan motioned for her to sit while he went to the counter to help Terese, who had ordered coffee.

"I hope you don't mind that I asked my wife to join us," he said upon their return with three cups. "This is the best place to meet at this time of night, but I don't want other students to get the wrong impression about our conversation. Besides, Terese may bring a perspective I might overlook."

"I don't think you overlook much, Mr. Morrow," she said, "but I understand what you're saying, and I appreciate why your wife is here."

"I'm Terese, by the way," she interjected. "He may

not overlook very much, but he does overlook proper introductions sometimes."

Lauren laughed. "Perhaps I spoke too soon."

"While introductions aren't my forte, Lauren, I did notice you in class this evening. Your phone call explains it. You believe your mother is embezzling?"

Lauren tucked a strand of strawberry blond hair behind an ear and nodded timidly.

"From where?"

"I don't really know for sure."

"How much? Do you have a rough estimate?"

"No, but it seems a lot."

"In what way?"

"It just does."

Callan paused and reached for his coffee cup. "You know what I teach in class, Lauren. You know that in the examination of fraud cases, evidence and evidence-based facts are crucial. You're not giving me anything of that nature, and embezzling is a very serious crime. I don't want you to scare yourself over something that may not be true."

"But it *is* true."

"What's true?"

Lauren didn't answer.

Callan nursed his hot coffee then lowered his voice. "Okay, then let's approach this from a different angle. Let's forget about any possible embezzlement for the moment. The bottom line is that something is bothering you."

Lauren acknowledged she did have a great deal on her mind. Most of what troubled her were issues at home in Indianapolis.

"Start from the beginning," Callan said.

"My mother has had two very successful terms on the City Council in Indianapolis," she offered slowly and deliberately.

"The party has encouraged her to join the mayoral race. She's a good politician in addition to being fair and honest. I'm not just saying that because I'm her daughter. People have told me so. She has a squeaky-clean past. She breezed through the primary a couple of weeks ago, and she wants to win the race in the fall. I don't think I've ever seen my mother want something so badly. She wants to take the city to the next level of development. Are you familiar with Indy?"

"Very much," Terese replied. "Callan and I have lived in Indy since college. We've raised our sons there. We consider it home. We only recently moved to Vermillion when Callan started the fraud and forensic accounting curriculum at the college."

"We're also familiar with your mother," Callan interjected. "She's Elizabeth Kimmerman, isn't she?"

"Yes. Everyone calls her Beth." Lauren reached for her latte and brought the hot drink carefully to her lips. "The last time I was home, however, there seemed to be some uncomfortable dynamics. I asked my brother about it, but he brushed me off. Gabe moved out of the house about a year ago. He said he didn't know what I was talking about. I told him he was hiding the truth from me."

"What did he say to that?"

"He said I should go back to Vermillion and forget about it. Well, I can't forget about it, Mr. Morrow. I can't forget how I feel. It's so unlike my family."

"What dynamics did you see? Did it have to do with their relationship? Was it financial? Health-related?"

"It's not any of those, at least, not in the context you're speaking. I mean, it's not tension between my parents. It's more like pressure from outside the home. Does that make sense?"

"Only if it means you believe your mother's embezzlement was discovered by someone who is pressuring your parents for restitution, or worse, blackmail in light of your mother's campaign."

"I suppose that's what I fear," she said, looking beyond Callan and Terese's gazes. She turned her head at the sound of someone entering the coffee shop.

Callan studied his student's internal suffering through the fear on her face. There seemed to be more she wanted to say. Whether she was debating whether to say what was on her mind or couldn't articulate the words, he couldn't discern. He finished his coffee and asked if he could get Lauren or Terese a refill. As he scooted his chair back, Lauren turned her head from the door to face him.

"A board member committed suicide this morning," she said.

Callan sat back down.

"My mother is board chair of this charitable thrift organization in Broad Ripple that helps youths in the city. One of the members of the board suddenly and inexplicably killed himself."

"Such things always appear sudden, Lauren, but they're rarely inexplicable."

"No one seems to know why he did it though. The most disturbing thing about it is that he killed himself just after returning a piece of furniture to an antique gallery that's owned by the executive director of Open Arms—the thrift store."

"Why is that troubling?"

"It seems that the man who died, William Davisly, ordered a bureau one day and returned it the next. He didn't seem to want it when he bought it. In fact, he was quite put out by the whole thing, but he bought it anyway then turned around and returned it. All very sudden. Now he's dead."

"How do you know all this?"

"Through my brother. Gabe works for the gallery where

Mr. Davisly purchased the piece. He handled the transactions. I talked with him after my mother called. She called me right before class to tell me. She was upset and wanted to talk."

"That explains your demeanor during class."

"Yes, but I should tell you something that Gabe also told me, but Mom doesn't know that I know. My mother also purchased an antique piece from the same gallery recently. It was a bureau like the one Mr. Davisly purchased. She bought it one day and returned it the next. Or, I guess, my father returned it. My brother is worried. He can't tell me that he isn't worried, Mr. Morrow. I know him too well, and when Gabe worries, I tend to worry too, because, you see, Gabe thinks things through logically. Everything has a logical reason for happening."

"The transactions worry him?"

"Yes, the two are too similar in nature to be coincidental."

"Tell me a little more about this Open Arms thrift store and the gallery where the bureaus were purchased. How are they connected?"

"Are you familiar with Open Arms?" she asked, putting her hand over the top of her cup when Callan gestured if she'd like more coffee.

"As a matter of fact, I am," Terese said. "I went there many times when we lived in Indy. I know it caters to a trendier and younger crowd than I am, but it intrigues me every time I go. There's always something new and different, something I wouldn't normally see in the box department stores."

"The proceeds go to programs and organizations that help youths in need," Lauren said. "They provide youths with a place to go, something to do, an identity of self-worth, that sort of thing. I work there during the summer months between sessions."

"What about the gallery?"

"You've walked by it, I'm sure, especially if you've eaten

at the Brewpub or had coffee in the village. The name of it is Cottage Gallery. Kate O'Neal, the owner, took a bungalow and renovated it to meet her needs. It's larger than it looks from the outside. Gabe's working there part-time until he can earn enough money of his own to move to Chicago. He went to culinary school. There are more opportunities there."

"So how did you, your mother, and Gabe get to be associated with Kate, Open Arms, and Cottage Gallery?" Terese asked.

"Kate and my mother have been friends for years. They're very close. They both went to Park Tudor for high school, but they didn't know each other that well then. They got close in college. They both went to Butler." Lauren talked more about her mother's friendship with Kate before looking casually at a clock above the cashier counter. "It's getting late," she said. "I'm sorry. I've kept you both far too long."

"That's all right," Callan said. "We want to make sure you're okay."

"I am," she said, presenting a smile. "I appreciate you talking to me. I feel better already. You probably think it's all in my head."

Callan leaned toward the young woman and said, "Listen, you're under a lot of stress about what you saw and heard when you were home last. You're thinking of worst-case scenarios. That's what we do when we don't have all the facts. We think the worst, but it may be far from what's really going on. Then you come into class and listen to my lecture on the psyche of a fraudster, you read the case studies, we discuss the case studies intently, and you start to put two and two together about what you believe is happening to your mother."

"When you say it like that, Mr. Morrow, my mother as an embezzler doesn't make sense, does it?"

Callan smiled to reassure her.

Lauren rose from her chair. "Thank you for the coffee. Thanks for everything."

"You'll be okay walking back to the dorm?"

"Yes. Campus security is good. I feel better. I really do."

Callan watched Lauren leave. She passed by the front of the café window on her way toward the college, her blond hair blowing freely behind her, spirits improved. Satisfied, he sat back in his chair and contemplated their conversation. "Want anything else before we go?" he asked Terese.

"No." She gathered her wrap. "If I have anything else, I'll be up all night from the caffeine." She grabbed her purse from the floor.

Callan didn't move.

"You're going to be up all night, too, aren't you?" she asked.

"Yes, probably, but it won't be because of the coffee."

"What is it? I thought you talked through the embezzlement issue quite clearly with Lauren. She seemed satisfied with your explanation."

"Yes, I'm glad," he said halfheartedly.

Terese leaned in. "So what's on your mind?"

"I'm not sure there isn't something behind Mr. Davisly's death that Lauren shouldn't be more concerned about."

"Then why did you let her go?"

"No use upsetting her more tonight. There's nothing we or she can do. I can't help but think, however, there might be a connection between Mr. Davisly's antique bureau and the Kimmermans' bureau."

"It could be coincidence. Don't you believe in coincidences?"

"Yes, sure I do," he replied before finishing what was left in his cup. "After I've audited them."

Chapter Six

The next evening Gabe Kimmerman poked his head into Kate's dimly lit office. He didn't say anything. She appeared to be deep in thought, sifting through sales documents.

"Did you talk to Meredith Patterswaite today?" she asked without looking up.

"No, was I supposed to?"

She lifted her head and looked him in the eyes. "I thought you would."

He shrugged, not knowing why she would think that.

"It should be obvious, Gabe. The bureaus Mr. Davisly and your parents purchased and returned belonged to Ms. Patterswaite. She's quite irate."

"I didn't know."

"She called and left a message while I made a quick trip to Open Arms. She had some harsh words about our liberal return policy. She reminded me she didn't lose one sale, she lost two."

His expression must have given away his astonishment.

"And you should be upset too," Kate said indignantly. "We lost two commissions."

"That's all you're concerned about? Our commissions?"

Kate hesitated. "What happened to Mr. Davisly had nothing to do with us."

The young man's eyes darted around the room, searching for a rebuttal. "But we don't know that."

She gave him a piercing glare. "I do know that, and I'd appreciate it if you'd give her a call."

Gabe nodded reluctantly. "I'll do it tomorrow."

"Are you leaving now?"

"Yes, it's getting late. I have some tidying up to do first, then I'm heading out." He waited for further instructions, but none came. "Very well, then, if that's it, I'll be gone. I trust you'll turn on the security system. You'll do that tonight, won't you?"

"I always do," she said.

Gabe bit his lower lip. No, he remembered distinctly that she'd neglected to set the alarm several nights in a row during the past week. He dared not refute her, however. She didn't appear in the mood for more of his rebuttals. "Good night," he said, and left.

~

Kate picked up two pieces of paper from the top of her desk. One was a sales order, the other a sales return. The name on the *Sold To* line belonged to William Davisly. She studied it carefully before setting it down, then picked up two more pieces of paper, also a sales order and a sales return. The names on the *Sold To* line belonged to Barry and Beth Kimmerman. The information on each order form was identical except for the names. Kate let the Kimmermans' papers slip from her hand and glide to the top of her desk.

Kate thought briefly about the oddity of both transactions,

then picked up the phone's receiver on her desk and dialed a number she had memorized. No answer. The call went immediately to voice mail. When the monotonous message was finished, she simply asked, "Was this bureau handiwork yours? Call me as soon as you can. No, better yet, make it sooner."

She replaced the receiver and looked about her office, rubbing her hand along the top of her desk. Satisfied her domain was intact, she sat back in her chair and contemplated how she would handle the irritated Meredith Patterswaite if Gabe was unable to do so. Time passed slowly as she mulled over her predicament, and when out of the blue, an idea popped into her head, she grinned at its brilliance. Why didn't she think of it before?

Kate picked up a ballpoint pen and a blank piece of paper, and wrote the names of as many customers and proprietors as came to mind. A soiree was in order. The more names she wrote down, the grander the party grew in her mind. The upcoming Indianapolis 500-Mile Race made the perfect reason to have a party at Cottage Gallery. Of course, the purpose would be to garner support and loyalty to the gallery in the shadow of William Davisly's death, but it didn't have to be obvious to those who attended. Yes, the Indy 500! What a great way to let everyone know that life goes on, and Cottage Gallery would lead the way.

She wrote several names and listed several tasks that needed to be performed before, on hearing creaks from the bungalow's floorboards down the hall, she stopped and listened intently. But she heard nothing more. Kate glanced toward the window to see if a spring storm was brewing overhead. The old bungalow often expressed its discontent at storms, creaking and sounding as if the roof or floorboards were coming undone. She rose and went to the window. Heat lightning flashed in the distance. The branches of the old sycamores swayed congenially as they did on any other fair May evening. A storm was imminent, but it was miles away.

Kate glanced at the open doorway. Her desk lamp shone only a little light into the hallway. On deciding to investigate, she took small, hesitant steps forward. The creaks under her own footsteps matched those coming from down the hall. Her heart pounded, and her head felt light.

She stepped into the dark hallway and, using her hand to guide her along the wall, moved toward the front display room. The light from several vintage table lamps provided the only illumination in the room. A car passed slowly along the street, casting shadows that formed a macabre dance with the antiques.

Kate stopped her advance to listen, but she heard only silence. "Gabe, are you still in here?" she called.

He didn't answer.

She stood for several seconds before making her way through the display room toward another room that lead to the back hallway. Kate reached the back door and twisted the knob. It was locked. She sighed with relief, then turned toward the security panel to her right. She entered the security code onto the keypad and armed the mechanism before turning back toward the poorly lit display room. After flipping several switches to help her see better, she decided to check the front entrance as well. She strode to the door and turned the knob. Locked securely. Deadbolt fastened too.

Kate looked out at the street in front of the bungalow. All appeared calm and unassuming. Another car passed just as slowly as the first, but it didn't alarm her.

Time to go home. She could finish planning for the soiree tomorrow.

Kate turned to hurry down the aisle from the entrance to

her office when her leg hit the corner of a vintage desk that stuck out into the aisle. *That's odd,* she thought. She didn't remember the desk coming into the store today, and she definitely wouldn't have placed it in the aisleway for customers to bump into as she had just done. Every setting had a purpose—a strategic place for it to sit to be merchandised properly. Kate bent down to find a tag that would tell her the proprietor to whom the desk belonged. No tag.

She straightened and marched to her office, where she picked up her phone receiver and dialed another memorized number. "Gabe, this is Kate."

"What? At this hour?"

She ignored him. "Who does that desk belong to in the aisleway near the entrance?"

Gabe stumbled for words. "I-I don't know what you're talking about, Kate. What desk? Can't it wait?"

"Did you receive a desk today from a proprietor?"

"No, not today. No one brought one in for consignment."

"I don't believe you. There's a desk near the entrance. I hit my thigh on the corner. It was positioned very poorly. You know better than to merchandise items that way."

"Kate, I don't know what you're talking about. Seriously. There was no desk positioned in any aisleway near the entrance. I told you I tidied up before I left tonight. I wouldn't have left a desk like that in an aisle."

Tempted to believe him, Kate didn't say anything. Whatever disagreements she had with the young man weren't about how he displayed merchandise.

"Is that all?" he asked sharply.

Kate tried to think. If it wasn't Gabe who put the piece where it was, then how did it get there? Who could've gotten into the gallery to put it there? And how could they expect to sell it without any identifying information attached?

Gabe didn't wait any longer for an answer. He didn't say goodbye, just hung up.

Kate held onto the receiver and punched in the number she'd called earlier. She listened to the monotonous message again and at its ending said, "Your handiwork was at it again, wasn't it? I just want you to know that this time I've had it."

She slammed the receiver onto the cradle.

Chapter Seven

Gabe arrived at Cottage Gallery the next morning at nine fifteen, forty-five minutes before he was to open the showroom to the public. He sat in front of a computer screen and scrolled through an online directory of proprietors who consigned their antiques with Kate. Meredith Patterswaite's phone number appeared. Gabe picked up the phone receiver.

"Ms. Patterswaite, this is Gabe Kimmerman calling," he said.

Her usual cheery voice sounded confused. "Gabe?" she asked.

"Yes, from Cottage Gallery. You called yesterday."

"Yes, I did. You're very sweet to return my call, Gabe, but, well, quite frankly, I wanted to speak to Kate. I believe I should speak to Kate, given the circumstances."

"I understand, but she asked if I would call you to see what I can do for you."

"That's just it, Gabe, you can't do anything for me. Kate should do it. I find it offensive that she'd ask you to do her dirty work."

Gabe hesitated before saying, "I don't mind, Ms. Patterswaite."

"That's not the point, Gabe. Kate must think I'm worried

about my sales. I am, of course, but I'm more concerned about what happened to Mr. Davisly, and if the bureau he purchased had anything to do with his untimely decision."

"I'm sure it didn't."

"How can you be sure? Kate hasn't looked into it yet." Meredith paused as if to gather her thoughts. "I understand your parents bought a similar bureau of mine and returned it almost immediately. Do you know why?"

"No, ma'am, I haven't asked."

"I'm sure Kate hasn't, either, but that's exactly what I want to know. I want to know why they returned it."

Gabe said he understood and that he'd talk to Kate before the gallery opened and have her get back in touch.

"I'm having the bureau changed," she said abruptly.

He hesitated, confused. "Changed? What do you mean? Changed how?"

"Any way your man in the workshop can. His name is Mr. Cordry, isn't it?"

"Yes, Chuck to be exact."

"I want it changed," she said boldly. "I'm sure he can do something to the facade so that people won't associate it with Mr. Davisly. I want something done to it. Anything."

"I'm sure he can help you, but let me have Kate call you anyway, Ms. Patterswaite."

"A lot of good that'll do. That's because she forgets one very important fact."

"What's that?"

"I can do more than change or remove my items from consignment in her gallery," she said. Her voice quivered with anger. "I can make life very difficult for Kate. With my connections in town, I can ruin her reputation professionally. She'll never be able to sell another antique again."

"That's very serious, Ms. Patterswaite. Surely you don't mean that."

"You don't know how angry and apprehensive I am about what has happened with my bureau, Gabe. I thank you for all your help. You've been very kind to me, but I couldn't be more serious about what I said of Kate."

Gabe hung up and rose from the chair. He shuffled his feet toward Kate's office, gathering the delicate words to relay the phone conversation he'd had with Meredith. The door was half closed. Gabe could hear Kate's voice as if she was talking on the phone. It wasn't a pleasant voice, and based upon her responses, Gabe assumed the person on the other end was just as disagreeable.

"Because that's the way I want it," he heard Kate say. "You scared me half to death last night, coming into the gallery unannounced, dropping off an antique I didn't know I was getting. That's not how it's supposed to work."

Gabe shifted his feet to get one ear closer to the door's opening.

"We have to be careful," she continued. "Because we just do. . . . No, I have no idea what's going on." She paused.

Gabe looked through the door's opening. He saw enough of Kate to see her standing behind her desk with one hand braced on its surface as if the desk were holding her up. She looked pale, her face pasty and gaunt. He pulled his head back from the door.

"What do you mean, how do I not know?" she asked. "What are you accusing me of? How dare you say such a thing. No, I will not listen. You just do as you're told." Another second of silence passed. "Because that's why I pay you." The phone slammed against the receiver.

Gabe backed away as gently as he could. When a floorboard creaked underneath the ball of his foot, he knew he couldn't back away any further without being detected, so he stepped toward her surefootedly as if he'd just arrived down the hall.

He knocked firmly and peeked in, pointing to the front. "I was just on the phone with Meredith Patterswaite," he said.

Kate plopped into her chair as if she wasn't sure she wanted to hear about the conversation. "You didn't get very far with her, did you? Does she still want me to call her?"

"Yes, and I think it would do some good."

She tapped her fingers on her desk and then lifted her index finger to make a point. "I'll tell you what will be better, Gabe."

"What's that?"

"Who are our most difficult proprietors? If you could get rid of any dealer that consigns their antiques in our gallery, who would it be?"

Gabe was taken aback by the question and stammered for an answer. "Well, I don't know. I don't normally think of our proprietors in that way. Ms. Patterswaite isn't exactly difficult, but she does have questions. I've never given it much thought. May I ask why?"

"Certainly. We're going to give them an award. Everyone loves to be awarded for providing quality customer service. We'll give all those proprietors that give us trouble an award at this grand reception we'll have. It'll be wonderful and just what we need to take our minds off what's been happening. It'll change their negative attitudes as well. What's the matter? You don't look pleased."

"I'm not sure an award is what they want, Kate. I think they'd rather we get our inventory in order, nail down our return policies, and be sure there are no conflicts of interest between Open Arms and Cottage Gallery."

Kate sat back in her chair, folded her hands in her lap, and gave Gabe a look of apprehension. "Don't you like parties?"

"I love a good party, but that doesn't mean I want to hobnob with the likes of angry proprietors, if that's what you're asking."

"That's exactly what I'm asking, Gabe. I don't understand why you have to be so difficult."

~

Callan walked through the campus mall toward his office as the sun broke through the sycamore leaves. The air was crisp and refreshing. He strolled without contemplating the tasks ahead of him. He so rarely allowed himself to enjoy a morning, but this one was particularly bright, clear, and hopeful, and he was determined not to shroud it with anything that would change his outlook.

That was until he saw a young woman walking toward him on the path, lugging a backpack that appeared to weigh heavily upon her. She focused on the sidewalk in front of her, head drawn, walking as if she were plodding through a thick layer of mud.

"Lauren?" Callan asked as he passed.

She stopped and turned, acknowledging the greeting with a halfhearted smile, appearing not to care who the voice belonged to.

"Everything okay?" he asked, but immediately retorted, "I can see everything's not okay. What's the matter?"

"I don't know."

Callan stepped closer. "What's changed?" He had a terrible feeling that something had.

"Nothing's changed except that Gabe's even more withdrawn this morning."

"He called you?"

"No, Gabe would never call. I called him after I couldn't get a hold of my mother. He sounded angry and determined on the phone. I don't know what to make of it. Apparently, he had a run-in with Kate over a proprietor. He overheard a disturbing conversation she had, but he wouldn't tell me what he'd overheard. In addition, she's planning a party for misfits. That's what he called it, anyway. I don't know what that means exactly." She looked at him gravely then turned quickly away. "You're thinking I'm overanalyzing the situation, aren't you? Oh, Mr. Morrow, I suppose I am, but I can't help but wonder the worst."

"I don't blame you, Lauren. You need answers." Callan detected something else Lauren had on her mind by the way she avoided eye contact. He asked her what it was.

"I'm not sure exactly, but in addition to overhearing Kate's phone call and learning about her party, he said he had something he wanted me to read that he'd found on the internet."

"Did he say what it was?"

Lauren shook her head. "He wouldn't go into it over the phone. He said he found transcripts from a trial that I should know about, so he printed them off for me to read." Anticipating Callan's next question, she added, "I don't know what trial. Gabe just said it explained everything."

"Where is this transcript?"

"In my room at home. He put it in a dresser drawer so Mom wouldn't see it sitting out."

"Do you have time to go home before finals—even just for an afternoon?"

She nodded. "But I don't have a way. I don't have a car on campus."

Callan gazed into the canopy of trees to think. "I'm very sure Terese would be happy to take you. She's rather bored. If I could arrange it, would you go to Indy for the afternoon with her?"

Lauren responded with a simple expression of relief.

"I'll take that as a yes," he said.

~

Terese picked up Lauren in front of her dorm and drove the hour to Indianapolis. Lauren talked intermittently but said little about her family or their situation.

Lauren arranged lunch with her mother at an Italian bistro off the canal, and Terese parked under a row of trees not far from the restaurant.

"Oh," Lauren said as Terese put the car in park. "We're close to Cottage Gallery here. It's on the next block. Would you like to see it?"

Terese thought carefully. "Not this trip. I'm not sure it's a good idea. Did you say your brother was working today? We might run into him, and if he's not in a good mood, I don't want to spoil lunch with your mother."

"Then let's not," Lauren said as she exited the car. "And let's not stop by the house, either, to pick up that transcript Gabe left for me. I'm certain Mr. Morrow told you about it."

"Yes, he did. Are you sure? It won't take but a few minutes to swing by and get it."

"No," said Lauren. "If it'll upset me, I don't want to read it before finals. It'll be fine where it is. After finals, I'll have plenty of time to process whatever's in the document, but not now." She pointed to a row of buildings nearby. "The restaurant is this way. We'll have to cross the canal."

They meandered over the pedestrian bridge to the village of Broad Ripple. Terese followed Lauren to the railing and looked out over the canal's water at several dabbling ducks swimming carefree in the still water.

"The canal is really beautiful, isn't it? Can you believe it'll be two hundred years old soon?"

"I have to admit I don't know much about the history in this part of the state, even though I've lived here for many years," Terese said. "I'm originally from the Crystal Valley, north of Goshen."

"That's Amish country, isn't it?"

Terese nodded.

"We have Amish around here, but Irish Catholics built much of the canal. It's part of the Wabash and Erie Canal system."

"Then I should get to know more about it," Terese said. "My husband's paternal family is Irish Catholic."

"I suppose the name Morrow would be, wouldn't it? I wonder if his ancestors helped build the canal."

"I don't know," Terese said, wondering herself. "He works a lot on genealogy, but it's like pulling teeth to get anything out of him sometimes."

Lauren turned to Terese with an empathetic expression. "It's no wonder," she said.

"What do you mean?"

"Their history isn't glamorous. The Irish weren't treated very well. His family may have been indentured servants, or something."

Terese turned back to the ducks flapping their wings, splashing water, and squawking loudly. She thought of Callan looking at pictures of his great-grandparents, especially a picture of his great-grandmother. "I hadn't thought of that. Yes, unfortunately they may have been treated very badly," she said under her breath, "or worse."

Terese brushed the thought of her husband's great-grandmother out of her mind and took Lauren's arm to walk the rest of the way to the bistro. Where the bridge met Westfield Avenue, they turned and took several more steps before spotting

Beth Kimmerman sitting between pots of red geraniums at an outdoor setting along the street.

Beth set down her glass of cabernet as they approached. "Lauren, welcome home," she said, embracing her daughter warmly, "even if only for the afternoon. Hello, you must be Mrs. Morrow. I'm Lauren's mother, Beth Kimmerman. I can't tell you how much I appreciate you driving here for this nice surprise. Don't tell me you're done with classes for the semester, Lauren. I thought you had some finals yet."

"Yes, I still do. We must get back this afternoon. Mrs. Morrow was coming to the city and was kind enough to let me tag along."

Beth turned graciously toward Terese. "And you know my daughter how?"

"She's a student of my husband's Introduction to Fraud class."

Beth faced her daughter once again, this time losing the pleasant smile on her face. "Fraud? I thought you were studying to become a systems analyst."

"This is only an elective."

"Well, see that it is." She grinned. "We already have a lawyer in the family with your Uncle Jacob. Can we handle an auditor?"

Lauren laughed. "It's premature to think of me as an auditor or a fraud examiner, Mother, but I should think it would be no more embarrassing than having a politician in the family."

"Touché," Beth responded. "Well put. I believe you're right."

A waiter came for their drink order. Beth declined another glass of wine.

"How is the campaign going for you?" Terese asked.

Beth nodded but didn't answer fully. "Too early to tell. I have the support of my constituents, but it'll be a tough race, as mayoral elections go. Indy is usually decisive about their mayors by election time, and I seem to have a lot of backing. That's a good sign, but it's too early to tell if it'll stick through the fall." She smiled at her daughter. "So you're taking a fraud class. How interesting."

"If that's your way of approaching from another angle the subject of me changing my major, Mother—"

"It isn't."

"Good, because I'm not. I still have an interest in systems. I hope it'll come in handy for you down the road."

"In what way?" Beth asked.

"I thought we might talk sometime about developing or purchasing an inventory system for Open Arms, similar in scope to what they have at Cottage Gallery," Lauren said.

"Who told you about needing an inventory system?"

"Gabe mentioned it."

The waiter came and set iced teas in front of Terese and Lauren and refilled Beth's iced water before laying three menus on the table. He departed quickly for the kitchen.

"I'm sure he's told you an earful then," Beth replied. "For someone who went to culinary school and wants to move to Chicago, he seems to have taken an unusual interest in the financial welfare of the gallery and the thrift store."

"As well he should. It sounds like it's a real mess between the two. I'm sure it bothers you, too, doesn't it?"

Beth eyed her daughter carefully before saying, "Yes, I suppose it does. I wish Kate and Eddie got along better than they do. That would help. I often wonder if we're mismanaging our inventory or mismanaging our management."

"Eddie?" Terese asked.

"Our back room operations manager at Open Arms. He accepts donations and sees what's fit to go to the sales floor, what needs to go to the workshop for repair, or what Kate will buy for the gallery."

"Mother, you can't go on not knowing what problems you

have. Is it inventory or management? Otherwise, Open Arms is ripe for errors or misappropriation. If I've learned nothing from Mr. Morrow's class, I've learned that. You could have a serious situation going on behind the board's back."

Terese lifted her hands in front of her to pause the conversation. "Look, I'm sorry, but this sounds confidential." She scooted back from the table. "Let me leave you two, and I'll return later. If our waiter comes, order me a salad with blackened chicken, and I'll be fine."

"No, it's okay," Lauren said. She turned to her mother. "Mrs. Morrow knows all about my concerns, Mom. I've discussed it with Mr. Morrow, and she was with me when I did."

Beth twisted the stem of her glass. "That's fine. I don't mind. Please don't leave, Terese. Besides, those words are your brother's, Lauren, not yours."

"They're mine too. And yours. You said it yourself when you said Open Arms's inventory problems may be more mismanagement of management. Something could be going on."

"Nothing's *going on*," Beth countered. "Don't put it like that. Something doesn't have to be *going on*, Lauren, for a business not to be running smoothly. I know you've taken this fraud class to heart, and I appreciate your thoughts, but we don't need to be investigated or examined, if that's what you're thinking."

"That's a curious choice of wording, Mother."

"What is?"

"Investigated. I wasn't talking about an investigation . . . unless there's something you're not telling me."

Beth sighed. "There's nothing going on."

Lauren leaned toward her mother and lowered her voice. "Then it might not hurt to at least have a review performed."

"You mean hire a consultant to review our system of controls? We don't have that kind of money."

There was silence for several seconds before Terese offered, "Then why don't you consider having my husband come in to do a simple review of procedures?"

Beth's eyes narrowed.

Lauren jumped at the opportunity. "Sure, Mother, maybe he could recommend some basic controls in the manual process that won't cost a lot of money but will provide you and the board the assurance you need to know that operations are running effectively. What do you say?"

"I don't know," she replied.

"It makes a lot of sense," Lauren added, "and it's cheaper—a lot cheaper—than hiring a consultant or implementing an automated system you might not need."

"I bet Callan will do the review for nothing," Terese said. "I'll talk with him. I'm sure he'll consider it a contribution to the work you do for the city's youth."

"You're saying that without consulting him first?"

"Yes, but he can be persuaded, especially if the request comes directly from one of his students."

Terese could see that Beth was considering the offer seriously, but something was holding her back. "What's the matter?"

"For one thing, what if something really *is* happening at Open Arms? What if he finds something that'll reach the news media? We can't afford bad publicity on the heels of William Davisly's death. I'm sure Lauren's told you about that, Terese. If his death is directly connected to Open Arms or Cottage Gallery, it could mean the activities of the board could also be affected."

"Then let me make another suggestion," Terese said. "I'll talk to Callan about becoming a volunteer within the operations of Open Arms to simply observe and gather information without performing a formal evaluation. He can report his findings directly to you and leave it up to you as to what you tell or don't tell the board—or even Kate for that matter."

Beth nodded. "Very well," she conceded. "Our bylaws give me the power to make executive decisions that are in the best interests of the organization. I'll touch base with our external counsel tomorrow."

"When would you like him to begin?"

Beth looked at her daughter.

"I'm starting my summer schedule at Open Arms the day after my last final," Lauren said. "How about then?"

The waiter approached the women's table, smiling broadly. "Are we ready to order?" he asked.

Beth took a deep breath. "Yes, I believe I am."

Chapter Eight

Beth didn't touch much of her Cobb salad. She rationalized it was too hot to eat lunch on the patio; they should've eaten inside. It didn't matter that Lauren and Terese said they were fine under the canopy of the umbrella in the light breeze. Beth contended it was too warm. Perhaps it was the wine. She asked to be excused to go to the restroom.

Beth entered the room and dabbed at the nape of her neck with a cloth towelette. She glanced into the mirror, thinking she looked haggard and drawn. She touched her skin, smooth and soft, though pasty. She took deep breaths to quell her anxiety, then dabbed her neck some more and left the restroom, using the hallway wall to steady her gait as she made her way outside.

When Beth arrived at the table, Lauren scanned her with a concerned expression and touched Terese's arm for her attention.

"Mom, are you all right?"

"I'm fine, dear," she said, though her eyes drifted away.

"Mother, I think we'll be leaving now."

"But you haven't finished your lunch."

"Neither have you."

Beth looked down at her plate. "Oh, but I'm having it boxed for supper."

"And what will Daddy have?"

She shook her head as if she hadn't given it any thought. "He's not helpless. He's fixed supper before."

Lauren rose and walked to the other side of the table to give her mother a kiss on her cheek. "All right, then. Will you be fine if we go?"

Beth smiled superficially, then turned to Terese. "Yes, thank you for coming. I appreciate all the help of your husband. It was a pleasure meeting you."

Terese rose quietly from the table and took Lauren's arm to pull her gently away from her mother. "It's time to go," she said softly.

The women left, and Beth watched them cross the street and walk across the bridge over the canal.

"Will there be anything else, ma'am?" the waiter asked.

She hadn't heard him approach. "What? Oh, no, thank you. Wait, yes. Yes, another glass of cabernet, please."

He obliged, and she sat alone with her thoughts. Lauren surely suspected something was amiss. Why else was she ready to leave so prematurely? Even Terese appeared ready to go. Was she that transparent?

It wasn't her fault, she decided. Mr. Davisly was on her mind and Open Arms's inventory issues required a detailed strategy to resolve. The campaign was looming before her, and Marilyn Wells-Brewer could cause a great deal of alarm with her constituents. Barry was supportive, of course, but he could be very insistent about how problems should be resolved. And Kate had been no help at all.

Yes, Kate . . .

Beth picked up her phone and punched Kate's number.

"Hello, dear," she said when Kate answered. "Did I catch you at a bad time? . . . No? Listen, I was wondering if you'd have dinner with me tonight, say seven? That's wonderful. No, no special reason." She leaned forward and rested her elbows on the table as she listened to Kate inquire again. "Just as I said, dear, no special reason. Do I need a reason to have dinner with my best friend?" Beth ended the call just as the waiter brought her glass of wine.

"Would you like a box for your salad, ma'am?"

Beth looked at her lunch and curled her lip upward. "No. Please take it away."

~

Beth chose a small, quaint restaurant within the Mile Square of Indianapolis for dinner. She arrived before Kate and asked to be seated away from the other patrons. The waitress asked if she could bring her something to drink. Beth declined, saying she'd wait for her friend. But the waitress poured her some iced water anyway.

She sat motionless, staring at the patrons spread sparsely throughout the room. Surely, out of all these people, someone had problems as deep as hers. She wondered what they were doing about them, how they could drink, enjoy their food, and laugh with their friends. She couldn't do any of that anymore. She couldn't even have a decent lunch with her daughter.

She sighed, then remembered the envelope she'd received when she arrived home just before she left again to meet Kate. A pang developed in her stomach, and she wished she'd taken the waitress up on her offer of a drink. The style of envelope was familiar—like the one she and Barry had received before. Someone had stuck it in the front doorjamb, near the doorknob, and she'd stuffed it in a side pocket of her purse to look at later.

Beth pulled the now-crinkled envelope from her purse and looked around to make sure no one was watching. She ripped open the flap and pulled out the one-page letter. It read the same as the last one, only the amount was different—much different. Larger and unpayable. She took a deep breath and started to hyperventilate. Beth grabbed the iced water and drank it quickly. Almost immediately, her head began to ache. Her hand shook and her heart pounded. She set the glass on the tablecloth and tried to think about what she should do.

Barry.

No! Barry mustn't know. He doesn't need to know.

This was *her* problem. It was *her* family. She could think of an answer on her own.

Kate stepped into the restaurant and scanned the dining room. Beth's heart pounded faster. A seething distress overwhelmed her at the sight of her friend. Kate mustn't know either. She took a couple of deep breaths to calm her nerves just as Kate saw her in the remote corner of the room.

Kate placed her purse on a peg under the table and looked at her host with a questioning gaze. A waitress interrupted their greetings to ask if she could bring them something to drink. They ordered basil smash martinis and smiled pleasantly, but their eyes peered warily across the table at each other.

"I was right when you called, wasn't I?" Kate asked. "This dinner meeting wasn't meant to be social."

"What do you mean, dear?"

"You had me drive all the way to Mass Ave."

"Don't you like Mass Ave?"

"That's not the point," Kate said. "I'm sure I was brought here because it was far away from Broad Ripple. As they say in real estate: Location! Location! Location! You didn't want anyone to see us."

Beth tried to smile. "Everyone knows we're friends, Kate. Just because we're in the aftermath of a suicide, that shouldn't cause people to talk, should it? Or how about those bumps in the night at the gallery? Does anyone know about them?"

Kate cocked her head and looked skeptically at her friend. "Gabe shouldn't have told you about that."

"He's concerned about you, Kate, just as I am."

"I've decided to have a party."

Beth shook her head at the absurd response. "What does a party have to do with our conversation?"

"Everything, Beth. There's nothing like a party to take people's minds off their problems. The issues with the bureaus will be resolved once everyone gets together and forgets their cares. I know you're thinking about the bureau you bought. That's why you invited me to dinner, isn't it? The bureau?"

The waitress arrived at the table, setting down their martinis. The women declined any appetizers.

"I don't want to talk about the bureau," Beth replied when the waitress left. "It's a symptom of a bigger problem between Open Arms and Cottage Gallery that I believe you know something about. I want you to be honest with me and tell me what it is."

Kate lifted the stem of her glass and presented a toast. "To good friends."

Beth halfheartedly lifted her glass and took a sip.

"What do you want to know?" Kate asked.

"Everything."

Kate smiled onerously. "As a friend?"

Beth shrugged. "I wish it could be that way, but let's just say for now as a board chair."

Kate sighed and set her glass down. "That means, depending

on my answer, my position as executive director of Open Arms could be at risk."

"Only if what you have to tell me is something unlawful."

"It's not!" Kate blurted, leaning toward Beth.

"Then what's happening? Even my daughter has drawn a conclusion that something ominous is going on, and she's been in Vermillion for the past semester. I had lunch with her today. She's very worried."

"I don't know what Lauren is worried about, Beth, but if it's Mr. Davisly's death you're concerned about, I can't tell you why he died. It didn't have anything to do with Open Arms or the gallery. I can't help what rumors Marilyn has been spreading around town either. They aren't true. That's why I want to have this party—to put what's happened behind us, once and for all."

"The answers are deeper than a party, Kate. That's what I'm trying to tell you." Beth sat back in her seat and studied the anguish on her friend's face. "Recent events have you as upset as I am, don't they?"

Kate looked at her with pleading eyes but gave no answer.

Beth took a sip of her martini and carefully thought about what she wanted to do or say. On one hand, she wanted to believe Kate. On the other, however, the sales and returns of Davisly's bureau and the bureau she and Barry had dealt with were too much to overlook. She remembered the envelope stuck in the jamb of her front door this afternoon. She couldn't ignore its significance. She couldn't ignore the fact that her friend may know who was behind the letter she'd received.

Beth opened her mouth but closed it immediately.

Kate sneered. "Just say it. I'd rather you say it out loud."

"All right," she shot back. "If what you say is true, Kate, then you won't mind what I did this afternoon. I've asked Lauren's professor at Vermillion College to join us when he can as a volunteer at Open Arms."

Kate's inability to speak was a sign that she didn't know what Beth was talking about.

"Lauren's taking a class this semester," Beth explained. "I understand she likes it very much. It's an Introduction to Fraud class, I believe. Mr. Morrow's a fraud examiner."

"What do you mean, he'll be volunteering? Did you say he's a fraud examiner?"

"I've asked him to help with operations at the thrift store. If what you say is true—that you don't know what's going on between Open Arms and Cottage Gallery—then I hope you're as interested as I am to find out for sure. Am I right?"

Kate didn't answer.

Beth studied her friend's face but couldn't tell if she agreed or was simply in shock. It didn't matter. Beth was ready to leave. "I'm not hungry anymore," she confided. "Are you? What's the matter? You don't look well. Why don't we just order another martini and call it an evening?"

Kate remained still.

Beth waited several seconds before softening her expression and asking, "Kate, dear, would you like another drink—or is one smash enough for you?"

Chapter Nine

Callan leaned against the counter of a cashier station in the Open Arms secondhand store and gazed out the store's plate glass window at the pedestrian traffic strolling past. Finals were over for the semester. He'd expected to spend this time preparing for the next semester, but he rationalized that his first day as a volunteer was just as important—at least to Lauren. He turned away from the window to look across the showroom.

The display floor was neat, orderly, and well-stocked with quality furniture, small appliances, knickknacks, and clothing. The building was old, but its ornate vintage accents enhanced the eclectic aura of the interior. The floor needed some work. He embedded the heel of his right boot onto the surface of the building's original linoleum, creating a black scuff mark that blended in with the multitude of other scuff marks already on the floor. The waxed surface had surely faded during the state's sesquicentennial in 1966, and as he waited for Lauren to join him, he amused himself by trying the guess which president was in office when the woodwork was last painted.

Lauren had said she wanted to be with him on his first day.

Now, she hurried through double doors from the back room, greeted him briefly, and began to perform opening duties to prepare for customers who were sure to arrive before the store's official opening for the day.

She looked up to see Callan watching her. "I'll be with you in a moment, Mr. Morrow," she said, acknowledging his patience. "This won't take long."

"Take your time, and remember, it's Callan, not Mr. Morrow anymore."

She giggled. "All right. Sorry. After I'm done here, I'll take you to the back so you can get started."

Callan glanced toward the rear of the building, to the olive-gray double doors that divided the sales floor from the back room operations area. "I don't think that guy I'm to work with is back there yet. I saw a woman when I came in, though. She let me in."

"Was it Amy?"

Callan shrugged. "I don't know who Amy is, and she didn't introduce herself. She seemed in a hurry. All I know is that she told me none of the men that work in the back were in yet. I forget the one guy's name I'm supposed to meet."

"Eddie."

"Will he be in shortly?"

"He should be there now. I'm surprised he's not. Are you sure you didn't miss him?"

"Could have, but I haven't met that Kate you and Terese keep talking about either."

Lauren brushed Callan's comment away with a flick of her wrist. "Kate comes in late. We're not her main priority."

Callan moved from the sales counter and strolled down an aisle of clothing.

"I'm going to warn you," Lauren called. "Kate and Eddie

don't get along that well."

"What's their problem?"

"I don't know. They snip at each other over nothing sometimes. Drives me crazy." Lauren slammed the cash drawer shut and rubbed her hands together, signaling she had completed the opening cash procedures. "Hey, I'm going to run to the restroom. I'll be right back." She looked at Callan, a smile spreading across her face. Her eyes softened, and her lips quivered as if she was holding back tears or words of endearment.

Callan smiled back but was relieved when she scurried away without expressing what was on her mind. He looked again at the old linoleum beneath his feet and, unable to contain his impatience, followed the badly scarred tiles to the back room.

The back room was nothing more than a large, open area surrounded by cement block walls painted smoky green, with a gray cement floor and exposed wooden rafters supporting the ceiling above. Two space heaters, one at each end of the room, appeared ample to heat the space in the winter, but the lack of air-conditioning ducts indicated that it would be a hot place to work in the next four to five months.

Categorization of donations into different parts of the room seemed to be in progress: one area for clothes—mostly women's—and other areas for children's apparel and toys, small appliances, craft supplies, framed pictures and paintings, and tools.

Four large windows along the back of the room shed natural light onto furniture near a workshop, including wood desks, upholstered chairs, end tables, lamps, and other home furnishings. He examined these donations, interested in seeing what had been brought in and whether they'd been marked for sale. Some had tags attached, others did not. He perused the items that had been tagged. Except for one or two pieces here and there, the items were of remarkable quality and functionality, and the items' tags appeared to reflect their value.

A car door slammed outside. Callan heard voices, both male and female. He scurried to one of the back windows to look. A woman, tall and smartly dressed in a professional business suit, stood on the driver's side of a Lexus. She placed her handbag on the roof of the car and turned her head. A man, about her age, wearing jeans and a pressed light blue denim work shirt, stood in the shadow of the building. His profile exposed a protruding belly.

The conversation between the two was barely audible but contained occasional quips that appeared to irritate each other. Callan wondered if he was watching the dynamics of Kate and Eddie in action.

Kate carried herself well, holding her own with an arrogant air of indignation when it appeared that Eddie became agitated and raised his voice. Callan heard words, but not enough to gain a perspective on their context. Kate made a comment that seemed to amuse the man, and they began talking in more amicable tones.

She reached into the back seat of her car and pulled out a cardboard shoebox that the man accepted as if it contained fragile contents. Kate gave him some instructions about the box. He didn't appear to take the commands well and turned to walk toward a back door. He stopped and made a few pointed comments of his own, as if he couldn't stand to let her have the last word.

Kate raised her voice in frustration. "I don't know what to expect," she said distinctly, the first words Callan could hear clearly. "We'll just have to make the best of it."

The man didn't respond. He looked down at his work boots and kicked a couple of small rocks by digging into the gravel with his right foot.

"Don't be a child," she added. "Just do as you're told."

Callan hurried from the window to the center of the room before the man entered the building.

At first the man didn't notice Callan standing quietly before him, and he appeared startled when he finally caught sight of him. The man shut the door behind him, then glanced toward the back window, where Callan had stood just minutes before.

Callan had seen glances like that before—silent admissions of guilt. The man's glance might be innocent, but his forensic experience told him the guy believed Callan had overheard his conversation with Kate. Callan took the man's mind off the window by introducing himself as the new volunteer and extending his hand.

"I figured as much," the man said in a strong Hoosier twang, accepting the gesture. "I'm Eddie Lee. I reckon I'll be showin' you the ropes around the place."

"Sounds good. I'm anxious to see what I can do for you here, Eddie Lee."

"Yeah, well, if you'll give me a moment 'fore we get started, then I'll see what I can do about that eagerness you have. Oh, and by the way, I better tell ya right off the bat that my name's Eddie. Lee's my last name."

"I'm sorry," Callan said.

A grin escaped Eddie's lips. He turned and walked to the front of the store just as Lauren entered the back room.

"I see you two have met," she said, grinning broadly.

Eddie passed her and exited the room without acknowledgment.

Lauren lost her grin. "You two okay together?"

"Yeah, once I got his name right. Did a woman walk into the front entrance by any chance—nice looking, well-dressed?"

"You mean Kate? Why? Did you meet her?"

Callan shook his head. "Saw her out back a few minutes

ago, talking to Eddie. She's a nice dresser and drives a nice car for someone who's the director of a thrift store."

"You have to remember she owns Cottage Gallery. You don't think she gets her money from what the board of directors pays her, do you?"

"I thought she volunteered her position."

"Oh, did she?" Lauren asked surprised. "I didn't know that. Very benevolent of her. Doesn't matter, really. She makes enough through the gallery. Hey, I need some help getting a box of shopping sacks to the sales counter. Would you mind taking a box from the supply closet and bringing it up front for me? It's kind of heavy."

Callan obliged. He walked to the closet where Lauren pointed, grabbed a corrugated box of sacks, and headed toward the retail floor, stopping abruptly as he peered through the windows of the double doors. Eddie and Kate stood at the cashier counters involved in an animated conversation.

"What's the matter?" Lauren asked. "Why are you just standing there?"

"Nothing," he said, hoping Lauren would stop asking questions and go about her business.

Lauren inched her way next to him and looked through the windows to see what he could see. "Those two are starting to get to you, aren't they? Pay no attention to them. Anyway, I was going to tell you there's coffee in the break room if you want some. Creamer is in a round oatmeal box-like container. It looks nasty but should whiten your coffee just the same."

She turned to go into a side door that Callan presumed led to the break room.

"And take your time with that stakeout you have going there," she said, "but I'll need that box of sacks before the store opens."

~

Callan pushed through the double doors and walked across the retail floor.

Upon hearing the doors open, Eddie stopped his conversation with Kate. He turned and walked toward the back room without finishing their discussion.

Kate appeared busy recounting the money Lauren had prepared earlier. Callan placed the box on the counter and emitted a grunt loud enough to be heard over the jingling of coins.

"Lauren was right," Callan said. "That was heavier than I thought."

Kate glanced at him quickly before turning her attention back to the register. "You don't need to do that. Eddie could've brought it up for you. He's used to it."

"I'll need to get used to it sooner or later. By the way, I'm Callan, the new volunteer."

Kate turned and gave him a glare, heightened by her piercing eyes—dark, deep, and lined in a brown tint—then she surprised him by returning a smile, one that appeared genuine. "Hi, Callan," she said. "I'm Kate O'Neal. Welcome aboard. I'm glad you're here." She maintained the smile and eye contact for several uncomfortable moments.

Callan matched her glare, refusing to be the first to blink. Eventually, he released his standoff and grinned, realizing there was no honor to be won from a childish showdown.

"I guess I'll talk to you later then," he said. "Better get to the back. I enjoyed our chat."

He sensed that Kate's icy stare continued as he made his way across the display floor.

He entered the back room, expecting a similar, cold reception from Eddie, but the room was vacant. A sliver of light shone between the outside door and its jamb. Callan walked toward it to see if Eddie needed any help carrying more boxes. Before reaching the door, however, he heard Lauren's voice calling from the break room. He couldn't tell if Lauren was calling for him or someone else. He walked into the break room, but Lauren wasn't there.

Callan looked around. The room contained vending machines of snacks and soft drinks. A refrigerator and sink stood on one side, while a large, rectangular table sat squarely in the middle, consuming most of the area. On the far side of the room was another door. Callan walked toward the door and opened it, discovering a hallway leading to the restrooms and another door into the sales floor.

A young woman in her twenties strode out of the women's restroom and entered the break room, searching the caverns of her purse. Callan barely managed to step out of the way. He recognized her as the young woman he'd seen when he first entered the store. Her thin, stringy hair hung lifelessly around a pimply face. Callan sensed her poor complexion was more about economics than apathy.

"Oh, I'm sorry," she said. "I didn't see you standing there. I could've knocked you down. I'm trying to find a couple of . . . here we go . . . quarters—Oops! No, they're nickels. Oh, I'm so sorry. I'm being rude. My name is Amy. Are you Callan?"

Her eyes widened with excitement when Callan said he was.

"It's so good to finally meet you. Lauren has told me all about you these past couple of days. She thinks very highly of you." Amy studied his face before adding, "Sorry about looking at you like that. You kinda remind me of Brian. Older, though, lots older." She returned to digging into the side pockets of her purse.

Callan reached into his pocket and pulled out five quarters. "Here, go ahead and take these. Who's this Brian guy?"

She looked at him quizzically. "Who keeps that many quarters in their pocket?" she asked.

"Just take them."

She continued to look at him the same way. "Are you sure? All I want is a diet pop out of the machine. You'd do that?" Before Callan had a chance to renege, Amy grabbed the coins and brushed a strand of hair away from her face, revealing the sincerity of her gratitude. "Brian's my boyfriend," she answered, depositing the coins into the machine. "Brian VanderPelt."

She glanced his way. Callan believed it was to see if the name she'd dropped prompted a reaction.

"Of *the* VanderPelts," she added.

The name meant nothing to him. "Have you been here long?"

Amy watched the plastic bottle roll into the receptacle. She tittered as if she'd won the jackpot out of a slot machine. She popped the cap off the bottle and quickly took a sip. "Ah! My lucky day. I never know what I'm going to get out of this machine. Now, what did you ask? Oh, yeah, I remember. You mean just now?"

"No, I mean, how long have you worked at Open Arms?"

"Not long. Maybe a year or more. I worked with Lauren last summer when she was here. I started about then. We helped each other get acquainted. Kate isn't exactly helpful. Mentoring her employees isn't one of her strong management skills. Don't worry, though. We'll help you out."

"Does Kate make things that difficult?"

Amy eyed him carefully as she took another swallow of her morning pick-me-up. "She's fine," she replied as if she'd said too much. "Why do you ask?"

"You brought it up."

"So I did. Sorry. I'm an open book, I guess."

And a little flighty too. "But you seem to have a reason for feeling that way," Callan said.

Amy looked off to the side. "No . . . Look, I like the job. I like being here. I gripe about how Kate runs the place and runs people like Eddie and me down, but this place is awesome. I love the clothes. I can dress for work, I mean, at my other job, for a fraction of the cost of going to Greenwood Park or Circle Centre Mall. I'm not that crazy about Eddie, but he seems to know what people will like and buy here. And then there's the youth this place helps. That's cool too, don't you think?"

"Very cool. Where else do you work?"

"My real job's at Tipton's down in Beech Grove. I waitress. Ever hear of it?"

"Tipton's? Sure. I haven't been there in years."

"Oh, you must come back. Best breaded tenderloins in the state. Hog fries too, if you're in for that sort of thing."

Callan cringed. "I don't think a night out on the town with my wife includes a bucket of beer and a plate full of hog fries."

Amy laughed. "She doesn't know what she's missing, then. She's probably not into brain sandwiches, blood pudding, or burgoo either, is she?"

"Not so much."

"Isn't she from Indiana?"

"Yes, but—"

"Bring 'er anyway, okay? You two oughtta stop in. It'll be fun. Brian stops in all the time just to chat, throw darts, play some pool, make fun of the locals, that sort of thing. They have a great menu, a live band on weekends—country, of course— iced longnecks in an aluminum trough, and we get all of our pork from the hog capital of the world."

"Let me guess. Tipton County?"

Amy curtsied and clapped, accidentally shaking her soft drink. The dark, sticky foam spilled over the top of the bottle and onto the floor.

"Oh, sheesh, I better clean this up." She hunted for something to wipe up the mess. "I wouldn't want to put anyone around here in a bad mood." She hurried to the counter and grabbed several white paper towels to sop up the spill. "There, maybe no one will notice until the bottom of their shoe sticks to the floor. Is that cleaned up good enough, ya think?"

Callan nodded. "Yes, but I'll wipe over it with a wet rag. You go on to the sales counter before they wipe *you* up with a wet rag for being late."

~

Callan finished wiping the floor and heard what sounded like items being brought into the back room from the outside. He made his way into the back room in time to see Eddie coming in, carrying a corrugated box with the word *Fragile* stamped in large, bold letters on the side. Lower, in the middle of the box, were the words *Merchandise Mart, Chicago, Illinois,* printed clearly in view. The box appeared to be lightweight and easy to handle.

"Need some help?" Callan asked.

Eddie shook his head. "Nah, I got it. Just a few more out there."

Callan didn't argue. Apparently Eddie preferred to do it himself. Callan watched Eddie bring in the remaining boxes and set them in a clearing on the floor. After a final trip from the trunk of Kate's Lexus, Eddie rubbed his hands together and straightened his body. "Ready to begin?"

Callan spent the rest of the morning accepting donations,

sorting and organizing merchandise, and restocking the sales room after pricing and recording the items.

Close to noon, Eddie's cell phone rang from his back pocket. He took the call and told the person he'd see them directly. "I'm heading out," he said. "Will you be okay?"

Callan assured him that he would. When Eddie left, he stood in the middle of the room and surveyed what seemed to be an unsurmountable job. When he heard the double doors open and close, he looked toward the sales floor and was surprised to see a man about his age, distinguished in stature and dress, standing just inside the door.

"Quite a mess, isn't it?" the man asked.

"Yes, it would appear," Callan said. "I was standing here trying to figure out how I'd organize this place if it was mine to organize."

"If you figure it out, I have a garage that could use your expertise."

Callan laughed. "My name is Callan Morrow. May I help you?"

"Barry Kimmerman," the man replied, extending his hand to reach Callan's.

"I take it you're Lauren's father."

"Yes, I came in to see how she was doing now she's back from school. I hear you were her auditing and fraud professor during the past semester." Barry stood close to Callan as they talked, lowering his voice to prevent it from being overheard. "I do hope you can make some sense of all this, for my wife's sake. My wife is Beth. She believes in this store and its mission for the youth of Indianapolis, but she worries about it. Someone like you can help make sense of it all." Barry turned around and looked at a closed door along the same wall as the windows. "Is Chuck's workshop locked?"

Callan said he didn't know but presumed it was. "He should be in this afternoon if you need anything."

"No, I'm curious to see what he's been working on. Have you taken a look?"

Callan shook his head.

"You must," Barry said. "He's a master at being able to transform the broken into new. It's fascinating to watch him at work. You must do it sometime when you're not too busy. Have you met Kate?"

"I have."

"What did you think of her?"

Callan simply nodded. He wasn't comfortable divulging his thoughts.

"A wise man to be cautious," Barry replied, "but you needn't be. I shouldn't have asked that question without prefacing that my wife and Kate are good friends. I trust Kate was kind to you today."

"Was there a chance that she might not be?"

Barry placed his hands in his pockets and grimaced. "Yes, I suppose there was."

"Why is that?"

"Simply because you're here."

Callan's apprehension heightened. "I suppose by that comment you know the real reason why I'm here at Open Arms?"

Barry nodded.

"Does Kate know why I'm here?"

"In addition to seeing Lauren, I wanted to meet you, and . . ."

"Warn me?"

Barry smiled, apparently impressed with Callan's quick ability of deduction. "Yes," he admitted. "Beth and Kate had drinks together last night, and I believe Beth told Kate your purpose for being here."

"I thought Beth wanted it kept a secret," Callan said. "Revealing my purpose could change Kate's behavior and the behavior of others. It may have even given them time to cover up the records of what they've already done, if they've been doing something fraudulent or unethical."

"I agree. I don't know what to say," Barry replied.

"It sounds to me like Beth was planning to tell Kate the purpose of my visit all along."

"I don't think so. No, I'm sure she wasn't planning to do that."

"Then what happened to change Beth's mind?"

Barry looked off to the side. "I wish I could explain it."

Callan accepted his answer at face value, although in the back of his mind, he wasn't so sure he should.

"I apologize that it happened," Barry said, "but I thought you should know. Lauren speaks highly of you."

"She was a great student. I enjoyed having her in my class."

Barry acknowledged the recognition and thanked him. "Well, I should be heading out, get back to the house. Say, was that Brian VanderPelt I saw outside as I was coming through?"

The question took Callan by surprise. "You mean Amy's boyfriend?"

"Boyfriend?" Barry hesitated then laughed. "Highly unlikely."

"I'm sure he is. Why do you say that?"

Barry chuckled again. "They're from different sides of the tracks. He's Chase VanderPelt's son, you know."

"No, I don't know, but I'm getting the feeling that I should."

"They're of money. Big money in this town." Barry lifted his hand and rubbed his fingers together. "Old money. They hobnob with the Auberts."

Callan made a face, indicating that the name Aubert meant as much to him as VanderPelt.

"What? You've never met Alex Aubert?" Barry asked. "Oh, you must. He's on the board of Open Arms. You two would get along. Alex is a financial guru; he'd relish talking to you about your experience as a forensic auditor. Is your wife in town for the weekend, by any chance?"

"Yes, we've rented a carriage house in SoBro for the time being. We'll be staying there."

"Splendid. Beth and I would like to invite you to our home for dinner this evening, if you can make it. Our son, Gabe, finished culinary school. He's working at Cottage Gallery until he can afford a move to Chicago. I think he should go to New York, but that's a father's opinion. Anyway, he's a great cook, and he wanted to do something special now that Lauren is back. His cooking is quite extraordinary. I think you and your wife will enjoy it."

"Perhaps you'd rather celebrate as a family. Some other time might be better."

"Nonsense! It was Lauren's idea, and having your company will take Beth's mind off the campaign and the horrid business of William Davisly's death. I'm sure you've heard about all that. Besides, Beth has asked Alex and his wife, Corinne, to join us. They're wonderful, down-to-earth people. We'd be pleased if you'd join us too. I'll tell Gabe to expect two more."

"Thank you. I'd like the chance to get to know you and your family better. Are you sure I can't help you find something in here? I know you said you came to see Lauren and to warn me about Kate, but I couldn't help but notice when you looked back at Chuck's workshop you were also looking for something in particular in the room. I may have seen it, if you can describe it to me."

"No," Barry said curtly. "I want nothing from this place."

But his eyes told a different story. Callan detected fear in them, not from what he saw in the room but from what he didn't see.

Barry's jaws clenched, but he snapped out of his light trance. "I must be going. Nice meeting you. We'll see you tonight. Bring nothing but your lovely wife. Knowing Gabe, everything is under control." When he removed his hands from his pockets to shake Callan's, a folded brochure fell to the floor.

Callan picked it up and handed it back to him.

Barry glanced at it before crumpling it in his hands. Noticing that Callan saw his expression of disgust, he explained, "It's an invitation. Kate's having a soiree at her gallery. She had it sitting up front for Lauren to give to me. Perhaps you'll be so lucky as to receive one also."

"Perhaps."

"If not," Barry said, noticing Callan's reticence, "I'll gladly give you mine."

Chapter Ten

That evening, as guests conversed over dinner at the Kimmerman table, Callan leaned toward Terese. "Barry didn't exaggerate his son's ability to prepare an extraordinary meal, did he?"

Terese agreed. Gabe had prepared a culinary feast of northern Indiana duck breast with a savory persimmon sauce and wild rice, culminating with a fluffy popover filled with walnut pudding for dessert. Conversation was pleasant as Callan and Terese got to know Alex and Corinne Aubert and the Kimmerman family better.

"Shall we take our coffee into the other room?" Barry offered when the meal was over, extending his hand to show the way.

"You all go ahead," Callan replied. "I'm going to stay behind until you're all out of the room so that I can lick my plate."

Everyone laughed, and Gabe thanked Callan for the inherent compliment.

Once in the other room, Terese sat beside her husband on a sofa and pinched his leg hard enough for it to hurt. He turned toward her. "We were having a lovely evening," she whispered as others engaged in small talk, "what with the champagne and you being such a gentleman . . ."

"So what's the matter?" he whispered back.

She pinched him again.

"Ouch!"

"I'm fairly certain these people aren't in the habit of licking their plates when guests leave the room."

Suddenly, and without warning, a gust of warm, late spring air burst through the room's French doors. Barry rushed to close them amid flying curtains and scattered leaves that blew about. They each took a moment to catch their breath, smelling the cool, damp draft that accompanied the gust.

"I daresay Mother Nature is trying to upstage your dinner, Gabe," Alex laughed.

"Yes, I agree," Barry said after thanking his son for the meal. "The weather report mentioned a slight chance for isolated storms, but that gust was more than slight. Anyone care for brandy instead of coffee? Cognac, perhaps?"

Callan's eyes lit up at Barry's offer. "Brandy de Jerez, by any chance?"

"Yes, but only the Solera Reserva," Barry said. "I don't have the Gran. Anyone else?"

Alex raised his index finger. Beth suggested a pink gin for the women, if there were any bitters.

"What did you say that you do, Callan?" Alex asked. "You said something about your career at dinner, but I don't believe I caught it."

"Oh, I'm sorry," Lauren interjected. "I should've explained. Mr. Morrow was one of my college professors this past semester."

"Yes, I knew that much, but was it for accounting?"

"Not accounting as you might think but in forensic accounting," Callan explained, "with an emphasis in process reviews."

"Ah, well then, perhaps you can do something about these robberies that have been going on in the area."

"Yes, I've heard about them," Terese said. "Are they still occurring?"

"As far as we know," Barry said, handing the first of the gins to her. "There were a couple just the other night. Too close to home, I'd say. One of them occurred at the home of one of Beth's friends."

"Oh dear, did they wipe them out completely?"

"No," Barry answered. "Strangely enough, the thieves were only interested in small, valuable items like jewelry, nothing else. I'd say it was kids."

"Kids?" Alex asked. "It sounded from the news to be more professional than what kids would take. Kids go after electronics, don't they?"

"Who knows, nowadays?" Callan replied.

"You should take a look into it," Alex proposed, receiving his snifter of brandy.

Callan shook his head and smiled. "I'm not a sleuth, Alex. Wrong type of forensics and investigating. I'm more into white-collar."

"Have you heard of the Grand Aire Airline incident in Chicago?" Lauren asked Alex.

A bolt of lightning and an earth trembling roar of thunder rolled overhead.

"That was you?" Alex asked after looking up at the ceiling. The look on his face indicated that he'd not only heard of the incident but that he was duly impressed. "A very high-profile case, as I remember."

"It's one of the reasons why I was able to obtain funding for a position at Vermillion and enhance a curriculum related to auditing and forensic accounting."

"You mentioned something about process reviews."

"Yes," Callan said modestly, "but not much more to add about it."

"I'm not so sure," Alex replied. He turned to his hostess. "Beth, what of it? Do you think Callan could help in some way? We suspect inventory control problems at Open Arms, you know."

Beth sat upright. "We're a step ahead of you, Alex." She explained Callan's involvement at the store.

Alex appeared delighted to hear the news. "I hope your work will also include a review of intercompany transactions with Cottage Gallery."

"I'm sure it will," Beth replied on Callan's behalf, "but what are you insinuating? I detect something more by the tone of your voice."

Alex appeared taken aback. "Do you? I'm sorry, Beth, I didn't mean there to be. I was just thinking about a lecture I heard this week."

"At the Columbia Club?" Barry asked.

"Yes, that's right. You were there, too, weren't you, Barry? I remember."

"Chase VanderPelt was the keynote speaker."

"Who's he?" Beth asked, half-interested.

Barry gave his wife a dirty look. "You know who he is."

She turned away.

"He's an investor."

"More than just an investor," Alex countered. "He's *the* developer in town. In fact, I hear he has a number of projects going on with Roger Montrose."

"What was so interesting about his talk?" she asked.

"Conflicts of interest, that sort of thing."

"Hardly riveting, Alex."

"Maybe so, but given recent events, it's at least relevant."

"I suppose you're hinting at Open Arms."

"And Cottage Gallery," Alex replied sternly. "I believe a review into how Kate conducts business with Open Arms may mitigate any repercussions that could come from William's death."

Beth jerked her head up. "I don't know what you're talking about."

"There's bound to be some."

"Marilyn Wells-Brewer is the only repercussion I can think of," Beth said sharply. "Kate's fairly certain Marilyn will go to all ends to find skeletons in people's closets, and I have to agree with her."

"I don't know, Beth," he said, apprehension rising in his voice. "Marilyn was fairly convincing."

"If I remember right, Alex, Kate told me you were as critical of her at the meeting as anyone," Beth argued.

"I was, but—"

"No buts. It sounds as if you're defending her now. I'll have you know that Marilyn is nothing more than a busybody who weaseled herself into the social circles of this town and made herself important not by what she's contributed through philanthropy but what she's conjured through scandal and hearsay. That's how she stays in the circles. That's how she got on our board. And that's how it's going to be with her. That's all."

Alex drew his eyebrows inward, looking at her intently. "Is it, Beth?"

Beth didn't have time to answer before a bolt of cloud-to-ground lightning struck nearby, flickering the lights in the room. A clap of thunder immediately followed. Everyone looked at each other, wondering if the lights would stay on or if a search for candles and kerosene lamps would end their conversation.

"Is it?" he asked again when it appeared the lights would remain on. "Is Marilyn so far off the mark this time? I've been doing some research since the board meeting, and I found—"

"I don't want to hear it," Beth said.

"Beth, let him talk," Barry urged.

"No, Alex, please. Some other time," Corinne pleaded with her husband on Beth's behalf.

"I'm not trying to be a rabble-rouser," he explained, "but I'm not sure we've heard anything but Marilyn's story and Kate's rebuttal on the issue. I'm not out to prove anyone right or wrong. I just think it warrants looking into before someone else does."

"Who else would be interested?"

"The media, for one," Alex replied.

Rain pattered outside, streaking the windows with sad lines of rainwater. The room felt chilly and damp. Everyone clung to their drinks and drank liberally from their glasses.

Alex took his wife's advice and sat quietly, allowing the conversation to fade away like the rolling thunder in the distance.

Callan broke the silence, wanting to hear more. "You said, Alex, that you had learned something about William that may be relevant to Marilyn's comments."

Alex looked at Barry for direction. Barry glanced toward his wife, who sipped her drink as if she didn't care what they talked about. He reluctantly turned to Alex and nodded for him to continue.

"I've been talking with my father. I'm sorry, Callan— Alexander Aubert is my father. He's known William Davisly for years. They were colleagues. In fact, my father is a wealth of information on the activities past and present of this city and the people in it. He told me some interesting history and mentioned where I could search for more details."

"What did he say? What did you find out?" Barry asked.

"There's a direct connection from William Davisly to the Brookside Park murders."

Beth sighed loud enough for all guests to hear.

Alex glanced at her then continued. "You may think it's only my opinion and presumption, but what I discovered through my father may explain Marilyn's comments at the meeting."

"How?" Barry asked. "You're saying there's information out there?"

"Yes, but how Marilyn came upon it is beyond me," Alex said. "It took a great deal of my time and tenacity to pull it together. In fact, if it weren't for my father, I'm not sure I'd have found it on my own. The information isn't transparent if you only do a superficial search of the murders or of William's life."

"But you found something?" Callan asked.

"Yes. It was Andrew Gammon who told us at the meeting of the sordid aspects of the Brookside Park murders. He said it was a murder that had it all—sex, theft, bribes, kickbacks, organized crime, that sort of thing—and it captured the city. He remembered or thought he remembered that Davisly's name was connected at some point in the investigation but recanted his statement when he remembered that Davisly lived away from Indy at the time of the murders, and so his involvement was improbable."

"Improbable, maybe, but not out of the question."

"Exactly, Callan. That's why my father recommended that I take a trip to Delphi in Carroll County to see if there was any background information on Davisly at the library and courthouse."

"Seriously, Alex," Beth interrupted. "You're no better than Marilyn, dredging vicious stories from the cobwebs of courthouse records."

"Marilyn opened the can of worms, Beth. The future of Open

Arms can't afford to let them crawl around the board room."

"What did you find out?" Callan asked.

"There could be another angle on the murders that doesn't involve sex, scandal, bribes, kickbacks, or any other sort of notorious activity."

"What other angle could possibly be left?"

"Information."

"On who? About what?"

"Everything," Alex said, "about everyone."

Beth glared at Alex and asked solemnly, "What are you talking about?"

"I'm talking about what the men who were murdered did for a living and what William was doing in Delphi at the time of their death. It was reported through Indianapolis news articles that the murdered men owned or were affiliated in information retention. They created confidential microfilm and microfiche for prominent financial, insurance, medical, and industrial companies in the Indianapolis area and beyond."

"Microfiche?" Terese asked, chuckling. "That's a term I haven't heard in decades."

"Keep in mind, these murders occurred in the 1970s," Alex said. "We don't hear of such medium anymore because microfilm and microfiche have been replaced by much more technologically advanced forms of retention, but at the time, they were the most efficient and affordable way of archiving information."

"I take it they had a very successful and profitable business going for them," Callan said.

"Yes, but while they were good at what they did, the men of Brookside Park weren't exactly the most upstanding citizens. They started their business from equipment they obtained in the Chicago black market. They procured clients from people they bribed or paid kickbacks to and received additional information from the women they pillow-talked in bed—women, by the way, who were married to some of the executives of these prominent businesses."

"Good gracious," Barry said, wiping his brow. "What did William do while these men were flirting with ethical standards?"

"William transplanted himself from Chicago to a tiny hamlet in the glacial fields of Carroll County north of Delphi."

"Doing what? I'm familiar with the area. It's in the middle of corn, mint, and soybean fields, nothing more. There aren't any city lights that would dazzle a man like Davisly from Chicago. What was he doing there?"

"He took an idea from a simple country farmer and turned it into a gold mine for organized crime, that's what he did."

"This is becoming an extraordinary story, Alex," Beth said unconvinced. "Too extraordinary for credence."

"It's not a story, Beth. Please, hear me out. My father didn't steer me wrong. Now, I don't need to remind you of the conservative leanings we have in Indiana. That was especially true in the 1970s, post-Cold War with the threat of a Soviet nuclear holocaust looming before us."

"What about it?"

"The son of a Logansport farmer who served in the Second World War asked his father what would happen to vital records and other highly confidential material should such an atomic threat come to pass. They came up with an idea to build a bunker in a hillside, reinforce it with concrete and radiation-proof steel, man it with a full-time guard, and then rent the space to clients who needed the protection such a vault could provide."

"I never knew such places existed," Beth said.

"They didn't. This was a unique business, but it was thoughtful enough that the venture took hold. The farmer and his old man had some hefty clients, including banks, insurance companies, government agencies, and the like. Eventually the farmers sold the vault for a pretty penny to two separate companies, who formed a joint venture. One company was from Chicago. The other was from Indianapolis." Alex stopped to take a sip from his brandy.

"Are we to guess who the owners of the two companies were?" Barry asked impatiently.

"You don't have to guess, Barry. I'm pretty sure you can figure it out," Alex replied. "William Davisly was the owner of the company from Chicago. He transferred to Carroll County, Indiana, to operate the vault and to generate contracts with more banks, more insurance companies, and more county government agencies. He even contracted with pharmaceutical and industrial companies who had patent and intellectual property assets that needed to be protected. What these clients didn't research very well was that the company Davisly owned in Chicago had ties to organized crime."

"It's almost ingenious," Callan said thoughtfully. "Davisly scared the hell out of important finance companies and government agencies with a fear of nuclear disaster and the loss of vital records."

"He then sold them space to protect their most vital records, formulas, and secrets," Alex added. "He hired guards to make sure that no one but him and his cronies had access to the information. Then, before anyone knew it, he had all the knowledge and information he needed on some of the most prominent citizens and companies in the state."

"Which meant the mafia in Chicago who Davisly was affiliated with now had control over the entire scheme."

"Complete control," Alex said, "over the lives of thousands—no, millions—of people and their livelihoods."

"That's incredible," Barry said. "I can't believe William could do all this from the middle of popcorn country."

"It was perfect, Barry. Don't you see? Delphi is nearly halfway between Chicago and Indianapolis—a great location. William was able to service clients in both directions and provide it expediently at a reasonable cost because overhead was low. It was just him and a few guards, plus electricity for power, and a generator in case the power went out."

"Okay, but what about the company in Indy who controlled the other half of ownership in this vault? What did they do? What was their role?"

Alex's expression became grave. "That company created the microfilm and the microfiche for the companies that stored their information in the vault. They also gave a copy of that microfilm and microfiche back to William Davisly for his organized crime ventures in Chicago. Sadly, though, that company had to dissolve when its owners were found tragically murdered in a tiny bungalow near Brookside Park."

"No!" Beth exclaimed. "This can't be true. I don't believe it! Surely, you're wrong. You have to be wrong."

"Tell that to my father," Alex said. "He should know. His investment company was one of Davisly's vault customers. The information of some of his most high-profile customers was stolen and sold to unscrupulous investors. His company was bilked out of millions, and my father's reputation was nearly destroyed because of the association."

"Oh, God," Beth wailed under her breath. She folded her arms around her stomach as if she was going to be sick.

"I don't get it," Callan said. "Why would William Davisly kill the men who made half of their scheme so successful?"

Alex shrugged. "My father believes that the men's lifestyles and indiscretions began to cause problems. Perhaps their boastfulness in a drunken state one evening leaked confidential information that made it necessary to have them removed before they ruined everything."

"What do you mean?"

"I mean that maybe the men confiscated some of the millions stolen from my father's company."

"But what does that have to do with William?"

"My father said he'd had a word with him about his suspicions."

"When was this?"

"One week before the men were killed."

"Dear God," Barry muttered. "That's the connection. That could be the connection, tying William to the murders. Don't you see, Beth?"

Rain pelted harder against the windows. Another squall of wind rattled the shutters along the house.

Corinne Aubert turned to Beth, who'd grown pale and drawn. "Beth, are you okay?" she asked. "Can I get you something?" When Beth didn't respond, Corinne turned defiantly toward her husband. "I think that's enough of your findings, Alex," she said angrily. "This wasn't the time or place to discuss your horrid research."

Callan disagreed. Despite the agonizing details, it was news that needed to be shared and mitigated. From the look Barry gave Alex, he figured Barry felt the same.

Lauren offered to stay the night to make sure her mother was okay, but Barry assured her she'd be fine. He'd watch over her.

"It'll all look different in the morning," he said. "Mornings have a way of doing that. It'll be fine."

Beth jerked her head up. "No, Barry, it won't be fine," she said vehemently. "It won't look different, and you can't say that it will. Did you not listen to what Alex said about the past?"

Chapter Eleven

Alex and Corinne were the last to leave the Kimmerman home. Barry shook Alex's hand and accepted a remorseful apology for upsetting his wife with the information on Davisly. "I made things miserable for Beth. I'm sorry for that."

"No, it wasn't your fault, Alex," Barry said. "I can't explain what I mean by that for Beth's sake, but trust me, it's not about you."

Alex said good night and left quietly with Corinne.

Barry looked sullenly upon his wife, who refused to look at him.

"What did you mean by that?" she asked.

He walked to the beverage counter and poured another Solera Reserva into his snifter. "What did I mean by what?"

"Don't be coy. I'm talking about your comment to Alex that my state of mind wasn't his fault."

He sipped his brandy and let it burn down the back of his throat, trying to ignore the question but knowing he couldn't. "We both know it wasn't Alex's fault, Beth."

"How would *you* know?"

Barry gave her a side glance and saw her look toward the stairs. She turned back around to catch a glimpse of his reaction. He took small, quick sips of his drink and pretended that her inching toward the staircase didn't bother him until she got too close.

"I wouldn't go up there if I were you," he said.

Anger glared from her eyes. She turned and, despite his warning, hurried up the stairs.

Soon after, he heard the rapid opening and closing of the drawers in the hallway dresser. An expletive blurted from Beth's mouth. He looked up. She hurried down the stairs with a wooden jewelry box in her hand and threw it over the banister onto the floor. It landed inches from Barry's feet.

"You had no right to take it," she said.

"I had every right, Beth. This problem isn't just yours to bear."

"But it's *my* problem."

"Don't even go there with me."

Beth trembled with anger. "It's *my* family, Barry. That letter was about *my* family."

Barry glared at her defiantly. "I said don't go there. It may be your side of the family, but it's affecting *our* family, the family you and I raised. It's affecting us too, so I have every right to stop you from throwing your life away. This election is what you've wanted for a long, long time, and I'm not about to let you ruin it for something that your side of the family was involved in decades ago, of which you had absolutely no part."

"Are you saying we should just forget about the letter?"

"Absolutely not. Do you think *they* are going to forget? Beth, get it through your head. If they haven't forgotten about Davisly's connection to a murder fifty years ago, and they haven't forgotten about something in your family's history one hundred years ago, I seriously doubt they're going to forget about a letter they gave to you yesterday."

"Then we should pay."

"No, we won't do that either. We won't pay, but we also won't forget."

Beth shook her head. "There are no other options, Barry."

He paused to sip his brandy. "There is one," he said. "We tackle this situation head on."

Beth stumbled while she rubbed her forehead with her fingertips. "How did you find out?"

"About what? The second letter? The one you just received and tried to conceal from me?"

"Yes, of course."

"I met Callan this morning at Open Arms when I went to see Lauren. I told him I knew about his process review. He was a little surprised, I think, because he understood that his role was to be kept confidential. I thought that was supposed to be the case as well. I was surprised when you told me that you told Kate about Callan's review during drinks last night. You wanted to see how she would react. Why? What changed your mind?"

Beth lowered her head.

"Callan asked me that question, Beth, but I didn't have an answer for him. He was adamant that something major happened to make you want Kate to know."

"It was nothing like that."

"But suppose it was. Suppose something did happen that made you change your mind about wanting Kate to know you were looking into who was behind the bureau transactions. Two possibilities existed for me. The first was realizing there could be a connection between William's death and the bureau he purchased from Cottage Gallery. The second was the possibility of another letter—to us."

Beth shook her head and turned away.

"You weren't going to tell me, were you? You were going to handle the letter yourself. It was the only reason I could think of why you would turn on your friend like that."

"Where's the letter?"

"In my possession."

"We should pay it, Barry."

"We're not paying a damn thing," he said adamantly. "They can go to hell before we pay another blackmail note. We couldn't afford the first one, let alone another one in which they want even more money than the first."

"I'm sure if I explained the situation to Andrew Gammon, he would lend us the money."

"He's a campaign contributor."

"This isn't a campaign contribution."

"You're not thinking straight, Beth. It doesn't matter. Any sum of money of that size being given to you by an existing contributor will be looked upon as a special interest payment. If it's done under the table as you're suggesting, it could be viewed even worse by the opposition, as a bribe of some kind."

"But the past—"

"Is not going to ruin you. Can't you see?" Barry took a step toward his wife, but she stepped back. "The past isn't going to ruin you, Beth, but how you handle the past could. We're not going to pay. It's time for the police. We have to bring these letters to the attention of the authorities."

"No!" Beth shouted. "No, not yet! Let me think. If not Andrew, surely you know someone else. What about that man Alex mentioned at dinner who spoke at the Columbia Club? He said you knew him."

"Chase VanderPelt?"

"Yes, that's him. What about Chase VanderPelt?"

"No," Barry replied emphatically. "We're not going to Chase VanderPelt."

"Why not? It's worth a shot just to inquire."

"I said no. He may not be associated with *your* career, but he's associated with mine. I'm a commercial lender. I lend money to him and to people like him, not the other way around."

"But we can at least talk to him."

"If not money, what else is there to talk about?"

"William Davisly, for one," Beth replied. "His perspective on William's death."

Barry laughed. "And how are we going to bring the topic up? Are we going to invite him to dinner and have your extortion letter fall from his napkin and then say, 'Oh, my goodness, how did that get in there? I wonder if William Davisly received one of those before he killed himself'?"

"Don't be absurd."

"Then don't you be," Barry said angrily.

"But the whole thing is absurd," she said. She paced in a circle before facing him again. "Don't you think so?"

"What are you talking about?"

"These notes, these damn notes, demanding money we don't have, stuck in a bureau we don't want but have to buy, no less. It's absurd."

Barry didn't answer.

"Well, don't you think it is?" she asked.

"It's unconventional, I'll admit."

Beth scoffed. "Unconventional? That's all you can say?"

"No," he replied remorsefully, "but that's how it works."

Beth stepped closer. Her eyes penetrated his. "What do you mean?"

"They're good, Beth," he said, softening his voice. "They're trying to camouflage their crime by making it appear that our bureau purchases are bona fide transactions. Their demands are less conspicuous that way, a bit of creative money laundering. That's why they use the bureaus. That's why we must go to the police now."

"No, Barry, please," Beth requested again, lurching toward him, arms outstretched. "A little more time is all I need."

"We don't have time. Kate is having that damn reception in a few days. I'm not feeling good about it. I think we should find a reason why we can't attend."

"Oh, but we must, Barry, we must. We have to go."

"Why?" he pleaded. "What reason could there possibly be to justify parading in front of those people?"

"We said it just the other night," she replied. "We have to show them that we're not afraid, that the letter makes no difference to us, whether we pay it or not."

Chapter Twelve

B eth watched her husband ascend the stairs to their bedroom. She wished she believed what she said to him, that the letter made no difference. At the time, it sounded convincing, coming from her mouth, and she thought it clever to use their own words to squelch a conversation she didn't want to have in the first place. Not being afraid took a strength she didn't know if she possessed. Not now, anyway.

It wasn't physical fear that confronted her, but one much more menacing and ominous—a fear of the unknown. Such fear created an unimaginable tear in the fabric of her being that others thought was impenetrable.

But this was different. As Barry indicated, the letter wasn't just about her. She had her family to consider. She didn't worry about her husband. Barry's job was secure. He'd made wise investments that could carry them through a financial crisis. Gabe would be fine too. He had an uncanny resolve to survive—to do what was needed to persevere through the challenges he faced.

Lauren was different because she was young and still naive to the world. She didn't want to shelter her daughter from life's experiences of hardships and mistakes. It wouldn't be right to do so. Sheltering her meant that Beth believed she was incapable of surviving on her own. She didn't believe that to be true. Beth knew Lauren could survive, but that didn't mean she had to expedite her maturation by making decisions about the letter that lacked discretion and consideration.

Beth climbed the stairs to their bedroom to join her husband. He said troubles were clearer and brighter in the morning. She decided to put that belief to the test. As she touched the knob to the closed door of their bedroom, she wondered for the first time about how much Barry could bear before he'd give up on her, before their relationship was no longer worth fighting for.

She remembered a time when she thought that of Barry. It was a time when they were first married. Money was tight, and their financial situation was more volatile than it was today. Barry made some poor real estate and stock market decisions that not only almost wiped them out financially but could have caused some legal difficulties. She remembered asking herself the same question about his worth to her. How many poor choices in their lives would he make? Was he worth persevering through the chronically poor choices he made? She loved him dearly, but that wasn't the point. Many a woman had come to financial ruin and even death loving a man so deeply because she thought of nothing more than love. She wasn't one of those women, and she didn't want to be.

But what about Barry?

Many men came to ruin and death for the woman they loved too. Was he one of those men? She wasn't sure if she had ever tested him to that point in their marriage. If there was ever a time to be tested, however, this was it. Their relationship and family were being tested, and she didn't know what to do.

She let go of the doorknob to their bedroom and went

into the room that belonged to Lauren. Innocent, unaffected by change, and uncomplicated, Lauren's room looked as if she hadn't quite crossed the Rubicon to womanhood with her decor of teenage posters, stuffed animals, and dolls.

Even the white hand-painted jewelry box with a dollop of lavender flowers on the corners seemed a bit too whimsical for a woman of Lauren's age. Beth reached for the box on top of Lauren's chest of drawers and cradled it in her hands, opening the top to reveal two decades' worth of earrings, bracelets, and necklaces that Lauren had collected over her life. She sifted through the delicate costume jewelry, smiling at the memories it represented.

Beth picked up one bracelet she recognized immediately. She'd picked it out of her own keepsake box and given it to Lauren on her sixteenth birthday. She sifted deeper into the box and found other jewelry of the same vintage that she'd given to her daughter over the years.

There was one piece she had not given to her daughter, however.

Beth could hardly breathe as she lifted an omega necklace of white gold with a diamond and black onyx pendant dangling from its center. She'd completely forgotten about the necklace her mother had presented to Lauren when she turned twelve. Beth eyed it carefully, looking to see if its history appeared in the glistening sparkles of its diamonds or the polished surface of its onyx. Her lower lip twitched as she felt the coolness of the silver upon her fingers.

The feeling inside her was real. She imagined her emotions were as real as they would have been when the necklace came into her family's possession.

Beth quickly returned the necklace to its place in the box and closed the lid. She held the box tightly, as if its wicked history would seep through the crevices and strangle her. She placed the box back onto the chest of drawers but hesitated. The rash of jewelry thefts in the area that Alex had brought up after dinner popped into her head. Perhaps, just to be safe, she should secure the box inside the chest instead of on top, in plain sight.

The top drawer creaked open, stuffed with undergarments and footies. Beth pushed some of them aside to make room for the box and in so doing exposed an unsealed, unmarked white envelope. The envelope flipped to an angle that would make closing the drawer difficult, so Beth removed it to replace the box before putting it back.

She glanced quickly at the envelope. Nothing was odd about it except that it appeared new, and with the flap unsealed, she could see Lauren's name written in Gabe's handwriting on the top page of the document inside. *Curious.* Gabe wasn't prone to writing anyone in the family a note, especially his sister. Upon a closer peek, he'd also written something else on the letter to Lauren: *About our great-great-grandmother.*

Her heart sank to her stomach.

Beth grasped the envelope tighter and reached for the arm of the cushioned rocker in the corner of the room to steady herself as she sat down. For a few moments, she rocked vigorously, leaning her head against the high back, and clutched the envelope against her chest. Her heart pounded. She didn't know what to think or do. Gabe was astute enough to know that something was happening within the family, but she was astounded to believe he'd risk writing anything in a letter to his sister.

Perhaps it's not about that.

Contrary to her better judgment, Beth pulled the document from the envelope and began to read. She soon realized that Gabe had pulled from the internet, or newspaper articles archived at the Central Library, depositions taken based upon events of a train ride from Indianapolis to Chicago one hundred years ago. Pangs welled in her gut. One of the depositions was in the words of her own great-grandmother, Evelyn.

Beth read the documents slowly, taking in each word. She thought she'd pictured the sordid event quite clearly from what she'd known before, but with every word of the deposition, she realized how limited her imagination had been—until now. The words pulled her in. The sway of the rocker was like that of a train in motion, and Beth found herself immersed in the event as if she were her grandmother, riding the train herself, living the moments just as her grandmother must've done. By delving deep into the story, imagining the fear and danger her grandmother had experienced on that train to Chicago back in 1925, she hoped she'd understand why she feared the past so much.

Evelyn stared out the sleeping compartment window, watching the farmland moving by with unnatural speed and furor. She frowned and turned away from the view, tilting her head, listening. Yes, the sound of sobbing was definitely coming from the next compartment. Evelyn sensed that the cries weren't from panic, so there was no immediate emergency, but they still came from someone in despair, and that required attention.

Evelyn rose from the cot, went to the wall and knocked three times. Upon the second set of knocks, the crying stopped. "Are you all right?" Evelyn asked. "Do you need help?"

No answer.

"May I come over?"

"No, please. I'm fine, just dreadfully sad."

Evelyn didn't know how to respond but suggested, "Maybe

another shoulder would—"

"No. Please, go away. I'm fine."

Evelyn let her be, but the crying persisted until she could stand it no longer. She stood, planning to check on the distressed woman, and caught sight of herself in a mirror that hung on the door leading to the hallway. She smiled. The straight line of her simple, multilayered dress with its scalloped hemline made her chest look flat. Very fashionable.

She unlocked her door and entered the hall. The train rolled as she stepped, making her walk a little like a drunk. She knocked rapidly on the woman's compartment and called out, "Ma'am? Ma'am, are you all right in there?"

"Please, I told you to go away."

"But I won't," Evelyn replied. "I won't until I know you're okay."

She heard movement, as if the woman had decided to rise from her bunk. The door opened slowly, and through the slim crevice she saw a sliver of the young woman's face, one so worn and harried that she appeared twice her twenty-something age.

"May I get you something?" Evelyn placed her hand against the door's surface to prevent the young woman from shutting it on her.

"I'm fine, thank you. Really, I am. You must go now."

"Surely there's something—"

"There isn't," she replied and began to close the door.

Anticipating the move, Evelyn pushed back. The woman didn't offer much resistance. "I could call for the porter."

The woman laughed, not a hearty or boisterous laugh, but one with an intonation of sarcasm and judgment directed upon her naivety. She tried to close the door again, but Evelyn stopped her.

"There must be someone here—"

The woman sighed in resignation. "There is. Please find Gentry or Clenck."

"Clenck?"

"Just find him."

"Okay, all right, Gentry or Clenck. I'll try to find them. Is there a message I should tell them?"

"Yes," she replied somberly. "Please beg them to kill me."

The extraordinary request took Evelyn off guard. She pulled back in surprise, and the woman seized the opportunity to shut the compartment door and lock it securely.

Evelyn pounded on it with the palm of her hand.

The woman, presumably wanting to avoid further disturbance, opened the door again, revealing a face marred by fear.

Evelyn tried to hide her astonished expression.

The woman staggered to her bunk and collapsed onto the mattress, a picture of hopelessness.

"Oh, my God, miss, you're frightened. What are you afraid of?"

"The *law*," the woman replied curtly.

"I don't understand. Are you running from the police?"

The woman shook her head.

"Then we have to get you some help."

"There is no help available. That's what I'm trying to tell you. There are only Gentry and Clenck on this train, but your words to them will be in vain, because they'll not do anything with the law on board."

"So you're telling me the police are on board?"

"No. He's bigger than the police. He's bigger than Gentry or Clenck. They're all his puppets. Don't you understand?" She got off the bunk and returned to the door. "Now go, please, unless you can find their guns."

"I have no intention of . . ." Evelyn stopped. Who was this woman with fear etched on her face? "I'm Evelyn Terrence. What's your name?"

The woman glanced briefly into Evelyn's eyes. "Madge Oberholtzer. Pleased to meet you," she said sarcastically in a tone that faded as she tried to close the door once more.

"No, wait, please. Clearly, you're in trouble. You can trust me. Are you going all the way to Chicago?"

"I heard him say to Clenck that we were going to Chicago," she replied. "But so far we've only been to hell and back. He says we're going to get married, but I don't know where he's taking me once we get there." She opened the door and gestured Evelyn into the compartment. "There's this deal, some transaction, with this company in Chicago that needs more coal or something; I don't know. All I know is that D. C. said we'd be married in Chicago after the deal was done."

"D. C.?" Evelyn asked. "You mean D. C. Stephenson?"

Madge nodded.

"The Grand Dragon of the Indiana Ku Klux Klan? How did you get mixed up with him?"

"Stop," Madge pleaded. "Go back to your cabin. Let me be."

Evelyn looked down and saw a laceration on the woman's arm. "You've cut yourself."

"I stumbled when the train rocked."

"Did you really? Or did he—"

"I stumbled."

"Well, then, when we get to Chicago, I'll see if Mr. Gentry or Mr. Clenck, whoever they are, will let us go to a five-and-dime and pick up some iodine or mercurochrome. Surely, they will allow that." Evelyn paused and thought for a moment before continuing, "Are you with him of your own free will?"

Madge just shook her head miserably.

"Then he'll be getting off in Hammond. He won't risk federal kidnapping charges by crossing the state line. He's only the law in Indiana."

"Then I have to get to Chicago."

Evelyn shook her head. "You think he'll let you stay on the train if he gets off? No. When the train stops in Hammond, you have to run for your life."

Madge leaned back on the mattress and began to sob again. "Oh, dear God, don't you see I have no other way out of this than to die?"

"No!" Evelyn implored. "Why would you say that?"

"To save myself the horror of my indiscretion. I can't bear seeing what this will do to my mother, being married this way. She was so hopeful for me. This job he had for me. I only went to his house because my mother—Oh, God! I can't bear going further. I can't bear going home!"

Evelyn caressed the broken woman in her arms as closely as she could without causing her additional discomfort. Madge seemed frail and weak. Her breath smelled of stale liquor and hunger, and her skin reeked of sweat and cheap cologne.

Madge allowed Evelyn to hold her as she cried. It seemed the only solace she'd had for some time, and she gladly accepted it.

"I'm sure your mother will forgive you," Beth said, consoling her. "There's no mother that would—"

"No," Madge interrupted. "You have it wrong. It isn't me she wouldn't forgive."

"I don't understand."

"It's herself. She'll never forgive herself for letting this happen to me, and I can't bear to see her torment when I return. I can't bear it."

"Then you have to tell me what happened, Madge. How did you meet this man?"

"It seems so convoluted now," the young woman said, wiping the tears from her eyes. "I don't know that I can remember it well. I don't even know why he was attracted to me, why he would want to be attracted to me. I was everything he wasn't, and he was everything I would never want in a man, but I didn't know it at the time. You see, I was a teacher, and I worked for the Department of Education in the State Program for Literacy."

"Where did you teach?"

"I didn't teach at a specific place. I taught illiterate adults how to read. I went into Ward Five and Ransom Place to teach the coloreds and some children how to read so they could read the Black newspaper, the *Recorder*, and to better themselves. That's why I attended the banquet at the Athletic Club in honor of Governor McCray last fall."

"McCray? I don't know much about him. Does he have an interest in education?"

"Yes, a sincere interest," Madge said, her eyes brightening. "Governor McCray built schools and believed in a reformatory system for delinquent prisoners. He also believed that coloreds needed and deserved better. That's why I went to support him. McCray rebuked the Klan and vetoed Klan-backed bills that were sure to pass in the statehouse. The bills would've hurt the progress we've made in programs for the illiterate."

"Is that where you met Stephenson—at this banquet?"

"No, I was dating Mr. Stanley Hill at the time—nothing serious. Stanley had done work for Governor McCray, and he was asked to plan the January inauguration of Governor Jackson. He asked me to assist with preparations, such as name tags and things. Of course, Stanley and I were prominently seated at a table during the inaugural dinner. It was there that I met Mr. Stephenson. He asked me to dance. Stanley said it would be okay, and so I did. Then Mr. Stephenson asked me out, and we went to dinner on a couple of occasions. Very nice dinners, they were. My parents approved, of course, him being from Irvington and a successful businessman. I thought . . ."

Madge hesitated.

"You thought what? You thought something was odd about his beliefs?"

"Oh, no, not at all. There was no reason to believe he wasn't a devout Christian—Protestant, of course—who was interested in education and the welfare of children. Why, he even . . ." Madge hesitated, embarrassed to continue. "He even commissioned me to write a book to be required as part of the curriculum in all Indiana public schools. It was about nutrition."

"You wrote it?"

"Yes. It was entitled *One Hundred Years of Health.* Mr. Stephenson was able to get a bill passed in the House requiring such a book be taught, but it wasn't readily apparent by the way the bill was written that there was only one book that could meet all the specifications required of the bill."

"*One Hundred Years of Health?*"

Madge nodded shamefully.

"I suppose even though you wrote the book, Stephenson owned it."

Madge nodded again.

"That means he'd earn the proceeds from the book sales. A book now required by the State of Indiana for all public schools."

"But I didn't know. I had no idea."

"How could you not know, Madge?"

"It was all secretive."

"Of course, but he's the Grand Dragon of the Indiana Ku Klux Klan, for crying out loud! He made the Klan in Indiana the most powerful in the country. My God, Madge, the city and the statehouse, except for McCray, are run by Klansmen.

Almost a third of the white population in Indiana are members. You live in one of the wealthiest areas of the city that supports him the most. He asks you to write a book that is suddenly the only book available to meet the requirements of a mysterious state education bill. You worked in the Indiana Department of Education, Madge. You surely knew about the bill?"

Evelyn's voice rose so loud that Madge put her hand over Evelyn's mouth to quiet her. "Please," Madge muttered. "I don't know how I didn't know, but I didn't."

"That's hard to believe."

"I didn't obsess over my life with the Klan," she explained. "I wanted no part of their evil. I spent my entire day, my life, and all the advantages I had to help those who couldn't read so they could have more of the opportunities that I had. I'm not oblivious to life within Irvington, but I didn't obsess over it, nor did it define me. So, whoever you are, if you want to judge me as others will, then please leave me here to die so that I may be judged by the One who has a right to judge me. Because He knows my heart, not you."

~

Beth closed her eyes, realizing that her own shame had manifested itself into her imagined version of the journey. Would her grandmother really have said that to the dispirited woman? If she had, would she have tried to think of words worthy of redemption to repair the damage she must have caused by her accusation? If so, she expected she'd find none. No words could ask for forgiveness here. Beth glanced back at the words of the deposition and placed herself back in the scene in her imagination.

"After about the third date we had," Madge said, "he revealed who he was. I knew that if he was who he said he was, he wasn't only the most powerful man in the state of Indiana, but he had most of the country in awe of him as well.

"I became ill at the table when I realized who was speaking to me and with whom I was associated. I told him very politely that I could no longer see him. He allowed me to leave the restaurant graciously, and I heard nothing further from him until last night.

"He called my home, and my mother answered the telephone. He asked to speak with me and said the matter was of a professional nature and urgent. He had a position within his company that he needed to fill with someone of my qualifications right away. The position and the money he offered enthralled my mother. I arrived home quite late, but it didn't seem to matter. He wanted to see me whenever I got home, and my mother encouraged me to go."

"What time was this?"

"I suspect it was around ten o'clock. He sent Mr. Gentry for me, and Mr. Gentry escorted me the short distance from my home on University Avenue to his mansion. The moment I arrived, I knew it wasn't right, that I shouldn't be there."

"How did you know?"

"Mr. Stephenson had been drinking. No respectable gentleman would drink that much and then invite a woman to his home to speak professionally about a position of reputable character. His chauffeur was in the room with him and this Mr. Clenck."

"Who is Mr. Clenck?"

"I don't know much about him. He was a business associate, I presumed at the time. Now I believe he's just one of Stephenson's men. It didn't matter though. What mattered was there were no other women in the house. Mr. Stephenson had even sent his maid out, giving her the night off. Anyway, it wasn't right. I'm fairly certain I was drugged with drink. I vomited and said I wanted to go home, but Mr. Stephenson said that wasn't possible. He said he couldn't send me back home to my mother in the state that I was in."

"What did you do?"

"What could I do? I don't remember what happened next but before I knew it, he told me that he loved me. That's when I learned we were going to Chicago to be married. I was astonished. How could he love me as much as he said he did when I loathed him and practically told him so at our last dinner?"

"Is that when you boarded this train?"

"Not right away. The men required revolvers before leaving the house, because we were going to Chicago where he wasn't the law. We left through the back to get into his automobile. I begged him to drive me home, but he wouldn't hear of it. I thought we were going to drive all night to Chicago, but instead, his chauffer drove us to Union Station, where this train was waiting for us. I think it's his private train. I didn't know anyone else was on board until you knocked on my wall."

Evelyn frowned, realizing that she hadn't seen anyone else when she got on. And no conductor had checked her ticket. If this was a private train, she'd got on the wrong one!

"There's just a skeletal crew," Madge said. "I only know of an engineer, a conductor, and a porter. Otherwise, it's just us, Mr. Gentry and Mr. Clenck. Mr. Stephenson, too, of course."

Fear raced through Evelyn. She'd become caught up in this woman's plight, probably inextricably so. Could she hide in her compartment and hope they'd not find her? And even if she could get off the train unseen, could she leave Madge to her fate? She sighed and shook her head. "What's to become of us?"

Madge didn't have time to respond before a porter rapped on the compartment to announce the stop at Hammond. "You were right," she whispered, her eyes wide.

Evelyn hurriedly gathered what clothes she could find of Madge's off the floor. "I'll help you get dressed," she said. "Do you have a brassiere? Are you able to wear one under your blouse?"

"No," she groaned. "I only have that side lacer."

Evelyn picked up the side lacer from the floor and shook her head. They didn't have time to lace it and pull it tight to flatten her breasts. Madge would have to forgo the fashionable boyish look.

The two suddenly jumped, startled by a fist pounding against the door.

"It's Hammond, Miss Oberholtzer."

Madge whispered to Beth that the voice belonged to Gentry.

"It's time to get up," he commanded. "We have to get off. Do you need me to get you dressed?"

Evelyn opened the compartment door and faced the bodyguard. "No, Mr. Gentry," she replied curtly. "We can manage on our own, but we must find a five-and-dime, if you wouldn't mind assisting."

Gentry frowned. "Who are you?"

"Madge's friend."

Gentry's eyebrows rose, but he made no comment, just tried to peek through the opening to get a glimpse of Madge. Evelyn blocked his view. He stepped back. "It's not up to me, doll. You'll have to take that up with Mr. Stephenson."

"Well, as you can see, Mr. Stephenson is the reason we must make this request. I'm thinking Mr. Stephenson isn't going to be very obliging."

Gentry considered her words. "Yeah, sure. I'll see what I can do. In the meantime, get as ready as you can, as fast as you can. We're heading over to the Indiana Hotel in about ten minutes. She's registered as Mr. Stephenson's wife." He frowned at Evelyn, then shrugged. "You can be her sister. Just note that he has his revolver, and he'll use it if you don't do as he says. You'll be with me."

Madge struggled to the door and pushed Evelyn away to ask, "Did he send my mother a telegram? D. C. promised he'd telegram my mother. Gentry, please help me contact my parents and let them know where I am."

Gentry's cold, brown eyes softened as he saw the anguish on Madge's face. He replied that he'd find out and get a message to her parents if Stephenson had not. "You're not going to be long at the Indiana, miss. He ordered Shorty to bring the Cadillac up from Indianapolis. He's sending you home."

Evelyn sighed with relief and spun to face to Madge as soon as Gentry left. "Let's hurry, then. We must hurry. The quicker we get you to the hotel, the quicker you'll be home."

"No," Madge cried. "I can't go home. Not now. I haven't the strength to face my mother. She can't see me like this."

Evelyn's own plans were inconsequential in the face of Madge's distress. "Okay, then you can stay with me. I'll telephone your mother from my home when we get to Indianapolis. You can talk to her from there. You can explain that you're with a friend and that you're all right."

Madge didn't look convinced, but it was the best solution they had for the time being. "I want a hat," she said.

Evelyn frowned. "I think a hat is the last thing that should be on your mind, Madge."

"But it isn't."

Beth assisted Madge with her dress and stockings. Gentry

came around again and told the women to be ready. They were about to depart the train and would meet Stephenson and Clenck at the hotel.

Madge scoffed. She couldn't find one of her ankle-strap button shoes. Evelyn suggested she look under the coat crumpled in a pile by the outside window. Madge found it there but did nothing with it. Instead, she sat on the bunk and stared helplessly into space.

Evelyn's heart ached for her, and she tried to do something with her hair. Though longer than most styles of the mid-1920s, it was still fashionable. The length, however, caused her to look even more ratty than she was.

"If we can just fix your hair, you'll be good enough to go to the hotel," Evelyn said.

"That's why I want a hat. I want him to buy me a black silk hat. It's the least he can do."

"Perhaps a necklace. Do you have a necklace or something that would detract from your hair?"

Madge looked about the room in a daze. She spotted her purse and pointed to it. "In there, but I don't want to wear it. He gave it to me last night. I'd rather throw it onto the tracks."

Evelyn found the necklace and was taken aback by its simplistic beauty. She pulled it from the purse and stared at the glistening silver omega with its black onyx and diamond pendant. "It's beautiful."

Madge was indifferent. She closed her eyes as Evelyn placed the necklace around her neck and shivered at the touch of the cool silver upon her tender skin.

Gentry called again from the hallway, this time more impertinent, encouraging their haste. They also heard the voice of the porter giving last-minute instructions for their departure.

Evelyn scurried to gather Madge's belongings, get her own

overnight bag from her compartment, and check her own hair and attire.

They emerged from the train into the chilly air, wanting to bolt but weary and afraid. Evelyn held Madge closely as they walked from the train station on Sibley Avenue toward the hotel. "There's a drugstore across the street," Evelyn said to Gentry. "It looks like it's open. I'd like to find something to spruce her up." As if to deflect any possible rejection, she also confided quietly, "I need to find a brassiere that will work."

Gentry nodded and flicked a cigarette he'd been smoking onto the sidewalk. He tightened his overcoat as a strong breeze blew from Lake Michigan around the corner of the building, then he pulled out a bill to cover the cost.

"I want to come," Madge said. "I'll sit on a soda fountain stool."

"Okay, I'll see what they have," Evelyn said. When they entered the store, she pointed to where the fountain bar was located, then darted the length of the store to a small apparel section before approaching the first aid section, where she picked up a bottle of mercurochrome. As she walked toward the cashier at the front of the store, she saw Madge walking away from the counter toward the fountain bar. Evelyn paid for her purchases, then approached Madge as she climbed onto a stool.

"I thought you were resting," Evelyn said critically.

Madge couldn't hide her guilt. "Oh, I-I . . . rouge," she stuttered.

"Rouge?"

"Yes, I could use some rouge, but I couldn't find it. Don't you think rouge would help?"

Evelyn hesitated. "I suppose it would. Not entirely, of course. Stay seated, and I'll pick out a shade. I mean it, though. I want you to stay seated."

Evelyn purchased the rouge, and the women emerged from the store with Gentry close at hand. He snuffed out another cigarette and led them across the street to the hotel. Two bellboys helped them to the suite where two men waited. Gentry greeted Stephenson, who paced the floor and didn't stop or show any interest when Gentry introduced her as Madge's friend from the train. Evelyn assumed that the man sprawled in a stuffed wingback chair must be Clenck. Gentry took a seat at the small table and began to roll a cigarette. Evelyn couldn't keep her eyes off Stephenson.

"I should like to visit the washroom, please," Madge said.

Stephenson nodded.

Evelyn watched Madge walk to the small bathroom, where she closed and locked the door behind her. Out the corner of her eye, Evelyn caught Stephenson's watchful eye upon her.

"What the hell are you looking at?" he blurted.

"Me? I should think it was the other way around, sir."

But she'd been staring at him from the moment she'd walked in, mesmerized by the fact that D. C. Stephenson was standing before her.

~

Beth came out of her imaginings and looked at the photo of Stephenson that Gabe had included in the envelope. The man repulsed her. He had boyish looks for a grown man, but in an unattractive way, and he wasn't as well built as some—clearly biased—historians described; rather, he was fat. He wasn't well dressed either. Though he wore a fancy tailored suit adorned with timepieces and gold jewelry, it hung on him like an oversized chair cover. His smile was unnaturally bland beneath deep-set, dark eyes, his tie crooked, his ears small, and his hair untrimmed and carefree. Most of all, Beth sensed that his soul was greasy. She flicked her eyes back to the deposition and imagined herself back in that hotel room, watching Madge emerge from the bathroom.

~

Madge walked to a settee that sat against the wall adjacent to the bedroom.

Evelyn perched on the edge of an occasional chair, satisfied that Madge was comfortable, until the young woman suddenly flinched as if in great pain. "Are you all right, Madge?"

"Yes, why?"

A rapid knock at the door interrupted Evelyn's inquiry. Clenck rose from his chair to answer. A small, tired-looking man in a light overcoat entered, smoking a cigarette. Clenck welcomed him as Shorty.

Stephenson finally stopped pacing. "What the hell took you so long?"

"Couldn't find the damn place. Not where you said it was."

"When can you be ready to take us back?"

"Where are we going?" Madge asked, belching under her breath.

"I'm ready anytime you are," Shorty said to Stephenson, ignoring Madge's question. "Give me a chance to smoke one first."

Stephenson turned to Clenck. "Go out and get us some booze. I'd like some whiskey. When you come back, we'll down a few and get on our way."

Clenck nodded and left the suite.

Stephenson sat in a stuffed wingback chair and smoked while Shorty turned his attention to Madge. He walked to the settee and sat next to her. "What's wrong with you?"

Madge didn't answer.

Evelyn looked closely and saw her flinch again.

"There's nothing wrong with her," Stephenson grunted.

"Where's your pain?" Shorty asked.

Madge licked her lips and confessed that she hurt all over. She tried to sit up to say more but couldn't and so beckoned Shorty to come close.

Shorty leaned down to listen.

"Can you keep a secret?" she whispered to him.

He nodded.

"I believe you can. You see, I've taken poison."

Shorty glanced at Stephenson with alarm.

"Call downstairs," Stephenson instructed him as he lurched from his chair. "Have service send a quart of milk right away."

Evelyn, also hearing her words, jumped up, rushed over to the settee, and took her hand. "Dear God, Madge."

Stephenson joined her. "Tell me what you've done!"

Madge closed her eyes and retched but didn't vomit. A spasm of pain convulsed through her. "I took three tablets that I bought from the drugstore," she admitted quietly, her expression tense with fear.

"You did what?" Evelyn exclaimed. "How did—"

"I don't believe you," Stephenson yelled.

Madge snorted. "You don't have to believe me. The evidence is in the bathroom."

Stephenson blurted an expletive.

Gentry stared wide-eyed at Madge.

Evelyn ran into the bathroom. A bottle labeled as containing eighteen bichloride of mercury tablets sat on the counter. Beth opened it and counted out fifteen tablets. Three missing. She threw the remaining tablets into the cuspidor, emptied its contents into the bathtub and watched them swirl down the drain. After setting the bottle down, she walked solemnly into the suite's parlor and nodded to Stephenson.

Madge smiled, appearing content. "What are you going to do now?" she asked him. "There's no fixing this. It isn't something you can snort an order for someone to fix or something you can throw your money at to make it go away."

"Don't be so sure," he spouted back. "Shorty, get the car."

"What about Clenck?" Shorty asked.

"He can take the train back to Union Station with Gentry," Stephenson said.

Shorty did as he was told.

Madge vomited, soiling her dress. Evelyn did her best to clean it up, but there was no time to change clothes. Bellboys arrived within minutes to take the grips. Evelyn helped Madge downstairs, and two young women from the hotel staff helped Gentry and Evelyn get Madge into the car's rear seat. Stephenson assured the women from the hotel that they didn't have time for an ambulance. He explained that they were taking Madge to St. Margaret Mercy themselves to expedite matters.

Evelyn climbed into the Cadillac Phaeton beside Madge, situating her feet among the luggage and personal articles while Shorty puffed on the last of a cigarette and threw it out the window. Cool, moist air from Lake Michigan, mixed with a light breeze, chilled the automobile. Madge shivered.

"Where's your coat?" Evelyn asked.

Madge didn't reply.

"Do you have her coat?" Evelyn asked Shorty. "The one with the fur collar."

He said he didn't know.

"It doesn't matter," Madge whispered softly.

"But it does," Evelyn replied. "Here, take mine."

"No, wait, this first," Madge said as if there was something more important to do. She struggled to lift her arms up over her neck.

Evelyn frowned. "What are you trying to do?"

"Unlatch my necklace."

"Why? No, let it be. It's not bothering anything."

"Please, unlatch my necklace and take it."

Evelyn stumbled for words, surprised by the request. "Take it? Madge, why would I want—"

"Please," she pleaded. "Take it. We may need it later. It's the only thing of value we have that could be used for money, and I want it safely with you."

Evelyn didn't argue. She unlatched the silver omega with the black onyx and diamond pendant and laid it carefully in the palm of her hand. Madge rested her head on Evelyn's shoulder and slumbered into what appeared to be a peaceful nap.

Stephenson started to climb into the front seat next to Shorty but changed his mind. "Get out," he commanded Evelyn. "You sit in the front."

"But she's comfortable now. She's resting."

Stephenson didn't say it twice. He opened the back door, flipped his lighted cigarette onto the pavement and waited silently for Evelyn to do as she was told. She did so reluctantly, not understanding the reasoning and urgency of him wanting to sit beside a woman with vomit covering the front of her dress, smelling salty and rancid, looking lifeless and drawn. He scooted in beside her and replaced Evelyn's shoulder with his. His large arms caressed her, and he kissed her lightly on the top of her head.

To Evelyn's dismay, they drove south, straight out of town. She wanted to beg Stephenson to get Madge to a hospital, but she knew it would be fruitless. The man was only concerned about himself, and once back in Indianapolis, he wouldn't have to worry about the police. Hopefully, someone on the hotel staff might have suspected something suspicious and called the police on Madge's behalf. Evelyn watched carefully for a modified black Ford or Chevy that might be a sign of law enforcement but saw none. By the time they reached the town of St. John, Evelyn had lost hope that anyone with authority was on the chase.

Shorty drove quickly through the Indiana countryside.

"Don't get pinched," Stephenson warned. "They don't know me here."

They entered Indianapolis from the north, speeding along Emerson Avenue now that Stephenson was in a town he owned. The clear sky revealed a moon shining brightly on the manicured lawns of Irvington, and the night air was much cooler. Shorty slowed. Evelyn assumed he didn't want to alarm the neighbors. She shot another worried glance into the back seat. Would Stephenson find someone to help Madge before it was too late? She wasn't looking good.

They turned into the drive of a stately home—Stephenson's, she assumed—and as they swung around the back toward the garage, Evelyn saw the silhouette of a woman on the front porch. Her heart pounded.

"Go and see who that is," Stephenson said sternly to Shorty when the car stopped.

Shorty did as requested, talking to the woman in what appeared to be a calm and appeasing conversation, while Stephenson muttered the word "damn" several times under his breath and Evelyn kept an eye on Madge, itching to make a run for it. But she couldn't go anywhere without her new friend, and Madge didn't look capable of running anywhere right now.

"It's her mother," Shorty said after he returned to the car. "I reassured her that Madge was well and safely in your company."

Madge tried to lift herself to see, but her mother had already trod down the sidewalk to University Avenue and was striding down the street. Madge tried to scramble out of the car—and Evelyn prepared herself to run with her if Madge made it out—but Stephenson pulled Madge back. She fell into his lap, too weary to fight, and her form stilled—too still for the living, all the breath suddenly gone from her.

Evelyn opened her mouth to speak, but Stephenson stopped her. "You must forget what happened tonight, you understand?" he said, pointing his finger at her. "What is done has been done. I'm the law and the power around here, and I wouldn't cross me, if I were you. When you leave this car, get to where you came from, and you get there now. Don't look back. When you wake up in the morning, you forget what you saw. It'll be a new day for us all, sweetheart, you'll see."

"I don't believe that," she said."

Stephenson laughed. "Why? Because of that woman on the porch? Doll, I've taken care of governors, of senators, of mayors, and the like. I've triumphed over police commissioners, IRS auditors, and district attorneys. I think I can handle someone's mama."

"Not this time," Shorty snorted. "That old broad's a spitfire. She could cause trouble."

Stephenson tossed Madge's lifeless body aside to reach over the front seat and grab Shorty by the throat. "You son of a bitch, if she causes trouble then I'll take everyone in this wretched city down with me," he growled as he choked Shorty into submission. He turned to Evelyn with his hands still stifling the breath out of his driver's lungs. Fire spewed from his nostrils and venom spit from his mouth now matted with stubble and reeking from alcohol and smoke. "Everyone!" he yelled. "You hear me?"

~

Beth must've fallen asleep at some point and her imaginings turned into a dream, because she woke with a start, covered in perspiration, her heart pounding in her chest. At first she thought Stephenson had finished Shorty's life and was pulling her over the front seat of the Cadillac toward him, his hands wrapped tightly around her abdomen. The pulling stopped, but the tight grip of someone's arms around her remained.

She struggled briefly before hearing a voice say, "You hear me? I love you, Beth."

The sound was soft and soothing, distinct, and near. The fog cleared from her brain, and she recognized the voice. "Oh, it's you." She sighed with relief and returned his hug.

"I mean it," Barry said. "I love you."

She knew that. Deep within, she always knew. She loved him too.

"We'll get through this," he added, squeezing her tightly, letting her know he was by her side.

She fell asleep. That was all she wanted to know.

Chapter Thirteen

Callan arrived in Broad Ripple in the late afternoon of the next day. The sky was overcast, but the air was humid and warm, holding in rather than warding off the day's heat. In spite of the traffic and commotion on the village streets, very few customers darted in and out of the shops, and even fewer entered Open Arms.

Amy Henzel stood alone at her sales register, filing her nails and waiting for customers. She took the heat and humidity in her stride, though beads of sweat formed at her temples and trickled down the side of her face. "It's not Memorial Day yet," she explained to Callan when he walked in and mentioned how stuffy it was in the building.

Callan wiped sweat from his forehead. "Is that why it's so hot in here? Kate believes in the Memorial to Labor Day rule for air-conditioning?"

Amy chuckled. "You think Kate would ruin her makeup by sweating? It's Eddie's doing. He's old school. Says he wasn't raised on air-conditioning, and the rest of us are spoiled."

"Huh, I would think comfortable customers would mean

increased revenue."

"Increased sales and decreased costs make everyone happy, I guess. I wouldn't know. I won't ever see any of it. Good thing I'm used to the heat."

"But you still like working here?"

Amy placed the nail file in her purse and reflected on Callan's question. "Didn't you ask me that already?"

"Did I?"

"Yeah," she said cynically. "Like, on the first day we met. It was in the break room. You're either obsessed with happiness or you don't like Kate and Eddie any better than I do." Her jovial spirit dissipated.

Callan opened his mouth to respond but hesitated as the front door opened. A woman in her midforties entered, but she didn't notice his customary greeting. She bypassed Callan and Amy and went straight to the double doors clearly marked *Employees Only*.

"I didn't realize people could go back there," Callan said.

"They're not supposed to, but they have been lately. Lauren asked me about it the other day too."

"What's going on?"

"Dunno. I asked Eddie. He said those people are customers and have business with him, and that it wasn't any of my business."

"Does he do transactions from the back?"

"If he does, I don't ring 'em up here."

"So how often do these customers go straight to the back?"

"That was the second one today," she replied.

"Who was that woman? Do you know?"

"Not really. She's been in before. Someone mentioned her name once, but I didn't pay attention."

"So then tell me something; if Eddie conducts business in the back, but you don't ring the transaction on the sales register, how does it get recorded?"

Amy grinned. "You're asking Amy Nobody? Look, all I'm told is that Lisa gets the transaction, and I don't need to worry about it." Callan gave her a quizzical look, so she added, "Lisa Stohler. She works part-time as a bookkeeper. Very part-time. She's so part-time that she hardly comes in. She's getting up there in years, and Kate doesn't have the heart to ask her to retire." Amy looked down at her watch. "I wonder where Lauren is."

"I haven't seen her. Is she replacing you for the next shift?"

"Yes. I thought so, anyway. She said she would."

Callan offered to go see if Lauren was in the break room.

"Do you mind?" she asked. "I need to get to Tipton's."

Callan went to the back, opening the double doors to the quiet back room, except for the presence of a high-school-aged boy who was looking over a desk. Callan went on to the break room and found Lauren at the counter, sweetening her iced tea.

"There you are," he said. "I told Amy I'd come find you."

"Find me? Why? Is she getting antsy out there? I didn't see that many customers."

"It's not customers. She says she has to leave for her other job."

Lauren glanced at her watch. "That's funny. All right, tell her I'll be there in a minute."

Callan exited the way he'd come, noticing the young teenager still with the desk. "Did that just come in this afternoon?" he asked.

"Yeah."

"Is it a gallery item?"

The boy shrugged. "I don't know nothin' about that. Some lady brought it in. Some guy of hers helped me."

"What'll happen to it?"

The boy scrunched up one side of his face, his expression suggesting he'd never given it much thought. "I reckon ol'

Chuck'll take a look at it to make sure it's okay 'fore Eddie says where it's to go."

"What sort of changes?"

"Dunno. I heard the woman who owns it wants changes made to make it look better so people won't keep returning it."

"I see." Callan didn't think there was much use asking the young man any more questions since he probably didn't have more answers to share. Besides, Callan saw Amy outside through the back windows out of the corner of his eye, primping her long, stringy hair. A young man, upper twenties, muscular, and handsome, came into view, smiling broadly, taking her in his arms to swing her around. A sensuous kiss along her neck followed. She giggled and tried to pull away but reached for him playfully when he let her go. Callan wasn't interested in seeing more. He turned and hurried to the sales floor, where Lauren was performing shift-changing procedures.

"Didn't take long for Amy to leave, did it?" Callan asked.

Lauren grunted. "And she left me a mess here. She was supposed to count the till before she left."

"She met her boyfriend, that Brian fellow, or at least, that's who I think it was. I saw them through the windows."

Lauren gave him a dirty look. "Apparently, Tipton's can wait, huh?"

Callan stuck his thumb toward the back. "Did you see that large desk in the back for Chuck to work on, by any chance?"

"Yeah, Jeremy said some lady and man brought it in."

"Is Jeremy that kid's name who's back there?"

Lauren nodded, trying to concentrate on her cash drawer.

"Do you know where it's going, how it's being accounted for, that sort of thing?"

"You're kidding, right? I haven't a clue."

Callan frowned. "Neither does Amy."

Lauren looked up. "What are you implying?"

"It's no wonder there are inventory issues, and that proprietors and other people are asking questions. Jeremy implied that Chuck might do some work for the gallery on certain pieces. I wonder how Chuck's time is being accounted for."

Lauren looked away in thought. She lifted her finger. "There's a way to find out. I know where the daily tickets are kept before Lisa, this woman who does the bookkeeping, records the activity."

"Is there a way I can get in there at night when no one knows I'm here to look at the tickets?" Callan asked.

Lauren smiled. "Only if you let me come along."

By the time Callan arrived at Open Arms that evening, Lauren had gathered a few days' samples of sales tickets, supporting inventory records, and other documentation. She brought the records to the break room and stratified the batches by day on a table.

The aroma of strong coffee welcomed Callan as he entered the room. He poured a cup and took a seat at the table as Lauren sifted through the documents. He sat watching her work, feeling uneasy.

"Something wrong?" she asked.

Callan shook his head. Nothing had to be wrong for him to get a sense of unease from a building at night.

"Unease?" Lauren asked.

"Maybe just different," he clarified. "This place is much different during the day with bustling people about, traffic along the street, and the sun blazing through the plate glass windows. I like to feel a building at night. The real sounds of a building come alive."

Lauren tried to smile as if she understood and agreed, but she said she wasn't fond of buildings at night and missed the familiar sounds of the day.

"How's your mother doing?" he asked. "We left her in quite a state of shock at the dinner party."

Lauren tried to brush her mother's behavior off as insignificant, but Callan saw her response more as her not wanting to talk about it.

"How's your father?"

She hesitated. "He's fine."

"Gabe, too?"

Lauren's shoulders dropped in resignation, as if she accepted that Callan wasn't going to give up talking about her family until she gave him something to satisfy his curiosity. "I haven't talked with him," she said.

"I thought you two were living together now."

"We are. I just haven't talked with him in the context you're asking. He's been disgruntled about his work at the gallery. It could be Kate, could be a number of other things."

"Like your parents, for instance?"

"What about my parents?"

"I'm just wondering, Lauren, if—"

"Look, okay, it's just that we're all a little stressed right now." Lauren paused to collect her thoughts. "Remember me telling you that Gabe gave me a letter before I came home from college? He put it in my dresser. Something about a grandmother he didn't want Mom to see just yet."

"I remember. What about it?"

"It wasn't in the dresser when I looked for it. Mom must've found it and kept it. It's the only logical explanation."

"Could your father have taken it?"

"Dad doesn't do things like that," she said. "I mean, yeah, he might find the letter and take it, but he'd confront Gabe about it later. That's how he is."

Before she could say anything more, Callan's head jerked up at the sound of a door closing. "Listen," he said.

Lauren heard a noise from the back room too. "Hurry," she urged. "You clear the table and hold onto this stuff and find a place to hide. I'll see who it is and try to intercept them if I think they're coming this way."

"No," Callan insisted. "I can't have you do that. It could be dangerous."

"My presence will be less suspicious than yours. I'll be all right."

Callan wouldn't hear of it. "No. We're not leaving this room, and you're not doing anything by yourself." He flicked off the light to the break room and opened the door to the back room just enough to get a glimpse.

Light radiated on the cement floor to their right. Before the light went off, they saw a shadow of a man, carrying an unidentifiable box, striding through the maze of unsorted clothes and merchandise to the door leading to the alley on the opposite wall. They continued their vigil until the man locked the door from the outside, started what sounded like an older-model pickup truck, and drove away.

Callan flicked on the break room light. "Did you recognize him?" he asked Lauren.

She nodded and caught her breath. "It was Chuck, the fix-it guy."

"What was he carrying? Did you recognize the box?"

"I don't know. Something was printed on the side, but I couldn't read it."

Callan frowned. "I couldn't either. Does he come in at

night often?"

"I have no idea. I can't see why he would."

"What's in his workshop?"

"Looks like a plain, old workshop to me, like what a lot of men have. It's been a while since I've been in it."

"Why? Does it hold some sort of secret?"

"No, I don't think so. I just don't have a reason to go in there. My job's at the sales counter or on the sales floor. All I remember is that Chuck has quite a setup."

"Hmm," Callan responded. "It might be worth catching him sometime during the day, when he's working."

They worked through several batches of tickets before Callan sighed, sat back, and told Lauren he believed they were getting nowhere fast.

"Don't you think we'll find something?" she asked.

"Not at this rate," he admitted. "I'm not spotting a pattern of anything out of the ordinary to make it worth continuing. The documentation appears clean."

"Maybe that's just it," Lauren said. "Maybe it's too clean."

"Maybe it is," he said, yawning, "but not tonight. Let's pack these up. I'm going home, and I suggest you do too."

~

Callan arrived early the next day at Open Arms. He figured he had a better chance of catching Chuck Cordry in his workshop then. The door to the alley was propped open to allow a light breeze to blow through the stuffy back room.

Eddie stood an arm's length from the door in the alley, talking to a neighboring shopkeeper. Callan stepped past the two and entered the building, noticing Eddie's skeptical glare directed his way.

Jeremy and another high-school-aged boy were in the middle of the room, sorting clothes into piles, trying to make a dent in the growing backlog of donations received but not processed. Callan walked up to the two to help but saw through the workshop's doorway that Chuck was busy upholstering a chair. Callan looked over his shoulder at Eddie. Although Eddie was still talking to the neighbor, Callan sensed one eye was on his movements. He decided to see Chuck when he wasn't being watched so closely.

"Any rhyme or reason to your sorting, guys?" Callan asked the boys. "Mind if I join in?"

Jeremy just shook his head. The other teen gave Callan some simple instructions, and Callan introduced himself. The boy gave him the once-over and said, "Ronnie."

Callan noticed an open wound on Ronnie's hand. It surely hurt, but the boy gave no indication that it bothered him in any way. "Haven't see you around yet," Callan said to him. "When do you usually work?"

Ronnie didn't look up. "Whenever they need me. A buck's a buck."

Callan tried to liven the mood with casual conversation, and he received bits and pieces of information here and there. They eventually opened up to him more, and he found out that they were estranged from their parents and didn't attend school. Both had dropped out of high school recently, leaving education to make it on their own. They found it difficult to survive, but felt that their chosen path was still better than the educational path and living with their parents.

"Somethin' better'll come along," Jeremy said, "once his hand heals up."

Callan looked at the wound again. "You oughtta see somebody about that."

"He'll be fine," Jeremy said.

Callan stared at Ronnie and added, "Just the same, you can't fool around with cuts."

"I'll be fine."

"Suit yourself. How did it happen?"

The boys gave each other side glances but didn't answer the question. Callan figured they hadn't discussed a mutually agreed upon response yet, so silence was the best answer for the moment.

"Did you get knifed or something?" Callan asked.

"A window," Ronnie blurted.

Jeremy closed his eyes as if he wished his buddy would've let Callan believe what he wanted.

"A window?" Callan asked.

"Yeah. They break sometimes, y'know."

"Yeah, I know, but not spontaneously. Did you happen to bust a window?"

"Yeah." He looked at Callan as if that should satisfy him.

Callan shook his head. "Why would you be busting in a window?"

Ronnie stammered a bit before saying, "Well, I'm staying at this place, y'know, but like, I locked myself out. I had to bust a window to get in. Cut my hand. It happens sometimes."

Callan studied their faces for the truth, but nothing reflected from their expressions. "You need to have it looked at," he said, "but I'm guessing you don't have a doctor, and you don't have insurance even if you had a doctor. But it needs attending to. It could get worse before it gets better, and you don't need that right now."

The boys stopped sorting.

"Am I right?" Callan asked. "Seems you two have enough on your minds the way it is."

Jeremy shifted his feet. Ronnie turned his head.

"I'll tell you what," Callan said, picking up a shirt. "If you want to get that looked at, I'll take you to a doctor and pay for it myself."

Before Ronnie could reject or accept, Eddie came up to the three and asked what all the talking was about. Eddie looked directly at Callan and said, "You may not be on the clock, but these two are. Let's get back to work."

The three watched him walk to the break room door and enter.

"Thanks, but I'm fine," Ronnie said to Callan's offer.

Callan didn't argue. Instead, with Eddie gone, he dropped the shirt in his hand, shuffled across the floor, and entered Chuck's workshop. An oily, metallic stench lingered in the air even though Callan couldn't spot any evidence of spills or open containers. A sawhorse holding a small square-framed chair that had been stripped of all fabric, padding, and webbing took up much of the workshop's available space. The chair's legs and two arms had been removed and were stacked neatly to the side, on the floor. The bare frame held only four newly installed black zigzag springs.

Chuck Cordry stood in front of the sawhorse, his back facing Callan. His worn, long-sleeved plaid shirt was tucked neatly into denims frayed at the bottom above scuffed boots. Sunbaked creases in the back of his neck confirmed Callan's first impression that the hard-boiled Hoosier was not afraid of hard work.

Chuck straightened up when Callan walked in. "Do those springs look right to you?" he asked in a raspy smoker's voice. "They're too low, ain't they?"

"Oh, I don't know," Callan replied. "Too low for what?"

Chuck ignored the uneducated comment and blurted an

expletive. "I sure measured the damn things wrong."

"The chair'll still be comfortable, won't it?"

The graying repairman looked at Callan as if he'd missed the point. "Sure," he said, "it'll sit just fine, nothin' wrong about that, but I'll always know it wasn't right, now, won't I?"

Chuck took a deep breath and reached into his toolbox for a self-made tack puller, a tool that was nothing more than a Craftsman flat-nosed screwdriver with the blade neatly hacksawed to form a *v*. He grabbed a hammer and placed the puller squarely on top of one of the clips holding the springs in place. With a sharp blow of the hammer, the tack that kept the clip of the spring tightly in place pressed firmly against the *v*. Chuck pulled down, using the wooden frame of the chair as leverage, and lifted the tack easily from the wood and out of the clip. He followed suit with each tack, carefully removing them without damaging the wood.

Callan watched, intrigued, as Chuck installed the new springs by stretching each one to the proper clips with precise measurements.

Chuck ran his large fingers through his thick, bristly hair, then pulled a Camel from a pack tucked inside his shirt sleeve and placed it between his lips. "Got a light?" he asked.

Callan shook his head.

Chuck frowned in thought, then his eyes brightened as if remembering something. He opened the drawer of a weathered cabinet, pulled out a book of matches, and struck a match. Chuck drew in a heavy breath and released a plume of thick, murky smoke into a room already saturated with unpleasant odors.

"You must be the new guy Eddie told me about," he said, leaning against the front of his workbench.

"I'm Cal."

"Charles Cordry here. Call me Chuck. I'm sure you

know that."

"You sure know your business. That was nice work on the chair."

The man shrugged and replied modestly, "Just stuff I do. Don't know much else, really."

Callan stepped around the workshop, surveying the assortment of broken small appliances, cabinets, and end table legs. He turned to look at a vintage lamp being refurnished. As he did so, he saw a shadowed silhouette appear on the shop's door. It stopped, however, before entering.

"There must be dozens of parts here to all kinds of items that can be fixed and resold," Callan said, studying a dovetailed drawer. "What are you doing here?"

Chuck stepped closer. "You can see it's broken on the other end. I'm hoping to superglue it or something, nothing fancy. It'll be good enough to sell."

"Here at Open Arms?"

Chuck nodded as smoke swirled around his nostrils.

"If it was in better condition, would it go to Cottage Gallery?"

Chuck took another puff and ignored the question.

Callan approached two old toasters and picked one of them up to eye it more closely. "You don't try to save these things, do you?"

"You might want to put that down," Chuck warned. "There's some loose parts on it, and the damn thing might come apart. Chasin' tiny sprockets and screws on a cement floor ain't my idea of fun."

Callan did as he was told. "People buy these things?"

"Not people like you, prolly."

Callan laughed. "No, you got that right. So, that's what you do then, isn't it?"

Chuck gave him the once-over. "What's that?"

"Build bargains."

A grin slid across Chuck's tanned face. "Yes, sir, I believe you're right. That's exactly what I do. I have a one-line job description."

Before Callan could delve deeper into what Chuck really did for Open Arms, the shadow emerged from the doorway.

"Chuck, got a sec?" Eddie asked, pointing toward the back room.

Chuck left the workshop, and Callan took the opportunity to study it in greater detail. He noticed the way tools were arranged, electrical outlets in convenient locations, spacious countertops, pegboards mounted with perfect alignment, and plenty of light to ensure precise craftsmanship. Although old, Chuck's tools were solid and clean, as if a job wasn't complete until everything was carefully wiped free of debris and grime. Callan noticed something else. The old guy had a discriminating eye for items that could be salvaged, refurbished, and given new life.

Callan decided he shouldn't stay long alone in the workshop. He stepped into the back room, where Eddie and Chuck were talking confidentially on one side of the room. Jeremy and Ronnie continued to sort clothing with the same lack of enthusiasm they'd had before.

Lauren burst through the double doors. "Can someone help up front?" she called. "I need some help for a woman who bought a desk."

One of the boys started for the doors, but Eddie called him back. "Hold on, Ronnie. What desk, Lauren?"

"Ronnie knows which one."

Eddie's eyebrows rose. "You'll talk to me," he said. "I asked you what desk."

Lauren sighed. "The one with the rosettes on the corners."

Eddie glanced at the desk. Chuck mouthed a couple of

comments that only Eddie could hear. Eddie acknowledged him with a modest nod and a tightening of his lower jaw.

"Who bought it?" Eddie asked.

"The name is Eckert."

"Tell her we'll have to deliver it ourselves," he said.

Lauren appeared confused. "But she's here to pick it up. She was told it would be ready."

"I understand, but something about the customization didn't turn out right. You'll have to tell her she can come back, or we can deliver it."

Lauren frowned but went back through the double doors. As soon as she was out of sight, Eddie called to Callan to help him move the desk with the rosettes to Chuck's workshop.

Callan obliged and grabbed one end. Eddie took the other and had to walk backward. In doing so, he accidentally jerked the desk away from Callan. Callan lost his grip and the desk hit the cement floor with a thud, barely missing his toes.

"Sorry about that," Eddie said. "Did I getcha?"

Callan looked at the expression on Eddie's face and wondered if the jerk was accidental. "No," he said. "Must be my lucky day."

"You need to get yourself better shoes." Eddie lifted his foot and stuck it around the desk for Callan to see. "Somethin' like these boots. We all wear them. Steel-toed. Hard as rocks. Tough-soled on the bottom too. You can step on anything, and anything can step on you."

Callan gave Eddie's boots a good look. "I'll keep that in mind."

"Good." Eddie looked Callan straight in the eye. "Wouldn't want you to learn the hard way."

Chapter Fourteen

Callan spent the remainder of the afternoon helping the two young men organize and inventory donations in the back room.

Eddie and Chuck spent most of that time behind a closed workshop door.

Within the hour, Gabe Kimmerman burst through the double doors and beelined toward the desks and bureaus area. He meandered through the maze of furniture, studying their exteriors, opening their drawers, and rubbing their surfaces and underbellies with his hands.

"Where's the desk?" he finally called out.

"What desk?"

"The one Lauren is upset about, the one with rosettes. I want to see it."

Callan shook his head. "I'm sorry, Gabe. It's unavailable."

"Unavailable? What does that mean?"

"You can't see it."

"Where is it?"

"Eddie has it, and based on the tone of his voice, I doubt

that he wants anyone looking at it."

Gabe scowled. "Is he with Cordry?"

Callan raised his hand to defuse Gabe's anger. "I don't think anything's going to be accomplished by confronting Eddie."

"I'm not interested in what happened before," Gabe replied. "I'm interested in the desk. Ms. Eckert is one of my customers. She does more business with me at the gallery than she does here with Eddie. He shouldn't have blown her off like that. She wants the desk. I want to know why she can't have it."

Callan suggested they walk to the front of the store to resume their conversation.

"Why?" Gabe asked, but he lowered his voice and calmed down. "Oh, I see. You don't want them to hear what you have to tell me. Okay, I get it. Then let's meet at the Brewpub along the trail leading to the village."

"When?"

"Take your time. I need to talk to Lauren about something first. I'll meet you there. I'll be sitting at a table outside."

~

The walk to the Brewpub was warm but that didn't seem to wane the enthusiasm of villagers ambling the canal greenway. Callan enjoyed the scenery along the canal more than the storefronts aligning the village streets. The green grass and the shady sycamores helped him unwind before delving into what could be a difficult conversation with Gabe.

Callan stopped to admire the ducks and swans in the canal. They glided peacefully along the still waters, unaffected by the people strolling past. They flapped water into the sultry air and dabbled their heads for pondweed. *It takes so much more to keep people amused than animals*, he thought. On an afternoon such as this, Callan wished all he had to do was swim with the swans, look up at the people along the greenway, and reflect on what a curious lot they were.

Callan rested his elbows on a post where the walking trail through the village crossed Guilford Avenue and gazed east along the canal. His daydreaming almost made him miss a young man crossing at the next bridge. His quick gait indicated that he was in a hurry to reach his destination. An older woman stood in the middle of the bridge, wearing a white sweater despite the heat. She greeted the man and joined him in his trek across the bridge to the village center.

Callan followed.

He didn't recognize the woman, but the young man was Gabe Kimmerman. What happened to the talk with his sister? Had he spoken to her, or was it a ruse to keep this meeting with the older woman a secret? Although the reason was none of his business, Callan was curious anyway. He quickened his steps to catch up to them without being detected, using other pedestrians as a screen. Gabe and the woman were so deeply engaged in conversation that Callan doubted the couple noticed him.

They turned, the woman leading, into the walkway to the front door of a small commercial building sided with clapboard and surrounded by lush prairie wildflowers. She unlocked the door and they entered, awakening a tingling bell that Callan heard even from his distance. The door shut behind them, but Callan continued to walk toward the building.

He wasn't interested in peering through the window to get a glimpse at what Gabe and the woman were doing. He was more interested in the sign identifying the establishment and, hopefully, the woman. The lettering was easy to read from a safe distance: *Patterswaite Designs.* The word *Designs* didn't tell him much. He couldn't tell from outside if the word meant the business was interior, architectural, or something in between. But at least he had a name.

He retreated toward the bridge over the canal and scampered along the trail until he came to the outside tables of the Brewpub. A peppy waitress assisted him and asked if he had a specific brew in mind. "If not, we're featuring our German and Austrian drafts today. Does a Warsteiner Verum sound good?"

Callan smiled. "Pour me two. I'm hoping a friend joins me shortly."

~

Callan didn't have to wait long. The waitress soon returned to the table with two tall Verums, just as Gabe walked up to greet him.

"One of them mine?" Gabe asked.

"If you like Warsteiner. Otherwise, I'll drink them both."

The men lifted their mugs simultaneously and gestured a silent cheer of goodwill. The first gulp was easy, and, as most beers were to Callan, it was also a relief. Gabe took a sip and wiped the suds off his upper lip.

A light breeze blew through the trees above them, cooling and soothing Callan in a way that made him acutely aware that it was still spring. Still, he noticed Gabe didn't appear to be enjoying anything, including the breeze or his beer. Gabe's attention was directed somewhere over his shoulder to another table. Callan turned. Brian VanderPelt straddled a bench next to a picnic table, talking with another man similar in age.

"You know him?" Callan asked.

"Sort of. I know his kind, anyway."

"And what kind is that?"

Gabe didn't answer.

"He seems to be omnipresent," Callan said. "I saw him at

Open Arms a little while ago. He's dating Amy."

Gabe chuckled, seeming to find the news hard to believe.

"Your father has the same impression."

"Yeah. It's a lopsided affair, if you ask me. You're saying Chase VanderPelt's son is dating a waitress at Tipton's? Naw, it doesn't add up. Believe me, Brian has money. He doesn't need to be dating a waitress for free beer."

"I take it you don't think much of him."

Gabe frowned. "It's not a matter of thinking."

"Is it trust, then?"

"Look, it doesn't have anything to do with that either. I don't trust anyone anymore, Callan."

"Does that include your mother?"

Gabe glared across the table.

"I'm not going to beat around the bush," Callan said. "I know about the letter you put in Lauren's dresser for her to read. Lauren suspects your mother took it."

Gabe's glare intensified. The men sat in silence before Gabe said, "Sorry I was late."

Callan shook his head as if being late didn't matter. What mattered was everything he'd seen and heard recently. He didn't know what to make of the missing letter Gabe had given to his sister. He didn't know what to make of Jeremy and Ronnie sorting clothes with Ronnie's injured hand. He didn't know what to make of Chuck's workshop and Eddie's reaction to Callan's presence in the workshop. He didn't know what to make of the exchange of unpleasant words between Eddie and Lauren, and he certainly didn't know what to make of Gabe's behavior in the back room, looking for the rosette desk, and him not mentioning meeting with the woman named Patterswaite in a shop along the canal.

He eyed Gabe drink his beer and reminisced that the young

man drank the same way he'd done some twenty-five or thirty years earlier—gulping for the sensation of drinking rather than the pleasure of its taste and craftsmanship. He laughed and made a comment to that effect.

"Craftsmanship?" Gabe asked with astonishment. "I have to say you're my first drinking buddy to describe his favorite beer that way."

Callan laughed. "Yes, I suppose I am. I tend to look at things much differently now that I've aged."

Gabe's eyebrows rose. "Ah, I see," he replied, setting his glass on the table as, his demeanor suddenly aloof, he watched a couple on a tandem bike roll past on the side street.

"You see what?"

"Some philosophical wisdom is about to be shared with me. I find people your age preface wisdom with a reason for giving it."

"Not me," Callan said, raising his hand. "Maybe after a few more beers you'll get some philosophy out of me, but I'm a little short on wisdom today."

"Good, because if it was a way to talk about my mother, I was going to have to ignore you again. I don't blame my mother for taking the letter. She does what she has to do. We all do."

Gabe took another drink, refusing to look at Callan. They sat in silence, feeling the breeze and watching people as they passed.

"The desk was in Chuck's workshop," Callan said to break the lull.

Gabe looked up. "You mean the desk for Marjorie Eckert that Eddie wouldn't let her have?"

"If that's the desk with the rosettes, then yes."

"More work to be done on it?"

"I don't know what you mean. What more needed to be done?"

"That's what I'm asking you," Gabe said. "Everything always needs additional work, it seems, if Eddie and Chuck are involved. Why else would it be back in Chuck's workshop?"

"I don't know. I thought it was just to get it out of sight until they delivered it themselves."

"Yeah, right."

Callan pushed his mug aside. "Tell me something. I want some honesty here. This desk for the Eckert woman is more than just business to you, isn't it? I can't help but think you have a personal stake in the whereabouts and welfare of this particular desk."

"You're taking my interest out of context. Ms. Eckert is my customer at Cottage Gallery, and I find Eddie entwined in too many transactions related to the affairs of the gallery. This isn't the first time Eddie's had his nose stuck where it didn't belong."

"Such as William Davisly's bureau?"

Gabe didn't answer.

"And the bureau your parents bought and returned?"

"How do you know about that?"

"Lauren told me about it in Vermillion, just like she told me about the letter you hid in her dresser. Why do you think I'm here?"

Gabe focused on the air bubbles floating to the top of his Warsteiner. "Yeah, well, creepy feelings, bad vibes, ugly rumors, and unsupported hypotheses are all I have to go on. It's like there's a conspiracy transpiring against my family's reputation, Callan. That hurts because we don't deserve it."

"What would anyone have on your family's reputation?"

Gabe took a deep breath. "Something very similar to the scenario Alex Aubert described at the dinner party about Mr. Davisly."

"A connection to the Brookside Park murders?"

Gabe shook his head. "No, nothing like that, but years ago just the same. It's on my mother's side of the family. The interesting difference between her situation and Mr. Davisly's is that my mother wasn't involved, yet it could still damage her career."

"You mean her mayoral campaign could be at stake?"

Gabe nodded.

"What happened that long ago, Gabe, that would affect her election today?"

"It's what I call the Hoosier cataclysm," he replied gravely. "The destruction of thousands of lives through persecution and unfair discrimination at the hands of the Ku Klux Klan in the 1920s. Are you familiar with the name D. C. Stephenson?"

Callan nodded.

"But are you familiar with what happened to hundreds of political figures in this state upon his conviction when Madge Oberholtzer died of poisoning?"

"No, I can't say that I am," Callan replied. "I daresay they didn't teach such things in school when I was growing up."

"Then let me give you a little history. Do you need another beer? I think you do."

Callan ordered another round, and Gabe leaned forward and lowered his voice to prevent being overheard. "I hesitate telling you our story," he said. "You may think I've made it all up."

Callan shook his head. "Why would I think that?"

"Because it's mind-boggling to say the least. It's not only complex but difficult to fathom."

"Then why have you tried to make sense of it? Wouldn't it be better to leave it alone?"

"I can't, Callan. It's affecting my family, and it's affecting me. I have to know. I have to know everything whether the facts are good or bad so that I can deal with the situation on my own terms and move forward despite the past."

Callan nodded. "Okay, so tell me. Start from the beginning. I want to know everything too."

Gabe took a sip to wet his throat. "It all started when Stephenson moved to Indiana. He was born in Houston but moved here as co-owner in a coal operation in the southwestern part of the state. He had an uncanny ability to capture audiences with his oratory skills. He also had an insatiable desire for power. He joined the Klan and soon became the state's Grand Dragon, infiltrating state government and becoming a prominent contender for national office. He was so powerful, with his wealth and political ties, that he was in contention for the presidential nomination in '28."

"I knew he had political ties, but I didn't think he was ever in office in Indiana."

"He wasn't. He was too busy building the Invisible Empire to be directly involved in politics, and given the vast fraternity of Klan members who were in office, he didn't need to be involved. He was so wealthy and powerful that by mid 1923, he was made the Grand Dragon not only of Indiana, but of twenty-two other states."

"I didn't realize that."

"It's public knowledge."

"I'm not saying it isn't. I just haven't had any reason to look into it. Obviously, you have. You seem to have done your research."

"Over and over," he replied. "I may have only gone to culinary school, but I'm nobody's idiot. My appetite extends beyond hors d'oeuvres and entrées."

"So what happened?"

"By the end of 1923, he became so confident in his powers that he severed ties with the national Klan and formed his own

Klan within the state. There wasn't any greater achievement by the Klan in any state of the Union than Indiana in the 1920s. The Klan was even able to make trouble and ruin the life of the governor at that time."

"Who was that?"

"McCray."

Callan nodded as if he vaguely recalled the man's name.

"McCray was a good guy," Gabe replied. "At least, most thought so. He backed several programs on education and the advancement of minorities. As you can imagine, that didn't sit well with the Klan. In addition, the Klan offered legislation, and he vetoed it. There was a constant political struggle in the assembly between McCray and the Klan. Finally, there was one bill passed by the general assembly that McCray vetoed. It was a bill that became the final straw for the Klan and the kiss of death for McCray."

"Let me guess," Callan said.

"It wouldn't do you any good. Unless you know exactly what I'm talking about, you'll never believe it."

"Something like the sterilization of prisoners so that no more criminals could be reproduced?" Callan gloated, hoping to prove Gabe wrong.

Gabe laughed and almost blew his beer through his nose. "No, Indiana was already doing that at Pendleton for years."

"Then what?"

"How about a Klan day at the Indiana State Fair?"

"What?" Callan asked. "Even back then, the State Fair was one of the largest and most popular fairs in the country. Are you sure about that?"

"Complete with cross burnings and other fun activities."

"You've got to be kidding."

"I wish I was. It was passed by the general assembly. McCray vetoed it immediately. That pissed the Klan off. It so happened the state attorney general was a Klansman, and with Stephenson's help, they found a weak link in the governor's life."

"You mean something he did morally wrong?"

"No, it wasn't immoral. It was financial in nature. McCray was having some personal financial trouble and even faced bankruptcy. To help keep his home in Kentland, he obtained a questionable loan from a state agricultural fund."

"I bet Stephenson found out about it."

"And the attorney general. They found out about it through the means they had as Klansmen."

"What did they do? File charges?"

"They charged the governor with embezzlement, throwing him into a costly legal battle. He was acquitted of the embezzlement charges, so they filed charges in federal court that he had obtained other fraudulent loans to pay for his personal property."

"They didn't stop, did they?"

"No, they were relentless," Gabe said solemnly. "McCray was convicted of those charges and sent to federal prison for a couple of years before Hoover finally pardoned him. By the time he was pardoned, however, he was no longer a political threat to Stephenson, and Stephenson was free to influence his own governor into office."

"Was that Jackson?"

Gabe gestured with his hand that it was indeed Edward L. Jackson.

"It's hard to believe one group could be so powerful," Callan reflected.

"Not hard to understand," Gabe said. "You only have to look at how radical viewpoints become totalitarian today. People are afraid to buck the trend so the trend festers and expands, whether or not it's accurate or truthful."

"But it took more than Stephenson to build the Invisible Empire in the twenties."

"Economics," Gabe answered, "or the fear of economic uncertainty."

"But people always considered the twenties to be a decade of prosperity," Callan countered. "Indiana was a hotbed for ragtime, jazz, and good times. Wisconsin was the gangster's vacationland, but Indiana was where they made money."

"But it was still Indiana, keep in mind. Very conservative and practical. There wasn't social security or insurance that was widely available at the time, and men wanted security to provide for their families in case they died or got hurt for a long period of time. The influx of Blacks from the South threatened jobs, particularly in the Great Lakes states. That's how fraternal organizations in general became powerful. Men joined these groups as a collective solution to such issues as life and health insurance, savings plans, and other services. The Klan capitalized on these organizations and preyed on the financial fears of these men."

"And women too," Callan said, reflecting on his own great-grandmother.

"Yes, and women too," Gabe acknowledged. "The Women's Ku Klux Klan had similar agendas and took advantage of the average woman's fears of being left behind to raise children and to feed a family, without an education or a skill, if their husband became lame or died. Differences in race, nationality, and religion threatened that security."

"But at some point, all that power and wealth had to come crashing down."

"Yes," Gabe said, "it did."

Callan was about to take another sip but saw a look of

despair in the young man's eyes. He placed his mug on the table and said, "Ah, I see. That's where your family comes in, isn't it?"

Gabe nodded as he drew a breath. "It all started with a train ride to Chicago with a woman named Madge Oberholtzer," he said. "Stephenson never had any intention of crossing the state line with her to Chicago, even though that's where she thought they were going. He knew kidnapping across state lines would be a federal charge, and he'd have less authority over federal enforcers. He didn't count on the woman taking her own life, though."

"I'm sure he thought he had too many connections to be held accountable for her death."

"I'm sure he did, but a jury in Noblesville had other thoughts. They held him directly accountable as to why Madge took the tablets in the first place. When Stephenson did nothing to help her after she took the tablets, making her death inevitable, his guilt was certain to the jury."

"I'm familiar with the Oberholtzer incident, but how does it tie into your family?"

"Stephenson sought the help of those in law enforcement and government to cover up the crime. After he was convicted, Stephenson wrote several letters to Governor Jackson, requesting a pardon. He expected a pardon. After all, Jackson owed Stephenson several favors for helping him into office."

"I can't believe a pardon would've been popular with the public, though."

"It wasn't," Gabe said. "Jackson ignored his requests, so a vindictive Stephenson wrote a few more letters. This time they were sent to the *Indianapolis Times*, listing political figures he bribed and helped into office. Governor Jackson was included, as were the mayor of Indianapolis, commissioners, and several leaders in cities across the state. In fact, the information sent to the newspaper had the names of over half of the elected officials of the Indiana General Assembly."

"There's a historical marker downtown where the Times Building once stood," Callan said, "commemorating the newspaper for winning the Pulitzer Prize after writing the article. I remember now. The story ruined the political lives and families of a lot of people back then."

Callan suddenly realized that Gabe told this portion of history not because he was fascinated by the events, but because he was a direct descendant of the history. His tale was also no longer an interesting story of the past, but an extension of recent events affecting the Kimmerman family. Callan hesitated before finally asking, "Who?"

"My great-great-grandfather. He was ruined politically in city government and financially with his own business. From what I understand, he was never the same after that."

Callan stared at Gabe for a few seconds. "But there's more to the story, isn't there, for it to affect your mother as it does."

"Yes, there was talk, I understand, that his wife, Evelyn Terrence, my great-great-grandmother, knew or befriended poor Madge Oberholtzer but did little to stop or prevent her death, even though she knew of Stephenson's propensity for violence. That's only hearsay, mind you, and one hundred years ago, but I think it abhors my mother that a woman in her family wouldn't have done more to help someone like Madge. It weighs heavily on my mother's mind."

"I'm sure it does, but it's just hearsay, as you said."

Gabe shrugged. "It doesn't matter. It's real in my mother's mind."

"It's been so long ago, Gabe. Surely voters won't be able to make a connection to your family's past," Callan said, appealing to his sense of reason.

Gabe smirked. "Yes, well, I wonder if that's what someone said to Mr. Davisly right before he shot himself. That it was too long ago, people wouldn't remember. Do you think they did?"

"We don't know what was behind Davisly's motive."

"Don't we? Don't you believe his past didn't cross his mind when he pulled the trigger? You don't need to protect me with false hope. I don't need to be sheltered from what is obvious to me. Do you really think someone didn't try to get to Davisly with a connection to Brookside Park? And do you really think my mother will win the mayoral election if our family history is revealed?"

Callan wanted to tell Gabe he believed that time healed everything despite the recent events, but he wasn't certain it was true.

As if Gabe had read Callan's mind, the young man started to tremble with anger. He shook his head vehemently. "I don't care how long ago it was. You know people and how everything is socially scrutinized no matter how long ago it happened. It depends on whose political agenda it benefits. No, I don't believe people forget something like this. It seems that some politicians survive scandal and voters forgive indiscretions such as affairs outside of their marriage, smoking dope in college, or even questionable investments that cost workers hundreds of jobs, but they don't forgive politicians with families linked to Indiana's darkest moment."

Gabe took a deep breath and glared into Callan's eyes. "Tell me something, Cal," he said. "Tell me that you'd vote for a mayoral candidate whose family was linked at some point to the Klan. Tell me that such knowledge wouldn't taint your thoughts about what their values and character were about. Then tell me such knowledge wouldn't make you think twice about casting your vote their way. If you wouldn't give such knowledge a second thought, then you're a different man than I am, Callan, because for me, it would be a cold day in hell before I'd vote for someone like that."

~

Callan drove to the carriage house he and Terese rented and found his wife sitting in an Adirondack chair under a canopy of trees, reading a book and enjoying the light breeze that blew across the shaded lawn. He tried to smile as he approached, but his conversation with Gabe made it nearly impossible to do so without her detecting that something was amiss.

"No, nothing's wrong," he reassured her. "The afternoon was just thought-provoking, is all."

"Then it's probably not the right time to present this to you," she said.

"What about?"

Terese pulled an envelope from between the pages of her book. "You received your own letter, of sorts."

Curiosity turned to concern. "A letter?" he asked.

"Of sorts," she repeated. "It's from your sister." Terese held the letter in her hand, reluctant to give it to him. "It was forwarded from Vermillion. Do you want to read it?"

Callan nodded and extended his hand. She gave him the letter and he looked at the return address. "She's still at the same old house, isn't she? Her life never changes."

"There's nothing wrong with that."

"There is if you expect others not to change with you."

"You don't know that."

"I will in a moment." Callan lifted the letter in front of him. "Let's see what the dear girl has to say. It can't be good."

"You don't know that, either."

"Oh yes I do," he replied adamantly. "She wrote a letter instead of calling. She could've called. People don't call when they've got something bad to say, because they don't want to hear the backlash. It's easier to write their scorn so that they don't have to see the ire in the faces they're trying to ridicule. That's why emails are so popular. It's a cowardly way to confront. She's one of those people."

He tore one of the edges of the envelope and ripped open the flap. The letter was written neatly upon quality letterhead. He frowned upon reading the greeting:

My dearest Callan,

"See? I was right. She called me 'dearest.' That means the letter's not only going to be bad, but it's going to be full of malarkey too."

"Read it and behave," Terese said.

> *My dearest Callan,*
> *You have me all wrong. That has usually been the case, or so I've learned over the years, but this time, I thought I should set the record straight.*
> *You've been making inquiries about our great-grandparents again. I heard from Aunt Priss about it. She mentioned that you had questions of her, and in return, she sent you some photographs. Given the premature death of our parents, I can see why our ancestors are so intriguing to you, but you have one thing wrong about me which only proves what I've known all along—that you don't know me at all.*
> *Contrary to what you believe, I do not object to your genealogy work. I also do not object to your inquiries about our great-grandmother and the philanthropic work she did for the women*

and children of the men who died in the City Coal Mine disaster one hundred years ago.

My reticence has always been about a much more recent and sinister event. Specifically, it is about the death of a young soldier during World War II. If you don't know the soldier to whom I am referring, then it is just as well.

I implore you to leave it be.

Please do not pursue your misguided curiosity any further. Our father was adamant that he wanted nothing more to be learned. If you cherish our father's memory as much as I do, you will let our family's history fade peacefully . . . with dignity.

Your sister,
Kathleen

Callan handed the letter back to Terese.

Terese read it quickly and returned the letter into its envelope. "I only have one thing to say."

"And what's that?"

"She doesn't know you very well either."

Callan smiled. "Yes. She shouldn't have implored me, should she have?"

"Is this Aunt Priss she refers to your Aunt Priscilla? The crazy one with all the cats—six or seven at least?"

"Yes, the one who lives in a trailer outside of Haubstadt."

"I never had someone in my family like your Aunt Priss. All the cats we ever owned were useful. They were farm cats put there for a purpose. I stepped foot into her trailer once, but I swore I'd never do it again."

"I'm glad you have that luxury," Callan said, turning to go

into the house. "As for me, a visit to Aunt Priss and her cats has now become my duty."

"To do what?" Terese asked, ready to object.

Callan smirked. "To spend an afternoon listening to cats cough up hair balls, my dear, what else? I may even dine on her pumpkin bread with its slight hint of tuna to tantalize my taste buds. Through it all, however, I hope to learn something about this soldier my sister so adamantly objects to me discovering. Her letter *implores* me to find out."

"What if I implored you not to go?"

He thought about it for a second then shook his head. "I would go anyway. You see, I had a rather candid conversation with Gabe Kimmerman about the past today. I have to go, Terese, not for Gabe but for myself."

Chapter Fifteen

Beth marched into the great room of her house, dropped her purse and briefcase on the floor, and plopped into a leather chair across from her husband, who focused on the evening paper. Barry peered at her through reading glasses over the top of the paper. He smiled and asked how her day was, but she ignored his greeting.

"I received a phone call this afternoon," she said pointedly.

Barry returned to his paper, squinting at an article he'd spotted. "I did too, as a matter of fact," he said with indifference. "Several of them."

"Don't be trite. You know very well who called me."

He lowered the paper into his lap.

"Why did you go to him, Barry? After our conversation the other evening, when you told me not to do so, you deliberately went to Chase VanderPelt and talked to him yourself. I don't understand."

Barry offered no apology or explanation. Instead, he asked, "What did he want?"

Beth's eyes widened. "What did *you* want is more of the

question. Because it seemed he wanted exactly what you asked of him."

"We discussed very little about you, if that's what you're implying," he replied. "The crux of our conversation was about the city and anything he thought I could do at the bank to be of assistance. It was benign, Beth. Absolutely benign."

Beth laughed. "Well, I can assure you that my conversation with him was anything but benign." She leaned forward. "He offered twenty-five thousand dollars toward my campaign fund." Beth didn't give him a chance to respond before adding, "I don't understand why you asked him for money after the lecture you gave me—"

"I didn't."

She lifted her finger. "You told me to be careful. Then you go and ask the very person you told me not to talk to."

"I said I didn't, Beth."

"And I don't believe you!"

Barry took a deep breath. "I swear, Beth, I didn't ask Chase for money."

"He was more than ready to give it to me."

"Did you accept?" His face paled at the thought.

"No, of course I didn't accept."

"Thank God," he muttered.

Beth sat back in her chair. "He said he'd been following my campaign and liked what I stood for. He wanted to ensure that I continued to succeed. I asked him what he liked best about my platform. He was evasive and vague, but he was adamant that he wanted to contribute and asked if twenty-five thousand would be sufficient."

Barry turned his focus away from his wife to think. "I don't know what I could've said to him that would've given him the impression that I was asking for funds on your behalf."

"I said his offer was very generous," Beth continued. "He began rambling about some development project somewhere downtown, but I stopped him. I said that I appreciated his interest in my campaign, but at this time, I would be satisfied if his support came in the form of a vote in November.'"

"It wasn't me who put him up to it," Barry said, wiping his forehead with the back of his hand.

"I want the truth."

"It is the truth!" he blurted. "I was against going to Chase to ask for money as you suggested. He's the go-to guy for money in this town. I know for a fact that Roger Montrose has dealings with him. So does Andrew Gammon. I've heard Cole Brewer does too. I'm not about to put our names on that list."

"Then why go to him at all?"

"I wanted to rattle his chains about what's going on in town from an investment standpoint. I wanted to know if there was any scuttlebutt that he's heard that would benefit me as a lender. It's called networking, Beth, and that's all I did. I touched base with him as a colleague."

Beth was unconvinced. "I wonder, then, how he went from scuttlebutt to contribution."

Barry shook his head. "I don't know. We did talk about your campaign briefly. I said it wasn't without its glitches, but that's all I said. Maybe he took that to mean financially, not fathoming what was really bothering us."

"You didn't."

"No, I didn't mention the letters, but I did want to know if there was word around town about letters of an unusual nature that he's heard about."

"What did he say?"

"Not a thing. Not about the letters, anyway. We talked about development projects and who was doing what and when, but nothing that hinted the least bit of scandal."

"I could've done that too, Barry," she said.

"Done what? Talk to Chase VanderPelt?"

"Absolutely. I would have approached it just as you did, from a community vantage." The look on Beth's face was hard and defiant. Creases cut across her forehead as her eyes demanded further explanation.

"I know, but I did it myself. It was for your own good."

Beth gasped, unable to comprehend what she'd just heard. "For my own good? Am I a child to you?"

"Of course not, but I know you, Beth. You're very direct sometimes. I had to play screen on this one for you."

Beth laughed out loud. "You mean you went to Chase because—"

"Because I knew you'd do it anyway. I don't care what you said to me. You had it in your mind to go to him anyway, and you'd have asked him for money right out of the gate."

She laughed again, but less menacingly.

"Don't laugh at me like I'm a fool," he said. "You'll never admit it, but that's exactly what you were going to do. I've never considered you a child, Beth, and I don't treat you like one. I do treat you, however, as a potential mayoral candidate who needs a filter."

Beth scoffed. "I have an aide and a campaign manager for that."

"Well, they're not doing a very good job."

Barry picked up the crumpled pages of the newspaper in his lap and quickly turned to the small article that he'd been reading when she walked into the room. He folded the paper unevenly, but the article appeared plainly in view on the page. He poked his finger on the headline to be sure she got the point: *Candidate Luncheon Draws the Ire of Italian Driver.*

"Apparently, Angela Bellefontino, one of the female drivers in the 500 race, thinks you need a filter too."

Beth snatched the paper from Barry's hands and scanned the short article. "Not sure what all the fuss is about," she said, handing the paper back to her husband. "It was just a luncheon—a lettuce wedge and a piece of chicken."

"That signified the sacrifices spouses give to their soul mates for the benefit of the 500-Mile Race and the sport of Indy Car racing," Barry said.

"Of course. This is Indianapolis."

"And it's a nice gesture, Beth. Hosting a luncheon to honor the drivers' spouses who have an important but often forgotten role in the racing experience of this town was a great idea. It had one flaw, though, that your aide and your campaign manager, who are women, overlooked."

"A simple oversight."

"It doesn't matter, Beth. Angela's husband wasn't invited and the husband of the other female driver in the race wasn't invited either. Bellefontino makes a good point. Do their spouses not make sacrifices too? Do you discount her husband's contributions because of his gender? Are women the only ones capable of supporting their spouses? Is that what the future mayor of this city thinks?"

"Of course not," she responded angrily. "I told you it was an oversight."

"That could cost you an election."

"Easily corrected. It's petty. It's just a small article on page four or wherever it was."

"People read page fours of newspapers, Beth. You're missing the point."

Beth peered at him sharply. "So you're going to tell me that you went to Chase VanderPelt on my behalf because of a lettuce wedge?"

"And a piece of chicken, you're damn right. My point is, Beth, if a small benevolent luncheon can turn into a campaign issue from an Italian race car driver, how much bigger do you think these letters and how you deal with them could be perceived by people in your own hometown?" He sat for several seconds in deep thought before adding, "What we're doing isn't working, Beth. We have to meet these people head-on."

Beth paused. "What are you suggesting?"

"We're a racing town," he said. "We're used to seeing drivers lose control of their race cars. Some slam into the walls. Others come out of their skid unscathed because they turn their wheel into the skid to bring their car under control."

"Are you saying we're out of control?"

Barry rose from his chair and approached his wife. He knelt on one knee in front of her and took her hand to kiss it gently. "No, baby," he said softly, "but we're sliding."

She sighed. "So what do you think we should do?"

"We have no choice. We have to do what drivers do when they're sliding. We have to turn into the skid, stand up to the past, and concentrate on the future."

Chapter Sixteen

Dark gray clouds rolled over Broad Ripple village, causing a misty fog to shroud the Central Canal. Pedestrians on the greenway clutched unopened umbrellas in preparation for a deluge that didn't come.

Gabe Kimmerman spent the morning dusting the gallery's collection, inventorying items, and preparing for Kate's soiree, which was to be held in the main parlor. He refused to dust the aisle along the north wall of the gallery, avoiding a certain bureau with rosettes that had been returned earlier in the day.

Kate walked into the room, looking through sales tickets, oblivious to Gabe's piercing attention to the bureau.

"If it's going to rain, I hope it happens soon," he said loud enough for Kate to hear.

She lifted her head as if surprised he was there.

"Outside," he explained. "I hope it rains before Carburetion Day at the speedway. People look forward to meeting the drivers up close prior to the 500-Mile Race. It would be a great disappointment."

Kate turned away, uninterested.

"And it would put a damper on your party if it continued into the next day." Still no reaction. "At least, no more of a damper than that bureau gives out."

This time, Kate looked at him. "Whatever are you babbling about, Gabe?"

He looked at the slips of paper in her hands. "Do you have the transaction receipt for the bureau Marjorie Eckert purchased and returned yesterday? Are you holding it?"

"You mean that ugly thing with the rosettes?" she asked, lifting the corner of her mouth with disgust. "I'd return it too, if I were Ms. Eckert."

"Did she give a reason for returning it? If I remember, she was in an awful hurry to receive the piece, but Eddie wouldn't let her have it. Here it is back on the showroom floor already."

"Perhaps she decided she didn't like rosettes," Kate said snidely, then turned and walked back toward her office.

Gabe stopped her. "This can't keep happening, Kate. You know it can't. These sales and returns are getting noticed by the proprietors."

"That's what the reception is for, Gabe," she said, "to rejuvenate the old into new. I suggest you get back to work on it, or we won't be ready in time. You worry like your mother, and I wonder why." She turned her back and hurried away.

Why? The word echoed in his head. *Why?* He was beginning to think Kate knew very well why. Either that or she was unable to face the reality of what was happening in her gallery. That could be the case. He believed Kate sashayed through reality as if it were an apparition, ignoring its significance so as not to deal with it proactively. That's what this soiree of hers was all about. He was convinced it was as much an apparition to her as the other events happening at the gallery.

That or Meredith Patterswaite's complaints about the desk

she owned was a smokescreen to hide her own involvement in what was going on. He also wondered if Kate was in collusion with Meredith, hiding her participation as apathy.

Gabe's concentration was interrupted when the bell above the entrance rang with its irritating tingle. He recognized the man immediately. His parents talked of him often, and he was a member of the Open Arms board.

"Good afternoon, Mr. Gammon," Gabe called. "Good to see you again."

"Good to see you as well," he replied although his attention was on the showroom.

"It appears you know what you're looking for, so I'll—"

Andrew lifted his hand, compelling Gabe to stop.

After several minutes of shadowing the prominent businessman, Gabe called out, "Are you sure I can't help you with anything, Mr. Gammon?"

"I can't seem to find it," he answered. "I'm looking for a desk . . . or a bureau of sorts. It was recommended to me by a Meredith . . ." Andrew looked at a sheet of paper he'd pulled from his pocket.

"Patterswaite?" Gabe asked before Andrew had a chance to find the name.

"Yes, Patterswaite. Meredith Patterswaite."

"I suppose it wouldn't have rosettes, would it?"

Andrew hesitated. "Rosettes? They may have been mentioned. I don't remember."

"Rosettes seem to be popular lately. Did Ms. Patterswaite give you an inventory number? If it's the piece I'm thinking of, it should be over here along the north wall."

Gabe led Andrew to Meredith's mahogany desk with a rectangular top and an inset leather writing surface. Intricate handmade carvings of rosettes embellished the drawers and the corners of the desk.

Andrew stared at it, then shook his head. "This can't be it."

"What number did Ms. Patterswaite write on the piece of paper she gave you?"

Andrew handed Gabe the piece of square note paper. Gabe looked at it, taking note of the details.

"Get Kate, please," Andrew instructed before Gabe had a chance to respond. "I don't have time to walk the gallery searching for something that may or may not be here. If Kate placed the bureau in a setting, then she'll know where it's located."

"I'm very certain this is the piece, Mr. Gammon. The inventory numbers match." Gabe returned the paper to Andrew.

He appeared both surprised and relieved. "I owe you an apology. I obviously don't know much about the piece."

Gabe smiled but couldn't help but wonder why the man was buying something he didn't know much about. "The desk is priceless, Mr. Gammon. You'll be pleased with it."

"How old is it?"

"Late nineteenth century."

"I see. I was worried about the rosettes. One hears the word rosette and doesn't think of it as being very masculine, but indeed it is."

Gabe smiled. "Then you like the bureau?"

Andrew glared at Gabe, his dark eyes piercing, his expression grave. "No," he replied solemnly. "I detest the damn thing."

"You don't have to buy it."

"Oh, but I do," he said. "I wouldn't live very long if I didn't bring it home."

Gabe's eyes widened in alarm.

Andrew laughed. "My wife, you see," he explained, appearing to notice Gabe's expression.

Gabe was unconvinced but documented the transaction

thoroughly and collected payment while receiving explicit instructions on where to deliver the bureau.

"Keep the directions I gave you on hand, Gabe," Andrew instructed further. "If it doesn't meet my wife's expectations, I'll be sending it back." He then left the shop, leaving the irritating bell and a bill of sale as a reminder of his presence.

"Who was that?" Kate asked as she entered from behind.

"Andrew Gammon."

"What did he want?"

Gabe shook his head. "I don't know. Not really, anyway. He bought a desk."

"He bought a desk, and you don't know what he wanted? That's marvelous, Gabe! I've been after him and his wife to stop in for months. I wonder what changed his mind."

Gabe gave her an icy glare. "He bought the rosette desk," he said, hoping for a reaction.

None came, except what he'd expect from her on hearing the good news about an expensive sale.

"It was Ms. Patterswaite's desk," he added. "The one Marjorie Eckert no longer wanted."

"Call Ms. Eckert," Kate said flippantly. "I'm sure we have something else on display to her liking. What I came to discuss with you were the arrangements for the reception on Friday. I have refreshments and entertainment lined up. Have we had a good response to the invitations?"

Gabe pulled the listing of attendees from a stack of unfiled paperwork. "I believe you'll find almost everyone you wanted to come will be attending. Except for Mr. Montrose."

"That's odd," Kate said. "He attends everything. He enjoys a good party, you know."

"No, I don't know him very well. I just know his name from the board of Open Arms. When he called, he seemed preoccupied, or something, and said he'd make it if he could."

"I see," she said, returning her attention to the attendee list. "I do hope he comes. Oh, good, I see the Auberts and several proprietors will be here. But what's this?" She pointed to a name.

Gabe checked the entry. "That's Amy Henzel and her boyfriend, Brian."

"I know *who* it is," Kate replied curtly. "I didn't ask *who* is this, I asked *what* is this? I don't remember adding her."

"You invited the VanderPelts."

"But not Amy."

"Kate, you can't very well leave her off the attendee list."

"I very well can. And explain this." She shoved the piece of paper in his face, and jabbed her finger at the name of a couple. "Who invited them?"

"I did, Kate. We can't very well not invite them."

"We most certainly can. I have no intention of inviting Callan Morrow and his wife."

"It shows good faith on our part that we appreciate those that volunteer for Open Arms."

"Oh please, Gabe."

"And customers like to see familiar faces. Amy Henzel and Callan Morrow may not be familiar faces at Cottage Gallery, but customers patronize both locations."

"I deal regularly with the tellers at your father's bank, but I don't see them at any of his financial receptions."

The landline phone rang at the counter.

"They've already been invited," Gabe said, placing his hand over the receiver. "I can't very well disinvite them."

"Very well then," she said with a huff.

Gabe answered the phone with his usual gallery greeting. A familiar voice, resonating with frustration, cut it short, however.

"Gabe, please tell me what's going on," a desperate Meredith

Patterswaite said. "The other day you asked me about a certain desk I owned in stock, and now I find that it's been returned by another customer as if she didn't want it at all. I don't understand."

Gabe looked at Kate to see if she was at all curious about the topic of conversation, but she focused on opening a small box she'd brought into the room. Gabe glanced at the contents. He wasn't sure, but a medallion that appeared to be made of amethyst or something similar lay inside. "I'm sorry, Ms. Patterswaite," Gabe said. "You were saying?"

"I said that customer had no intention of purchasing the desk in the first place," she replied.

"How can you be sure of that?"

Kate looked at him, suddenly interested, and extended her hand. "Let me take this," she said, grabbing the receiver. "Meredith? Hello, this is Kate O'Neal. If there's a problem, you'll need to tell us specifically what it is and what proof you have that . . . hello? Hello?"

Kate removed the receiver from her ear and handed it back to Gabe. He listened for Meredith's voice, but after receiving only the monotonous buzz of a dial tone, he replaced the receiver on the hook.

"What was that about?" Kate asked.

"I don't know."

"You surely must. Why did she call you, then? Why wouldn't she talk to me? I do hope she's not considering removing her items from the gallery before the reception," she said. "What would this place look like without *Patterswaite Designs*? What would the other proprietors think?"

"Is that all that matters to you?" he asked.

Kate scowled. "Yes, that's all that matters, and it's all that should matter to you too."

Chapter Seventeen

The Friday of Kate's soiree arrived without fanfare. Gabe wanted to believe Kate had been maintaining a low profile in the days leading to the reception because she was as concerned about the sales and returns of her merchandise as he was. Whether that was true, he was unable to discern. All he knew was that the mood within the gallery was as overcast as the skies over the village. One wouldn't have known a lively reception was just a couple of hours away.

Kate posted a *Closed for Private Showing* sign to prevent customers entering the showroom so she and Gabe could finish last-minute preparations.

"I should think the sounds of a piano bar would do better than chamber music this evening," Kate replied pretentiously. "Much better to start race weekend with Hoosier-born music, such as Cole Porter and Hoagy Carmichael, than something like Bach or Beethoven, don't you think?"

"You let the trio go?"

"I paid them and sent them back to Ft. Wayne."

"They didn't take up as much room, Kate. That piano you

rented is mammoth."

Kate ignored him. "What time did Ms. Patterswaite say she was arriving this evening?" she asked, closing the subject.

"Arriving?" Gabe asked, thinking it an odd thing to ask. "Oh, I have no idea."

"Haven't you talked with her?"

"No, not recently."

Kate frowned. "That wasn't very considerate. She's been upset at the return of her rosette desk. I see it's back again."

Gabe glanced toward the north wall where, indeed, the rosette desk had been returned. "Apparently, it didn't work for Mrs. Gammon."

"She didn't have it long enough to give it a chance."

Gabe sighed. "If you ask me, I doubt she knew Mr. Gammon even bought it."

"What do you mean?"

"I doubt Mrs. Gammon had anything to do with its purchase. This is what I've been trying to get across to you, Kate. Something about that desk—and others like it—has been happening. It has nothing to do with customers not liking the pieces. It has everything to do with them not wanting to purchase them to begin with."

Kate raised her hand for him to stop. "That's not what's bothering me. Ms. Patterswaite is upset. That's all that concerns me. She's accused us of lending certain pieces out of the gallery so that customers can display them during their personal parties only to return them once their affair is over. How can I explain to her that it isn't our policy to lend consignments out when her rosette desk keeps bouncing back and forth like a pinball from home to home?"

"Maybe you won't have to deal with her."

Kate grimaced. "What are you talking about?"

"Maybe she won't show tonight."

"But she must," Kate said. "She has to come. She simply has to be here. I want her know the kind of business we run."

This time, it was Gabe who grimaced. "Do you think that's such a wise idea?"

A knock at the door signifying the caterers had arrived broke the standoff between Kate and Gabe's glares. The caterers' arrival, including the bartender, tested their patience, but Kate accepted the caterers into the gallery with poise.

The caterers placed hot and cold appetizers in prominent locations, and the aroma of 500 Race Festival cuisine quickly saturated the gallery, lifting Kate and Gabe's spirits and teasing Gabe's ability to stay clear of the food.

"Go ahead," Kate said to him as a peace offering. "If you down a fried biscuit, I'll only notice if the entire bowl of apple butter is gone."

Gabe smiled in appreciation. Even though he thought the baby grand piano was excessive, the cuisine idea was brilliant. He asked Kate if he could bring her something from the bar.

"Has he set up yet?" she asked, then looked at her watch. "Oh my, I should think people will be arriving soon."

The first to enter were Barry and Beth Kimmerman. They surprised Kate by standing in the center of the showroom, assessing the venue. The look on Beth's face was one of indifference but tolerance. Barry's expression wasn't much better.

"Let me get you both something," Kate offered. After she ordered cocktails, she returned and took Beth's hand. "Come see what I found."

She led Beth to the sales counter and pulled a small box

from a shelf. Kate handed it to Beth, who took it reluctantly.

"What's this?"

"Just open it."

Beth lifted the lid and looked inside. An amethyst medallion lay atop a thin layer of soft cotton. "I don't understand," Beth said.

"Don't you recognize it?" Kate asked proudly.

Beth shook her head.

"It's an amulet."

"I can see that. I know what an amulet is, Kate. I don't know why I have it."

"Turn it over," she insisted.

Beth did so. The engraving on the back was worn but unmistakable.

"Now do you remember? I believe it's yours."

Beth looked again. "Yes, the initial is mine, but—Oh wait, yes! I do remember. I gave it to a friend when she was going through a rough time. They recently had their home broken into. Where did you get this?"

"It was in some of Eddie's inventory at Open Arms. It caught my eye, and I bought it. I bought it for you. It's a gift."

Beth shuddered and pushed the medallion with the box back into Kate's hands. "I couldn't," she said. "It doesn't feel right."

"Of course it's right, Beth. I bought it outright."

"But where did Eddie get it? This belonged to my friend. I gave it to her."

Kate stepped back. "It's not stolen merchandise, if that's what you're thinking."

"That's exactly what I'm thinking."

"Your friend donated these items. She dropped a box off at Open Arms. This was in it."

Beth shook her head with disbelief. "No, she would never give it away."

"But she did, and it's an amulet, Beth. Not only that, but it's an amethyst amulet, the most valuable ever made. You must take it. Ancient soldiers wore these to keep calm, to protect them in battle. If there's ever a time you need to keep cool and be protected, Beth, this is it."

"A stone isn't going to do that, Kate. I keep my faith in a power larger than a rock that has an inscription of my initial."

"Relax," Kate said, handing the amulet back to her friend. "Keep it, please. Everything is under control. I have a plan to intercept Marilyn Wells-Brewer before she taints the conversation circles this evening, if that's what you're worried about."

Beth's eyes narrowed. "It's beyond Marilyn, don't you think?"

"No, I don't believe that."

"You're in denial, then. This gift and the timing of this reception are smokescreens."

"No, dear," Kate said confidently, "this gift and the timing of this reception are perfect. Life goes on, and I'm going to make sure that it does."

Chapter Eighteen

A cool breeze blew through Callan's suit coat as he and Terese walked toward Cottage Gallery on the trail. She wrapped her arms through his and nestled closely as he dug his hands deeper into his pockets to ward off the light chill. The temperature seemed to drop considerably as the afternoon turned to dusk. Fog hovered over the canal, wisps floating along the trail ahead of them.

Laughter and music from within the gallery greeted them as they reached the entrance. Callan opened the door, and Terese quickly stepped into the brightly lit room. Another woman, who'd been following close behind, took advantage of Callan's kindness and entered behind Terese.

When the woman looked up to thank him, he caught a glimpse of her face. "I believe we've met before, haven't we?" he asked.

She studied him briefly and shook her head. "I don't believe so. Are you a proprietor at Cottage Gallery?"

"No," he replied, trying to place her face. "My name is Callan Morrow. Does that ring a bell?"

"I'm sorry, it doesn't, but I'm not good at names. I'm a customer of the gallery, but aside from that, I really don't know anyone. I'm Marjorie Eckert. And you said your name was . . . ?"

Callan didn't respond right away. He recognized the name but realized he was mistaken about having met.

"Did I hear correctly?" a different woman asked Callan when Marjorie Eckert continued into the gallery. "Did you say your name is Callan Morrow? I was telling my husband that I was hoping to get to meet you this evening."

"Oh?" Callan asked, surprised.

The woman smiled coyly. "I make it my business to stay in touch, you see. My name is Marilyn Wells-Brewer. Perhaps you've heard of me. I'm on the board of directors of Open Arms. That was my husband, Cole, who passed you, running off to the bar. I do hope you don't think him rude, but his interest in such affairs is rather limited. I, on the other hand, am fascinated by the recent events of Cottage Gallery. But of course, I'm sure you are too. That's why you're here, isn't it?"

"I'm sorry, Ms. Wells-Brewer, but I don't—I mean, I have to say that I'm not—"

"I believe you are," she said. "You see, there are too many unanswered questions at the gallery for you not to be. Wouldn't you agree? But I have no doubt that you'll get to the bottom of them. One only has to read the papers to learn of your recent accomplishments."

"I'm sorry?"

"Chicago."

"Chicago?" Callan asked, then hesitated. "You have an excellent memory. The Grand Aire case in Chicago was months ago."

"I did my research," she replied proudly. "As I said, I—"

"—make it your business to know, yes. I understood that."

"Oh, please don't get me wrong. Contrary to what others may think, my interest is only for the good of the organization. Open Arms, that is. You understand, don't you?"

Callan smiled in a way to appease her even though he wasn't sure he did. He changed the subject with small talk and eventually left Marilyn so that he could take his wife's arm to lead her away. "May I get you a drink?" he asked.

"You may," Terese said. "Do I look like I need one?"

"No, but your expression could use one."

"It comes and goes naturally, especially when around people like her."

"Yes, but I may have to separate myself from you," he said teasingly. "I'm here to observe, converse, and learn. I'd rather people here not know what I'm thinking based upon the look on my wife's face. Let's save your expressions for moments when I might actually need them."

"Such as now?" Terese asked, nodding toward their host.

Kate strode toward the couple to greet them.

"Hello, Kate," Callan said. "Congratulations. It appears you have an excellent turnout tonight."

"You're very kind, Callan, thank you. Terese, thank you for coming. Don't you look lovely? Gabe mentioned that he put you two on the invitation list, and I gave him a great big hug for remembering. How thoughtless I am sometimes with guest lists. Too much to think about, I suppose. Well, anyway, I saw you come in. Who could miss you, Callan? You look simply dapper. I love the Indy Car tie. So appropriate. And don't you love everyone wearing black and white tonight? The room simply looks like a checkered flag!"

Kate went from incessant rambling to deafening silence in an instant.

Callan turned to see what had captured her attention. A

woman stood near the entrance, wearing a large spring bonnet with a flowing floral sundress. A handbag hung heavily on her right arm. She adjusted her belongings as she searched the room. Callan didn't recognize her, but he found her eccentric features and mannerisms curious. He sensed that Kate found them annoying.

"Please excuse me, won't you?" she said.

Kate called Patricia Reinholdt by name. "Here, dear, why don't you set your purse, uh, your bag in my office, or something? You'd be more comfortable."

"I'm fine," Patricia insisted. "Is that Marilyn and her husband over there?"

Kate turned and looked in the direction Patricia pointed. "I'm not sure, dear."

"Why, yes, it is," Callan answered as he approached the women. "My wife and I walked in with them."

"But that's impossible," she said.

The comment took Callan by surprise. "Well, as impossible as it sounds, I'm afraid it's true. You can see for yourself."

Patricia emitted a distressing sigh. "Oh—I—Well, I must've missed them on the trail." She put her hand to her temple. "I'm not quite . . . You see, they were right behind me. I guess I didn't see them pass."

"It's no wonder, dear. Your handbag slows you down." Kate tried to pry the bag from Patricia's hands.

"No," she replied, holding tighter to its handles. "I must've been daydreaming."

"Or something else caught your attention," Callan said.

"What? Oh, yes. Something did, in fact." Patricia scanned the room. "It was probably nothing."

"Someone you were following?" Kate asked.

"I don't follow people."

"Of course not, dear. Here, let me get you something to drink." Kate turned to leave, not realizing that Patricia could see her doubtful expression.

"She doesn't believe me," Patricia said when Kate was gone.

"Never mind her. It doesn't matter," Callan said.

"Oh, but it does, in a way."

Callan hoped she would elaborate, but Patricia Reinholdt stood clutching her handbag, staring into the crowd. "I'm Callan Morrow, by the way. This is my wife, Terese."

"Yes, I know."

"I didn't realize we'd met before."

"We haven't?" Patricia asked surprised. "Oh, well, I must've just known. I've heard your name before." She looked about the room once again. "Haven't Andrew Gammon and Roger Montrose arrived?"

"I haven't seen them yet."

Patricia craned her head around Callan for a better look. "That's odd," she said. "I do hope there isn't trouble. You do know who I'm talking about, don't you?"

"I know of them, yes."

"*Everyone* knows *of* them, Mr. Morrow. They're movers and shakers. They make things happen in town."

"Why would there be trouble, then?"

Patricia sighed. "Because I couldn't help but overhear on the trail. I'm not prone to eavesdropping, but I couldn't help but hear their conversation." She leaned closer to him. "They were arguing."

"Sports, perhaps? Men do argue about sports."

"Don't be silly. Their argument wasn't frivolous."

"I assure you, Ms. Reinholdt, we don't take our sports frivolously in Indiana."

"What I meant was that their conversation was much more

pointed than that. I'm sure they have opportunities to argue often. After all, Mr. Gammon is a financier, and Mr. Montrose is a developer. But to argue on the trail near Cottage Gallery—"

"I'm sorry, I don't understand. Why is their argument troubling you so much?"

"Because Mr. Gammon mentioned Meredith Patterswaite's name as I passed, but I don't see her here, either."

Callan paused. "That doesn't explain why you're troubled."

Patricia looked at Callan as if she suddenly realized she was talking to a stranger. "I'm sorry. I've probably said too much, but I thought you'd have an interest as well. You're a forensic auditor, aren't you?"

"Yes, but—"

"That's why you're here, isn't it?"

"People seem to think so, yes," he replied, recalling his conversation with Marilyn Wells-Brewer.

"Surely, you can see, then, Mr. Morrow. It's in everyone's eyes."

"What, exactly?"

"Fear," she said. "You can see it. I can tell that you sense it. In Mrs. Kimmerman, especially."

Callan took a deep breath and studied Patricia. "Is that why you've been following her?"

Patricia brought her bag up to her chest and held it tightly. "I'm not sure I understand what you're asking," she said after a long pause.

"I was told you were seen following Beth on the afternoon of the last board meeting. You followed her for several blocks, in fact."

"Is that what Marilyn told you?"

"I didn't say it was Marilyn. If it's the truth, it doesn't matter who said it. What I want to know is if your observation of fear is why you followed Beth before the last board meeting, and if so, what you hoped to gain from it."

Patricia straightened her back. "It sounds as if you agree with Kate that I'm nothing more than a prying busybody, Mr. Morrow."

"I'm looking for a reason why you aren't."

"I don't know any more about the underlying reasons for the ill feelings than you do, but one can't deny that William's death, Beth's odd behavior, Andrew and Roger's argument outside, and Ms. Patterswaite's lack of attendance here can't be coincidental."

"Ms. Patterswaite? What does she have to do with any of this?"

Patricia stuttered. Callan felt that if she could take back mentioning Meredith's name, she would have. "I don't know," she replied nervously. "The name just came out of my mouth. Why, even you know about Ms. Patterswaite."

Callan frowned. The only encounter he'd had with the proprietor was when he followed her and Gabe to her shop in the village. "How would you know of any interest I have with Meredith Patterswaite?"

Patricia's eyes bulged from her head. She clutched her handbag again and made a side glance toward the exit.

"If you want to go, Ms. Reinholdt, you may," Callan said, realizing that she suddenly remembered how she knew. "Terese and I will just follow you. We'll follow you the same way you followed Beth before the board meeting. We'll follow you the same way you followed me when I trailed Gabe to Meredith's shop before going to the Brewpub. It all boils down to motive. I know why I was following Gabe and Meredith. I had good reason to do so. What was your reason for following *me*?"

She didn't answer.

Callan became uneasy with her silence.

"What's the matter? Do you believe something is going to happen to Meredith?" he asked. "Tell me, please. Is something going to happen to her? Has something already happened? Is that why she isn't here at the reception?"

Chapter Nineteen

Patricia Reinholdt walked away without excusing herself. Callan let her go, knowing there was little more he was going to get out of her—at least, little more tonight.

"Let's forget about her," Terese urged. "You still haven't gotten me my drink."

"Ah, yes, the drink. Funny. Most parties we go to, the bar is the first place we hit."

"That's because at most parties, the stories don't start until *after* people have downed a few."

They walked to the bar and stood in line. As Callan perused the guests, he directed Terese's attention toward the entrance, where Alex and Corinne Aubert had just walked in. Alex spotted them and waved, gesturing to hold a spot in the beverage line for them. After meandering their way through the crowd of familiar faces, the Auberts reached the Morrows and greeted them warmly.

Terese commented on Corinne's shawl, covering her shoulders. "It's beautiful and definitely needed this evening. Unseasonably cool, don't you think?"

"It's the fog coming off the river and the canal," Corinne replied. "It's getting quite thick and makes things chilly. Ah, is that Beth?"

The four turned to see Beth approach with Barry not far behind, carrying their drinks. Beth seemed to lack her usual grace and levity. She greeted the foursome, but her voice lacked enthusiasm. Corinne touched her arm and asked how she was doing. Beth shrugged. The two talked briefly, but her demeanor didn't change and the lackadaisical expression on her face didn't waiver.

Barry, however, made no bones about wanting to be anywhere but at the reception.

"Where's Lauren?" Beth asked suddenly. "Have you seen Lauren?"

Barry's eyes darted around the room. He looked at his watch, then said as if he, too, was concerned, "I'll give her a call."

"No, wait," Terese said. "Is that her? She's with another woman. I think it's Amy, isn't it?"

Beth stepped aside to look around Corinne and get a better look toward the entrance. Lauren and Amy were both dressed to the hilt and enjoyed the compliments of those they greeted as they made their way to the center of the room. Callan noticed that Beth's relief at seeing Lauren was quickly offset with discontent.

Berry grasped his wife's hand and squeezed it gently. "Now, don't say anything," he said. "She was invited like the rest of us."

"What is it, Beth?" Corinne asked.

"It's nothing," Barry responded on his wife's behalf.

"Barry's right," Beth replied. "I'm being silly."

"Are you talking about the girl Lauren came in with?" Alex asked.

"Amy Henzel," Callan replied.

"Henzel? Wasn't there a Henzel executive at VanOsdol

Industries?"

"Good heavens, no," Beth replied.

"I know who you're thinking, Alex. You're close, but his name wasn't Henzel," Barry said.

"She seems pleasant enough."

"You say she works with Lauren?" Corinne asked.

"Yes," Callan answered. "At Open Arms. She works the front counters with her. She's also a waitress."

"Nothing wrong with a young woman working her way up," Alex added. "Where's she a waitress? I wonder if we frequent the place."

"You've not heard of it," Beth responded eagerly as if she hoped the subject would drop.

"Tipton's," Callan said.

Alex erupted into laughter, nearly spilling his drink. "That's a name I haven't heard in a long time. Tipton's? Are you kidding?"

"You might want to keep it down," Beth scolded.

"It's been ages since I've puked on beer and hog balls from that place," he said, reeling from memories that kept him choking.

Corinne joined in the scolding, being more assertive than Beth.

"I'm not out of hand," Alex contended. "Besides, Tipton's is a great place. Man, the fun we used to have in college there. That young woman should be making decent money, if she's working at Tipton's. It's quite the place and has been a Hoosier icon for years. I don't know what you have against it, Beth, or against Amy, for that matter, but—"

"I don't have . . ." Beth interrupted sternly, taking a deep breath to redeem the intrusion. "I don't have anything against a good time or against Amy. She does a good job for us at Open Arms, and she and Lauren get along admirably."

"Then what's the problem?"

"I don't have a problem. I just have more in mind for my daughter than to have her hang around people who squirt ketchup on a plate full of fried pig balls and call it dinner."

~

The chuckles simmered as the young women approached. After introductions, the men left for the bar to refresh their drinks, laughing as they chided and joked with each other. Terese and Corinne admired the smart evening garments the two young women had chosen for the reception.

"I love the necklace you're wearing, Amy," Terese said. "It's stunning. It really is."

Amy blushed as she stroked the heirloom with her fingertips. A genuine sense of pride from her eyes shone as bright as the Lindy star sapphire around her neck. The silver strand flush against her chest sparkled as well.

Terese couldn't take her eyes off it. She noticed Beth couldn't either. Amy smiled uncomfortably under the scrutiny. Corinne, however, remarked how infrequently one saw women wearing Lindy stars anymore.

"It *is* beautiful, Amy," Lauren said. "Was it passed down through your family?"

"I'm embarrassed to say that I don't really know. My father gave it to me when I turned sixteen. I think it was his mother's, but I'm not sure. He said I was of age to receive something special, whatever that means. He wanted me to have it."

"It means you must make him very proud, and that he loves you very much," Corinne explained. "Otherwise, he wouldn't have given you something that was special to him."

Amy blushed again. "I suppose you're right. It's just that I don't have the sense of heritage that you all seem to have."

"Then hold onto it, dear, and never let it go," Corinne said. "Those gifts of family are the most treasured, and the longer you live, the more you'll appreciate them. Maybe one day your daughter will turn sixteen, and you'll pass it on to her so that she can experience the sense of family you never had. That would be a gift she would treasure all her life."

Terese smiled at the lovely thought. Lauren's expression, however, turned grave. She lowered her head so that she wouldn't have to look at anyone. Terese turned to Beth and saw her staring harshly upon her daughter as if she was ashamed and embarrassed.

Silence shrouded the women until Beth said pointedly to her daughter, "Not everything given in family should be treasured, Lauren."

Uncomfortable glances were exchanged.

"Whatever are you talking about?" Corinne asked sternly.

Beth didn't answer.

"Come now, Beth, you're being silly. What is it? What are you talking about?"

"Lauren knows," she said.

Terese turned to Lauren. As her mother stared unforgivingly, Lauren's right hand twitched as if she wanted to raise it to her neck. Terese looked at the necklace Lauren wore and thought it equally stunning as Amy's. A leaf-shaped black onyx and diamond pendant on a silver omega adorned her black and white outfit.

Terese turned to Beth and asked, "Do you mean the necklace?"

"I said it's nothing," Beth replied. "I apologize for opening my mouth."

"No," Corinne said, "we won't accept that. The only apology we'll accept now is an explanation."

"It'll have to wait," Beth said as she turned toward the entrance.

"Mayor Kendall just walked in. I didn't realize he was invited. I'm sorry, but I have to see him about something important. I have to intercept him before Marilyn Wells-Brewer does."

~

Callan noticed the women disperse as Beth left the group. He wanted to rejoin his wife, but Kate intercepted him before he had a chance to do so.

"Ah, Mr. Morrow, the reception is going well, isn't it? I hope you're enjoying yourself," she said with a slight slur. "There are many dignitaries in town for the 500-Mile Race, you know. I don't suppose you've met Mayor Kendall. He just walked in."

"Yes, he was hard to miss," Callan said. "I saw Beth dart like a bullet toward him as soon as he walked into the room."

Kate laughed. "She's counting on him to be a staunch supporter in her campaign. He's not running for reelection, so his endorsement would be important."

Callan watched Beth in conversation with the mayor while Kate teetered near him, grabbing his coat sleeve at one point to steady herself. He noticed Beth speaking close to the mayor's ear, as if in confidence. Mayor Kendall pursed his lips as he drank his cocktail, but Callan didn't believe his lips puckered from the alcohol. Beth said something deliberate and alarming.

"Do you think their conversation is going well?" Callan asked Kate, nodding in their direction so she'd take notice. "They seem to be in a deep conversation over there."

"It's an important election coming up. I'm sure they have plenty of things to discuss."

"In the middle of a reception, where everyone can see?"

Kate shrugged. Even in her inebriated state, Callan didn't believe the scenario looked right to her either.

Callan watched as Beth said something that appeared very pointed. The mayor gave Beth a look of disdain and glanced at his watch. Without a closing comment, he left Beth's side and walked toward a woman standing near the piano. He made some brief comments to her, and she appeared moved by what he had to say. Though she didn't respond, Callan could tell she didn't approve of what he'd said.

"Who's that woman the mayor is talking to now?" Callan asked Kate.

Kate leaned too far toward Callan and almost toppled over. "Janice Perkins, one of my new proprietors," she replied after regaining her composure.

"A new proprietor? She sells antiques?"

"Yes, just recently. She placed a table lamp by Serge Roche on consignment in this room. She's an economic development consultant and does quite a bit of work for the city. I'm not surprised she knows the mayor, although I didn't know she did. She's not from around here, you see. She's originally from up around Warsaw."

"That's interesting," Callan said.

"Warsaw?"

Callan frowned. "No, not Warsaw, Kate. Ms. Perkins. She's interesting."

Kate shook her head. "I don't see what's so interesting about her, except that she's talking with the mayor."

"Exactly. It's called coming full circle. She's a new proprietor, who is a consultant for the city, who was hired by the mayor, who is campaigning for Beth, who just had a serious conversation with her and is now in a serious conversation with Ms. Perkins. It's a full circle."

"It's still not very interesting."

"I find full circles always interesting. Why is she here?"

"Why shouldn't she be?" Kate asked. "I would think having a Serge Roche on consignment would be self-explanatory. I doubt she has any other motive for being a proprietor at Cottage Gallery than to make some extra money on something she no longer wants."

"How many items does she have on consignment?"

"Just the lamp."

"Isn't that odd?"

"Really, Mr. Morrow, you don't know much about consignment businesses, do you? Did you not hear me say the lamp is a Serge Roche? It's good for me that it's there. It'll sell quickly. Besides, I like having her here. She's a good friend of . . ." Kate's voice trailed off. Her eyes focused on a gentleman who approached Beth with hand extended. Kate's face gradually paled, and she wet her lips slowly with her tongue as if they'd suddenly become dry.

"What's the matter, Kate?"

No reply. She took two steps toward the center of the room as if something alarmed her, then turned back to Callan to hand him her glass. "Would you hold this, please?" Without an explanation, she dashed away toward the back of the gallery.

~

Beth Kimmerman smiled as the gentleman approached. She noticed his large diamond ring and smart cufflinks. "Mr. VanderPelt, is it?"

"Mrs. Kimmerman, we finally meet. We've only spoken on the phone, haven't we?"

"But you know my husband, I believe."

"Yes, I know him quite well. A good man. I rely on his financial expertise."

"And he respects yours."

"But I owe you an apology," he said humbly.

"Nonsense," Beth replied. "Whatever for?"

"My intrusive phone call, for one thing. I handled it very poorly, and it was inappropriate."

Beth lost her smile and eyed him cynically. "Did my husband call you to tell you that?" When he didn't respond, she added, "My husband doesn't speak for me, Mr. VanderPelt. I didn't find your call offensive in the least."

"You're very kind, Mrs. Kimmerman."

"You're making more out of my rejection than necessary, I'm afraid. Your call was very much appreciated, and the contribution offer meant a great deal to me."

"But the answer is still no?"

Beth's smile returned, thinking back to her conversation with Barry about considering things thoroughly before acting. Having not met the man personally before, she now had a sense of his humility and grace among overwhelming success.

"The answer now is maybe, Mr. VanderPelt," she said.

Callan disposed of Kate's glass and approached Barry Kimmerman, who stood alone off to one side of the room, agitated, and sipping his cocktail.

"People-watching?" Callan asked. When Barry ignored the comment, he qualified his question. "Or watching someone in particular? Who is that man Beth's talking to?"

Barry released his clenched jaw. "His name is Chase VanderPelt."

"He looks important. Is he?"

Barry shrugged and took a sip of his drink. "He's

highly regarded."

Callan watched Barry, whose eyes never departed from his wife and the distinguished man. "I assume you saw the mayor," he said.

"Someone said he was here, but I didn't see him."

"Surely you must have. He and Beth chatted for quite a while."

"So I heard," Barry said as if he didn't care.

"Now he's gone."

Barry's eyebrows rose. "So soon?"

"Prematurely, if you ask me," Callan said.

"He must've had another engagement."

"Or it was something Beth said that disturbed him."

Barry turned. "Mayor Kendall has been a strong advocate for Beth's candidacy," he said. "They confide in each other. Beth is able to talk freely with him, without fear what his reaction will be."

"It still doesn't make sense to me," Callan replied. "Do you know what she would've said?"

Barry hesitated, then said, "No. He's always been a constant source of inspiration and motivation. She may have said something regarding her concerns about the election."

"I think she said more than that. He left their conversation in disgust and talked to a woman briefly before leaving the reception without finishing his drink. Do you know who that woman was?"

Barry shook his head. "I've seen her around at functions, but I have no idea who she really is."

"But you know who I'm talking about. You must've been watching her too."

Barry ignored the comment.

"Kate tells me her name is Janice Perkins," Callan said.

"I don't know her."

"She's also a new proprietor here at Cottage Gallery," Callan added. "What do you make of that?"

"She likes antiques."

"She only has one item on consignment. It's a lamp."

Barry shrugged and took another sip. "She likes antique lamps."

Callan took a step closer so Barry could see how aggravated he was getting. "Or, Barry, she's not really a dealer of antiques at all. Do you get what I'm saying?"

"No, but I bet you're going to tell me."

"I think Beth told him there may be a connection between Davisly's death and activity with either Open Arms or the gallery that could expose a past her family has, that could embarrass her campaign. I think the mayor asked Ms. Perkins to consign something—anything—to see what is going on in the gallery."

"You mean consign something as a decoy? Why would the mayor ask this Perkins woman to do that?"

"Because I think Beth is considering dropping out of the race for mayor because of the events. Having Janice Perkins as a proprietor is a covert way of determining whether Beth's fears have any credence."

Barry grinned and shook his head. "How do you come up with your hypotheses, Callan? Are they evidence-based, or do you simply throw mud into the air to see where it lands and sticks?"

"I'd think recent events would have you thinking adamantly about your own hypotheses, Barry, but you're apparently content drinking highballs and gritting your teeth."

Barry sucked a couple of ice cubes into his mouth and crunched loudly. "It won't work," he said.

"What won't work?"

"You say this Perkins woman has a lamp she's using as a decoy?"

Callan nodded.

"Then it won't work. I doubt the two of them will get any information at all."

"You sound fairly certain of that," Callan said.

"They're not into lamps, Callan, trust me."

Callan stepped closer. "Who isn't into lamps?"

"The people Mayor Kendall and this Perkins woman want information about. The people who were after William Davisly. The same people who are after Beth."

"And who are these people?"

"I wish I knew the answer to that," Barry said solemnly.

"Then how are you so sure a decoy wouldn't work?"

Barry crunched on another cube of ice. He didn't answer. Instead, they watched Chuck Cordry enter the reception area. He'd spruced up nicely, although he still looked out of place among the other guests. He carried a white envelope and perused the room as if hoping to spot the individual to whom the envelope was addressed. Neither Callan nor Barry was surprised when Chuck made a beeline in their direction.

Callan glanced at Barry for his reaction.

Barry finished the contents of his cocktail and took a deep breath. "I knew from the beginning that Beth and I shouldn't have come tonight," he said. "You can quote me on that, Cal. Nothing good will come of this evening."

Chapter Twenty

Chuck extended an envelope for Barry to accept and said, "Some guy out front said to give this to your wife. I saw you first. I 'spect that's just as good."

"What is it?" Barry asked without taking it.

"I don't know, sir. He didn't say."

"Who gave it to you?"

"Damned if I know. Never saw the kid before."

"Kid?"

"Young man. Twenties, perhaps. Younger than he looks with that scraggly tumbleweed on his chin."

"I don't know him," Barry said.

"Well, I sure as hell don't either, but I said I'd give it to you just the same."

"How do I know there was a kid out there?" Barry asked. "How do I know it's not someone you want me to believe is out there?"

Chuck smiled with amusement as he scratched the top of his head. "You can look at it like this: Either there was a kid out there with a letter for you, or I sat down at my workbench and wrote you a dandy just because I like you so much. Now, which one do you think it is?"

Barry huffed. "What I'm saying is that Beth and I don't need a middleman to help us do our business. Whoever this scraggly kid is could've come into the reception and delivered the letter personally, if it was important."

"You gonna take it?" Chuck asked, apparently weary of the bantering. "I don't give a flying rat's behind whether you do or not. The sooner you take it, the quicker I can grab a beer, say my hellos to Ms. Kate, and get the hell out of here."

Barry stared into his eyes. Callan figured it was for no other reason than to let Chuck know he wasn't intimidated by him or the letter.

Chuck seemed to recognize the look in Barry's eyes. He smiled onerously and said, "Or I can grab a beer and find a seat someplace in one of these fancy chairs I reupholstered and read the letter for myself. That sounds even better, don't you think?" He turned to leave.

Barry grabbed his arm. "Hand it over."

Chuck did as he was told and symbolically tipped his hat. "Good evening, gentlemen. I trust you'll have a more enjoyable evening at this party than I will." He turned and walked straight to the bar.

"Damn smartass," Barry scoffed. "I don't like him."

"Any reason why?"

"Yeah," he replied sharply. "He's part of Eddie's crew, and I don't like Eddie."

Barry ripped open the envelope addressed to Beth and read its contents quickly. Fire consumed his eyes. His face flushed with anger, and his teeth clamped and began to grind. "I'll kill the son of a bitch."

"What is it?" Callan asked. "Let me see."

"No." Barry wadded the letter into a tight ball. "It'll only alarm Beth for no reason. I'd appreciate if you didn't mention anything about me receiving this letter until I've had a chance to talk to her."

Callan nodded.

"I'm serious, Cal."

"Hey, it's not my place to tell her."

"Son of a bitch," Barry repeated.

"But I do wish you'd tell me what the letter's about," Callan said. "I don't know how we can get to the bottom of this situation if you won't open up and let me help you and Beth."

Barry shook his head. "If you'll excuse me, I need a moment."

Callan stood alone, looking about the room. *Where was Patricia Reinholdt?* he wondered. Of all the times her curious eavesdropping and espionage skills could come in handy, she seemed to be nowhere in sight. He may have been a bit harsh on her earlier. He hadn't meant to break her spirit, only the odd behavior she exhibited toward others.

Callan sucked on ice cubes tainted with bourbon as he pondered what else Patricia knew that she hadn't told him. He wondered if her amateur spying had more purpose than what appeared on the surface. If so, how did she obtain the information to follow those that she trailed? Was she going on specific knowledge, or was she simply at the right place and the right time—all of the time? He wondered also why Patricia had felt it necessary to trail him as he followed Gabe and Meredith Patterswaite to Meredith's place of business the other day. Was she following him? Or had she known in advance that Gabe and Meredith were going to meet, and Callan got in the way? Perhaps she'd even seen the scraggly kid outside the gallery who supposedly gave Chuck the Kimmermans' ominous note.

Callan looked around the room.

Where was Patricia Reinholdt now?

No sign of her, but he saw Barry and Beth alone in animated conversation. The letter Chuck had given Barry was no longer in Barry's hand. The couple's discussion wasn't loud or conspicuous but was, nevertheless, noticeable. He wondered what they were discussing. If it wasn't about the letter, perhaps it was about Beth's conversation with the mayor. He watched them carefully. Beth apparently said something sharp that silenced Barry, because she left him standing to grind his teeth alone.

"Mother's been in rare form tonight, hasn't she?" a voice asked.

Callan spun around. Lauren and Amy stood beside him.

"I'm sorry you had to see that last exchange between your parents," Callan said.

"It's okay," she replied. "It comes with the territory."

"Besides," Amy said excitedly, "we've been watching Andrew Gammon over there with Marjorie Eckert." She pointed to the couple for Callan's benefit.

Lauren raised an eyebrow. "They appear to be inspecting a bureau."

Callan's gaze swung to where Amy pointed. "It's not just a bureau," he said. "It's the one with the rosettes, and they're inspecting it very closely."

Marjorie asked Andrew several questions, which he answered. Then he squatted on his haunches, reached underneath the desk and felt the bottom of it with his right hand. Marjorie watched him, asking more questions, to which Andrew did not reply. His face was expressionless as he surveyed the desk's underbelly with his hand, giving Marjorie no indication that he found anything of interest.

Andrew stood and faced her. She smiled and extended her hand to shake his, then appeared to make closing small talk before turning and walking across the reception floor, leaving

Andrew alone with the desk. He opened a drawer and examined it carefully.

"What's he doing?" Amy asked. "What's he after?"

After closing the drawer, Andrew opened another and scrutinized it in the same manner. After a few moments, he stood, ran his fingers through his hair as if exasperated, then looked about the room at the guests.

"I wonder who he's looking for?" Amy asked.

Callan wondered the same thing. "Where's Kate?"

Lauren shrugged. "I don't know. I haven't seen her for quite a while."

Amy reached into her purse and pulled out her phone, turning away so Callan and Lauren couldn't hear who she called. After making the call in a hushed voice, she turned back and explained that it was time for her to leave.

"Now?" Lauren asked.

"Yes, I'm sorry. Please excuse me."

Amy left abruptly.

"Well, that was odd," Lauren said. "Don't you think?"

Callan smiled. "Probably not. She's young and in love with that Brian fellow. I did impulsive things myself when I was captivated by Terese."

"But how do you know she left because of Brian?"

"Didn't you see her blush?" Callan asked. "No, that's not the mystery. What I'm wondering is why Brian didn't come with her to the reception tonight."

Lauren lifted her finger to remember. "I asked her about that when she asked to meet me so that we could come together. I said I thought Brian was invited. She didn't have much to say, only that he had something to take care of first."

Callan paused to think. "That's odd. Most people simply have something else to do when they don't want to attend a reception. When he has to take care of something first, it makes it sound as if he'll appear later."

"But he didn't," Lauren said.

"Exactly."

He returned to looking at Andrew Gammon at the rosette desk.

With his composure regained, Andrew buttoned his jacket and weaved his way through the crowd, smiling graciously until he reached Gabe. The two conversed. Andrew asked a question, but Gabe shrugged and shook his head. Andrew moved on, finding Beth. He said something seemingly cordial, but her response was too subtle to work out any intent behind it.

"Guests are starting to leave," Callan said to Lauren. "I wonder where Kate is. She should see them off. I think she should also take a look at that rosette desk with me to find out what all the intrigue is about."

"No," Lauren said with alarm. "Please don't look at it. I don't feel good about that piece. Something isn't right. Please don't go over to it, at least, not with people still at the reception. You never know who's watching."

Gabe hurried toward them, his eyes alert with excitement. "Have you seen Kate anywhere?"

"No, but people are starting to leave," Callan said. "She should be here."

"She told me she was going back to her office to give Ms. Patterswaite a call," Gabe explained. "Kate was hoping she'd come tonight, but she hasn't. I went back to Kate's office, but she wasn't there."

Callan had just opened his mouth to speak when a commotion from outside turned their attention toward the entrance. People gravitated toward the noise, craning their heads around others to get a better view. Callan pushed his way through the crowd to the door, then stopped. The village lights through the river mist created an eerie glow and cast silhouettes of people running toward the Central Canal. Though he couldn't see why they ran, he heard the patter of their running feet on the trail, and the quickening cadence of their steps heightened his anxiety. Were they running to or away from something? Only one way to find out. He ran with them toward the bridge over the canal.

When he arrived at the water's edge, he realized there weren't as many people running through the fog as he'd first thought. Only a handful of people were scattered around a focal point on the canal's bank. Curious, he slowed his gait and stopped upon hearing his name.

An agitated and perspiring Alex Aubert ran toward Callan through the mist. "Callan," he called again. "I thought it was you." He appeared relieved to spot a familiar face in the confusion.

"What's going on? Do you know what's happening?"

Alex bent slightly, using his knees as support as he caught his breath. "Come," he gasped, taking in a waft of fresh air that made him cough. "Come quickly."

"Where? To the canal? Why? What's going on?"

"Who is he?" someone yelled in the distance.

Alex looked up and turned toward the questioning voice. "Oh God," he said.

Callan grabbed Alex's jacket sleeve. "What happened?"

"Quick," Alex answered. "You must come. A body has been discovered." He shook Callan's grip from his coat and beckoned Callan toward the water.

But he didn't budge. Bewilderment clouded his senses. Why did Alex believe he, of all people, needed to be at the site where a body had been found?

Alex grabbed Callan and tried to drag him forward, to no avail.

"Why, Alex?"

"Because," he puffed, "the authorities may need our help."

"Do you know who it is?"

Alex nodded. Mist and perspiration dripped off the end of his nose. "His face . . . It looks like . . . Andrew Gammon."

Hearing Gammon's name stunned Callan. Fear penetrated him. Though Alex again encouraged Callan to hurry with him, Callan remained steadfast.

Alex couldn't wait. He turned away and ran back to the canal bank.

More people ran past Callan. Others stood solemnly like statues in the fog. The surreal mix of shapes and voices obstructed Callan's thoughts. He could hardly believe the insanity of the entire evening. Suddenly, however, he became acutely aware of his surroundings. A sudden chill crept up the back of his neck, as if someone other than Alex knew he was standing there. He turned in time to see a silhouette, obscured by mist, slither behind a series of trees and hurry toward the bridge to the main avenue. While people were being pulled toward the greenway along the canal, one person moved away.

Callan watched until the person moved from sight. Then he joined the others on the bank of the Central Canal.

Chapter Twenty-One

The news of the murder had spread quickly throughout Broad Ripple even before newspaper and television crews converged and police made official statements regarding their initial investigation. The sensational spins by the media numbed residents with the reality that a person such as Andrew Gammon could be killed along the banks of the village's most prominent icon. That it could happen on the eve of Indianapolis's festival weekend compounded the horror.

Terese was surprised that Beth and Lauren Kimmerman accepted her invitation to get out of the house for lunch. While most of the city was gathered around Monument Circle and on the sidewalks of downtown streets in anticipation of seeing the thirty-three drivers of the 500-Mile Race in the festival parade, the three women chose to stay in Broad Ripple.

Terese offered to take Beth and Lauren to Keystone Crossing to give them a reprieve from the sadness in the village, but Beth insisted they stay in Broad Ripple. The morning fog had lifted quietly from the canal by the time the three settled into a booth at a small café not far from Cottage Gallery.

"Shop owners are going to need our patronage," Beth said as a mimosa was placed before her. "Murder isn't exactly good for business." Beth spouted the words hatefully against the attacker.

Terese quickly changed the subject. "I left Callan at the carriage house. He's into genealogy, you know."

Beth and Lauren looked at her as if they had no idea what to say. They didn't appear to care.

"Genealogy," Terese repeated.

"Yes, we heard you," Beth replied. "Family history interests some people, but not me."

"What about?" Lauren asked, ignoring her mother's brashness.

"He has a great-grandmother he's been researching. She has an admirable past." Terese took a sip of water to give her time to think of something more to say. As she did so, she glanced at Lauren, who gestured for her not to continue. Lauren pointed to her neck, and Terese remembered the pendant Beth had admonished Lauren for wearing at the reception. It seemed there was a connection with great-grandmothers that Lauren wanted to avoid.

"And Andrew Gammon as well," Terese quickly added to change the focus away from grandmothers.

Beth's head jerked toward Terese. "Andrew Gammon? Why in the world would Callan be looking into Andrew's family history? What business does he have in doing so?"

Terese realized she'd made another blunder. "I'm not quite sure, Beth. He wants to cover all bases, I assume. Callan is a strong believer that family has a lot to do with a person's character, based on their upbringing and—"

"Not necessarily," Beth contended.

"Well, no, you're right, not necessarily, but if Andrew was being blackmailed as Mr. Davisly was, then perhaps it has something to do with his past . . . or his family's past."

Beth repositioned her silverware and glass of water. "Callan has his reasons for delving into Andrew's genealogy, I'm sure, but it sounds like a waste of time to me," she said. "And I'm not sure I can stand to hear of any more scandal with members of Open Arms's board."

"I'm sure Open Arms will . . ." Terese stopped when she noticed Beth's icy expression. She lowered her tone of voice. "I was going to say that I'm sure Open Arms will be fine through all this."

Beth took a deep breath and exhaled slowly. "I don't think Open Arms was fine even before what happened last night. Open Arms was . . ." Beth stopped and looked into her daughter's eyes as if she suddenly realized how cynical she sounded to Terese, who was only trying to make small talk. She lowered her voice and said, "Oh, I'm sorry."

"There's no need to be."

"Yes, there is. I need to apologize. Not just to you, but to everyone around me, lately. I was a troll last night at the reception. I should apologize to everyone from my husband to the mayor, from my children to the board, from Corinne to . . ." Beth stopped before mentioning another name.

"Who, Mother?" Lauren prompted. "Who else needs an apology?"

Beth sipped on her mimosa then ordered black coffee from the waitress, who came to the table with a brimming smile.

After the waitress had taken her order, Lauren leaned toward her mother and asked, "Are you the reason Kate left the reception last night?"

Beth looked at Lauren but gave no indication that her daughter was correct.

"I found it rather odd, and unacceptable, that Kate wasn't around to see the guests off," Lauren added. "At first, I thought it was because Meredith Patterswaite hadn't arrived as Kate hoped, but then I figured it could be something else. Someone could have spoiled her evening. Criticism from someone like Marilyn Wells-Brewer would be taken for granted, but unkind words from someone she counted on for support would've devastated her."

"You're being dramatic, Lauren," Beth replied. "I didn't say anything to her. Kate just needed a break and retired to her office."

"That doesn't make sense."

"It does if you know Kate."

Lauren shook her head in disbelief. "I don't know her like you do, Mother, but why—"

"She'd had too much to drink, Lauren," Beth said sharply.

"As had many."

"But her overindulgence was not, in my opinion, good business."

Lauren thought for a second. "Drunken stupor or not, she wasn't in her office when Gabe went to call on her."

"She wasn't there?" Terese asked. "Where could she have gone?"

Lauren stared at her mother.

"I don't know what to say," Beth said, taking another sip of her mimosa. "If she wasn't drunk, then she was sulking."

"That isn't a very flattering remark about your best friend."

"Best friends aren't immune to making unflattering remarks, Lauren. Just because I like her doesn't mean I like all that she does. It also doesn't mean that I will stand idly by as she destroys her business and the reputation of those around her. Just like that onyx and diamond pendant you wore."

"The pendant? You mean to tell me that I embarrassed you because I wore a pendant?"

Beth twisted the stem of her glass and stared off to the side. "It's not just a pendant, and it's not what you think, Lauren. None of it is what you think, whether it be Kate or the pendant."

"May I ask something?" Terese asked out of the blue. "You don't have to answer, but I hope you will."

Beth reacted with indifference.

"Did you go to the canal last night when the commotion started?"

"Yes," she said. "Many people from the reception went. What's that got to do with the pendant Lauren wore?"

"Probably nothing, but I had a thought."

Beth frowned. "I went there with Barry."

"Who did you see there?"

"Well, I don't know. I haven't thought about it. I'll have to remember. From the board, Alex Aubert, of course. He was one of the first ones at the canal after someone found the body. I saw Marilyn and Cole. Cole and Alex talked quite a bit and made an identification of the body for authorities. Callan was there too. I suppose that was it."

"Did you see Patricia Reinholdt?"

"Patty? No, she left the reception early, I believe. She could've been at the canal, but I didn't notice her. It would've been the type of sordid event Patty would've been attracted to, however."

"How about Eddie or Chuck?"

Beth shook her head, then turned away to think. "Wait a minute. There *was* someone else I recognized. I thought it odd, because she stood off to the side. She had a look of utter fear on her face."

"Who was that?" Terese asked.

"A proprietor of Cottage Gallery, I think. No, wait. Not a proprietor but a customer. Barry knew her. He saw her before I did. He said her name to me, but I can't recall."

"Marjorie Eckert?"

Beth hesitated. "Why, yes, I believe that's the name Barry mentioned."

"She was frightened?" Lauren asked.

"I don't think I've ever seen such fear before."

"When did Kate learn of Mr. Gammon's death?" Terese asked.

Beth seemed to hear the question but her mind was apparently on something else. "Oh," she replied several seconds later. "Kate? I'm not sure I know. As Barry and I were coming back from the canal, we saw her coming from the rear of the gallery across the side yard."

"From the rear?" Lauren asked.

Her mother nodded. "If she was in her office, the back door is the closest way out. She could slip out of the gallery easily without being seen by those at the reception. Of course, by then, almost everyone had left the reception to go to the canal to see what the commotion was about."

"But she wasn't in her office, Mother. Gabe checked, and she wasn't there."

"I don't know what to tell you. Your father and I saw her coming from the rear of the gallery across the side yard. He gave her the news about Andrew before she reached the canal. The scene on the greenway wasn't going to do Kate any good, so your father told her not to go. She shivered terribly, I remember. The fog made it quite chilly. Your father had given me his coat, and I took it off and placed it over Kate's shoulders. Even though she was shivering, she didn't appear to be cold. It was as if the shock of Andrew's death shielded her from the cold. Either that, or she was too intoxicated to notice."

"Then why was she shivering?"

"Fright, no doubt," Beth said. "She kept repeating that she couldn't believe Andrew was dead, that Andrew was the one who'd been killed."

Terese's eyes narrowed. "I'm sorry, but that sounds like Kate suspected someone else was going to be harmed last night."

Beth leaned forward and lowered her voice. "Yes, it was very odd how she said it. I can't remember her exact words, but it was almost as if she had a premonition. The news of a body found on the canal didn't seem to surprise her, but she certainly didn't expect it to be Andrew Gammon."

"Who did she suspect it would be?"

"I don't know," Beth said. "I could kick myself now. I think she was trying to tell me last night, but she was in such a state of shock, and I was so put out with her anyway, that I thought she was talking gibberish. Apparently not, however. She may have been trying to tell me something important."

"Not to worry," Terese said. "It so happens that Kate called Cal shortly before I left and asked him to meet her at the gallery. After he finished his genealogy work, he was going to head over."

"Did she say what about?"

"If she did, Callan didn't tell me."

"I hope this is a turnaround," Beth said. "I hope she's reaching out to Callan for help."

"And I know what she needs help with," Lauren said. "It's that rosette desk. Both Mr. Gammon and Ms. Eckert purchased that desk and returned it within hours of each other."

Terese frowned. "I wonder what it means."

Lauren shrugged. "I think it's cursed, if you ask me."

~

Callan crossed the bridge over the canal at Guilford Avenue, sipping on a latte and taking in the solitude of walking through the misty remnants of a foggy morning. Although not chilly, the low-hanging clouds reminded him of early autumn rather than late spring. A few onlookers stood a safe distance from where investigators had worked the night before, but otherwise, the greenway looked as if nothing had occurred.

Callan completed his trek across the bridge and walked along the treelined street toward Cottage Gallery. The canopy of sycamores released periodic droplets of water that splatted around him as if in competition as to which tree could hit his unprotected head. Or perhaps it was tears they released. Callan wasn't a man prone to symbolic melodrama, but today he would make an exception. The sycamores had every reason to cry.

Kate's phone call had taken him by surprise. She sounded upset and tired, exactly what he would expect given the events of the previous night. He was cautious, however, to hypothesize what had upset her. Why would Andrew Gammon's death upset her more than William Davisly's? Was she finally realizing there was a link between Cottage Gallery and the murders? Or was she simply upset about what the murders would do to her business?

A sign on the door indicated the gallery would be closed for the Memorial weekend holiday. Gabe answered the door when Callan knocked and welcomed him into the foyer. The overhead bell rang with a piercing clang.

He followed Gabe to the Cardinal Room, where Kate was hanging a collection of framed aristocratic German red-wax seals. She stepped back to survey the arrangement on the wall and appeared satisfied—at least for the moment. As Callan approached, she turned to shake his hand, thanking him for taking the time to meet her. Her swollen eyes and sunken facial features marked the emotional toll of a bleak morning.

"I see you brought some coffee for yourself," she said, "but may I offer you a refresher?"

Callan refused, so she offered him a seat on a mahogany tub

chair. "It's all right," she said, anticipating his hesitancy to sit on the nineteenth-century relic. "It's one of my pieces. It's not going to sell, I'm afraid. Where's Gabe, by the way?"

"He was in the next room. Would you like to go somewhere more private?"

"It's not necessary."

Kate moved a mantel clock, setting it on a rosewood game table, making it more noticeable when customers entered the room. Then she quickly moved it back to its original setting. "I'm not ignoring you, Callan," she said as she examined the face of a bureau for scratches. "I'm groping for words, you see."

Callan sipped patiently on his coffee.

She soon stopped her meaningless tasks and took a seat near him. "I'm sure you're wondering why I called."

"I don't mean to be presumptuous," he replied, "but I felt it would be a matter of time before you would. It's been a difficult time for you and the board of Open Arms recently, and you've had much on your mind. You didn't need a murder on top of it all."

"No, and now what I'm about to tell you will seem particularly extraordinary. I hardly know how to say it."

"Is it about last night?" he asked.

"Not entirely—although last night confirmed my suspicions. I have a desk that Chuck Cordry worked on for me in his workshop at Open Arms. It's located in the Sycamore Room right now. It's been problematic for me, to say the least."

"The one with the rosettes?"

"Yes, then you're familiar with it. I've been in denial, for lack of a better word, regarding its history. It was first sold to Marjorie Eckert of Carmel. She apparently didn't like how it fit in her study once she got it home. She returned it immediately. Not long after that, Andrew Gammon bought the same piece."

"And returned it as well?"

Kate nodded. "The proprietor was irate. Two returns of the same piece in a matter of days. She accused me of renting it to prominent customers for staging purposes at private gatherings, with the ability to return the piece once the event was over."

"How was this to profit you?"

"I'd charge a fee for the rental. She accused me of not passing the rental fee on to her."

"I see, and did you?"

"Did I become a Rooms To Go? No, Mr. Morrow, I did not. I run a fine antiques gallery, and I make a good living. I don't need the headaches of administering rentals and worrying about damage to the pieces for a tawdry fee. The risk of liability and reputation isn't worth it."

"Who was this proprietor who accused you?"

"Meredith Patterswaite."

Callan smiled, recognizing the name.

"She amuses you?" Kate asked.

He shook his head.

"Then it should amuse you even less to learn that she's missing." Kate rose from her seat and paced, touching pieces she seemed to favor. "I believe you now, Callan," she said somberly. "You always had a theory that William Davisly's death was somehow connected to Open Arms or to Cottage Gallery. I opposed such a thought. I suppose others in town have thought like you all along, haven't they? Well, now you can add me to that list, because I need your help. I've avoided your help before, but I need it now. Ask me whatever you need to ask, if it'll help us get to the bottom of these strange notes."

Kate took a hanky from a side pocket and dabbed at her nose.

Callan paused to let her regain her composure. "Are you sure you're okay with me probing into the case?"

She nodded halfheartedly before sighing and nodding again more convincingly.

"Where were you last night?" he asked.

"In my office. I wasn't feeling well."

"Were you there all night?"

Kate grimaced. "Have you talked to the police? These are the same questions they asked me last night and early this morning. No, I wasn't in my office all night. I went out into the side yard as everyone was coming back from the canal."

"Coming back? Is that true? There was a commotion long before everyone was coming back, Kate. Why didn't that prompt you from the office?"

Kate loured, as if she realized she wasn't going to be able to bluff her way through his questions. "All right. If you must know, I did go out into the side yard from the back when the commotion occurred, but not right away. I saw Barry and Beth. You can ask them."

"But at the reception, Gabe said he was looking for you, and you weren't in your office."

"No, I wasn't," she said, pacing some more. "When the commotion started, I heard a knock at my back door. It was Patricia Reinholdt, of all people."

"That's odd."

"I thought so too."

"What did she want, and why would she come around to the back of your gallery?"

"She said she saw a light through my office window. Patty is never overt in what she does. Rather than walking to my office in plain sight of prominent guests, she'd rather peer through a windowpane at night. You know how she is. We had words with her at the reception, if you remember. That's why she came to see me. She wanted to set the record straight. She was annoyed with our accusations that she was a stalking meddler, for lack of a better term. She didn't come to apologize; she came to *get* an apology. Can you believe it?"

"How did you react?"

"How do you think I reacted? I was quite angry. Here was a woman asking for an apology for calling her a stalker after she'd just peeked through my window at night to see if I was in my office. Why, I was furious!"

"So what happened?"

"She burst into tears and ran away. I didn't see where she ran. I didn't care. I just wanted the crazy woman away from my gallery!"

"Is that when you went into the side yard?"

"Yes, and that's when I saw Barry and Beth coming back from the canal. But really, Callan, I don't want to talk about the canal. I didn't call you to talk about Barry and Beth, or even Patty. I want to know what I should do about Meredith Patterswaite."

"I'm sorry if it appears that I'm not interested, but so much happened last night. It all might be connected. When did Meredith come up missing?"

"That's hard to tell. One never really knows someone is missing until they are unaccounted for, but that doesn't mean that was when they went missing. I don't know what to tell you. All I know is that she hasn't returned any of the phone calls I've left for her."

"Does she have family or friends associated with the gallery who might know?"

"Unfortunately, we don't have information like that on Meredith. We try to keep extensive contact information on our proprietors so that we can get a hold of them in case a customer wants to make an offer on a piece but would like to negotiate first. We have limited information on Meredith, however. I think she likes it that way."

"Is she a private individual?"

"*Private* isn't the right word. *Controlling* is a better description. She limits information about herself to maintain control over who has access to her."

"That's the definition of privacy, Kate."

"When it's limiting information from *me*, I call it control."

Callan acquiesced. "Very well. Did she make an appearance at the reception?"

"No, I tried to call her, but I didn't receive an answer."

"It *is* Memorial weekend, Kate. People do go to the lakes over the holiday."

"I've heard that from others. Yes, I know. People go away for the weekend. People use the holiday to springboard into summer by going to the lakes. Blah, blah, blah, Mr. Morrow. I've heard it all, but I believe it's more than that. I have to get to the bottom of where she is, and I don't know what to do." Kate sat back in the chair across from Callan and rubbed her temples. "Then there's Beth, you know?"

"Beth?"

She looked up. "Surely, she's told you how impatient she's getting with me. I suppose I shouldn't blame her. She's at her wit's end with me and how I've been managing Open Arms and Cottage Gallery. She says I'm not transparent. I need to be more transparent. What more can I do, Callan? What more can I do?"

Callan studied the creases on her face and the weariness in her eyes as she bemoaned her situation. She seemed sincere in asking what more she could've done, as if she truly believed she was doing everything in her power to be transparent about the organizations' activities. He found it hard to believe that it took last night's murder for her to become suspicious.

Another thought crossed his mind. Perhaps Kate was guilty

of the unnerving events and believed her scheme was unraveling. Seeking his help bought her time to cover her tracks. Perhaps she wanted to use him to gain information so that she could stay one step ahead of what people thought. She could have even planted something—a document of some kind—for him to discover that would implicate another person to deflect suspicion from her.

"I'll need access to your records," he said bluntly, "for both Open Arms and the gallery. I'll need access immediately and without interference. That is, if you're serious about wanting my help."

Callan noticed a twinge around the creases of Kate's right eye. She nodded reluctantly before giving him permission to look at anything he wanted. Then he expressed his appreciation and left quietly.

Gabe stood in the doorway of the main showroom and gestured for Callan to follow him. Without hesitation, Callan followed him to the rosette desk against the wall. Gabe pulled open the middle drawer, and the drawer on the right. He reached inside the middle drawer. Callan heard a click and assumed the young man had pressed some kind of button. Gabe reached inside the drawer on the right and pulled a panel away from the back, revealing a hidden compartment. Callan stooped to look inside. The men glanced knowingly at each other. Although the secret compartment was empty, they had finally made some headway as to the desk's intriguing history.

"When did you find this?" Callan asked.

"Just now. Something other than what appeared on the surface had to be going on with this desk. I know from selling other valuable antiques like this that hidden compartments often accompany such pieces. I did some research on this style and period of desk but came up empty-handed. This particular desk isn't noted for its cubbyholes or hidden compartments."

"So what made you so curious?"

"It wasn't my curiosity that intrigued me, Callan. It was Mr. Gammon and Ms. Eckert's curiosity last night that was too much for me to ignore, so while you and Kate were talking in the Cardinal Room, I spent my time frisking the desk."

"Good job. It took a while to find the button, didn't it?"

"I found the false back to the drawer first. Something wasn't right about it, and it was different from the drawer on the left, but I couldn't figure out how to release the backing."

"So how did you figure it out?"

"I noticed earlier that the middle drawer here had a hole on the right side, but there wasn't a hole on the left. I discovered that you have to pull the drawer open to where the hole lines up perfectly with the button that releases the backing. Once you do, then you push the button. It's ingenious because the hole by itself isn't a clue that there's a secret compartment. You also have to find the button which is hidden until you match it with the hole."

"Man, they were creative back then, weren't they? I guess they had to be, to protect their valuables from unscrupulous individuals. How old did you say this piece is?"

"That's just it, Cal. While the desk is over a hundred years old, the compartment isn't. The compartment is recent."

Gabe pulled the false backing out of the drawer and held it in front of Callan's face. Callan leaned forward and took a sniff. "It's new. Smells like freshly cut wood."

"And it's live edge wood, allowing it to blend in more easily with the desk's age."

Callan could see the wheels turning in Gabe's mind. "What are you thinking?"

"I was thinking back to when Meredith requested Chuck to

add the rosettes to make the desk more appealing. I wonder if she asked him to do more than add rosettes."

He stood and looked at Gabe, rubbing his chin. "What are you doing this evening?"

Chapter Twenty-Two

Callan and Gabe arrived at Open Arms around eleven o'clock. Late night revelers in the village rocked the bars, enjoyed the theaters, and laughed at second-rate comics. Callan pulled onto a residential side alley off Sugar Bob Lane and parked in rear of a shop with a distant but perfect exterior view of the door that led into the back room of Open Arms. They could also see the windows along the back wall.

Callan leaned against the headrest and watched the rear of the building. "There's a light coming from the workroom," he said. "I guess I didn't expect a light to be on, but when else would Chuck and Eddie have time to build such intricate creations as hidden compartments in antiques so they'd be undetected? Do you want to leave and come back when we know they're not there?"

"No," Gabe said earnestly. "I want to know what's going on *now*. I'm willing to wait, if you are."

They didn't wait long. Headlights illuminated the alley. A late-model foreign hatchback rolled to a stop near the back door.

Two young women with long hair emerged from the car,

scantily clad and presumably dressed for the nightclubs. They surveyed the surroundings and walked carefully in their heels to the back door. The woman who wore a blue halter top knocked on the door while the other drew her shawl closer around her shoulders and kept watch.

The back door inched open, revealing Eddie standing in the dim light shining through the doorway. His words to the woman appeared short and to the point. They nodded in agreement and entered.

"I want to see what they're doing in there," Callan said. "Let's take a look."

Gabe was just as eager. They exited his car and stepped onto the gravel, not realizing how loud gravel and broken pavement sounded underfoot in the stillness of night. They tiptoed to solid asphalt then hurried to the windows at the back of the building.

Eddie stood by Chuck's table, while the two young women stood near the door, holding small boxes. Eddie slipped something into his pocket and gave the women instructions that he and Gabe couldn't hear. The women nodded and left the workshop.

Callan motioned to Gabe to hide behind the dumpster near the corner of the building. They did so just before the two women drove past in their hatchback. When the car was safely out of sight, Callan and Gabe emerged from their hiding place and went back to the windows along Chuck's workshop. They were surprised to see Kate in the doorway, hands upon her hips. She appeared angry, her voice stern.

Eddie wasn't any happier or kinder with his gestures. Bursts of anger spouted from his mouth, but with the muffled sounds of music from the nearby clubs, Callan and Gabe couldn't make out the words through the glass.

After a minute of bantering back and forth, Kate and Eddie's conversation quelled when Eddie pointed to the sales floor. Kate shook her head and marched out of the workshop. Eddie picked up a rubber mallet from Chuck's worktable and slammed it on the surface of the table in frustration. Then he tossed the mallet to the side and followed Kate.

Callan scanned the lighted room. Two boxes sat near the doorway with smaller green cardboard boxes with words printed on the sides stacked on top.

"What are you looking at?" Gabe whispered.

Callan pointed to the boxes. "I wonder what's in them."

"I've never seen them before."

Eddie walked back into the workshop just as lights from another car came down the side alley parallel to the building. Callan motioned that they move behind the dumpsters again. The lights of the vehicle grew brighter and came into full view at the corner of the building. It wasn't a car of young women this time. This vehicle was a windowless charcoal van. The driver stopped and killed the engine, which killed the radio blaring from inside.

Eddie emerged from the door to the alley. He slapped his hand twice on the van's double doors, then retreated quickly back inside the building. On cue, both the driver and passenger doors opened. Two young males jumped from their seats onto the rocky drive and went into the building. Callan recognized them as the young men with whom he'd sorted clothes the other day—Jeremy and Ronnie. They soon returned with what appeared to be small kitchen appliances, toys, and other gadgets that they placed through the van's double doors. Large brown corrugated boxes marked with the *Merchandise Mart* logo came next. After two more trips, Eddie turned off the workshop lights and joined the young men in the alley.

Eddie closed the van's doors, slapped his hand twice on

them, and Jeremy drove away, radio blaring, past Callan and Gabe in their spot behind the dumpsters. Eddie didn't go inside the building but appeared to wait for another car. One came down the side alley, and Eddie put up his hand for the car to stop, but instead of doing so, it swerved and accelerated, kicking gravel in its wake. Callan recognized the car as Kate's. Eddie jumped aside to let her pass. As she did so, he cursed and gave her the finger.

Eddie stood alone for a several seconds before cursing again, then turned to go down the side of the building where Callan and Gabe couldn't see. They did, however, hear the clicking of a key in a door lock, then footsteps upon gravel, before a truck fired up and started down the alley. Eddie turned the corner and drove away.

"What the hell?" Gabe said, still on his haunches behind the dumpster.

"Yeah, I know," Callan agreed, standing.

"So what do you want to do? Do you still want to go inside?"

Callan shook his head. "No, I've seen enough."

"What do you think's going on?"

"Something not related to operating a thrift store, that's for damn sure."

Callan paused to think. His mind raced with more questions than answers. Were Eddie and the young men using Open Arms to smuggle and sell stolen goods? Why was Kate there? Was she upset by what she'd discovered or upset by how the operation was being executed?

"I want to talk to Kate," he said. "I want to see her documentation. There's more going on with the gallery and Open Arms than she's letting on. I won't know until I see her paperwork."

"She'll never agree to that," Gabe said.

"She already has. I received a verbal commitment this afternoon. She appeared genuine, but now I'm not so sure."

"Okay, then, I'll pull some records for you tomorrow."

"Tomorrow may be too late. I told her I wanted complete access to her documents. Do you have your keys to the gallery with you?"

"Yes, of course, but—"

"It won't take long, but I need to see what documents she has and what they look like tonight so that I can see if she alters them tomorrow."

He drove the short distance to Cottage Gallery and parked off to the side.

Gabe pointed to Kate's Lexus on the opposite side of the street. "She's in her office," he said. "That's it, where the light's on."

Callan blurted an expletive under his breath. "I was hoping she'd wait until morning before she started altering documents. Okay, do this for me. Give her a call to let her know we're coming in. I don't want to scare her, but I also don't want to give her time alone with the records."

Gabe grabbed his cell phone from inside his pants' pocket and placed a call to the gallery's main line. When he didn't receive an answer, he left a quick message and dialed Kate's cell number. Again, there was no answer.

"I don't understand what Kate was doing in Chuck's workshop at this time of night," Gabe said while they waited for her return call. "I'm really disappointed in her right now. I don't know if I can keep my mouth shut when she lets us in."

"It may not be what you think, Gabe," Callan said. "Was she there because she was working together with Eddie, or was Eddie as surprised to see her in the workshop as we were?"

The two sat in silence for a couple of minutes.

"Does she usually take this long to return a call?" Callan asked impatiently.

"No, she doesn't, as a matter of fact. I'll give her another minute before calling again."

"No, let's go in," Callan said. "She may be on the up and up with Eddie, but she also may be stalling for time in there."

The two strode to the front entrance and opened the door. The bell tinkled gently overhead.

Callan didn't like the feel of the place. Stale potpourri and the creaking of old floorboards under his feet were the only smell and sound in the front room. Accent lighting from lamps for sale by proprietors illuminated their way to the hallway to Kate's office.

They moved quietly through the room, but it was almost too quiet for Callan. If Kate was in her office, they should've heard the shuffling of papers or the moving of boxes.

He called out her name.

No answer.

A sliver of golden light shone faintly into the hallway from her partially closed office door. Callan and Gabe stood outside, listening for signs of activity.

"Kate?" he called again, using his fingertips to carefully open the door.

Kate didn't look up. She was slumped over her desk onto a disorganized stack of papers, an open wound on the back of her head.

Callan sprang to her side and placed his fingers to the side of her neck. A faint but clearly identifiable pulse brought a sigh of relief, calming his pounding heart. He reached into his pocket to retrieve his cell phone. The emergency dispatcher answered his frantic call immediately.

He looked at Gabe and noticed a pasty pallor on his face.

"You okay?"

Gabe looked at Kate and shook his head. "I gotta get out of here." He turned and stumbled out of the office.

Callan knew how he felt. He had a sick feeling in his stomach and imagined he looked just as gray and pasty. In addition, he didn't know what to believe anymore. He looked about the room, being careful not to disturb anything. Papers were strewn about as if she'd been frantically calculating numbers and reconciling inventory. Her coffee cup was half full and still warm, marked with lipstick, the shade she currently wore. Several pens lay haphazardly among paperclips. A stapler rested on its side near her, jarred open as if she'd been wrestling with jammed staples inside. She'd obviously been in the middle of her work when interrupted.

Something caught his attention. Gabe had noticed it too, before he said he had to leave. An amethyst medallion lay on the floor beside her chair. Callan didn't know why the medallion had such an impact on Gabe, but at the moment he had a bigger problem slumped over her desk in the middle of the night. Finding Kate fighting for her life was so unexpected at a time when he believed they were close to obtaining some answers. He wondered what his next step would be. He was running out of suspects.

One, at least, was dying.

Chapter Twenty-Three

The cold morning rain pattered on top of Callan's umbrella as he hurried up the sidewalk to the Kimmerman home, shielding Terese from the deluge. It wasn't just the elements or what had happened to Kate that made their walk so dismal. It was race day. Of all mornings, the community needed a fine spring day, one that was sunny and temperate. Race day in Indianapolis was something special. Nobody wanted to see rain. It meant the race would be postponed to later in the day or, on rare occasions, the next day. Rain was a sacrilege of sorts—intolerable and disappointing—because it was a cancellation of anticipation and excitement.

For Callan and Terese, the rain also meant the reality of an evil presence in their midst.

It poured harder as Lauren answered the door. She gestured them into the foyer, and they followed her quietly into the large family room. "They're in here," she said. "I'll go see if Gabe needs help with coffee and brunch." She left, leaving Callan and Terese alone with her sullen-faced parents and the Auberts.

Beth didn't attempt to offer pleasantries. She appeared

to have a deep sense of apprehension and hopelessness about her as if she'd succumbed to the realization that the charitable organization she chaired and the mayoral election she hoped to win was now all but lost.

Barry offered Callan something stronger than coffee, but Callan declined. A bourbon seemed too harsh and too early, a mimosa too lighthearted, and a Bloody Mary inappropriate no matter how good it sounded.

Corinne stepped across the room and handed Beth a coverlet to wrap around her shoulders. The room wasn't chilly, but the pattering rain, dreary cloudiness, and subdued mood within the room called for the warm comfort of the coverlet. As Beth wrapped it around her, an edge flipped out and skirted across an end table next to the couch, knocking a gadget to the floor that hit a cloisonné vase, causing the vase to ring and Callan to glance that way.

"What have we learned?" he asked Barry.

"Kate is stable but alive," Barry replied. "The intruder obviously thought he left her for dead. She's in a drug-induced coma until the swelling around her brain subsides. Until then, it'll be touch and go. We won't know if she'll make it until . . . well, we just won't know."

"And the police?" Alex asked.

"Detectives left about forty-five minutes ago. They didn't ask us to go downtown. They weren't here to tell us anything, just to ask questions. It was all very one-sided."

"It was the same with me," Callan said, "although I answered all their questions last night at the gallery. All those they knew to ask, anyway."

All eyes turned to him, alight with curiosity.

"What does that mean?" Barry asked.

"Shall we have coffee?" Beth asked. "I could use a cup."

"I'll get it for you," Corinne offered. "Black?"

"Yes, black, very strong, no sugar. Anyone else?"

"I think we all could use some," Barry said eagerly.

Terese stood and left the room to assist Corinne. Now alone with just the Kimmermans and Alex Aubert, Callan asked Barry to repeat his question.

"You said that you answered all the questions the detectives knew to ask," he said. "That implies there were questions they didn't ask. What did you mean by that?"

"Where were you last night, Beth?" Callan asked pointedly.

Beth glared with contempt. "I hardly know anymore. It's difficult for me to think, let alone remember anything."

"Were you there?"

"Was I where?"

"I'm not going to beat around the bush. The police are asking questions, but I daresay they're not asking the right questions. There's too much at stake here. It's more than a mayoral race or your pride, Beth. There's Andrew Gammon's murder and an attempted murder on Kate. Apparently, there's a missing person as well, with Meredith Patterswaite."

"Don't you think I know that?"

"Then let's not play games with each other. I believe you knew exactly what I meant when I asked if you were at Cottage Gallery last night."

"What?" Barry interjected. "Is that where you went? You went to see Kate?"

Beth looked away. "What makes you think I was there?"

Callan walked toward the end table where something had fallen to the floor. He picked up the fallen piece, studied it, then extended it for Beth to see. "How did you get this?"

Callan recognized the amethyst amulet as the one that had lain on the floor beside Kate's chair. How it went from Kate's desk to Beth's end table was the question he hoped Beth would answer honestly.

She shook her head as if she couldn't remember where she got it and, more pointedly, that it didn't matter.

Callan glared at her, noticing the defiance growing on her face.

"Come now, Callan," Barry stated, "it's clear she doesn't know."

"But I think she does. I think she confronted Kate last night with the amulet. I don't know why, and I don't know the significance, but I believe it played an important role in the events of last night. Did the police ask you about the amulet, Beth? Did they know enough to ask?"

Beth uncrossed her legs on the couch and let the coverlet drop behind her as she rose. "This conversation is over, Callan," she said as she passed him to be with the other women in the kitchen.

Barry followed her, leaving Alex alone with the auditor, who clutched the vintage medallion in his hand.

"What the hell was that all about?" Alex asked, grabbing Callan's arm, forcing Callan to face him.

"I'm through with these people, Alex. I saw this amulet lying on the floor beside Kate right after we found her."

"Surely, you're mistaken."

"I am not . . . mistaken," Callan said adamantly. "Not about this or the fact that Beth was in Kate's office last night."

"Calm down, please," Alex urged.

Callan ignored Alex and shook loose from his grip. He couldn't believe what he was experiencing: Silence from a family in desperate trouble while colleagues were being murdered and a close friend was close to death. This wasn't a time for silence, and the more Callan thought of the situation, the angrier he became.

He marched into the kitchen, where he stood defiantly in the doorway and pointed the amulet at young Gabe. "I want a word with you!" he said firmly.

Alex took Callan's shoulders from behind to hold him back.

Barry stepped forward and stood between Callan and his son.

"Let me go!" Callan said to Alex, trying to shrug him off. He craned his head around Barry to look at Gabe. "You took this amulet from Kate's office last night, didn't you? You knew your mother was there, and you took it so she wouldn't be incriminated. Didn't you, Gabe?"

"Callan, please," Barry implored.

"I don't know when you did it—sometime when I stepped away, before the police came—but you took it. I know you did. When, Gabe? When did you take it?"

Alex tugged on Callan's shoulders, pulling him away from the kitchen and back into the living room. "Calm down, Callan," he said. "What's gotten into you? They're all scared. Can't you see that?"

"But I'm not the one they should be afraid of," Callan countered. "Beth takes me for a fool. Gabe takes me for a fool. The Kimmermans worry and lament, but they won't share what they don't want anyone to know, and they connive and hide things behind our backs because they think we're fools. We can't help them if they're going to be like that."

"I know. I understand. They must have their reasons for doing so, however."

"That doesn't mean I have to be a part of it," Callan said, straightening his shirt sleeves. "I'm sorry, Alex. My behavior is inexcusable, but I'm at my wit's end. I think it's best if Terese and I return to Vermillion immediately."

"You don't mean that, Callan. Give the Kimmermans time."

"Time? There is no more time, Alex. You think Kate has

more time?"

"That's not what I meant. Look, I've been doing some more research. I'm sure you have too. Together, maybe we can make some sense out of this mess without the family's help."

Chapter Twenty-Four

Alex suggested they go onto their covered stoop to talk, and Callan agreed.

"You know how I've been looking into the background of William Davisly with the help of my father?" Alex asked once outside. "Well, I decided to do the same on Roger Montrose."

"Why him?"

"According to Patricia Reinholdt and Marilyn Wells-Brewer—"

"Oh, brother," Callan said, shaking his head.

"No, hear me out. My father agrees with me. There's some interesting stuff out there. How well do you know Roger?"

"Not at all. Only what I read in the papers."

"He happens to be well respected. One of the reasons for this is because he's able to get complex projects started and completed promptly."

"So what's the problem?" Callan asked.

"His reputation is wavering within the business community. Roger's not coming through on the Wyandotte."

"You mean the Wyandotte Ballroom? The renovation of that old jazz ballroom downtown is one of his projects?"

"Yes, he and another financier by the name of Chase VanderPelt."

Callan raised his eyebrows at hearing the name.

"You probably know by now that Chase is another bigwig in Indy. Does most of his business on the south side, in Greenwood, and some of those architectural wonders in Bartholomew County and French Lick. He's put cash into the Wyandotte, but the project was also heavily backed by preservationists who were not only interested in bringing the building back to its original glory but also in establishing a jazz and ragtime museum to honor Hoosier musicians of the era."

"But that's been in renovation since before I moved away. You mean they haven't made any more progress in, what, two years or more?"

"At least two years. That's my point," Alex said. "Montrose got some big money to invest in the project, including from Andrew Gammon, who not only put up some money of his own but also helped to conjure interest in others. These investors bought stock in the Wyandotte venture to help fund the renovation."

"So what happened?" Callan asked. "Once Indy has a worthy project going, it usually gets finished like gangbusters, especially historic projects like this one."

"I know. That's why investors are asking questions."

"Investors like Gammon?"

"Yes. They want the project to get going again, but Montrose says he needs more money."

"What happened to the money already invested?"

"Montrose has a reputation for honesty, Callan, so I hesitated in asking some of my colleagues to research into him further. What they found is curious. While they don't suspect embezzlement of any kind, he may have bent the rules of integrity just a bit."

"In what way?"

"It isn't overt."

"It never is," Callan replied, "starting out."

"What they suspect is the diversion of funds to other projects without transparency," Alex said. "According to my colleagues who know Montrose well, it seems that Montrose wasn't satisfied with the five or six million dollars he and VanderPelt had raised. They wanted more so that they could make the Wyandotte a truly grand wonder that would draw national, not just regional, attention. Instead of securing additional investors, he did a little investing of the funds he had on his own."

"Something risky, no doubt."

"It wouldn't appear that way on the surface. I think Roger thought they were safe deals. They were safe in other real estate projects on properties in Arizona, Florida, and Maine. For the past several months—at least the last year—Montrose and VanderPelt have invested in companies that were doing similar projects as the Wyandotte by exchanging Wyandotte stock for these projects. They made the deals so the purchasers couldn't sell the stock right away, restricting them from selling."

Callan scratched his head. "How were they doing that? Restricting the investors from being able to sell?"

"Yes, for several months, apparently. This gave Montrose enough time to invest in something else. Unfortunately, though, the venture in Arizona went belly-up. Investors in Arizona wanted their money, so Wyandotte stock was given to them for repayment."

"You'd think the investors in Arizona would be screaming at the top of their lungs, being paid with stock that wasn't any better than the project they were in."

"Oh, but that's just it," Alex said. "At the time they were

paid, Wyandotte stock was doing very well. The Wyandotte venture was still young and a hot investment. They didn't mind the exchange because it was a heck of a lot better than what they had."

"And it was lucrative for Montrose because no money left his hands," Callan added. "From what you're saying, Alex, he got cash in exchange for Wyandotte's stock."

"Exactly. And Montrose's plan would've worked if the Arizona investors were interested in a project in Indiana, but they had no interest in Indiana. They were satisfied taking the Wyandotte stock because it was good, but they wanted their money, so when the time restriction on the Wyandotte stock expired, they took what the stock was worth, draining what had been raised for the ballroom."

"I take it the Arizona project wasn't the only project that went belly-up."

"No, it wasn't. It was almost like a Ponzi scheme in real estate. The project in Maine soon followed. The project in Florida and the one in Colorado are still going strong, but they're not enough to carry what Roger and Chase gave away in Arizona and Maine."

"So what happened?"

"Andrew apparently got wind of the exchange of Wyandotte stock for these botched real estate deals."

"I think I see where this is going," Callan said, wiping some of the rain's mist from his forehead. "You think Andrew threatened to go to investors with the truth of what happened to their money? Do you think Roger killed Andrew because of it?"

"I don't know about that. I'm not going to speculate."

Callan thought for a moment, remembering his recent genealogy research on Andrew. "I think I do know. He may have been after Andrew from a different angle."

"What are you talking about?" Alex said.

"I'm into genealogy, Alex. I've traced my family history back for generations. I decided to take a look into Andrew's family tree, using some resources I have online. His family doesn't have a squeaky-clean past."

Alex's mouth gaped for a moment. "You mean Roger could've been blackmailing him?"

"Or extortion. Andrew's from Anderson. We all know that. Apparently, one of the most corrupt public officials in Illinois history was also from Anderson—a guy from back in the fifties. He was the first auditor of public accounts for Illinois who used his elected position to bilk millions of dollars from under the State's noses.

"Not only that, but because he was the auditor, no one looked over his shoulder. If he told the legislature that he needed more money to do his job, the State gave it to him. He ended up with millions of dollars and used the funds to purchase private jets and about thirty cars, including a Rolls-Royce that he had shipped from England."

"How did you find this out?"

"The man's name came up when I researched Andrew's family. Being an auditor, I recognized it. From there, it was an easy search online to find out exactly how Andrew was related."

Alex shook his head. "If I were stealing from the government, I'd never be brazen enough to buy that much stuff. It would only call attention to me."

Callan nodded. "Apparently, it didn't go unnoticed by the *Chicago Daily News*. They looked into the issue and wrote a story that earned them the Pulitzer Prize and changed the way the state of Illinois dealt with the auditor's office."

"But what does it have to do with Andrew?"

"It doesn't, not directly. That's what's sad. Andrew is a well-known financier in the Anderson and Muncie area. He's made a lot of friends in Indianapolis as a result of contributions to the universities in those cities. I think Roger played on Andrew's fear that if people in Indianapolis found out that he had embezzler blood in him, they might reconsider the financial deals they'd made with him."

"I see what you're getting at," Alex said.

"So . . . let's think," Callan said. "How can we simplify this? I mean, can Andrew's death be tied to Roger and if so, what commonalities are there with William Davisly's death, the attempt on Kate's life, the disappearance of Meredith Patterswaite, the Kimmermans' behavior, and the odd actions of Marjorie Eckert with Andrew Gammon on the night of the reception? One thing that comes to mind right off the bat is that they all have a past or are ashamed of a past in their families."

Alex nodded just as the front door opened.

Terese stepped outside, handing Callan his umbrella. "I think we should go," she said. "It's not getting any better in there, and I don't want you going back in."

"That's fine." He wasn't planning to go back. "Yes, I think Alex and I have discussed everything we need to discuss. I'm ready to go—in more ways than one."

Alex frowned.

"I'm sorry," Callan said to him. "What you and I have discovered is significant, but it's only circumstantial, and we don't have the cooperation of the Kimmermans to be able to prove anything. We need them to open up, but they won't."

"Think of it from their standpoint, Callan," Alex pleaded. "Asking them to help could destroy what they've worked so hard to develop. It could destroy their careers and any chance for normalcy."

"I know," he replied. "That's why I have no right to make their choices for them. It's up to them. That's why I believe it's in my best interest, and the best interest of everyone involved, if Terese and I take our leave and return to Vermillion immediately."

Chapter Twenty-Five

A light mist continued to dampen Callan and Terese's spirits as they drove to the carriage house. Callan turned on the radio to find a weather forecast and learned that the low-pressure system that covered Indianapolis extended north to the Great Lakes, but southern Indiana was relatively dry.

"If it's going to rain in Indy for the rest of the day, then I think I'll visit Aunt Priss down south," he said out of the blue. "Would you like to come along?"

Terese curled up her nose. "Just thinking about all those cats in her small trailer makes me sneeze and itch. Besides, I think you'll be more productive if you talk with her alone."

Callan agreed. He made some coffee and poured it into a thermal cup, then set off toward Haubstadt. The weather forecaster appeared to be right, for once. An hour south of the city, the clouds dissipated to a partly sunny sky, exposing vibrant colors from the wooded forests and hills.

His Aunt Priscilla had moved from St. Joseph to the small German American community of Haubstadt when Callan was in high school. She was his father's youngest sister and a bit of a black sheep. Outspoken and eccentric, she'd moved away due to differences in lifestyle opinions between her and the rest of the family. That was all Callan could remember. The most he knew was that she lived from trailer to trailer with men who had no more in their pockets than she did.

The trailer park where Priss lived was a few miles out of town, on a small dirt road with two lanes of old, worn-out mobile homes scattered over a couple of acres. The sunlight beaming through dotted clouds did little to brighten the landscape around her home, but Callan disregarded the surroundings, and would have disregarded the old man lying prostrate on the stone walk to the trailer, except that he blocked Callan's way.

Callan nudged the man with his foot to see if he was alive. The man grunted and told him to go away, so Callan let him alone. Before he reached the trailer, his aunt came to the door and stood with a cigarette hanging from her jowls, her gray flyaway hair wadded back with a plastic hairclip. She tittered at the sight of him, and he smiled in greeting. She'd weathered since he'd last seen her.

Her expression changed when she caught sight of the old man asleep on her doorstep. "Oh!" she uttered. "Bert! Wake up, you old fool. Callan, give him a kick."

"I already did. He told me to go away."

She shook her head. "Not enough sense to walk three trailers down. No more boyfriends for me, I tell you. He's the last one."

"I'd say he hasn't been a boy in years, Aunt Priss."

She winked before leading him into the trailer.

Callan closed the door. The inside of the trailer hadn't changed since his last visit, years ago. Clutter was his aunt's decorating motif. A velvet wall hanging needed a good dusting, an end table needed leg repair, and a seat cushion on the couch had worn through to the foam.

"You have more cats," he said, as a golden tabby with white paws gave him a walk-by leg rub.

"What? Yes, I suppose I do. I attract strays, it seems. That one is Benjamin Footstockings. You'll never get rid of him. Just shoo him away."

"Does he shoo?" Callan asked. He found most cats didn't unless threatened with bodily harm.

"Not very easily. Now, what can I get you? I made some burgoo, just the way you like it. I should have let you help me stir the pot. Oh, how you used to enjoy stirring the pot as everything simmered together."

"Yes, well, I'm not six anymore, Aunt Priss."

"Then you may not want a peanut butter and jelly sandwich with it either. I have some round steak and gravy in the fridge. Bert was too drunk to eat last night, so you can have that, if you'd prefer."

Callan sat at the small Formica table by the window under a faded floral curtain and smiled at his aunt. "No, grab your drink and come sit with me," he said. "I want to talk with you."

She extinguished her cigarette and grabbed a glass that had ice melting in a bronzy liquid. Contentment radiated from her eyes as she gazed at him. "You want to know about your great-grandmother, you said on the phone."

"And about this," he added, pulling his sister's letter from his shirt pocket.

Priss took the letter in her gnarled hand and read its contents, shaking her head and tsking with her tongue several times. When she was through, she set the letter on the table. "She doesn't mince words, does she?"

"No. And I can hear my mother's tone of voice in that letter. Can you?"

Priss smiled and winked. "We'll not talk about your mother's tone of voice. Why do you think I moved away? First, let me tell you about your great-grandmother. I know you must be curious, and even concerned, in a way."

"Yes, I am."

"You needn't be. She was as good as gold and benevolent as all get out."

"But what about that auxiliary?"

"Oh, that. Well, she started that auxiliary for the families affected by the City Coal Mine disaster one hundred years ago."

"Yes, I know, but they can have a dark side, Aunt Priss, and I don't know whether to be proud or ashamed."

Priss sat back in her chair and empathized by nodding. "I see. Well, my dear boy, you didn't give me a chance to freshen my drink before you threw me that curveball. I don't know what to tell you about that."

"Why? Don't you know?"

"Oh, yes, I know everything. A woman like me knows everything scandalous, but I don't know how much comfort what I know will be to you."

"And why is that?"

She smiled fondly. "Because I don't know where your heart is. Your heart has a lot to do with matters of family, you know."

"Yes, I'm well aware."

"Then let me begin. You do know who ran many of these women's auxiliaries back in the 1920s, don't you?"

"Yes, I have an idea. The Klan had a foothold in many of them around the state. They weren't as strong down here as they were in central Indiana, but I understand they flourished among women by creating fear, using the threat of insecurity and destitution should the menfolk become incapacitated."

"Your grandmother's auxiliary was taken over by the Klan."

Callan took a deep breath and shook his head. "That's what

I came to find out. What I hoped not to hear."

"Oh!" she exclaimed, taking his hand. "Don't be dismayed. She was kicked out of the damn thing!"

"Kicked out?" he asked surprised. "That seems unfathomable to me. Was there a scandal?"

She chuckled. "No, there doesn't have to be a scandal for someone to be kicked out of something . . . or to move to Haubstadt like me, for that matter. She just wasn't one of them."

"One of who? You mean, a Klanswoman? What about my great-grandfather?"

She patted his hand. "No, dear, he couldn't be. Oh, goodness, your grandfather could never be in the Klan."

Callan didn't understand.

"Honey, you don't have to be Black for the Klan not to like you. Your great-grandfather was born and raised in the little village of Cumback in southern Daviess County. If you remember your geography, those of German ancestry settled along the Ohio River. The French settled from Vincennes to Terre Haute. The Anabaptists settled in northern Daviess County, but in the southern part of that county is where the Morrow family lived."

"With the Irish."

She laughed. "Not just the Irish, mind you, but the Irish Catholics," she said. "The Klan didn't like Catholics any more than they liked Jews and Blacks. So you see, dear, the Klan wasn't interested in your grandfather or your grandmother. Your grandmother wasn't Irish. She was German, but she was Catholic, so she was nudged out of the auxiliary."

Callan picked up the letter and held it out to his aunt. "But my sister is so angry. What connection is my sister making with her World War II accusations? If it isn't the Klan, then what could it be?"

"Do you remember the controversy when President Reagan

visited Bitburg in the mid-1980s?"

"Yes, but very vaguely."

"He visited Kohlmeshohe Cemetery, where dozens of members of the Waffen-SS from World War II were buried. It created feelings of deep hurt and resentment by Jewish Americans that he did so. Apparently, all American servicemen remains had been removed from German soil. There was no reason for Reagan to go there. It was only at the request of Chancellor Kohl that he did so."

"And this bothered my parents? My sister said that if I cherished my father's memory, I wouldn't look into our family's past. What does Reagan's visit to Bitburg have to do with my genealogy interest?"

"Because buried at this Kohlmeshohe Cemetery is a Nazi soldier with the same maiden surname as this great-grandmother of ours who was kicked out of the City Coal Mine auxiliary."

"This soldier was a relative of ours?"

"I didn't say that," she replied guardedly. "I said he had our surname. That doesn't mean he was related, but his name was too close for comfort for your father. He was convinced we were related, and he believed that if this man at Bitburg was a Nazi, then we must be Nazis too."

"But that's ridiculous, Aunt Priss."

She reached for his hand again. "I know. I also enjoy genealogy. Contrary to what your sister believes, because of what your father believed, I researched this soldier myself. First, our family came to America sixty years before this young soldier was even born. Second, this young soldier wasn't even from the same part of Germany as our family. Third, even if this young soldier was a far-distant relative of ours, like a tenth or eleventh cousin six times removed, it makes you or me no more a Nazi than we are cousins to the pope."

"So my father was guilt-ridden with an association that wasn't his to bear."

"And if your sister wants to carry that guilt like a ball and chain around her neck then let her wallow in her shame all she wants, but I'll have nothing of it, Callan, and I suggest you don't either. Continue your genealogy and forget about that soldier in Bitburg. He was nothing more than a lost soul to us."

Callan took a deep breath.

Priss studied his face. "What are you thinking?" she asked. "I can tell you're not convinced."

"What? Oh, no, no, I agree," Callan said. "I was just thinking. Not about me, but of someone else. There's someone else who wears a ball and chain around her neck because of guilt and remorse that isn't hers to bear."

"Who is this person, dear? Someone in our family?"

Callan shook his head and sat back in his chair as Benjamin Footstockings caressed his pant leg. "No, someone else who feels guilty by association. Someone I gave up on but now wish I hadn't."

Chapter Twenty-Six

Callan returned to gray clouds and light mist when he reached the beltway that circled Indianapolis. His phone rang from his left front pants' pocket as he dodged late afternoon traffic. He ignored the call, but his phone rang incessantly. Callan stuck his fingers into his pocket as far they would go, but his phone was wedged deep within, smashed between his tight denims and the stubborn seat belt.

The ringing stopped but soon started again.

He pulled off the interstate at the nearest exit and returned the call. An excited Alex Aubert was on the other end.

"Marjorie Eckert's home is for sale," Alex said before Callan finished saying hello. "Just listed."

"Okay," Callan said blandly. "Interesting, but not relevant."

"Oh, it's very relevant," Alex countered. "Marjorie lived near Spring Mill Road since she was a child. I should know. I grew up in the neighborhood. It's the only home Marjorie's ever known. Why move now?"

"I'm sure I wouldn't know."

"Of course you do. Wouldn't you think it could have

something to do with the bureau she returned, the same bureau that Andrew Gammon bought and returned, and with Andrew's subsequent death?"

Callan paused, trying to think of any plausible reason why Alex's theory made any sense. "I'm not following you, Alex."

"I bet she feels that she has to leave town for her own safety."

"I suppose," Callan said, trying harder to believe the possibility. "Still, though . . ."

"Hear me out, Callan, please. I was able to track down Mr. Douglass. The Douglass family was one of our former neighbors."

"Does he live next door to Marjorie?"

"No, but not far from her. Old man Douglass still lives in the house. He's not in good shape, but his daughter Gabrielle is there, caring for him."

"How do you know this? Did you call her?"

"Yes, this morning. I've known her practically all my life. I made a courtesy call to see how her father was doing. We talked, and I managed to steer the conversation toward Marjorie Eckert."

"And?"

"Well, her father was in no shape to recall any facts, but Gaby sure was. She remembers plenty and had plenty to say."

"Like what?"

"I didn't get into it with her," he said. "I got the feeling it was a rather complicated story. She said she could meet us this afternoon, however."

"Why would Gabrielle know so much?"

"She and Marjorie's mother practically grew up together. It won't take but a few minutes for Gaby to tell her story. I'm not sure it will lead us anywhere, but if there's a clue as to why Marjorie may have received an extortion note and why she's now putting her house up for sale, I think she's worth a listen."

Callan sighed.

"I'll pick you up," Alex insisted. "Or meet you somewhere. We could go together."

"Yeah, yeah," Callan relented, glancing at his watch. "The day's practically shot anyway."

The two men met at the Ruins in Holliday Park on Spring Mill Road, shrouded in a gray mist. The drive was short. Alex barely had time to finish another pep talk about what he thought was the meeting's significance before they arrived.

Gabrielle Douglass greeted Alex warmly and introduced herself to Callan before turning abruptly to whisk the men to a small den. "I apologize," she said. "I left my father unattended without something to occupy his mind."

Callan entered the room behind Alex and found her father sitting placidly in a wheelchair in front of a blaring television.

"Daddy, let me get you a pillow for your back. You don't look very comfortable."

Alex bent down to shake Mr. Douglass's hand.

The old man ignored him and looked up to his daughter. "Who's he?"

"You don't remember?" Alex asked. "I'm Alex Aubert, sir. You knew my folks quite well when we lived in the neighborhood. We were neighbors once."

Mr. Douglass stared at Gabrielle blankly. "Was he the one who always ran his damn bike through my irises?"

"No, Daddy," she said, grabbing the television's remote. "Here. I've changed it to *The Rifleman*. And here's a blanket to put over your legs. I'm not turning on the heat. It's late May, Daddy." Gabrielle covered her father's legs and turned to the gentlemen. "That should keep him busy. May I offer you something to drink while we talk? I'm having a Riesling in the sunroom, but I have bourbon. Lemonade, too, if you'd prefer."

The men accepted a Maker's Mark and followed Gabrielle into the airy sunroom, where she welcomed them to sit on cushioned wicker chairs.

She sighed when she finally sat down, appearing to relish the chance to relax. Gabrielle brushed a strand of auburn hair from her face and smiled at Alex, a smile of contentment, as if seeing Alex again was a fond remembrance.

They sipped their drinks as she and Alex made small talk while Callan took the time to study their host. Gabrielle was stylishly dressed, adorned in fine accessories, a bit too overdressed for an afternoon of caring for an elderly parent. He surmised that Alex thought so too, given the attention he gave to the three bracelets she wore.

"Oh, these?" she said, embarrassed. Gabrielle twisted the bracelets several times. "They were my mother's. You remember my mother, Alex. This ring was hers also. I can't part with them." She glanced at the men's faces. "I wear them to bed, in fact. You've heard of the robberies in the area lately, surely."

Alex said he had.

"Well, I can't be too careful. Some of the neighbors have been robbed here in Crow's Nest. It's vain, I know, but until they catch the intruders, I'll wear whatever's in my jewelry box if I have to." She released her hold on the bracelets. "But you're here to talk about the Eckert house, aren't you? That's what you said over the phone, anyway, Alex."

"Yes, I find it strange that Marjorie wants to leave after all these years."

Gabrielle leaned forward. "Yes, isn't it? But you know as well as I do that the women in the Eckert family aren't known for their discreet behavior."

"No, I don't know what you mean at all."

"Doesn't it ring a bell?"

Alex shook his head.

"Perhaps you were too young," she replied, twisting the stem of her wineglass. "You're about Marjorie's age, aren't you?"

"She's a bit older, but not by much."

Gabrielle smiled. "Ah, yes, I remember, and so does Daddy. He was right, you know. You were the one who used to ride your bike through his irises."

"Thank you for defending me."

"I had to say something to keep him from chasing you with his walker. Anyway, I'm more of Marjorie's mother's age. Her mother's name was Helene. It's not important if you don't remember her. Helene and I were friends, or we were supposed to be, until she stole my boyfriend and became pregnant by him."

Callan tried to hide a grin behind his highball glass as he took a sip.

"Does our tight, little community amuse you, Callan?" Gabrielle asked, grinning also.

"Everyone seems to know everyone here."

"Yes, we do," she said. "We always have."

Alex leaned forward. "Then I'm getting the feeling that Helene's past could have some relevance to Marjorie's actions, if everyone knows everyone that well."

"Oh, I believe the past has a great deal to do with Marjorie's behavior," she replied coyly. "Do you remember your folks talking about the Marjorie Cromwell murder when you were just a tike? It was a murder right here on Spring Mill Road."

"You mean the heiress of the grocery chain? But that was so long ago."

"It feels like yesterday to those of us still here, Alex. The Cromwells lived nearby. Mr. Cromwell passed away and his wife, Marjorie, lived in that big stone home all alone."

"She became a recluse, I remember my mother saying."

"Yes, and every eccentric. She trusted no one, especially corporations, even though she was the heiress to one."

"I think I read about the murder when *The Star* did a 'Remember Back' article a few years ago," Callan said. "It's still unsolved, isn't it?"

"To the authorities," Gabrielle replied, twisting the stem of her glass again.

"What does that mean?"

She chuckled and set her glass on the wicker table in front of her. "I believe one has to be a moron not to figure the murder out. How it's escaped the authorities all these years is beyond me."

"It started with an embezzlement, if I remember correctly," Callan said.

"That's putting it mildly. Yes, Marjorie Cromwell had funds embezzled from her trust account by a bank employee. After that, she didn't trust banks. She began hiding thousands of dollars in her home, stuffing whatever valuables she could behind her plaster walls and then having contractors patch them up. She wrapped twenty-dollar bills in aluminum foil and tagged them as gifts for Jesus."

Callan turned to Alex and smiled. "Should you ever feel compelled to do the same, Alex, the name is Cal."

"No, thanks. I'm pretty sure that's what got her killed," Alex replied. He turned to Gabrielle. "So how does Marjorie Eckert's mother, Helene, fit into all of this? She lived in the neighborhood, but what connection did she have with Mrs. Cromwell?"

"Helene Eckert was a young, unmarried woman who visited Mrs. Cromwell at her home," Gabrielle explained. "Mrs. Cromwell was fond of her and mentored her. They made these aluminum packages for Jesus together. I was fond of Helene too. She was a very likable girl."

"Why do I feel there's a *but* coming on?"

Gabrielle smirked. "Because she also had a bit of a dark side to her and was quite self-centered. As Helene got older, she started to run with an unsavory crowd. She schmoozed my boyfriend and became pregnant. I was furious, and Mrs. Cromwell didn't approve, of course, but Helene stayed in the woman's good graces by naming the baby after her."

"Ah, the Marjorie Eckert we know," Callan said.

"That's right. As time went on, Helene became concerned for Mrs. Cromwell and tried to coax her into putting her money back into financial institutions."

"I may be cynical," Callan said, "but I wonder if Helene really tried doing that, or if it was a roundabout way to divert the money to herself."

"I'd say you and I are of like minds. Long story short is that before Helene was successful in getting Mrs. Cromwell's cash back into a bank, Mrs. Cromwell was murdered. Thousands were taken, but thousands were left alone in the house, untouched."

"How uncanny," Alex said, "especially since the murder remains unsolved to this day."

Callan took a deep breath. "So, Gabrielle, I'm trying to think of plausible suspects. Considering we're of like minds, I'm sure you've thought of plausible suspects as well."

She laughed heartily. "I have to tell you that I've read all of the detectives' hypotheses and the newspapers' editorial comments, but they didn't know Helene Eckert like I knew her. Yes, I've given the list considerable thought, and in my mind, it all boils down to the work of two men."

Callan leaned closer. "Who were they?"

"Contractors Mrs. Cromwell hired to work on her house."

"To patch the walls?"

"I'm sure it was to do some patching, but I bet they did more tearing down than building up. You see, they were hired at

Helene's recommendation."

"Need I guess who one of the contractors was?"

Gabrielle picked up her wineglass and encouraged Callan to do so.

"Marjorie's father, who was Helene's lover and your former boyfriend," he said.

"Jackpot."

The men took deep breaths simultaneously.

"Is that who the authorities suspect as well?" Callan asked.

"Yes, but they're unable to prove it enough to bring him and his accomplice to trial. The bottom line is that thousands of dollars were unaccounted for after the murder. I believe the assumption is that Helene Eckert took the money, with the help of her lover boy, and hid it somewhere."

"Somewhere her daughter, Marjorie, could find upon her death," Callan said. "Someone may be threatening Marjorie because they believe she has the money somewhere she's not telling."

"That's what I think, but who knows for sure? I've talked to the police numerous times over the years, to no avail. I'm not sure they know what to believe out of me."

"Why is that?"

Gabrielle Douglass frowned. "I believe they've always wondered if what I had to say about the murder was a bona fide theory of the crime or an unfounded accusation by a scorned lover against the woman she loathed."

Callan and Alex left the house with Gabrielle's last comment on their minds.

"What do you think?" Callan asked as he climbed into the car.

"Like Gaby said, who could know for sure?"

"True," Callan replied thoughtfully. "But one thing is for

certain. Gabrielle said the Cromwell murder is in her mind as if it was yesterday. It's apparently in someone else's mind as if it was yesterday too, and worth extorting Marjorie Eckert for."

Chapter
Twenty-Seven

Lauren clutched her windbreaker as she reached for an umbrella through the bucket seats of her car. The umbrella was wedged under the front passenger seat, caught on its sliding mechanism. She tugged gently but gave up. She didn't need the umbrella, she decided. She'd simply lift the windbreaker over her head to ward off the elements and run to the building.

That didn't fare well, however. The light mist seemed to find its way through the open caverns of her windbreaker. It wasn't cold, necessarily, but she felt cold. The dreariness of the day, the disappointment of the canceled race, the horror of Andrew Gammon's murder, and the shock of Kate's attack sent ominous chills through her body.

Hearing that Callan wasn't going to help her family anymore caused her to shiver the most. She felt it was now up to her to get to the bottom of what was going on between Open Arms and Cottage Gallery. Sugar Bob Lane was devoid of traffic. It was just as well Open Arms was closed. No one would've been in the village to shop. It was also the perfect time to peruse the records she'd pulled for Callan the night they saw Chuck Cordry taking boxes from his workshop.

Lauren paid little attention to the charcoal van parked by the door leading to Open Arm's back room until she tried to unlock the door and found it already unlocked. She entered cautiously but lowered her guard when she saw Ronnie coming out of Chuck's workshop with two boxes in his arms, favoring his injured hand.

"What are you doing here?" she asked.

"What are you?" he responded, stunned to see her.

She looked around the room. "Where's Jeremy?"

Ronnie continued his trek through the alley door to the charcoal van.

"I asked you a question," Lauren said, following him to the door.

"Jeremy's not here."

Lauren watched him return to the back room to retrieve more boxes. "Why not? Ronnie, what's wrong? Something's not right. What are you doing?"

"Don't, Lauren," the young man replied. "Just leave me alone. I've got work to do for Eddie. You know if I don't get it done, he'll have my ass."

"I know, but . . . I don't understand."

"You don't need to understand. Look, it's better that you don't."

"Don't say that, Ronnie," she said. "If you only knew what I'm going through, you wouldn't say that to me. Tell me what you're doing. Tell me why Jeremy isn't here. I've got to know."

Ronnie sat his load of boxes on the floor and ran fingers through his wispy hair. "Okay." He hesitated for a moment. "It's obvious you don't know yet. It's not a secret, and I'll tell you this one thing, but promise me you won't ask me any questions about it, okay?" When she nodded, he took a step toward her and said, "Jeremy was arrested last night in Crow's Nest. He's in deep trouble, and I'm gonna be too, if anyone finds out."

"Arrested? What was he doing in Crow's Nest? Why would you be in trouble?"

"Nothing. I told you. No questions. Keep your mouth shut." Ronnie picked up the boxes and hurried to the van.

Lauren stepped away, not sure what to do.

The young man returned empty-handed and grabbed the doorknob. "I mean it, Lauren. The less you know, the better. I'm outta here. Go home. I mean it." Ronnie slammed the door shut.

Lauren heard the van start. Music blared from its speakers, fading as Ronnie drove away. She stood in the large room and turned 360 degrees. Nothing looked familiar to her anymore. Everything she knew and enjoyed about working at Open Arms had changed. She didn't even recognize it.

She stared at the open doorway to Chuck's workshop. In his haste to leave the building, Ronnie had forgotten to close and lock the door. She walked toward it as the rain pelted harder on the roof then tapered to a methodical drumming.

Lauren remembered being in the workshop only a handful of times. It was just as she remembered—cold and oily, but organized. She didn't know what she expected to learn, but Ronnie's jaunts from the workshop to the van compelled her to look. An unfinished chair sat atop a sawhorse. A desk with its drawers pulled from their ranks and set on top of each other stood next to it. The lower right drawer was still intact inside the desk. She pulled on the drawer to look inside, but it didn't budge.

Lauren turned her attention to a set of cabinets hung above a workbench. One cabinet was ajar. She inched it open to find it full of jars, boxes, and other gadgets that Chuck used to fix the small appliances that lined the bench below. Underneath the workbench were more cabinets. She bent down and opened one and found the shelves within empty. Other cabinets were empty as well. Had Ronnie cleared them all?

Lauren straightened and looked at the row of can openers, blenders, and waffle irons that lined the back of a workbench. They all seemed so pointless. She picked up a metal toaster to examine why Chuck would bother to fix the used relic. *Clang!* The bottom suddenly fell out. Springs, sockets, nuts, bolts, screws, and heating elements fell to the floor, scattering on the concrete in a million different directions.

She stood, overcome by surprise, holding the upper part of the toaster. Her eyes darted across the floor to assess the damage. "Oh, shit," she said under her breath.

"Oh, shit is right," a man said.

Lauren jerked up and saw Eddie Lee standing in the doorway.

"You might want to make yourself a pot of coffee," he said. His eyes glared; his face reddened with anger. "Looks like you're going to be here awhile, cleaning up." Eddie took two steps forward, kicking a sprocket at her with the steel toe of his boot. "Then I want you to gather your things and get the hell out of here . . . for good."

Chapter Twenty-Eight

The rain was falling harder by the time Alex dropped Callan off at his car, following the men's discussion with Gabrielle Douglass. His phone rang on the seat beside him, and a glance at the display told him it was Terese. She could wait until he reached the carriage house. He wasn't that far away.

The phone rang again, however. He pulled off to the side of the road and answered it.

"Are you on your way home?" she asked urgently.

"Not far. Why? What's up?"

"Beth Kimmerman called. She'd like to speak with you. She'll meet you downtown."

Callan grimaced. "Aw, Terese, I'm really tired. Can it wait until tomorrow?"

"I don't think so," she replied. "Beth sounded . . . Well, she sounded desperate."

"She should sound desperate," Callan said unforgivingly. "She has a desperate situation on her hands that she's doing nothing about."

"Yes, I know, but I think something has happened to make

her feel even more so. I could tell in her voice."

He sighed and told Terese to tell Beth he'd meet her at the Bierhalle in the Athenaeum. "I'll be there in about fifteen."

The Athenaeum, formerly *das Deutches Haus*, was a massive nineteenth-century redbrick and stone building on the eastern edge of downtown Indianapolis, just north of the Lockerbie Square district. Colorful banners hung from the large hall that scaled two to three stories high. The hearty wood tables and monumental stone walls combined with the rich aroma of wiener schnitzel and red cabbage comforted Callan with their familiarity. He loved the camaraderie of the patrons, the bands that could transform any song into a polka, and the boundless energy that came from good food, music, friends, and laughter.

He chose a table away from a robust crowd of out-of-town revelers so he could hear what Beth had to say and find out what was so urgent.

"I'd sit alone too, if I looked as glum-faced as you do tonight," said a voice from behind. "How are you, man? It's been a long time. I haven't seen you for ages."

Callan looked up to see Wayne, his longtime bartender friend from his life in Indy. He greeted him heartily and made small talk to catch up.

"Just so happens I have a Warsteiner Verum with your name on it," Wayne said.

"Then keep 'em comin', buddy. Gonna be one of those evenings, I'm afraid."

When Wayne left, Callan's gaze wandered about the old hall, taking in the aura that he'd missed since moving from the city. It wasn't long before his eyes landed on a small table for two off to one side of the room, recognizing the two diners. The woman fidgeted with a napkin and adjusted her suit jacket frequently. The older gentleman sat stoically, refined and reserved, seemingly content, watching her demeanor. Callan hadn't expected, in his wildest thoughts, to see Marilyn Wells-Brewer and Chase VanderPelt sitting together just tables away.

Wayne approached and set a cold pilsener on the table. "There you go, man. Now, you sure you're okay? You want a couple of soft pretzels or sauerkraut balls to sop up those tears you got?"

Callan smiled. "No, Wayne, just tired. But tell me something. Do you see that couple over there? Are they your table?"

"Yeah, man, but if I 'spect to make the rent this month on what they're drinkin', I'm going to be hard-pressed."

"What do you mean?"

"They're not drinkin' much." Wayne stuck his pinky in the air. "They're trying to impress each other with their sophistication and refinery."

Callan smirked and glanced at the couple again. "What are their conversations about?"

"Oh, I dunno, man. I don't get paid to stand around and eavesdrop. Haven't paid that much attention."

"But you have an idea," Callan said. He reached into his pants' pocket, pulled out a twenty, and slid it toward the waiter.

"Money," Wayne said. "Her kind? His kind? It's always about money. I didn't get the full scoop, but it sounds like she needs some cash real fast-like. I heard her say she's run out of options."

"Did he respond?"

"Not around me. He was very careful not to speak details in front of me." Wayne pointed to Callan's Verum. "Do you want your check when you're finished with that?"

"No, I'm meeting someone in a few minutes."

"An imaginary someone?"

Callan smiled. "No, a real someone. My mood's improved." Wayne started to leave, but Callan called him back. "No pretzels,

Wayne, but how about a *Kaseplatte* with pumpernickel. Include an order of cheese curds. I want my guest to feel welcomed. I don't want her to think I'm not open to reconciliation."

Wayne nodded and pushed the twenty back toward Callan before he walked away.

~

The massive wood door at the entrance opened, and Beth Kimmerman walked in, lowering an umbrella to her side and primping her hair with her fingertips. Callan side-glanced at the table Chase VanderPelt and Marilyn Wells-Brewer had left just minutes before, wishing Beth had arrived earlier.

Beth extended her hand and offered her appreciation for Callan taking the time to meet her.

"My pleasure," he said. "No reason why I shouldn't."

"Alex tells me you're returning to Vermillion," she replied, setting her things on a vacant chair beside them.

"Yes, we'll head back tomorrow afternoon sometime. It depends on if they're able to run the race. I'd like to stay in town if they do."

Beth smiled, as if she understood but didn't care. "I apologize for being rude to you this morning. I didn't mean or intend to be. It's just, well, it was just that I thought you were going to implicate me in Kate's attack. I would never do such a thing to Kate, you know."

"You had me wrong," Callan said. "I didn't say you attacked Kate. I said you were in the office with her last night."

"But the implication was there. If you didn't believe I attacked her, then what difference did it make that I was in her office?"

"You may have seen or noticed something or someone unusual that could provide a clue as to what happened."

"Oh, but I didn't," Beth replied. "I was so angry at Kate that I didn't notice anything out of the ordinary. Even my conversation with her is a blur to me now."

"Then you *were* in Kate's office last night, as I suspected."

"Of course I was," she said indignantly. "You know I was. You figured it out when you saw the amulet."

The two sat quietly. Wayne arrived with the cheese platter and bread. Beth asked if there was fresh mint behind the bar, and when Wayne said there was, she ordered a julep, and he left again. Callan and Beth sat staring at each other without comment or expression, until polka music started in the back. They recognized the tune as one of the city's favorites.

"I saw the amulet on the floor beside Kate," Callan said, raising his voice, knowing the lyrics would get louder. "When I saw it fall from the end table at your house this morning, I knew there was only one way it could've gotten there. Gabe snuck into the office and retrieved it without my knowledge before the police arrived. He had no reason to take it unless he was trying to protect the one person he suspected of having been in the office in the first place. What I can't figure out is why you went to her office at that time of night. Was it to return the amulet?"

"No," Beth replied after considerable thought. "I had it when I went to the office, but I didn't go there specifically to return it. I only went there to confront her about it."

"Why then? It was so late."

"I wasn't going to sleep with that thing on my nightstand, Callan," she said. "Kate simply couldn't understand why I didn't want that keepsake in my possession. She reminded me that it was mine, that it had to be mine, based on the inscription on the back of the medallion. I handed it to her and said the same thing I said to Lauren at the reception when I saw her wearing that diamond and onyx pendant."

"And what was that?"

"I said not everything given in family should be treasured," Beth replied.

The volume of the song increased suddenly. When it did, the crowd took each other by the arms and danced in a wild fashion, swinging each other in circles, spilling beer, and slipping on the fallen brew.

"Why would Kate think that this amulet had been in your family before?" Callan asked above the revelry.

"Kate and I go back many years. Our mothers were good friends. We've been friends since we were young, lost track of our friendship in high school, then rekindled it in college. The amulet she found came into her possession as part of an estate collection that Eddie came across. It belonged to a longtime friend of both of our families. That's what Kate said, anyway. That she found the amulet among things at Open Arms."

Callan gave her a dirty look.

"Oh, now, it's not what you think," Beth replied harshly. "She didn't take the amulet from Open Arms. I'm sure she paid for it."

"Why did she want it for you in the first place?"

"Because it had my great-grandmother's initial engraved on the back."

"Kate knew this?"

"Certainly. We were good friends. My grandmother and I had the same initial; her name was Evelyn, mine is Elizabeth. She knew this and knew that on any valuable piece of jewelry my great-grandfather bought for my grandmother, he had her initial engraved on the back, if there was room."

"And did this pendant Lauren wore to the reception have your great-grandmother's initial engraved on the back also?"

"No, but it wouldn't have."

"Why not?" Callan asked. "Didn't it belong to your great-grandmother?"

Beth hesitated. "Yes, but my great-grandfather didn't purchase the pendant for her."

Callan hesitated to think. "So there was no reason for him to have it engraved," he said. "Now, I get it."

"Do you?" she challenged.

"Yes, I believe I do," he said respectfully. "Although the amulet belonged to your great-grandmother, the pendant Lauren wore was given to your great-grandmother by someone other than your great-grandfather. It belonged to your great-grandmother's friend, Madge Oberholtzer, didn't it? Madge gave it to her."

Beth sat upright with astonishment.

Wayne approached with Beth's julep and set it in front of her. "Is there anything else?" he asked. Callan said no. "I see you two aren't dancing," Wayne commented, turning to Beth. "I don't blame you. He's not much of a polka dancer."

"No, he isn't," Beth replied, looking directly at Callan. "A good polka dancer needs to know how to dance in circles. Callan doesn't dance in circles."

Wayne departed, and Beth asked, "How do you know about my grandmother's friendship with Madge Oberholtzer?"

"And association with D. C. Stephenson," Callan added. "Don't forget about that notorious madman. It was easy. Gabe told me all about it."

She sat back in her chair, appearing relieved. "I'm glad it was Gabe who told you and not through some anonymous letter you received. It was my mistake, going to see Kate in the first place. I thought she gave me the amulet as a covert way of letting me know she knew I was being blackmailed. Do you know about the letters and the demands I've received for payment?"

Callan said he had a good idea but knew none of the details.

Beth told him about the letters and the bureaus she and Barry purchased and returned.

"I thought Kate was behind them," Beth said. "She knew about my family's history and how it could ruin my political career if voters knew. I was sure she knew something about William Davisly, Andrew Gammon, and that Eckert woman who bought the rosette desk. I thought for sure she had used what she knew against them . . . and me. We argued. If she wasn't the person behind the demand notes, then I suspected she was an accomplice, or at least knew the perpetrator, and allowed the ruse to happen."

"But why would she allow it?"

"To avoid the embarrassment of a horrible conspiracy within her own business and Open Arms."

Callan popped a couple of cheese curds into his mouth and thought as he chased them down with his beer.

"There's a couple of other things you should know too," Beth said. "Lauren was fired from her job today, and Jeremy Forrest, one of the boys who assists Eddie in the back room, was arrested by the police last night in Crow's Nest for home invasion and theft." Beth shook her head and suddenly looked as if she was going to throw up. "This is becoming unbearable, Callan. This is becoming totally intolerable."

"But it isn't the time to give up," he said, leaning forward to urge her to hang on.

She glared at him critically. "But isn't that what you've done?"

Callan returned the glare. "Given up? Me? Oh, no. Don't characterize your unwillingness to cooperate with me as a sign that I've surrendered to this whole sordid mess. If that's where this conversation is going, attacking my integrity when I've done nothing but have concern for you and your family's welfare, then consider this conversation over, Mrs. Kimmerman." Callan pushed his chair back from the table and stood. "I will not be manipulated in the same way you allow the person who is blackmailing you to do."

"Oh, sit down," Beth replied angrily. "My only motive for not being transparent has been discretion."

"But you can't do it on your own, Beth. This isn't a situation—and never has been a situation—where you can handle it on your own. How many murders, suicides, disappearances, attacks, thefts, conspiracies, and God knows what else must occur before your pride and values take a back seat to the welfare of your own family?"

"I understand that now," she said remorsefully.

"I don't think you do," Callan said, pulling his billfold out of his pocket to lay cash on the table. "I really don't think you do."

"What do you mean?"

A sudden chill went up Callan's spine as he thought about what he did mean by the statement. Knowledge of the letters, thefts, arrests, and murders converged into one thought he couldn't deny. He sat back down. "Did you say Lauren was fired today?"

"Yes, Eddie caught her in Chuck's workshop. She lifted a toaster or something and the inner workings fell to the floor. He was angry."

"That's it? That's why she was fired?"

Beth paused. "That's the reason Eddie gave her, but Lauren also said that he accused her of prying in places she had no business to pry."

"Like Chuck's workshop."

"I suppose."

Callan popped another curd into his mouth as he thought. "There's more than toasters and sprockets in that workshop,

Beth, don't you think?"

"No, I don't follow you."

"I believe Kate realized something illegal was going on at Open Arms and confronted Eddie the night she was attacked. Now she's fighting for her life." Callan stood again. "We have to go," he said.

"Why? What's the hurry?" she asked, reaching for her things.

Callan paused, staring at Beth's ashen face. "If I'm right, Lauren could be in the same danger Kate was in, if Eddie believes she now knows what Kate knew."

"What do they know?"

He wished he had the answer. It would resolve why he believed more lives were in danger.

Chapter Twenty-Nine

"Do you have a car?" Callan asked Beth as they stepped under the canopy outside the entrance.

"No, I came with Barry." She raised her umbrella. "He was meeting colleagues at the Columbia Club. Why?"

Callan didn't answer. He led Beth across the street to his car. Evening had fully set in, causing the streetlights to turn on automatically. Their beams danced in the puddles as raindrops fell.

"Where's Lauren now?" Callan asked.

"At home at Gabe's house. But I want my car first. If there may be trouble, I want to bring her back to our house with me."

Beth said little and asked nothing as they climbed into his car and headed north from downtown. She stared through the car window at the rain-soaked lawns of the Butler-Tarkington district but remained quiet. "I suppose William Davisly was technically murdered, wasn't he?" she asked eventually.

Callan emerged from a trance. *Murder? Was William Davisly murdered?*

"I mean, I suppose he had no choice," Beth explained in a

sorrowful voice. "Poor William. I suppose there was no other way out for him but to kill or be killed, and he chose to kill."

"But he killed himself," Callan replied.

"Precisely, because he didn't know who to kill. So he kills the man with the wretched past that no one knew so that the man everyone admired and respected could live on. Do you see what I mean? I'm sure William thought of himself as two men—one with an evil past and one he wanted to be remembered. He killed the evil one."

Callan nodded reluctantly. He understood but didn't know where Beth was going with the conversation. "Are you saying that you've thought about suicide as well?"

"No, not physically, but professionally, I have. I've thought a lot lately about giving up all that I've worked for, to preserve what I've done."

"But you can't think like that, Beth."

"It's hard not to, when the situation is as desperate as it is."

"This, too, shall pass," he said, trying to reassure and comfort her.

"But it won't," she countered. "It hasn't yet. This is the third letter I've received so far. The first payment wasn't sufficient, nor was the second. They didn't pass, Callan. This, too, shall *not* pass."

"What are you afraid of, Beth?" Callan asked. "It's a fair question."

"I know it is, but you have it wrong. I'm not afraid of anything. I'm angry."

Callan turned and saw the expression on her face in the dim green light from the dashboard and in the reflection of passing automobile headlights. He sensed her posture tense and heard her breathing become more pronounced.

"I don't . . ." she began to say. "I don't know how to reconcile how I feel about the Madge Oberholtzer situation with what my great-grandmother did about it."

"What do you mean?"

"She didn't do enough, Cal. My great-grandmother was this woman's friend. She knew Madge was dying, but she didn't do anything upon returning from Hammond to help the poor woman get medical help or receive justice. She left that entirely to her parents."

"You don't know that's true," Callan said adamantly. "You have no idea what your great-grandmother did or didn't do."

He softened his voice. "I'm not saying you shouldn't be angry, Beth, but I believe some of your feelings are misdirected. You have a right to dislike and be angry about your great-grandparents' past, but it seems you're also angry at Madge Oberholtzer for dragging your great-grandmother into the situation and giving her that pendant."

"I'm not angry at a stupid pendant."

"No, but you're angry at what it represents. You're angry at your grandmother or your mother for giving it to Lauren as a gift. You're even angry at your own daughter for choosing to wear the pendant at a silly reception. The anger is misguided, Beth. That's what I want you to think about."

Callan turned to look at her expression again. Her face had softened. The passing headlights now glistened off tears in the corners of her eyes.

"You're right about the pendant," she said, "and I'm angry it was given to her as a gift. It's not Lauren's fault, but I don't know what to do."

"What you have to do is the hardest thing for humans to do. You have to look at the anger for what it is . . . and forgive . . . or it will destroy any joy you have in this life."

Several seconds of silence passed, punctuated by passing

traffic, before Beth said, "But it's hard to forgive with these letters looming over my head. Each letter I receive makes me even angrier."

"Then tackle the situation of the letters first. Tell me about their timing again."

Beth stammered as if she didn't know where to begin. "I received the first letter before William committed suicide—or was murdered, depending on how you want to look at it. The second letter came shortly after his death. They were all transacted, using the same method—a secret compartment in an antique desk. The letter received at the reception demanded more money."

"Okay, stop there. I'm going to be brutally honest with you. When you paid the first letter, there was a hope that the demands would stop. They didn't. In fact, they escalated. The demands will never stop if you continue to give in. You have to work with law enforcement on this, Beth. They're experts at handling such issues."

"And risk disclosure to the public? That would surely ruin me, Callan."

"Or risk the public finding out later that you're a public servant open to being blackmailed. That doesn't invoke public trust either, you know."

Beth lowered her head. "Oh, I know. We talked about that this morning."

"You and Barry?"

"Yes, Barry used to feel the same way you do, before he came up with a plan."

Callan stared at her, alarmed to hear that Barry had devised a plan without the use of proper authorities.

"You won't be happy with us," Beth said. "We paid the third demand."

Callan didn't say a word. He wanted to blurt an expletive and ask what they were thinking, but he didn't. He couldn't without the conversation turning into a full-blown row.

"Before I met you at the Athenaeum, Barry and I went to Cottage Gallery. Gabe helped us pick out a bureau—one with a compartment much like the other ones we used."

"And you put the money in the compartment?"

"Not all they requested, though. I wasn't honest when I said that Barry dropped me off to meet colleagues at the Columbia Club. He went back to Broad Ripple."

"To return the bureau to Open Arms, I presume," Callan said.

"Yes. He's probably returned it by now."

"I wonder if Eddie will be there to see that it's been returned. If so, then I suspect Eddie will be busy reaping the reward you gave him."

"Then you're not worried about Lauren?"

"Yes, I'm still worried," Callan confided, "but I'm not as panic-stricken as I was before. Although I don't like what you've done, and I don't understand why Barry had a change of heart, I think it'll keep Eddie preoccupied so that Lauren isn't his main concern."

"Then you believe Eddie has something to do with the letters in the bureaus?"

"Don't you?" he asked.

"I don't know," she said. "I don't know what to believe. But you'll still come with me to see Lauren, won't you?"

Callan shrugged. "I'm not sure that's necessary anymore. Like I said, I think Eddie'll be more interested in getting the money out of the desk than pursuing Lauren over what she might know. Get your car and drive to her place. Bring her back if you're more comfortable doing so. Call me if you need anything."

Callan pulled into the Kimmermans' driveway and cut the

engine. The headlights remained on but eventually shut off automatically. They sat in silence as the rain diminished to a light mist on the windshield.

"Are you okay?" he asked eventually.

"I would be if I knew you'd stay in town to help us," she replied.

Callan took a deep breath to hold in his thoughts. "Let Lauren know I'm still in town," he replied noncommittally.

Beth stared into the darkness. "Thank—" She suddenly stiffened. "What was that?" she exclaimed, eyes wide with fear.

Callan shook his head. "I didn't see anything." He tried to focus on the house through the streaking windshield, but it was almost impossible to do so.

"Did you see that?" she whispered.

"See what? Where? I don't see anything."

Beth couldn't speak. Callan sensed her choking up with fear. She pointed toward the house.

This time, Callan saw movement—a shadow slithering from the large spruce tree to the corner of the house, behind the hedges.

Chapter Thirty

Heart pounding, Callan peered through the darkness, his gaze darting from one end of the yard to the other.

"They're coming after us!" Beth screamed. "There! By the side of the house—someone's there!"

"Where's your cell phone?" Callan asked as he reached for the ignition.

Beth grabbed her purse from the floor of the car. In her haste, some of its contents fell from the opening and scattered on the floor. She rummaged through her purse between glances at the house.

Callan looked up as he turned the ignition key, and this time, he clearly saw a man dressed in dark clothing moving toward them. The intruder seemed unafraid of detection, interested only in reaching the car.

"There he is!" Beth screamed.

"Stay low and find the phone!" Callan yelled. "We gotta get out of here."

"Oh, God, I don't know where it is. I can't find it!"

Callan put the car in reverse and dug his fingers into his

front pants' pocket. He could feel his phone with his fingertips, but the seatbelt was wrapped securely around his torso. The belt wedged the phone tightly in his pocket. "Look on the floor, Beth!" he yelled in exasperation. "Find it!"

As Callan maneuvered, tires squealing, onto the street, the figure ran across the yard toward them. "Did you find it?" Callan asked.

Beth scratched at the carpet on the floorboard and eventually raised her arm, phone finally clutched in her hand. "I've got it!"

"Call the police!" Cal said, speeding through the neighborhood. He glanced behind him but no longer saw shadows, and no car followed. "Then call Lauren and tell her to take cover until we get there. Make it clear she's not to answer the door for any reason."

"Yes, yes," Beth responded.

"And call Barry and Gabe!"

Beth punched Lauren's number on the display, but nothing happened. The screen remained black. "Oh, no!" she cried.

"What?" Callan yelled. "What is it?"

"It's dead!"

Callan slowed the car and unbuckled his seatbelt, lifting his rear off the seat so he could remove his phone from his pocket while they kept moving. "Here, use mine. I've got juice."

Beth punched Lauren's number, but the call went to voice mail. Beth ended the call and tried again. Nothing.

"Does she often not answer?" Callan asked.

"Sometimes. She was so disheartened when I left her this afternoon that I doubt she wants to talk to anyone. She's never been fired before, and getting fired from a place where I'm the board chair, well, she was in an awful state, Callan. Where are we going?"

"To get Lauren. Is Gabe at the house with her?"

"No, he's with Barry."

"Then we'll go straight to their house."

Callan maneuvered through the streets to the small, isolated neighborhood where Gabe and Lauren lived. The car's headlights shone against low, white patches of mist and fog from the nearby river. The illumination cast an eerie glow as they crossed the bridge into the community. The street was wooded, quiet, and narrow among older, comfortable homes. Every house looked the same in the fog.

"Pull over," Beth said. "I think this is it."

Callan turned off the ignition and opened the car door. The dome light above them revealed a scared, uneasy expression on Beth's face.

"What's the matter?" he asked.

Beth shook her head. "It looks like the house, Callan, but I don't remember the steps being like that. I don't know anymore. It looks different in the fog. I just don't remember the steps."

"And I don't have her address in my phone to be sure. Call her again."

Beth did so but again, there was no answer.

Callan looked carefully at the 1920s-style bungalow and determined there were a dozen such homes in the neighborhood. He was familiar with Rocky Ripple. To preserve its sanctity and independence, only two bridges segregated the town's environmental and political elements from Indianapolis, but its uniqueness meant little to him in an enclave of sameness shrouded in fog.

"I say we move on," Beth said, growing more anxious. "I'm sure this is the street, Callan, but not the house."

Callan did as he was directed and inched up the street. Soon there were no more bungalows. The road made an easy turn close to the river's edge, where homes sat on stilts to escape the winter and springtime floods. His heart pounded faster and the gnawing pang in his stomach grew stronger as they entered another fog bank. He bit his lower lip, creeping through the thickness.

"Do you believe it was Eddie?" Beth asked, her voice cracking.

"You mean back at your house?" The question surprised him.

"And at Kate's," she added.

Callan tried to soften the alarm in his voice. "I don't know who else it could be. From what Gabe and I saw through the windows of Open Arms when Kate was there, it only makes sense."

"And Lauren? Do you really believe Lauren's in danger too?"

"Beth," he said, taking a deep breath to prevent blurting what he thought was obvious. "She was just fired. You and I were just attacked. I don't think the two are a coincidence, but just to be sure, we have to stay ahead of whoever it is and get Lauren out of Gabe's house."

"At least there's one thing going for us tonight. He won't be able to see any easier through this fog than we can."

Callan gave her a nod. She was right. He looked at the fog differently and welcomed its disguise.

Bungalows appeared again on the left side of the street, and Beth pointed to one. "There, Callan, it's that house, the first one. See? No steps off the street, only by the porch. This is it, I'm sure."

Callan pulled alongside the curb opposite the house and looked at the dimly lit home through the misty air. There were no apparent signs of activity except for a reading lamp shining through the sheers in the front living room and a small light illuminating from an upstairs dormer.

He opened the car door and turned to Beth. "I want you to come with me," he said. "I want you to speak first. You're her mother. Tell her she needs to come with us."

Beth nodded. The two exited the car quickly and ran up the path. A handcrafted bird-in-hand sign hung on the front door with the words *Welcome, Friends*, an obvious addition by Lauren to Gabe's bachelor residence. This night of all nights, he hoped Lauren didn't mean it.

Callan knocked firmly on the metal screen door that was locked from the inside. There was no answer, so the two pounded together, desperate for Lauren to respond.

Groggy and alarmed, she opened the door and unlocked the screen with bewildered clumsiness. The sound of a steel guitar from a speaker inside the bungalow fit the mood expressed by her body language. She appeared to have been crying and, based on her disheveled clothing and tangled hair, had been melancholy for most of the day. Lauren tried to present a shallow smile to cover what was obvious, but it didn't last long.

"You have to come with us, Lauren," her mother said, pushing herself through the door past Lauren's shaken frame. "Please, you need to come with us now. We'll explain in the car."

Lauren didn't move. She looked at Callan for confirmation.

"Please, Lauren," he said calmly. "We need you to come now."

"What's this about?" she asked. "You're frightening me."

"It's about what happened to you today at Open Arms," Beth explained. "It's about your termination. It's about Jeremy's arrest. It's about Eddie . . . and Kate. It's about all of it. We'll explain in the car."

Lauren didn't seem to doubt what her mother said, but she stood in the living room appearing petrified of going anywhere.

"It's true," Callan said.

Beth touched her daughter's arm. "Callan and I were out this evening. When we returned home, we surprised a man in dark clothing lurking about our house. We left immediately to warn you. Please come with us."

"Stop!" she cried, placing the palms of her hands over her ears. She began to tremble.

Beth wrapped her arms around her daughter.

Callan walked to a corner table and turned off the light he'd seen through the front window. He wanted to make the house appear as if no one was home. He looked through the sheers to see if there were any shadowy figures.

"We need to get out of here," Beth said softly to Lauren. "We need to go to the police and tell them what we know and what's been happening to us. Will you come with us?"

"But what will I tell them?" Lauren asked.

Callan ran out of patience. "We'll talk about it along the way," he replied urgently. "Right now, we need to do as your mother said and get out of here."

"Okay," Lauren conceded. "Let me get my purse . . . and my shoes. I don't have any shoes."

"Where are they?" Beth asked. "I'll help you find them."

Callan remembered kicking something that was sticking out from under the end table when he turned off the lamp. He took a second look. "Here it is," he said, reaching for the handles of a small leather handbag. "Is this what you're looking for?"

"Yes," Lauren replied, but changed her mind after seeing its silhouette in the darkness. "No, it doesn't have my cell phone in it. The phone's in my other purse, in the back bedroom."

"Get it," Callan said. "We could use it. I'm going to turn that light off upstairs."

Beth followed her daughter into the bedroom.

Callan had just placed his foot on the staircase when glass suddenly shattered from the kitchen. *The back door!* Callan hurried to the back bedroom to join the women.

"We're going to be fine," he whispered, crouching with the two women beneath the side of the bed away from the door.

"We have to stay calm and think. First, did you find your shoes and the purse with your cell phone?"

"No," Lauren answered. "They must be upstairs or in the kitchen."

"Get your phone, Callan!" Beth whispered. "Hurry! Call the police."

Callan patted both pants' pockets with his hands. "I don't have it," he said, wondering why he didn't. He suddenly remembered. "I gave my phone to you."

"Oh, no!" Beth cried. "I was so rushed, I left it in the car."

More glass shattered and the sound of someone trying to reach through the broken pane to find a doorknob made the realization of their imminent danger more vivid and terrifying.

Callan's eyes darted about the room but saw only a window and what appeared to be two closet doors. "That window is our best option," he said.

"No, the door," Lauren whispered.

Callan squinted through the darkness. "What door? The one in the corner? The closet?"

"It's not a closet. It leads to the back of the house, past the basement stairs to the back door in the kitchen. We can go outside or down into the basement and try to crawl out of a basement window from there."

"Let's go out the back door. It's our safest bet."

The intruder started to move. Glass cracked under the soles of their boots as they walked across the floor. The intruder's footsteps entered the living room, sounding slow and methodical. They stopped suddenly and paused.

Callan held his breath, exhausting what energy he had. His left leg had started to twitch involuntarily from holding his crouching position for so long, but he dared not move to relieve it.

As if the intruder sensed their energy and presence, they began to walk again toward the small hallway to the back bedroom.

Callan could feel Lauren beside him, wanting to bolt out the back. He touched her so that she'd stay in place and remain quiet. They crouched closer to the bed, careful not to make any sound against the bare floorboards.

The upstairs light cast a man's elongated shadow down the hall. The towering shadow approached slowly, then stopped suddenly at the doorway. Callan moved his head slightly to get a glimpse of the intruder's position and try to sense his intentions. His eyes widened when he saw the man's boots—muddy, wet, and discolored. He recognized them immediately. They belonged to Eddie Lee.

Dread consumed Callan. *If we could just get to the door.*

Eddie's feet shifted slightly, giving hope that he was contemplating leaving the room to go upstairs, but they remained stationary for several more seconds.

Callan could almost hear him breathing. He was sure Eddie was listening for them as much as they were listening for him. Every second of silence meant that something would soon give way to freedom or demise.

Just when Callan was sure he could smell his own fear permeating from his skin, Eddie's boots moved slowly back down the hall, returned to the living room and made their way to the staircase. The stairs creaked and moaned with every upward motion until Callan believed he had reached the top.

"Let's go," he whispered. It was their chance, their only chance. Callan jumped up and helped Beth and Lauren to their feet. He motioned for Lauren to lead the way through the door to the kitchen and outside to freedom.

Beth stood but hesitated to move. "What if someone's out

there?" she asked, frightened.

"I don't care," he said and pulled her toward the door.

Lauren led, in stocking feet, through the corner door to the back door of the kitchen. She stepped outside through the broken glass and stumbled onto the wet grass below. She got up and tried to run but fell again in agony.

Callan and Beth leaped off the porch.

"She's cut bad," Beth said.

Callan didn't hesitate to reach toward the grass to scoop Lauren into his arms. Eddie was between them and the car, so he asked Lauren, "Is there a place we can go?"

"Yes," Lauren said, panting. "Gabe's got a friend around the corner. He should be home."

They ran. Fueled by fear and adrenaline, they darted through and around clumps of peony bushes, trees, and other landscaping to avoid detection by their intruder.

Gabe's friend was standing outside, emptying a bag of trash into the garbage can as the trio staggered from the rear of his house. The young man saw the urgency on their faces and the blood on Lauren's stockings. He asked only a few pointed questions before leading them into his home through the back door and hurrying to a medicine cabinet for first aid supplies.

Callan reached for the wall phone and called 911.

Beth grabbed the receiver when he was done and called Barry and Gabe. As she held the receiver in her hand after the calls were completed, she leaned against the wall and sobbed, overcome with emotion and the realization of what they'd been through.

Callan took the receiver carefully from her hand and replaced it on the hook.

She lifted her head and stared into his face, wiping a tear from her cheek. Unable to face him just yet, she turned to focus into the darkness of an adjacent room. Facing away from him and anything he had to say to her, she stumbled slowly to a side chair in the dark living room and dropped onto its seat cushion.

"Please leave me alone," she said. "Please. There's nothing that can be said right now."

Chapter
Thirty-One

Callan woke the next morning under a wad of covers and bedsheets, evidence that his sleep was as restless as he remembered. The sun shone brightly through the window of the carriage house. A change of weather, maybe a change of luck, he hoped. He looked at the time. It was midmorning. He'd slept longer than he thought.

Terese was not beside him. He scratched his scruffy head and walked clumsily into the kitchenette, where she stood by the sink.

"Do you have the dexterity to pour it yourself?" she asked, pointing to the coffee pot. She took a better look at him. "Better not. Go sit down, and I'll hand it to you."

Callan plopped into a love sofa and looked at the dancing shadows the trees made upon the panes of glass.

"They're running the race today," she said, handing him a cup. "It'll be on the radio soon."

He yawned. Any other Indianapolis 500 race day, Callan would've jumped to his feet to tune the radio to the race that was blacked out annually by television in the viewing area. The grill would've been smoldering with brats dunked in Warsteiner. As it was, however, there was none of that. No macaroni salad was freshly prepared, nor corn husked and ready for roasting. There wasn't even a tin trough iced down and filled with cold beer and pop. No checkered banners, no humming of "Back Home Again in Indiana," and no lawn chairs strewn hastily about the yard. Any other race day, Callan would've pitched a fit if this hadn't come to fruition by eleven o'clock.

Today, he laid his head against the sofa and took a deep breath of relief that the long weekend was almost over.

"They arrested Eddie Lee," Terese said, sitting next to him.

"Where did they find him?" he asked, closing his eyes.

"Not at Gabe's house as you thought they would. The news this morning said he was arrested without incident at his home."

Callan took another deep breath but didn't say anything.

"The early morning news on TV had a tape of him being brought into the county jail," she added. "His attorney made a statement. Are you listening to me?"

"Yeah, I'm listening. My eyes don't have to be open to hear."

"His attorney said they arrested the wrong man," she said.

Callan shook his head.

"His attorney says Eddie is innocent of all charges."

"He would, wouldn't he? What else could he say?"

"Are you sure the man in Lauren's house was Eddie Lee?" she asked.

Callan opened his eyes and turned his head toward her. "You're asking *me*?"

She nodded.

"I should know, Terese. I was there. I saw his boots."

"Okay," she said, rising from the sofa and walking back to the kitchenette. "But—"

Callan sat up. "But what?"

"Did you see his face? Eddie's attorney said he has an ironclad alibi."

Callan tried to recall. He remembered the dark room, crouching beside the bed. He saw the boots, Eddie's boots. *But his face?* He hit the couch with his fist. "No more questions! I don't care anymore. I've had it, Terese, I really have. After the race, we're heading back to Vermillion. I'm tired, and I don't care."

Terese poured herself some coffee and leaned on the counter. "You received a phone call while you were in bed."

Her serious tone made him turn toward her.

"Some lady said you'd want to see her. She didn't leave her name. She wasn't comfortable doing so."

"Then what makes her think I'm comfortable seeing her?"

"I don't know, but I think you should."

"Did she leave a message of any kind?"

"Nothing that made sense to me," Terese said. "She said you'd understand. I told her we were renting a small place in SoBro. She said she'd drive this way to save you any trouble."

He waved his hands. "Not here at the carriage house."

"No, not here. Somewhere close by." Terese hesitated a moment before adding, "I said you'd meet with her."

Callan frowned. "And I suppose you told her that I'd meet her sooner than later, meaning I better get my ass in gear to go talk with this mysterious woman."

Terese smiled as if she was grateful that he understood.

He approached her and gave her a kiss.

"Now you better get going," she insisted. "It sounded critical. Not urgent, but critical. Pants, though, please."

~

Even though he didn't have any idea who would be there to meet him, Callan spotted the woman immediately upon entering the café. An older woman, perhaps late sixties, early seventies, she looked at him and smiled. Callan couldn't tell if the wrinkles etched into her face below her cheek bones were from hard work, a smoking habit, or poor genetics. Based on the silky richness of her professionally colored and styled hair, she appeared to have money. Her clothing was modest but tasteful, and he presumed she was used to appearing in public well-presented. She even looked familiar to him, in a way, but he couldn't place where he might have seen her.

"Mr. Morrow, so good of you to come on such short notice. I heard everything on the news. I'm sure you're exhausted. I must apologize for my secrecy over the phone to your wife, but I hope you understand my need for discretion until I was able to meet with you in person."

"Quite frankly, I don't understand," Callan replied, "but it is what it is. I'm here. Who are you?"

"Someone who was afraid to come out from hiding until I heard the news of Mr. Lee's arrest last night. I'm someone who has had strong suspicions about Mr. Lee but nothing to substantiate those suspicions, and I'm someone who has something to give to you, Mr. Morrow, and I want to give it to you right away."

The woman reached inside a handbag that matched the shawl around her shoulders. She pulled out an envelope and slid it across the table toward him. "Oh, how rude of me. Would you like some coffee?" She motioned for a waiter.

The waiter came right away.

"Coffee for the gentleman, sir," she said. "Do you take cream, Mr. Morrow? Yes, with cream, and how about an order of those wonderful fried biscuits you serve with apple butter? Such a treat this time of year. And, oh, a refill on my coffee, please. Thank you."

Callan used the time the woman had with the waiter to open the envelope wrapped tightly in three rubber bands. The flap to the envelope had not been sealed. He lifted the flap just enough to get a glimpse of the envelope's contents. What he saw shocked him.

"It should all be there, Mr. Morrow."

"How much is here?"

"Twenty-five thousand dollars, if I've counted correctly."

"What the h—"

"You should count it as well," she said. "You're an auditor. That's why I called you this morning first thing after I heard about the arrest. I wanted to be diligent in that regard, but I couldn't, oh, I just couldn't reveal that I had the money before I knew it would be safe to do so. You understand, don't you?"

Callan leaned toward the woman. Her eyes begged for leniency and mercy. "Who . . . are . . . you?" he asked again.

The woman looked shocked. "Well, I thought it became obvious when I gave you the money."

"No, it didn't. Please tell me who you are."

The woman stared at him with a curious gaze. "You're quite serious, aren't you?"

He didn't answer.

"Oh, dear." She blinked several times. "Oh, dear, then you haven't missed the money at all, have you?"

Callan pursed his lips but said nothing.

"Oh, dear. Oh, my goodness. Oh, Mr. Morrow, I may have done everyone a great injustice, and I fear that I was in much greater danger than I thought I was. I may have placed others in danger as well. It's quite shocking to find this out, you see. This money may have been the reason Mr. Gammon was killed, if no one knew it was missing. They probably thought he took the money and killed him for it. Oh, Mr. Morrow, I may have even been responsible for the attack on Ms. O'Neal, don't you think? They may have thought she took the money."

The waiter arrived with fresh coffee and a plate of Hoosier fried biscuits.

Callan didn't reach for his coffee. Instead, he pushed the envelope of money closer to the woman. "You're avoiding telling me your identity, ma'am. I'm afraid I'm going to have to leave." He started to rise.

"I'm Meredith Patterswaite, for goodness' sake," she replied indignantly. "I thought it should be quite evident."

Callan nodded and reached for a hot biscuit, letting it drop hastily onto the plate in front of him as he rubbed the scalding heat from his fingertips. "I'm not a mind reader, but I did wonder," he said. "The money threw me, though. Where did you get it?"

"From a returned desk," she said. "Quite by accident, I might add."

"The rosette desk?"

"Yes, it belongs to me. I found the money the afternoon Mr. Gammon returned it."

"Then you'll have to tell me the sequence of events, Ms. Patterswaite, if you would. I apologize if I was impatient and impertinent with you moments ago."

"I completely understand, Mr. Morrow. I'm rather impatient and impertinent with myself right now, not realizing the danger I placed myself and . . . oh, my goodness, you don't suppose I'm responsible for the death of Andrew Gammon, do you?"

"Did you have a knife on the canal greenway?" Callan asked.

"I beg your pardon?"

"I asked if you had a knife, stabbed Andrew Gammon, and then ran like hell."

"Why, no, of course not. Goodness, Mr. Morrow."

"Then how are you responsible?"

Ms. Patterswaite didn't respond.

"Let's start with the sequence of events," Callan said.

Meredith shook her head and stared down at the small bistro table. "I can hardly enjoy these biscuits now," she muttered.

"You will once you tell me the sequence of events."

"Yes, well, the sequence is quite clear to me, really. You see, I bought the rosette desk at an estate sale in New Castle. It was a beautiful piece, and I loved it dearly, but it needed some work, so I asked Kate if I could hire the services of the men at Open Arms to do what needed to be done to restore it."

"Restore or embellish?"

"What?" Meredith appeared genuinely confused. "Oh, when asked of me in that way, I guess I should've said embellish."

"With rosettes?"

"Yes, I had the rosettes added. They did the work, and I placed the desk on the show floor of Cottage Gallery where it commanded a handsome price and was sold right away."

"Can you tell me who the customer was?" Callan asked.

"Why, yes. It was Marjorie Eckert."

"What happened after she bought it?"

"She returned it almost immediately with no explanation."

"Then it happened again? I mean, the desk was purchased and returned again?"

Meredith nodded and leaned closer to him. "The same desk, the same scenario. Only, this time to Andrew Gammon. He was very knowledgeable about fine antiques, or so I had heard. I was quite flattered that he was interested in the rosette desk."

"But he returned it as well."

"Yes, Gabe thought I should know. Kate wouldn't hear me out when I complained, so I wanted to take the desk from the premises. Gabe told me it was returned to Open Arms. Now, why such furniture is purchased at Cottage Gallery and returned to Open Arms is beyond me. I didn't like the arrangement at all, and I went to Open Arms to claim the desk."

"Was anyone at Open Arms when you went to get the desk?" Callan asked as he grabbed another biscuit and lathered a thick layer of apple butter on top.

"Lauren was there," Meredith said thoughtfully, "and an odd young man in the back who wouldn't look me in the eyes when he spoke."

"No one of management?"

She shook her head. "Are the biscuits good, Mr. Morrow?"

Callan replied with his mouth full. "Yes, they are quite good. You should have one."

Meredith continued to shake her head. "No, I don't believe I could, knowing what I know now. It would seem wrong for me to enjoy such a thing with Mr. Gammon dead and poor Kate O'Neal lying in a hospital bed, fighting for her life."

Callan swallowed. "Yeah, I know what you mean, but tell me . . . How did you come to all of this money, and what do you expect me to do with it?"

"I was hoping you would turn it over to the authorities for me, Mr. Morrow, or at least accompany me to the police station. I want you to verify that I turned the money over to you, an auditor, in its entirety—all twenty-five thousand dollars of it."

"How did you get it?"

She took a sip of her coffee and grimaced as if it had gotten too cool for her. "As I mentioned, I took the desk from Open Arms back to my shop near the canal with the help of a gentleman friend of mine. I wondered what was wrong with it, why customers were returning it so quickly. I thought it might be damaged, so I looked it over rather closely. I had my gentleman friend look it over too. He said, 'What's this?' I said, 'What's what? I don't know what you're talking about.' He pointed out a button that was in the middle drawer. When the button was depressed, it released a panel inside the right hand drawer that revealed a compartment I didn't know was there. Well, there it was, Mr. Morrow, a secret compartment. I had no idea that the desk had such a compartment."

"It wasn't pointed out to you at the estate sale in New Castle?"

"No, I swear I didn't know. In fact, I would swear on a Bible that it wasn't there at all when I purchased it. In fact, if I had to guess, I'd say it was added by Mr. Lee when I took it in to have the minor repairs done on it before I set it on the sales floor at the gallery."

"Interesting," Callan commented, "because that's exactly what Gabe Kimmerman pointed out to me before it was returned to Open Arms. But we didn't find any money."

"I took the money, then felt guilty for not properly terminating my consignment contract with Kate, so I had my gentleman friend return the desk to Cottage Gallery before the reception."

"And then you went into hiding?"

Meredith nodded timidly. "I was scared. Kate kept calling me the night of the reception, asking me to attend, but I couldn't go. I just couldn't go. Do you blame me?"

"But you did let someone know you were still in town, didn't you? Didn't someone try to see you while the commotion regarding Mr. Gammon was occurring on the canal?"

Meredith sat back in her seat, stunned. "How do you know about that?"

Callan smiled. "It was just a hunch, because I saw someone crossing the bridge over the canal while people were gathering on the greenway. While curious onlookers gravitated toward the crime scene, there was one person who was repelling away.

I knew your shop wasn't far from the point where I saw this person crossing the bridge. After hearing your story just now, it was a wild hunch that the person on the bridge was on her way to see you."

Meredith lowered her head.

"Who was the woman? Patricia Reinholdt?"

She lifted her head abruptly. "I don't know anyone by that name. No, it was someone else, but I couldn't see clearly from the window who it was. I can't give you a good description, unfortunately, but she looked young."

"In what way?"

"I couldn't see that well, but I say she was young simply by her mannerisms and the way she carried herself."

"So, what did you do?"

"I refused to open the door. I asked her to leave, and she did so on her own. I didn't have to threaten her by calling the police or anything. It was as if she slithered back into the fog along the canal from where she came—back into the cursed mist that descended upon the village."

"Yes, that's how it looked to me, too."

"It really frightened me," Meredith said convincingly. "I couldn't take a chance that the person would come back, perhaps with a heavy hitter. It crossed my mind the woman may have suspected I had the money in my possession. So I packed a few things in a bag and left for my cabin on Lake Maxinkuckee near Culver. I have a place near the military academy. It's secluded. I thought it would be a better place to be."

"And you say you didn't mention a word to anyone about the money."

"Definitely not. Only to you just now."

"And you took the money with you to Maxinkuckee?"

"Yes," she said, "but I didn't spend a penny. I stuffed it in an old Amish trunk I purchased years ago in Nappanee until I returned to town this morning. I want you to count it all, Mr. Morrow. It's all there."

"I don't doubt that it is, Ms. Patterswaite."

"But you look like you're in doubt. You're thinking about something. If you're thinking about any impropriety on my part, Mr. Morrow, I assure you that taking the money was my only lapse of good judgment."

"On the contrary, I'm not thinking about that at all," Callan said. "I'm wondering who's missing the money."

Chapter Thirty-Two

"Are the shops closed today?" Callan asked Gabe over their cell phones. He could hear an announcer from a radio in the background.

"Well, yes, the race is running. There's no point in opening during the race. Besides, Kate's still unconscious, Eddie's been arrested, Lauren's been fired, Chuck is fishing, and Amy is too terrified to come to work. It's just me."

"Chuck is fishing?"

"That's what I said."

"With all that's going on, he decides to go fishing?"

"I don't know, Cal," Gabe said impatiently. "Memorial weekend, I guess. He left right after the reception to go up north to the lakes. He's probably not heard about everything that's happened yet, but let's face it, he's not exactly our employee of the month. Fishing will always take precedence."

"I don't believe that."

"Cal, I'm tired. What is it you want?"

"Are you at either one of the stores?" Callan asked.

"You're kidding, right? Memorial Day, the race is on, it's

sunny outside. I'm drinking beer and eating brats. Why would I be at the stores?"

"Then you're not going to like what I'm going to ask," Callan said.

~

Callan screeched to a halt in the alley outside the back door of Open Arms. A disgruntled Gabe Kimmerman was already there, unable to look him in the eyes. Callan offered an apology.

"I still don't get why you've asked me here," Gabe said in response.

"I told you over the phone."

"Yes, forgive me, but when you called, Bellefontino and two Brazilian drivers were battling it out on Turn Four. I had both ears tuned to something slightly more entertaining and less disturbing."

"I understand, but we'll be able to tie down Eddie's involvement with the blackmailing scheme that's been perpetrated on your family, William Davisly, Andrew Gammon, Marjorie Eckert, and others. I thought of this idea as I was talking to Meredith Patterswaite this morning."

Gabe looked intrigued and allowed Callan to continue uninterrupted.

"I don't suppose you knew that Meredith had spent the past few days at her cottage on Maxinkuckee."

"Not at all. What does she have to do with why I'm here and not enjoying the race in my lawn chair?"

Callan told Gabe briefly about Meredith finding money stashed in the secret compartment of the rosette desk just before she brought it back to the gallery, and before Gabe found the secret compartments himself. He described Meredith's suspicions about Eddie extorting money from Andrew and Marjorie and her fear that taking the money out of the rosette desk may have escalated the violence against Andrew and Kate. He lifted his index in the air to make a point. "Your mother told me yesterday that you and your father decided to pay the demand from the letter your father received at the reception."

"Yes, it's true. We knew you wouldn't approve."

"Never mind about that. What piece of furniture did you put the money into?"

"It was an early nineteenth-century oak bureau, kind of a George III, if I'm not mistaken."

"Did you let Eddie know that it was returned?" Callan asked.

"Yes, I made certain of it."

"When did you let him know?"

"Late yesterday afternoon. I can tell you exactly because I remember it was just about the time my father left to take my mother downtown to see you."

"Was Eddie in the store with you?"

Gabe shook his head.

"Good," Callan said, smiling.

"How is that so good?" Gabe asked. "He was waiting in ambush. My mother and sister were almost killed with you last night, Callan. I hardly find any good in that."

"But it means," Callan explained, "that if you and your father were placing demand money in the bureau at the time Eddie was waiting in ambush, and then Eddie was arrested shortly after the attack at your house—"

"—the money should still be in the bureau," Gabe said.

"Bingo."

Gabe turned to unlock the door and enter the back room of Open Arms. He strode to an oak bureau with raised bracket feet, plain but solid and beveled inward to provide character and depth. Gabe opened its slanted cover, revealing a rich interior with several smaller drawers of various sizes.

Callan watched as Gabe felt the interior of the bureau. He heard a click in one of the drawers as if a panel had loosened, ready to be removed.

Gabe appeared hopeful and eager to retrieve the envelope that he'd placed in the bureau himself. Callan leaned forward to get a better look through the open drawers. As Gabe reached inside, the contented look he had moments before faded into an expression of dazed confusion and doubt. He reached further, patting the drawer firmly with the palm of his hand and tapping his fingertips to the end and sides of the drawer as if he'd missed something.

"Is there another compartment?" Callan asked.

"No, this is the compartment I put the money in. The money's gone—but it can't be."

"Are you sure you have the right bureau?"

Gabe turned abruptly and scowled. "Yes, I'm sure. I'm not an idiot. I'm not in the habit of placing twenty-five thousand dollars in a bureau and not remembering where I put it. This is it. This is the damn bureau, but the money's not here. It's gone!" Gabe stood and ran the palms of his hands desperately through the hair on his scalp. "Son of a bitch," he blurted.

Callan stepped forward and looked for himself, reaching inside the compartment and feeling the perimeter to see if there was any possible way that an envelope with that much cash could have fallen into the drawer below or into the back of the bureau. He opened each of the other drawers, feeling the top, sides, and bottom of each drawer. Eventually, he stood beside Gabe and stared at the ornate bureau with its drawers hanging out in disarray.

"Oh my God, Callan, how can this be?" Gabe said, shaking

his head.

Callan wondered. He was so sure of the timing of the events of the night before that Eddie had no way of getting into Open Arms to retrieve the money before waiting in the shadows of the Kimmerman home.

"Unless," he said, raising a finger, "he did have time after he broke into your house and before he was arrested at his house. Terese told me he wasn't arrested at the scene but at his home."

Gabe thought hard but shook his head. "I can't see it, Cal, but then who's to know? I mean, we were obviously wrong about the money still being here. We could be wrong about the timing of events and when Eddie got the money."

"You're right, though, it doesn't make sense," Callan said, refuting his own supposition. "If that were the case, Eddie would've had to have been one cool dude last night with the ability to think logically and clearly amid utter chaos. Could someone else have been here?"

"Yeah, Amy," Gabe said. "Amy was the only one here."

Callan turned abruptly. "Amy? What was she doing here?"

"The same reason as Lauren. Amy said Lauren's firing upset her deeply. She said she came to finish the job for Lauren, to find out what Lauren came to find out before she got caught. Amy doesn't like Eddie any better than the rest of us."

"What about Chuck? Where's he fishing?"

"Lake Tippecanoe."

"That's an hour and a half from here. Is he still there?"

"As far as I know."

"It's feasible that Chuck could drive from Lake Tippy, do the dirty work we thought Eddie did, then return to the lake." He narrowed his eyes at Gabe. "Are you sure this is the bureau?"

Gabe threw his hands in the air. "Yes! What does it take to convince you? If you don't believe me, go ahead, look around.

There's nothing else like that bureau in here."

"Not even in the workshop?"

"Go look," Gabe said with frustration. "I'm not going to answer that. Look for yourself."

Not out of doubt, but out of curiosity, Callan walked into the workshop, turned on a light, and perused Chuck's unfinished projects. Everything on the counters and sawhorse looked pretty much the same as the last time he was in the room.

Callan accidentally kicked a ball of twine that had fallen to the floor. It unraveled as it rolled, leaving an easy trail to where it finally stopped. Callan would've ordinarily left the twine where it was, but he wanted everything to be the same when he left as when he arrived. He followed the string until he reached the ball at the corner of a table. He picked it up and began to wrap the twine tightly around the ball, careful to use the pattern already in place. As he looked down to focus on his work, his eyes drifted to two familiar objects under the table, pushed back out of the way to be unnoticed. Callan set the twine ball on the table and picked up one of the objects.

"You find something?" Gabe asked, entering the workshop.

Callan held out a tan work boot for Gabe to see. Dried mud from a recent rain was on the soles of the boot. Discoloration from having been recently wet was also evident. He looked at Gabe who was concentrating on the boot.

"These were under the table," Callan said. "You recognize them?"

"Yeah, they look like Eddie's."

"I saw them last night as I peered out from under the bed," he said. "I saw these exact boots. They were muddy and wet just like this."

He turned the boot over and looked closely into the boot's grooves on the bottom. Callan took a finger and broke a piece of mud from inside the groove. He rubbed his fingers together. The mud was sharp and abrasive. Callan was sure it would cut him if he continued.

"What is it?" Gabe asked.

"Glass. Slivers of glass embedded into the sole."

"But how did Eddie's boots make it back . . . ?" Gabe said as he thought. "And why would they . . . ?"

"Exactly," Callan replied. "If Eddie was arrested and took his boots off when he got home before he was arrested, then why didn't the police see the boots last night, and how did they get into Chuck's workshop this morning?" Callan thought some more. "Tell me something. Does Chuck own a pair of boots like these?"

"Sure," Gabe said reluctantly. "We all do. Eddie swears by them. He tells us all to get a pair in case something drops on our feet. But those boots can't belong to Chuck."

"Why not?"

"He'd have taken them to Tippy," Gabe said. "He wears them everywhere. I'm surprised he wasn't in them when he came to the reception. He's the kind of guy who'd sleep in them."

"He's not wearing them now, I'm afraid."

"You think it was Chuck that tried to kill you last night? Oh, my God, Callan, Eddie was arrested based on your account of the events. Are you saying you're not convinced it was Eddie last night?"

"No, I'm saying I'm not convinced it was Chuck either. You say he wears these things everywhere? If so, that can't be true, because he isn't wearing them right now fishing on Lake Tippecanoe this weekend. They're in my hand."

Gabe leaned against a table and lowered his head. "I don't know what to think. I don't know what to do."

"There's a way to find out for sure if it's Chuck," Callan said with resolve, "but we need another letter to go out in a bureau and be returned."

Gabe looked up. His eyes were wide with thought.

"What is it?" Callan asked.

"There was a sale," Gabe replied. "An odd, very similar sale."

"To someone on the board, perhaps?" Callan asked, thinking back to who he'd seen sitting at a table in the Athenaeum. "Would it have been to Marilyn Wells-Brewer?"

Gabe gave him a look of astonishment.

"Tell me about it."

"It was crazy," Gabe said. "Cole Brewer called me yesterday, insisting that I open the gallery so that he could purchase something."

"Eddie or Chuck must've sent the Brewers a letter before all the fiasco broke out. I bet my next paycheck the item you sold to Cole will be coming back like all the others."

"But it hasn't yet," Gabe said.

"Then make it happen. Give Cole or Marilyn a call and tell them you're making a routine customer service call to see if they're pleased with their purchase. If they say they're not satisfied, tell them they must return it tonight because another customer wants it. Hopefully, they'll think you're calling on behalf of the blackmailers."

"Will I get arrested?"

"No, we're going to the police right after this. I want them involved. Then I want you to call Chuck and tell him you've had another return. Ask if he'll be back from the holiday weekend this evening."

"That would raise suspicion," Gabe said. "I'm not the one who normally calls about a return."

"Who does?"

"Lauren or Amy from the sales counter."

Callan thought for a moment "Lauren is out, so call Amy and see if she'll call Chuck."

"Okay," Gabe said. "Then what? What's next?"

"We wait," Callan replied smugly. "We wait for Chuck to return from his fishing trip."

Chapter Thirty-Three

"Is there a Lisa?" Callan asked Gabe, referring to Lisa Stohler, Open Arm's part-time bookkeeper.

They crouched in the darkness behind the dumpsters at Open Arms. Lights in the alley weren't positioned in a manner for him to see clearly, but Callan suspected by the young man's silence that he was assessing the question. It was a legitimate question. Lisa was the one person in the mystery he hadn't met, seen, or heard from yet. He wondered if it was Lisa, whoever she was, who they were waiting for in the darkness.

"Of course there's a Lisa," Gabe whispered.

"I've never seen her," Callan said. "We've been dealing with high-profile transactions, yet I've never seen or talked with the bookkeeper in charge of it all."

His comment was met with silence once again. He prompted Gabe for an answer.

"She wasn't in charge of it all," Gabe said. "Lisa wasn't in charge of anything."

"Didn't she do the books? If not, then who is she? Where is she? What does she do?"

Gabe sighed loud enough for Callan to hear. "Just leave her out of this, Cal," he said pleadingly. "She's not a threat, because she's nothing to the organizations. I do what Lisa is getting paid to do. Don't tell Kate that. She keeps Lisa around in title only because she doesn't have the heart to let her go."

"I'm not trying to be cruel or anything, but I'm stooped behind a dumpster on a rocky drive, wondering if we've brought the authorities here on a wrong assumption."

"Is that what you think?" Gabe asked.

Callan didn't know anymore. He'd have preferred to be inside with the police to see it all play out, not as a matter of interest, but to see the scam in real-time. There was no doubt in Callan's mind that Chuck didn't do the extortions alone. He believed Eddie was involved too. He may have been mistaken about Eddie's attempted assault on his and the Kimmerman women's lives the night before, but he believed it was only a matter of time before Eddie would be indicted.

"I have to say it would surprise me more than anybody if it's Lisa who hobbles into the building to get the Brewers' cash," Gabe said, still whispering. "The poor dear is about seventy-eight years old. She has a hard time getting around. She's as coarse as burlap underwear and has a gruffness that can make a bulldog shy away. Lisa's accuracy has gotten worse over the past year because she can't see worth squat, and she can't hear a cannon boom from the next room, but she's been with Kate for many years in different capacities. It's one of the most compassionate things Kate has ever done, keeping Lisa on the payroll."

"I still don't know what to think about Kate's lack of transparency though," Callan said. "I wish she'd been more up-front with us from the beginning. Instead, she had this image she had to maintain. Look where it got her and look where we are."

Gabe sighed again.

"What is it? Did I say something about Kate you don't agree with?"

"No," Gabe replied. "I wish she was more genuine myself. No, I'm thinking about something else—the boots we found in Chuck's workshop. It doesn't make sense that they were there, does it?"

This time it was Callan who sighed. "No, I've thought a lot about that as well. Knowing Chuck, he wouldn't leave the boots behind while he went fishing."

"Do you think they were planted?"

Callan said that he believed they were. "But I'm not ready to divulge what I think happened."

"Why not?"

Callan turned toward Gabe who waited eagerly for a response. "Because I haven't a clue," Callan replied, keeping his voice suitably low.

After a half-hour of silence, Callan tapped Gabe on the shoulder and pointed to a shadowy figure making its way down the alley toward Open Arms. The hooded shadow seemed to slither along the sides of buildings and fences that hugged the alley. As the figure approached, Callan was sure, from his size and the way he walked, that it was a man.

The man turned his head back to where he came from, as if to check if he'd been followed. He stopped and pulled what appeared to be a cell phone from his pocket. The man punched some buttons on the phone, said a few words that Callan couldn't hear, then replaced the phone in his pocket. He made one final observation of his surroundings before walking briskly to the back door of Open Arms.

The man reached into his pocket again—this time, to retrieve a set of keys. He seemed to know exactly which key fit the lock and opened the door with ease, then entered the building slowly.

Callan and Gabe waited patiently. They couldn't see any movement from the windows. No lights turned on, and they heard no sounds. The deafening quiet was almost unbearable. Each minute ticked slowly away.

Surely, Callan thought, the intruder had found the bureau he was after by now. He had to find the secret compartment within the drawer though, and that could take a while. It would also be dark. Callan remembered how difficult it was to find the drawer during the day, let alone how difficult it would be now in complete darkness.

Once that task was accomplished, however, the intruder would search for the latch or lever that would unlock the specific compartment in which the Brewers had placed their money. Callan imagined an intense but exhilarating look upon the man's face, a rush of satisfying adrenaline pulsing through his veins, sweat beading on his forehead beneath his hood. He probably also changed his crouched position a few times and looked and felt around the bureau at different angles to be sure he found the right lever. Soon, a faint smile would cross his face, and after three or four seconds, he'd hear a sound from the drawer that he was near the treasure.

Of course, the authorities would hear and see the action unfold from their hidden positions inside the back room, but Callan was sure the intruder wouldn't be fazed by their obscured presence as he opened the final drawer, containing a loose panel that would be easy to remove.

Grabbing the envelope and pulling it from the compartment would be the man's last step—and the easiest and most gratifying. Callan imagined he did it with ease and found it as satisfying as when he took the money from all the others.

Then the police would make their move.

Callan and Gabe heard scuffling and a muffled commanding

voice say, "Drop any weapons and lie face down on the floor!"

The man did as he was told as far as Callan could tell. He imagined someone spread eagled on the cold cement floor.

Lights flicked on from the back room. Gabe stood to get a better view through the windows.

"Get down!" a directive came from nearby.

Callan pulled him back to the ground. "It's not over, Gabe. It isn't safe yet."

They stayed in position away from the central point of action to be sure they didn't interfere with law enforcement protocol. It wasn't until the figure was escorted from the premises, heavily guarded, that Callan and Gabe were able to approach.

Callan strode ahead of Gabe, studying the figure in dark clothing. He could see that the man was broad and masculine. His hood had been pulled back, revealing short hair, and when he turned, Callan was taken aback by the man's facial features. This man had a scraggly goatee.

"Is it Chuck?" Gabe asked.

Callan didn't answer. Chuck didn't have a goatee. He continued forward, reaching the first of the law enforcement officials who blocked a direct view of the man by standing in a circle around him. Callan stood between two of the officers to get a good look at the intruder.

A policeman flicked a flashlight on, illuminating the man's face.

Callan's mouth gaped.

Another officer pulled the man's wallet from a back pocket and searched for identification. "Driver's license here says his name is Brian Vander-something." He turned to Callan. "Ring a bell?"

Callan stared at the young man in disbelief. The Brian VanderPelt he'd seen before was at a distance, but he didn't have a goatee.

Brian glared back. The officer led him to a patrol car.

Gabe approached, standing beside Callan who remained motionless on the rocky alley. Gabe started to speak, but Callan raised his hand.

"Don't," Callan said, rubbing his eyes with his fingertips. "I'm as confused as you are right now."

Chapter Thirty-Four

Callan looked over the top of his newspaper the next morning as he tried to sip through the steam rising from his coffee cup. Broad Ripple was quiet. The gourmet coffee shop was even more so, and he was glad for that. He'd spent a tedious night with authorities, answering questions and receiving information about the events leading up to the surprising discovery that Chase and Brian VanderPelt were the perpetrators behind the extortion notes. There was one piece of the puzzle he couldn't resolve, however. Callan needed her help. He was pleased when she appeared in front of the glass entrance door.

Marilyn Wells-Brewer slipped in and glanced around the café, seemingly relieved that it was almost empty.

Callan rose to greet her.

She inched closer, clutching her handbag as she sat on the edge of the chair next to him.

"Coffee?" he asked. "I'll get you a cup. Their house blend is quite good. Stay still and be comfortable."

Callan soon returned. Marilyn grasped the mug, eager for something warm to hold.

"I appreciate you coming to see me," he replied. "I'm sure it's been a difficult night for you and Cole."

"Embarrassing is more like it," she said. Her voice quivered.

"I don't understand why. Being extorted wasn't of your own doing."

Marilyn paused. "No, but when the details of what happened are exposed to the public as I'm sure they will, our reputation in town will be tainted."

Her red, swollen eyes indicated that it would be best for Callan not to respond. He had to ask one question, however. "What troubles you the most?"

She sipped her coffee, hesitating to answer.

"Whatever you're willing to tell me won't go any farther than this conversation," he said.

"But why do you want to know?"

"To understand," he replied. "To put all the sordid pieces of this puzzle together so that I can help others move on with their lives."

Marilyn's eyes narrowed. "Such as Beth Kimmerman?"

"For one," he said. "Her daughter, for another. My own life too."

"Yours?" she asked, surprised.

"My family's past hasn't been squeaky clean either, Marilyn. We all have segments of our history that we're not proud of and hope others will never discover."

"Yes, but my troubles include the present as well as the past," she said sullenly.

"Financial problems, I assume."

She studied his face, appearing to search for empathy.

"I saw you and Chase VanderPelt at the Athenaeum the other day," Callan confided. "Meeting him didn't make sense to me at the time, but now it does. From what I've learned of

Chase, he's the go-to man for movers and shakers in this city, especially when it comes to needing money."

"I'm hardly a mover or shaker, Callan. I'm not the persona I like to portray."

"Then you were at the Athenaeum, asking for money."

She nodded. "Cole and I received a note to keep certain information quiet. We didn't have the amount demanded of us. Certainly, you can see the irony of my asking money from the very person who was calling the shots with his son. Chase must've been laughing under his breath the whole time I was groveling for a loan."

"But he gave you the money, didn't he?"

Marilyn chuckled. "Partially. He wouldn't lend it all to us. Cole put what Chase gave us into the bureau with our IOU. Can you believe it? We're so pathetic with our money, Callan, that we had to give an extortionist an IOU."

"For what?" Callan asked. "What did the VanderPelts have on you worth paying to keep silent?"

Marilyn took a deep breath. "You sure this is confidential?"

Callan reassured her that it was.

"Very well. My father was in the entertainment business," she said.

Callan paused. He could think of only one entertainment business worth blackmailing a person of Marilyn's status over, but she shook her head as if she knew what he was thinking.

"It was nothing illicit or promiscuous, I can assure you," she said.

"Then what?"

"My father owned a novelty mystery tour company. He put everything the family owned into this business. He took people on tours throughout the state, all fun and harmless."

"Such as what?" Callan asked, still perplexed.

"The business toured eerie and supposedly haunted places, like hideaways along riverbanks that Chicago gangsters were known to frequent, odd cemeteries, and places around Vincennes, where serpents lurked in the French bayous and cypress swamps along the Wabash, that sort of thing."

"Sounds like innocent fun."

"Oh, it was. He'd also go to places where ghosts could be seen at midnight, according to local legends, such as Purple Head Bridge and the trestle over the Embarras River. His best money-makers were the midnight shows at Hell's Gate near Diamond, Crybaby Bridge near Pendleton, and Dogface Bridge near San Pierre. He had elaborate setups at these places where he created illusions that scared the wits out of people."

"I'm sure they loved it, Marilyn. All in good fun. Not my cup of tea, mind you, but harmless, like you said."

Marilyn held her cup tighter in her hands. "Until one evening at 100 Steps Cemetery in Brazil, Indiana," she muttered. "Are you familiar with the place?"

"No, not at all."

"There's a set of stone steps at the cemetery. One hundred of them, to be exact. You're to count the steps as you climb upward. Legend has it that when you reach the top and turn around to look out over the cemetery, you'll receive a vision of your own death."

Callan sat back. "Why would anyone want to do that?"

"I don't know, but people did. They paid my father good money to do it too. All went well until a woman from Greencastle climbed the steps, turned around, and screamed at a vision she saw. No one is certain what the vision was, and we'll never know. Three days later the woman died. Her last words were 'It came true.'"

"But that doesn't mean it had anything to do with your

father's tour."

"Does it matter? The appearance of truth is often more damning than the truth itself."

"Yes, I know," Callan said, reflecting on his sister's misdirected anger at his family. "So what happened?"

"The family of the woman from Greencastle blamed the vision at 100 Steps Cemetery directly on my father. Other families jumped on the bandwagon and falsely claimed their relatives died after taking the tour also. The theory was that my father conspired to have this woman killed as a publicity stunt."

"Was it proven?"

"No, of course not," Marilyn said emphatically. "His attorneys were able to defend my father against wrongful death suits brought against him. But it didn't matter. He was never able to shake the stigma of the case from the public's mind, and he spent his life savings defending himself."

Callan couldn't take his eyes from Marilyn, who slumped sadly in her seat.

"And ours too," she added.

"You spent your life savings?"

"I had to. I couldn't let my father be accused of murder or sued for wrongful death, now, could I? What would people think of me, of what I've done for the community, being the daughter of a man like that? Tell me honestly, Callan. What would people think?"

Callan didn't give an answer. He thought it best not to have one to give.

Marilyn sipped her coffee and lamented her and her husband's financial situation a while longer before she rose to say she'd stayed long enough.

Chapter Thirty-Five

Callan watched Marilyn until she stepped out of the café's door. She stumbled once, as if the reality of her family's history had left her without any clear direction of what to do or where to go next. He tried to make it clear when she stood that what happened in the past wasn't as important as how she conducted herself going forward, but she didn't want to hear any of it. He refrained from telling her what he really thought, that she'd spent her life savings to save her selfish pride rather than to defend a father she loved. So he watched her leave until she was out of sight, unable to comfort her about what people would really think.

Callan was still gazing at the door long after Marilyn left when another woman appeared. This woman opened the door with difficulty and strode to the leather chair beside him.

"May I?" the woman asked.

Callan looked up. He folded the paper evenly over his lap and gestured for her to sit in the leather chair next to him, hoping to disguise his surprise at her presence.

"Thank you." Before sitting, Beth took a moment to assess

the café. "Did I startle you?" she asked.

"On the contrary," Callan began, then changed his mind. "Well, no, yes."

Beth smiled. "Which means I did. I know how we speak in Indiana."

"Then how about yes, no, maybe, for sure? That would've summed it up better."

She nodded. "Which means I might've; can't say for certain. Let's change the subject. We're not a very direct people, are we?"

"To a fault," Callan said. "But you speak and understand Hoosier well. You'll make a great mayor. I'll admit, you did startle me. You were the last person I expected to see this morning. Patty Reinholdt, perhaps, but not you."

"Patty is omnipresent." Beth looked over her shoulder again, this time to the coffee counter.

"May I get you some?" Callan offered.

"In a bit," she said softly. "I'm not quite sure why I've come." She removed her purse strap from her shoulder and let the handbag drop to the floor.

"How did you—?"

"I phoned the carriage house. Terese said you'd be here."

"I see. How's Kate doing?"

"She's come to, finally. A little bit, anyway. She's better. Not out of the woods by any means, but at least we know she's going to make it."

Callan allowed the conversation to fade naturally. He sensed Beth hadn't come to the coffee shop to talk about Kate.

"I wanted to talk with you privately," she said. "The events of last night have me confused, and I'm trying to, well, trying to assess . . ."

"Your future?" Callan suggested.

She smiled faintly. "Yes, I suppose you could say it like that."

"Are you seriously contemplating ending your mayoral campaign?"

She hesitated. "Yes, no, maybe, for sure."

Callan didn't acknowledge her attempt at humor over something that wasn't humorous to him. "You're a much stronger woman than you give yourself credit for, Beth."

"That's what I hear. Barry has left the decision entirely up to me, as it should be. He wants me to stay in, but I haven't decided whether it's worth the fight, given last night's events. At this point, I don't feel I have much fight left. The media won't be kind about this, you know."

"So what is it you want to know that'll help you decide what to do?" Callan asked.

"I need to understand more about what happened. There wasn't one crime, was there?"

Callan shook his head. "There were two schemes going on— two separate crimes perpetrated by two separate groups."

"From what I understand, Eddie confessed to leading a jewelry theft ring but not to the extortion notes left in the bureaus. Was it the stolen jewelry from those break-ins around Crow's Nest?"

"I'm afraid so. They put the items in boxes that looked like they'd arrived from the Merchandise Mart in Chicago to be transported to customers. The boxes were printed and stamped to look like they came from the Mart, but the 1-800 number printed on the outside of the carton was bogus."

"How did you find that out?"

"I called it. Gabe and I saw firsthand what went on at night in the back room. We saw two young women about late teens or early twenties who arrived and went in the back door. They didn't stay long. We suspected they'd made an illegal purchase of some kind. We didn't know what at the time."

"Were those boys there at night?"

"Yes. Ronnie hadn't gotten caught then, unlike Jeremy, but it's just a matter of time now, with Eddie's arrest."

"What do you think will become of them?" Beth asked.

Callan shook his head. "I have no idea. I'm not familiar with juvenile law. Eddie preyed on their vulnerabilities. He exploited their needs, their lack of family support, their homelessness, and substance abuse issues. He used their weaknesses to keep them under his control, especially to keep them quiet."

Beth looked away. "He was a modern-day D. C. Stephenson, in a way, wasn't he?"

"Maybe not as ruthless, but the Stephensons of the world come in all forms—all genders, all races, all socioeconomic statuses. Evil has no stereotype."

"I know," Beth said reflectively, "but I can't help but feel sorry for the boys anyway."

"I don't usually feel sorry for people like them," Callan confessed, "but I have to admit that it saddens me to think about the trouble they've gotten into."

"I'm surprised Eddie had the wherewithal to pull off such a jewelry theft operation as he did."

"I'm not so sure he did. Jeremy and Ronnie started to get sloppy. There was too much to keep track of, I guess. As Eddie became more successful, he grew arrogant and took risks he shouldn't have taken. That's how Kate found the amulet she gave you."

"I asked her about that. I asked how she got it, because amulets weren't something Eddie dabbled with at Open Arms."

"It struck Kate as odd, too, even if she didn't let on to you that she felt that way."

"Tell me something," she said, frowning. "That Lindy star necklace that Amy wore to the reception. She said it was a family heirloom. Terese and Corinne were taken in by her story, but I believed it was contrived. She didn't strike me as the type of person who'd have such a necklace."

"Her story was completely fabricated. Her father didn't give her the Lindy star necklace. She purchased it from Eddie."

"I don't understand what Brian saw in Amy," Beth said. Contempt for the couple glared from her eyes. "He comes from good money in town. Old money."

"Could be that Brian was attracted to Amy because she was everything opposite from that. You have to admit that Amy was unpretentious and down-to-earth. I'm sure he enjoyed life at Tipton's for that reason."

"I'm surprised Kate didn't say something to Eddie about her."

"Maybe she did," Callan said. "I believe Kate confronted Eddie about things she didn't understand at Open Arms the night she was attacked. Gabe and I saw Kate in Chuck's workshop that night, as we peered through the back windows."

"Then if Kate confronted Eddie about things she didn't understand, it would be plausible that Eddie followed her back to the gallery to confront her again, wouldn't it? They argued, and Eddie hit her."

"Yes, but that's not what happened," Callan said. "Eddie didn't follow Kate to Cottage Gallery."

"What did he do then?"

"He made a phone call."

"To Chuck?"

"No, remember, Chuck went fishing." Callan let the statement sink in for a second before saying, "Eddie called Amy."

"Amy? But why?"

"When questioned by the police, Amy confessed that Eddie did make such a call to her. It was a vile call. He screamed that she was a fool to wear the Lindy star necklace she'd purchased from him at a reception full of people the jewelry was stolen from. Keep in mind, many of the attendees lived in the general area of the robberies."

"So Amy, in her distress, called Brian."

"Yes, because Brian was part of the extortion notes, the second crime separate from the jewelry operation. You see, the detectives told me early this morning that it was Brian's father, Chase, who orchestrated the elaborate scheme to extort money from Open Arms board members and customers."

"But why did Brian go after Kate?"

"She was coming out of denial," Callan said. "Andrew's death was a wake-up call she needed to heed. She began asking questions about issues she'd never asked before. She noticed things that she'd previously ignored. She finally realized all that glittered wasn't gold to the gallery."

"So it was Brian who attacked her," Beth repeated under her breath as she thought about the events.

"Brian wanted to know how much Kate knew about the notes in the bureaus in addition to the jewelry thefts. He went to see her after Amy phoned him. I don't know if they got into an argument, or if Brian took advantage of the opportunity to shut her up before she said something to authorities, or what. In any case, the amulet was lying on the floor next to Kate. It may have dropped during the scuffle. The amulet meant nothing to Brian, so he didn't take it, but it did mean something to Gabe."

"I know," Beth said regretfully. "He was only trying to protect me by taking it. Gabe told me something else that struck me as odd. He said it wasn't Eddie who tried to attack us."

Callan nodded. "That's right. Again, it was Brian."

"But you were so sure it was Eddie. The boots. Remember the boots?"

"Yes," Callan said. "I'm embarrassed to say he was arrested

based upon my account to the police. I knew I was wrong as soon as I spotted Chuck's boots in his workshop."

"You mean Brian's boots, don't you? You just said Brian was the one who ambushed us at my home and followed us to Gabe and Lauren's house."

"No, I mean Chuck. They were Chuck's boots, but Brian wore them."

Beth frowned, puzzled. "That doesn't make sense. I heard something about Lake Tippecanoe from the wires this morning. What was that about? It sounded as if reporters were tying an incident on Lake Tippy to our set of events. Is that true?"

Callan paused to reflect on the news reports he'd heard as well. "Apparently, a capsized fisherman's boat was found in Kosciusko County last evening, at the Oswego end of the lake. Authorities were looking for a middle-aged man, fitting Chuck's description, who was last seen fishing in the area. Chuck's truck and boat trailer were found nearby. I personally believe they'll find his body at the bottom of the lake, made to look like an accidental boat drowning."

"Good heavens," Beth said. "But why? Was it because of the jewels?"

"No, I don't believe so, because Brian had very little to do with the jewelry scheme, if anything at all. Chuck helped Eddie modify small appliances like toasters and blenders to hide stolen jewelry, but that was done just for Eddie."

"Then how does Brian fit in?"

"Chuck also modified the desks that were used to hide the notes and stash the extortion funds. He was killed by Brian for what he knew about the extortion schemes."

"But killing Chuck the way they did seems like a convoluted way of getting rid of him."

"I know. I've thought about that a lot. What I believe, and

this is only *my* theory, is that Brian and Amy knew Chuck had taken the holiday weekend to go fishing. Brian went to Lake Tippy specifically to kill Chuck."

"But again, I have to ask, why? That's what I don't understand."

"The scheme was falling apart. Money was missing. They had no idea that it was Meredith Patterswaite who'd taken the cash out of her own bureau. At first, they suspected Andrew had double-crossed them. That's why Andrew was killed. So they suspected Chuck as having it. Besides, Chuck knew too much about what was going on. He could've easily made a deal with prosecutors to nail the VanderPelts."

"But how did Chuck's boots make it back to his workshop?"

"Before dumping Chuck's body into the lake, I suspect Brian took Chuck's boots and wore them to ambush us. He then planted the boots under Chuck's workbench, using Amy's key to get into the back room. It was all done to implicate Chuck in the attack. I believe Brian counted on the authorities connecting their investigation of the attack to Chuck, and that they'd find him dead from an accidental drowning and close the case."

"They counted on a lot for that scenario to work, if you ask me."

Callan agreed. "But they were getting desperate."

Beth took a moment to digest Callan's explanation of the events. "I don't know very much about Brian," she said. "I mean, he had life in the palms of his hands, coming from such privilege. Anything he wanted, his family would've given it to him. I don't get it."

"Greed, I suspect. Some people always want more than they have. That's why he and his father targeted prominent members of the Open Arms board."

"Including me," Beth said.

"Yes, including you."

Beth twisted a small tassel that dangled from the zipper of her purse. "He didn't know me very well."

"He didn't have to," Callan said. "He only had to know enough about your weaknesses to get what he wanted."

Beth twisted the tassel faster.

"Are you sure you wouldn't like some coffee?" he asked. "You look like you could use some."

Beth glanced at the counter and nodded. Her face was suddenly ashen, and her eyes drawn. "Yes, I think I could use a cup now. I'm not in the mood for a latte, but I'd like something a little stronger than regular coffee."

"They have what they call an Americano, a diluted espresso, if you will."

She smiled. "Yes, that'll be fine."

Callan went to the counter and soon returned with two coffees. "Chase will be indicted before this is all over," Callan said, hoping to give her some peace that would bring color back into her cheeks.

Beth nodded. "So what did Amy do? What was her part in all of this?"

"Amy provided the means for collecting the extortion money," he said. "Once the Potters had targeted a victim, a letter would be sent to that person requesting they go to Cottage Gallery and purchase a certain desk or bureau."

Beth raised her hand for Callan to stop. "No details, please. I'm pretty familiar with the process, unfortunately."

"It was all done to make the scheme covert. Not as blatant as kidnapping or phone calls that could be traced." Callan refrained from reciting information she already knew, but he did want to mention one aspect of the case of which she wasn't aware. "Although Chuck helped build and install some of the secret compartments in the furniture used in the plots, he wasn't privy to when the furniture would be returned to the gallery and when the money could be picked up."

"Okay, but if it wasn't Chuck, then who? Amy? Did Amy retrieve the money?"

Callan nodded. "She knew when a bureau was returned to Open Arms, and who returned it, because she worked there. She could slip easily into the back room and retrieve the envelopes of money without detection or raising suspicion."

"It was a perfect plan, wasn't it?" she asked. "Or it could've been."

"The VanderPelts started with you and Barry because of your high profile in the mayoral race. They tried it next on Roger Montrose, threatening to expose faulty investments in the Wyandotte Ballroom renovation, but Montrose didn't have the money to pay their demand. Their perfect plan wasn't so perfect if the people they victimized had no money to pay them. So they tried to hit William Davisly."

"But William wanted no part of it," Beth said.

"Exactly. Davisly simply returned the bureau with a note telling them to go to hell. He shot himself to end their scheme against him, and suddenly, Chase's perfect plan was full of holes. By the time Davisly died, several notes had already gone out."

"Tell me more about Andrew," she said. "I miss his common sense and friendship. His death hit me as hard as Kate's attack. You see, he tried to talk to me about what he knew of the bureaus as he left the reception, but I brushed him off. The reception wasn't the right time or place to hear the evidence he had. I should've listened, however. He told me it also involved Marjorie Eckert."

"Yes, when Andrew and Marjorie ran into each other at the reception, they began talking as they eyed the bureau each of them had purchased and returned. Lauren, Amy, and I saw them talking, but we didn't know what they were talking about. I assume now they'd found out each other had been victimized. Amy came to the same conclusion, I'm sure."

"Yes," Beth remembered. "Lauren did say to me that Amy had to leave the reception abruptly, something about Brian being out front to give her a lift."

"That wasn't true," Callan said. "Amy had to leave the reception to tell Brian about what she'd seen. She apparently made a call to him about the time Andrew left the gallery. Brian was already in the area. He was the messenger who delivered the demand letter you received through Chuck Cordry."

"Do you think Brian followed Andrew to the canal?"

"He may have even confronted and threatened him, believing that he didn't put the demand money into the secret compartment of the desk as he was told to do. Gabe probably told you that Meredith Patterswaite took the money from the desk, leaving the VanderPelts with nothing. Andrew may have gotten angry at Brian. They probably scuffled on the greenway and poor Andrew was fatally injured."

"I can't believe there were no witnesses. I know it was foggy and difficult to see that night, but I can't understand why no one saw anything. Didn't you speak of a woman you saw on the bridge over the canal? I wonder if she saw something."

Callan shook his head. "At first, I thought she was Patty Reinholdt, but then I remembered Patty had an oversized satchel with her at the reception."

"She carries it with her wherever she goes," Beth confirmed.

"The woman on the bridge didn't have a satchel."

"Then who was it?"

"Amy Henzel," Callan said. "She knew, as Brian did, that there was no money in the bureau Andrew returned. She realized someone could have found and taken the money. The obvious person, to her, was the person who owned the bureau—Meredith Patterswaite. Amy was who I saw on the bridge. She was on her way to Meredith's shop."

"It's all incredible," Beth said. "It seems the only person who came out of this whole mess unscathed was the one person who made it so scandalous in the first place."

"Who was that?"

"Marilyn Wells-Brewer, of course."

Callan smiled. "Not sure how you're going to take this, Beth, but Marilyn and Cole didn't exactly escape unscathed. The Brewers received a demand note too. In fact, it was their note that was used to catch Brian in the act. Do you remember when we sat and talked at the Athenaeum? I happened to see Marilyn in the bar right before you arrived. She was with Chase."

"What in the world was she doing with him? That seems very unlikely."

Callan smirked as if the meeting wasn't unlikely at all.

Beth leaned forward. "Don't just smirk, Callan. Please, tell me."

"She was asking for money."

"Are you kidding me? I know this isn't a laughing matter, but I can't help but see the humor in it. Why, to listen to her talk, you would think she and Cole had more than enough money to pay a demand note."

"I'm sure Chase was as blown away by what he was hearing from her, knowing full well why she needed the money."

"Yes, unknowingly going to the very person who was blackmailing her so that she could give the money right back to him. I wonder what he had on her. She was so self-righteous and above scandal, you know."

"I shouldn't say. I met with her right before you came in. My curiosity got the best of me, and I had to know the connection she had with the crime. I felt guilty for asking after I found out. All I will tell you is that there's a stigma attached to her family that she'd prefer to have silenced. If you ask me, however, her imagination is getting the best of her. I doubt that anyone really cares."

"Imagination can scare us more than reality," Beth said. She stared at Callan. "I suppose that's what you think I'm doing—allowing my imagination to get the best of me over this mayoral race."

She sighed. "You may be right, Callan. Perhaps that's exactly what I'm doing, but the crux of my problem is this . . . I don't know what to do about it."

Chapter Thirty-Six

"That's because your pain has lingered far too long for you to think clearly, Beth," Callan said.

"I know, but I can't get it out of my mind. I can't forget."

"Perhaps you shouldn't."

Beth winced as if it was a strange thing for him to say. "But that's what I hear people tell me I should do—silence the past."

"Forgetting the past and silencing the past are two different things," Callan said. "Silencing isn't healthy. It infers that you should shut down all emotion, all the anger and hurt you've carried throughout your ordeal. Forgetting isn't healthy either, because it affects the mind rather than your emotions. What you need is a commitment to your overall health and well-being. Such a commitment takes time."

Beth shook her head. "You'll think I'm being trite, Callan, but I'm angry about something that happened a hundred years ago that I had no control over. I'm angry that my constituents might judge *me* for something that happened to my family before I was born. That makes me angry at my great-grandfather for getting caught up in the Klan. It makes me angry at my great-grandmother for not helping Madge Oberholtzer more than she did, and it makes me angry at Madge for being so naive that she didn't know she was dating a Grand Dragon until it was too late."

"We're all naive about things we're not involved in. From what I remember about Madge, the Klan was something she stayed away from, that she didn't concern herself with. She was going to be naive about them and their ways. The same could've been true of your great-grandmother."

"We all know ignorance is a lousy defense, Callan," Beth said harshly, "and although it sits better on my palate to think my great-grandmother was more naive than indifferent, I don't believe that to be the case. I'm not that way, and neither was my mother or my grandmother. I doubt my great-grandmother was either. No, she was indifferent to my great-grandfather's involvement. I'm the angriest at him."

"Then think of him as a good man who did something wrong," Callan retorted. "We all make mistakes."

"His mistake, however, was monumental. It wasn't like putting salt instead of sugar in a recipe. His mistake had a huge impact on people's lives."

"And he paid dearly for that mistake. Gabe told me what happened to his career."

Beth shook her head and breathed heavily. "But he must have been bad deep inside, Callan, to have been associated with those people."

"That's why you have a greater responsibility to come to terms with your anger," he said.

"Me?" she asked defiantly. "What responsibility is mine? I'm the victim of my great-grandparents' lives."

"Yes, you are a victim, if that's how you choose to see yourself. That's why this situation isn't going away. Victimization is what Chase VanderPelt used to control you. You're the one, Beth, who's perpetuating the hurt and anger of something that happened one hundred years ago. Not your great-grandparents, Madge, or Chase. You're the one unhappy because of it. You're miserable, and it's affecting your family and your career."

"Then what do you suggest I do?"

Callan sat back in his seat. "Concern yourself with now, the present," he said. "You can't change the past, but you can change how it affects your life. Your constant reflection keeps the past in the present, making it impossible to move forward. Aren't you tired of it?"

"Of course I'm tired," she said.

"Then let go. Allow yourself to be at peace and feel compassion for yourself, your family, your great-grandparents . . . and Madge. There's only one way to do that," he said. "It's not forgetting, and it's not silencing. It's called forgiveness."

Beth's eyebrows clenched together on her forehead. "You expect me to forgive?" she asked accusingly.

"I don't expect anything. It's you who should be expecting it. It's you who has to decide deliberately to release your anger and resentment."

"They don't deserve it," she said.

"You don't deserve it either," he said bluntly, "but that doesn't stop the Lord from forgiving you when you ask."

Beth's eyes softened. "Yes, but that's different. It's all a bit easier if you're God."

"No, it's not just because of God," Callan said, reflecting on his faith. "It's because God is love. Love forgives whether it's deserved or not. If you can't love yourself or love who you're forgiving, then at least try to love having peace of mind."

Beth eyed Callan cynically She wasn't quite convinced.

"At least it's a start," he said as a compromise. "I don't know what more I can tell you. The rest is up to you. That is, if you want to."

Beth sighed and asked pointedly, "You're not very happy with me, are you?"

The question took Callan by surprise.

She repeated the question when it became obvious he wasn't going to answer. "Is it because you're not happy with yourself in this investigation?"

Callan nodded. "You're very astute," he said. "I missed some important marks. I broke a sacred vow of my profession by wrongly accusing someone without gathering all of the facts completely."

"Are you talking about Eddie?"

Callan nodded again. "I accused him of the wrong crime, essentially. What I do as a profession must be done delicately, Beth. There are procedures and facts that need to be verified before going further. I didn't do that."

"Then you must make a commitment to forgive yourself as well."

"I know, and I will, but I judged you wrong too," he said apologetically. "Being a fraud examiner must be done in much the same way that an actor prepares for a role. An actor must submerge himself into that role completely, understand his character so that he thinks, acts, breathes, talks, and even smells like him. He must do so whether or not that character is of his own principles and values. I failed to do that with you. I judged you throughout this affair without considering all the facts and what you were going through."

"I wish my family felt the same way."

"Let your family speak for themselves," Callan said. "I think if you'd ask, they'd tell you they understand the position you're in. They know it's a difficult position to be a wife, a mother, and a candidate for public office, but they'd want you to move on. Gabe looks up to you. He looks at the decisions you and Barry make as examples of the decisions he'd make for himself in similar circumstances. He looks to see how honorable and true your decisions are to yourself. That's all he's ever wanted to see in your family's past."

"And Lauren?"

Callan reflected thoughtfully. "She has a special bond and relationship with you, but I'm not sure you fully understand how important that relationship is to her."

"No, you're wrong, Callan. I do understand."

"Then stop being a victim. Stop playing defense and start playing offense. Show her what you stand for, and let her know what you stand upon."

Beth paused to reflect. She clasped her purse tightly and stood, prepared to go. Neither one of them said a word for several seconds.

"I'm glad the situation is over, nonetheless," she offered. "This conversation could go on and on without a victor, but at least I'm glad this matter of silencing the past is finally over."

"Not quite," Callan replied sharply.

Beth raised her brows, appearing perturbed that he would continue to confront her but intrigued by what more there could possibly be.

"There's someone I'd like you to meet," he said.

Chapter Thirty-Seven

Beth peered through the window of Callan's car at a rural area on the far-east side of the city. Though within the city's corporate limits, this portion of the city contrasted sharply from the rest of Indianapolis. Modest, neatly trimmed homes dotted the landscape, giving way to an occasional farmhouse with a small red or white barn standing on the premises. Most of the residences and barns had large stars of gold, red, or blue on their front facade, a sign of rural Indiana friendship and hospitality.

Above her, white, fluffy cumulus clouds floated evenly interspersed against a canvas of bright blue. The imposing sun cast a maze of well-defined cloud shadows on the roadway.

Beth looked at Callan as he drove south on German Church Road, appearing not to notice the green pastures or cows grazing near the fences where wild tiger lilies grew. She turned to her daughter, Lauren, who sat in the back seat staring blankly out her side window, unfazed by the simple beauty of the Hoosier landscape.

Callan suddenly turned west.

Beth side-glanced him. When he turned on Mitthoefer

Road to go south once more, she could stand the silence no longer. "Where are you taking me?" she asked in bewilderment.

Callan continued to drive, unwilling to answer.

"Do you know, Lauren?"

Lauren turned her head toward her mother but didn't respond.

It seemed to Beth as if she wasn't supposed to know where they were going until they got there. She didn't like the feeling of not knowing. It unnerved her. "I've decided I'm going to teach," she said abruptly.

The comment drew a reaction from her daughter, as she'd hoped. "When did you decide this?" Lauren asked.

"I've been thinking about it for quite some time. I think I may see if Butler University has a position."

Lauren turned back to the passing landscape.

Callan continued to focus straight ahead, on his destination.

"Perhaps Vermillion College is looking for a professor with my qualifications," she said to Callan.

"Perhaps," he replied, "but you wouldn't like it."

"Why not? I think I could adapt quite well to a small college environment unaffected by the outside world. Colleges and universities seem to have developed their own fantasy utopias unattached to real life. I could get used to that."

"But it's not where you built your life, Beth."

Beth laughed. "Yes, and quite a utopia it is."

They drove further, reaching the National Road, Indianapolis's main east–west thoroughfare. Callan turned west once again.

"I do want to know where you're taking me," she insisted.

This time, Callan turned to her and smiled. He pulled into a neatly manicured drive, leading to Memorial Park Cemetery. A sign welcomed them to the walled burial ground, reading simply: *A cemetery is a place where a life lived becomes real, memories spring to life, and future generations come to remember.*

The words resonated harshly with Beth. A pang in the pit of her stomach ached. After what she'd been through recently, she didn't want certain memories of her family's lives to spring to life. She certainly didn't want her children to remember them.

Callan meandered through the lanes of the cemetery before stopping the car in what appeared to Beth to be a nondescript area. She peered out of the car's window toward a meadow of granite headstones arranged perfectly into tranquil rows of order. The shadows of the clouds dotted the meadow and floated effortlessly in front of her.

"Why are we here?" she asked.

Callan pulled the car off to the side, allowing enough space for another car to pass on the lane. He opened the car door and stood on the pavement, looking toward a specific area of stones.

Lauren followed his lead.

Beth sat in the car.

"I'd like for you to come," Callan said, bending down to look at Beth through the open car door.

She didn't respond.

"Okay," he relented. "Then if you'll excuse us, there is someone I want Lauren to meet."

With his fob, Callan released the lid of his trunk and extracted a small bouquet of spring flowers and a small plastic sack. He handed Lauren the sack.

"How's your foot?" he asked. "Can you walk?"

"Not very well, but I want to do this," she replied.

Beth watched as he led Lauren to an area off the lane surrounded by a grove of maple trees and sparsely dotted with headstones rising from the ground. She believed Callan meant for this trip to bring closure. Even though she was fighting the emotional urge to join them, she decided it was the right thing to do and exited the car to catch up to them.

They stopped in front of one stone—granite and light gray. Time hadn't diminished the name carved permanently into it.

Oberholtzer.

Off to the side was a smaller stone, one barely noticeable, hardly large enough for mowers to avoid.

"I wanted to bring you here," Callan said to Lauren as he stepped closer to the smaller stone, "and I wanted your mother to be here, too, so you could meet her. The bronze plaque you saw when we drove in is true. Lives are real here. They don't go away in death, and memories good and bad are remembered. We have to remember so we can move forward, so that future lives will honor what was good and not dare repeat what was bad."

Beth stepped through the soft bluegrass and stood solemnly behind them. She watched Callan place the bouquet of flowers on the small monument. The petals nearly covered the stone entirely, but the breeze blew them slightly, revealing the name that she could read easily.

Madge A., 1896–1925.

There was nothing more.

Beth was stunned. Surely, this wasn't all that memorialized Madge Oberholtzer. She looked at the other stones around her but found nothing more. She couldn't believe it. Surely, the torment Madge suffered, and the city that suffered in the months following her death, were worthy of a stone much larger and more commemorative than the one she stood beside.

An immense sadness consumed her.

"Even though what happened to her was shameful," Callan said in retrospect, "the life of Madge Augustine Oberholtzer was not."

He pulled a folded piece of paper from his pocket and opened the flaps.

Beth craned her neck to look at what was written on the page. Madge's full name was printed boldly at the top. The rest of the page appeared to be nothing more than scribbled notes that Callan had written in bullet points while researching her history.

"Madge's life was short, but it was rich and dedicated to the least of those that made this city their home. She was a teacher, Lauren. I don't know if you knew that. She dedicated her life to teaching children in the slums how to read. She taught their parents, too, hoping that each word would eventually make a difference in their lives. At a time when the Klan was an influencing factor in Hoosier politics, she persevered, with other good people who knew the difference between right and wrong, to change the community. It didn't happen overnight, and it didn't happen before she was murdered. Unfortunately, it wasn't her life that changed the community. It was her death. But through her death, her life was illuminated by the contributions she made and the type of city we wanted to become."

"It's sad, isn't it?" Lauren reflected. "Rather than the good an individual does, people often remember them for the bad they're associated with."

"It's human nature, I guess," Callan replied, "but it doesn't have to be that way. You can change that, Lauren. I want you to break out of your family's fear of the past. You're a good woman, and you have a great future ahead of you, if you can break away from fear and see the events of the past for what they are. They don't define your family any more than they define Madge, especially in the eyes of God."

A broad smile crossed Lauren's face.

Beth saw her daughter's smile then looked at the stone and thought of the future ahead.

"Live bigger than fear," Callan challenged.

Lauren smiled again and opened the plastic sack she had

in her hand. She turned to her mother and asked, "Would you mind holding this?"

Beth held out her hand. Lauren gently placed something delicate into her palm. When Lauren pulled away, a silver omega slithered over the side of Beth's hand, revealing the diamond and black onyx pendant that Lauren wore to the reception at Cottage Gallery.

Beth took in a deep breath and sighed, surprised to see it in her hand.

"I want to give it back to Madge," Lauren said.

Beth didn't say anything. Shrouded in regret, she bit her bottom lip, not knowing how to respond or if the decision was hers to make. "Why?" she uttered.

"It belongs to her," Lauren said. "I want to give it back. I have as much use for it in life as she does in death if you're ashamed of me wearing it."

Lauren reached into the sack and withdrew a small trowel, like one used to pluck weeds from the ground or to plant bulbs for flowers to grow. She turned the handle toward her mother and asked, "Would you like to do the honors? Would you like to bury the past, silencing it forever?"

Beth looked at the ground at the base of Madge's stone, green and full beneath her feet. It would be easy to dig a small hole to give the necklace back to the woman who gave it to her great-grandmother decades ago. It would be easy to be freed of the memory it represented, but it wouldn't release the shame. Beth looked into her daughter's eyes and realized the necklace represented something much, much more than a shameful memory. It was something meaningful and life-giving. She wasn't sure she was ready to accept what Callan had said to her daughter about Madge's life, but it was time she stopped associating her feelings with the wrong person—and forgave her.

Rather than reaching for the shovel in Lauren's hand, Beth unraveled the chain that held the pendant in place and clasped it behind her daughter's neck. She readjusted Lauren's hair and touched the pendant gently where it lay flat against her chest. "No, Lauren, I think it looks fine on you. Madge would be happy that it belongs to you. You understand her, and you wear it unashamed. You should keep it."

"But you're the one I want to respect," Lauren replied.

"You have," Beth assured her as she gave her a hug. A smile crossed her face. "Yes, I mean it. It looks beautiful on you, and not only does it represent the beauty you have inside, but it symbolizes the woman Madge was, and who I want to be."

Callan looked upon Beth with an expression of hope and revelation. "Who do you want to be, Beth?" he asked. "Mayor?"

Beth Kimmerman smiled again. The diamond and onyx pendant around her daughter's neck glistened brightly in the sunshine.

A Note to My Readers

Historical scandals have always intrigued me. I never knew how much until I became an avid genealogist. My mother, Barbara Kreigh, sparked my interest with romps in old local cemeteries with paper and charcoal in hand to rub the etchings of tombstones to reveal information about our ancestors. Her cousins, James Willard Brown of Venice, Florida, and Mildred McCord DeRue of Frankton, Indiana, left me with published accounts of our Irish, Scottish, and English predecessors. My cousin-in-law, Jack Lawrence Enloe of Creve Couer, Missouri, shared an interest in our Swiss and German heritage and provided valuable insight into my family's past.

When a cousin, once removed, passed away and I inherited family pictures and historical documents, including birth certificates, marriage certificates, land deeds, naturalization papers, and Civil War and WWI military records, I found a poem attached to an obituary sent by my Great-Great-Grandmother Clark to a great-aunt. It was a poem, author unknown, that went something like this:

Only the present hour is mine
I may not have another in which
to speak a kindly word or
to help a fallen neighbor.
The path of life is straight ahead
I can retrace it never.
The daily record that I make will
stand unchanged forever.

One could take the words to heart and live a life worthy of time and remembrance, but I wondered about those who choose the opposite? Some forget or don't care that their life will be recorded, and their names will be forever a blot in genealogical records like the ones my cousin-in-law and I keep. I began to plot *Silence the Past* with that in mind. The words of the above poem were with me as well as I wrote.

I owe so many people for helping me with this book. Of course, Tahlia Newland and Rose Newland of AIA Publishing in New South Wales, Australia, saw something within the pages and added their creative minds to perfect it.

Authors Barbara Scott-Emmett of Newcastle, England, and Brent Meske in South Korea and editor Katherine Kirk in Ecuador provided incredible insight about the strengths of the manuscript and what I could do to improve it.

I couldn't have finished without the encouragement and feedback from Becky Jackson of Peru, Indiana, Matt and Andria Harrison of Indianapolis, Jan Vest of Diamondhead, Mississippi, and Alvin Mullins, originally from Newport, Arkansas, and the spiritual insight of my dear friends, Eric Duggins of Queretaro, Mexico, and Brett and Deb Henson of Mooresville, North Carolina.

And, of course, a special thanks to Phyllis Shnaider of

New Orleans who helped me understand the importance of grounding myself in the present and recognizing the healing power of forgiveness.

If you enjoyed this book, I'd be very grateful if you'd write a review and publish it at your point of purchase. Your review, even a brief one, will help other readers decide if they'll enjoy my work.

If you'd like to be notified of new releases from myself and other AIA Publishing authors, please sign up to the AIA Publishing email list. You'll find the sign-up button on the right-hand side under the photo at www.aiapublishing.com. Of course, your information will never be shared, and the publisher won't inundate you with emails, just let you know of new releases.

And please be sure to visit my personal website at www.garykreigh.com.

Gary Lee Edward Kreigh
Gulf Shores, Alabama
June 12, 2022

Born in Anderson, Indiana, Gary Lee Edward Kreigh graduated with an accounting degree from Ball State University. He also studied at the University of Indianapolis for Computer Technology and the Gonzaga University for Organizational Development.

Gary uses his thirty-five years in the fields of forensic accounting, fraud examination, and internal auditing to write about corporate and social issues, and experiences that affect ordinary people in extraordinary situations. His experience spans the banking, retail, finance, education, and medical industries. He now juggles his time and residence between New Orleans and Gulf Shores, Alabama.

This is Gary's third book. His first, *Why Birds Fall*, is a mystery about corruption in the aviation industry. His second and third, *Masquerade of Truth* and *Payola*, are Reverend Fountain mysteries set in New Orleans.

www.ingramcontent.com/pod-product-compliance
Lightning Source LLC
Chambersburg PA
CBHW060737190726
48285CB00001B/243